D0043113

 ueen

Without a Country

To Val – fellow
author – and –
newly founded again friend,
Rachel Bard

Rachel Bard

Literary Network Press
Burton, Washington, USA

Copyright © Rachel Bard 2000

First published 2000 by Minerva Press, London
Published 2001 by Literary Network Press
All Rights Reserved

Cover design by Laurel Black
Text design by Sheryl Mehary

ISBN 0-9710333-8-2
Library of Congress 2001-091004

No part of this book may be reproduced in any
form, by photocopying or by any electronic or mechanical
means, including information storage or retrieval
systems, without permission in writing
from both the copyright owner and
the publisher of this book.

Literary Network Press
P.O. Box 13523
Burton, Washington 98013

Queen
Without a Country

To the Logians

Preface

Queen Without a Country is a historical novel about Berengaria, daughter of Sancho VI, King of Navarre, and wife of Richard I, King of England. The major events and characters in the book are based on the historical record, with one exception: Pierre Savary. We do know where and when he lived, that Berengaria was acquainted with him and that he gave her the rights to the town of Montbazon and its revenues. However, his subsequent relationship with the Queen is based on hints in the archival records, including one historian's testimony that "he remained devoted to her throughout his life."

The author is grateful for access to documents in the British Library in London, the Bibliothèque Nationale in Paris, the Médiathèque of Le Mans and the Library of the Basque Studies Center in Reno.

Readers who wish to learn more about the medieval world that Berengaria inhabited are encouraged to consult the bibliography at the end of this book.

Berengaria's Europe, 1200

The Middle East during the Third Crusade

BULGARIA

Black Sea

Danube

Constantinople

ASIA MINOR

Tigris

Athens

RHODES

CYPRUS

SELJUK EMPIRE

Euphrates

CRETE

Damascus

Tyre

Acre

Mediterranean Sea

Jaffa

PALESTINE
Jerusalem

Ascalon

Alexandria

Cairo

EGYPT

rincess Berengaria stood at the rail of the small galley as it sped across the Strait of Messina toward Sicily. Except for the man at the helm and two seamen at the stern she was alone on the deck.

She had never been to sea, and her senses were heightened by the thrill of the swift passage over the water. Her eyes darted from the vessel's sharp bow, slicing its way through the foam-crested waves, to the blades of the invisible oarsmen on the lower deck. Rhythmically, all in perfect harmony, the oars dipped into the sea and rose, and the sheets of water that fell from them caught the light and glittered like miniature waterfalls. She was enchanted. Above her, the square sail with its bold red and white stripes was taut, filled by the strong following breeze. Her cloak billowed about her and she held her slight body as straight as though she were a mast and the cloak her sail. She had let down her hood and her long brown hair streamed behind her like a banner. Her cheeks were rosy from the wind, and her lips were parted in a smile of pure happiness.

The burly captain, standing forward with his hand on the helm, glanced with appreciation at this handsome woman, who seemed to relish the exhilaration of a swift sail in a stout craft as much as he did. The other ladies in her party were cowering below decks — perhaps fearing seasickness, all unaware of what they were missing.

Catching his look, she smiled and made her way forward, keeping a firm grip on the rail. "How much longer do you think, captain, before we reach Messina? Not that I wish this voyage to end, it is so wonderful!"

"Why, we should be seeing the lighthouse before long, miss." He caught himself; he had never had royalty on board. "I mean your ladyship, and then we're practically there; we'll be in harbor by sundown."

Berengaria stood there a moment, looking ahead at the blur on the horizon — the island where her future lay.

"I am sorry for the others, they should not be missing all this beauty. Maybe I will go down and persuade Queen Eleanor to come up." She smiled at him again, and he saw that her eyes were the same blue-green as the sea.

Turning aft, she looked up at the pennant that flew at the top of the mast: the coat of arms of the Plantagenet kings, three golden lions on a field of crimson. And she felt again the tremor of uncertainty, almost fear, that had been her companion for two months. In the care of her future mother-in-law, Queen Eleanor, she was on her way to meet the man she was to marry: Richard Plantagenet, King of England. After the wedding he would embark on his Crusade to Palestine, and she would go with him as his queen.

What will it be like, she wondered for the hundredth time, to be a king's wife? What will he be like?

She had seen Richard once before, when she was only six. He had come to a tournament in Pamplona hosted by her father, King Sancho of Navarre. She remembered being dazzled by the handsome, golden-haired young prince, and her terror when he jousted with her idolized older brother, Young Sancho, and unhorsed him. She remembered running after the two lads when they walked off the field after their encounter.

"Sanchito, Sanchito! Are you all right?" she had cried out.

"Of course I'm all right, Berenguelita. Why shouldn't I be?"

"But Richard gave you such a lot of terrible blows — I was afraid you might be hurt." She looked at Richard accusingly. "You did, you know."

"I'm none the worse for the trouncing, and Richard won fair and square," Young Sancho told her. "It's only a great game, you know."

"If he won, what is his prize?" she had asked.

Both boys laughed. Then Richard knelt so he was eye to eye with the little princess.

"It is the custom, Princess Berengaria, for fair ladies to give a trophy to the victor in a tournament, as a mark of their esteem. Have you some trophy for me? That will be my prize."

She looked around. What trophy could she give him? She caught sight of a bush bearing bright yellow flowers and broke off a sprig laden with blossoms, and, eyes sparkling with the fun of this new game, handed it to Richard. "Your trophy, Sir Knight," she said, hoping that sounded right.

Richard rose and stuck the sprig of broom in the band of his plumed hat. "You have given me the one prize that means the most to me, little princess. The broom is the sign of my family, the Plantagenets, always worn in our helmets when we go into battle." He bowed low and took her hand to kiss it. "Thank you, my lady. I shall wear your trophy throughout the tournament, thinking of you."

So they parted, the boys running ahead to return to the jousting, Berengaria following more slowly. But suddenly a bright yellow something in the path caught her eye. It was the sprig of broom — it must have fallen and Richard had not even noticed. She picked it up crossly and was about to throw it away. If that was all he thought of his prize! But then she put it in the pocket of her cloak. Maybe she would see him later and give it back — and maybe he would accept it with an apology and maybe he would kiss her hand again.

But he hadn't. The next day he had left to go back across the mountains to France. The episode faded into a blur of childhood memories. She had hardly thought of Richard since, not until her father and Richard's mother, Queen Eleanor of England and Duchess of Aquitaine, had arranged this marriage. But after Eleanor had come to snatch her from her studies at the monastery of Leyre, she had thought of little else.

Standing on the deck and lost in her memories, she forgot her intent to go below. She clung to the rail, buffeted by anxiety yet buoyed by tremulous anticipation. She was sure she could learn to love Richard, if he truly loved her. But what did she know of love?

Though in her twenty-fifth year, she was an innocent where men were concerned. Her mother had died eleven years ago and her father had never thought of explaining anything about marriage beyond impressing on her that she must think of the good of the kingdom, not her own preferences. King Sancho was very choosy about who might woo his daughters. Not only must the suitor be nobly born; the alliance must have political advantages. So, though suitors had appeared, none had taken her fancy; and if once in a while she was attracted to some young man, her father thought him ineligible.

This only reinforced her conviction that she was meant for the life of the mind rather than affairs of the heart. She and her younger sister Blanche would endlessly discuss their different views of what they hoped for from life.

"If you would just make a little effort, Berenguelita, you could enjoy yourself more when we have receptions at the palace. You don't have to judge a man as a possible future husband, just let yourself go and flirt a little. You are very pretty, you know. Men admire you, but you scare them off."

"That's all very well for you to say, Blanche; you're a romantic and you're the beauty of the family. But when some silly young count tells me how well his hounds can track down a deer, or why the horse he just bought is superior to the one he just sold, I lose interest very quickly, and wish I could go away somewhere and read my Latin books. I have no illusions that a knight in shining armor will come to sweep me off my feet."

By the time she was twenty she could read and write Latin, and she had learned everything the brothers at the Cathedral school could teach her. Then she began dreaming of learning to be a scribe — of copying precious manuscripts to preserve them for future scholars. This was not a seemly occupation for a royal princess in the twelfth century, but she finally got her wish. Her father, himself an accomplished reader and writer of Latin, at last consented to her pleas. She went to study with the learned monks at the monastery of Leyre, in the Pyrenees Mountains that bordered Navarre on the northeast. And in that secure haven Queen Eleanor had swept in like a whirlwind to collect her and begin the long journey to Sicily.

Almost at once her hopes that she could confide in Eleanor had been dashed. She quickly learned that her aloof companion cared only about getting the bride to Sicily before Richard left the island on his Crusade; seeing the two safely married; and returning home to Aquitaine. There were to be no reminiscences about what Richard was like as a boy, no interest in Berengaria as a person, no heart-to-heart talk about marriage.

Musing on the strange turn her life had taken, wondering if her peaceful days of study were all behind her, she was startled by the clack of swift, purposeful footsteps on the deck. Here was Eleanor, walking briskly forward to confer with the captain. She came back to where Berengaria stood and began speaking at once.

"We will soon be in Messina, and before we land there are some matters we must talk about." Regal, self-assured, still a striking woman in spite of her nearly three-score years, she held her midnight-blue woolen cloak closely about her. The fur-lined hood enveloped her head so that little showed except her piercing blue eyes, fixed on Berengaria.

"Tell me, my girl" (she had never called her "daughter," despite Berengaria's request), "how many children did your mother have? How many sons, and how many daughters?"

"Two sons and three daughters," Berengaria replied, mystified. "Why do you ask?"

Instead of answering, Eleanor asked another question. "And are they all living?"

"No, my sister Sancha died as an infant of but two days."

"And your mother's mother — what was her brood?"

Berengaria had to stop and think. "Two daughters and two sons, I believe, who lived. There may have been others who died young. But I never knew my aunts and uncles. My mother was from Castile, and her family never came to see us."

Eleanor was pursuing her own thoughts. "That bodes well. And on Richard's side of the family, there is certainly ample evidence of prolific parenting. Nobody can say that King Henry and I did not do our share, in our day! Eight babes in twelve years!" She smiled wryly. Berengaria did not know if a reply was expected, but Eleanor went on.

"So. We shall pray that God will grant to you and Richard at least a brace of sons to ensure the succession, and several daughters too, to marry off." She looked out to sea a moment, then turned to Berengaria again, speaking softly but distinctly. "But remember this. Whether that comes to pass or not depends most of all on you. Richard is older than you and he will not find marriage easy. He has never been given to longterm attachments to any woman. But like any man, he can be cajoled. He is not indifferent to female beauty and the seductions of the bedchamber. It will be up to you to learn how to handle him — how to make him want to lie with you."

Berengaria turned red as a beet. Such blunt talk! What could she say? Eleanor saw her discomfiture and put a hand on her arm. "Now do not worry, my girl. All this will come naturally, once you and Richard are wed. God knows, his father never lacked for lust! But for you, the task will be to channel his love toward you, and not to let him fritter his affections on other, unsuitable partners." She doubted if Berengaria completely understood, but better to leave it for now. She went below.

Berengaria did not completely understand. Unsuitable partners? But she would remember every word, and try to sort out the meaning, during the days to come.

Suddenly the cry of "Land ho!" rang out from the lookout in the bow. The galley was approaching Messina. She forgot everything else in the drama of coming into a strange port and its confusing activity. Her maid Cristina and the other women had come on deck and together they watched and exclaimed in excitement.

A long hook of land with a lighthouse at the end bent about the harbor. Within these sheltered waters vessels large and small were scudding about and dozens more were anchored near the shore. Off to the left she could see a field crowded with tents and huts, almost obscured by blue woodsmoke.

"That must be the Crusaders' camp!" exclaimed Cristina, as excited as her mistress. Beyond all this lay Messina, nothing like the drab, gray, crowded-together cities she was used to, but every house flaunting its colors — ochre, white, sunflower-yellow, rose. Here and there a minaret raised its slender spire. The city climbed the slopes of the mountain range to the west. The mountains were really rounded hills — nothing like the sharp-peaked, snowy Pyrenees of home. At the thought of the Pyrenees she felt a pang of homesickness. Why was she not still at Leyre, looking up in the morning at the craggy peaks that framed her little world? She reached deep down in her cloak's pocket for her little psalter, a parting gift from her friends at the monastery that she kept with her always.

But soon all this was forgotten. Suddenly they were bearing down on the pier, and there stood Richard awaiting them: a tall, solidly built man, with a luxuriant red-gold mane and beard. He bore himself with easy grace and his short crimson cloak was blown back by the same wind that had brought her here. Catching sight of his mother, he raised his hand in greeting. Then his eyes fell on Berengaria. He smiled slightly and made a little bow.

He was, she thought, the handsomest man she had ever seen.

She felt almost dizzy. At last, Messina! Where the next chapter of her life would begin.

hough Berengaria had been thinking of little but Richard lately, she would have been dismayed to know how seldom she had been in his thoughts. Preparing a force of 5,000 men to sail off to do battle with a powerful entrenched army — unbelievers, true, but nevertheless formidable — absorbed all his attention. Added to that was the matter of the obnoxious King Philip of France. He was being remarkably difficult. Richard was beginning to wonder if they could even function as co-leaders of this Third Crusade.

Philip had demanded a meeting yesterday, and the two monarchs had faced each other across a table in Richard's tent. They were as unlike as could be. Richard, tall, sturdy as an oak, dominated in physical terms. His ruddy face was open and he made no effort to hide his feelings, whether amusement, scorn or fury. Philip, slight and sallow-visaged, was inscrutable, and his darting eyes missed nothing. The coldly polite conference became a shouting match, each man holding to his notion of when the fleet should sail for the Holy Land. Richard claimed he had to wait until his mother arrived because she was bringing his bride.

Philip said that was frivolous, in view of the Pope's call for speed and zeal in the Holy Crusade. "Furthermore," he said, "I know you prefer to stay to pursue your little war against the Sicilians. Meanwhile, the real enemy awaits us in Palestine, getting stronger all the time."

"That may be. But this 'little war' is giving my men training in the kind of fighting they will have to do in Palestine. Saladin and his men wait for us there, snug and smug behind their thick walls. When we go at them with my battering rams, they won't be so cocky!" He looked at Philip belligerently, as though he were confronting Saladin himself.

Philip merely sneered, and rose to leave. "Suit yourself. Whenever you find it convenient to sail, I am sure you will. Meantime, I shall wait no longer. If you arrive in Palestine to find the infidels already vanquished by my brave Frenchmen, let the shame of it be on your head."

Out he went, to begin gathering his troops and loading his ships. To everybody's surprise, he had left before sunrise.

Now, having seen the last of Philip's fleet disappear over the horizon, Richard sat on a seawall by one of the long piers that poked into Messina's harbor. From here he could watch for the galley from Reggio. He studied the horizon. Nothing yet. He picked up the parchment that had been delivered to him a few days ago and reread it, trying to face up to the news that it contained; for until he received it, he had no inkling that he was soon to be a bridegroom.

My beloved son:

I write you from Genoa, where the Princess Berengaria and I are breaking our journey to Sicily. I pray this reaches you before you depart for the Holy Land.

I have told you many times that you must take a wife, in order to assure the succession to the throne. I have urged you to betroth yourself to Princess Berengaria, whose father, King Sancho, could prove a strong ally on our southern borders in France where the Count of Toulouse continues to threaten us.

Since you have taken no action, I am doing so. King Sancho has agreed to the marriage — he is aware that his daughter is getting no younger. We will arrive early in April and the wedding will take place at once, since I must return within a week.

Please tell your sister Joanna that it is my wish that she accompany you and your queen to Palestine; now that she is widowed, she has no occupation to keep her from it, and she will be a companion for Berengaria.

So. At last he would have to marry. His mother was right; it was his duty to produce an heir.

Yet he did not look forward to marriage. All his previous involvements with women had been impulsive, short-lived affairs, pleasant but quickly forgotten. He could not even remember the face of the girl who had borne him a child so long ago and he had never seen his son. He had, however, of course made sure that his bastard would be properly brought up and that he would receive an appropriate title and fortune.

Now, as often as not, he took his pleasure with partners of his own sex. He was not the first monarch to do so. There are always willing men and boys among a king's courtiers and soldiers, and no shame attached.

"And why should there be?" Richard asked himself. "I am generous to those I invite to my tent. I know it is a sin in the eyes of the Holy Church, but one of these days I will confess all and do penance."

He rose and walked down to the shore. Idly, he picked up a few pebbles and let them trickle through his fingers. In the harbor, the tireless vessels came and went. He could hear shouts of men loading the galleys that would bear them to the Holy Land. But here it was quiet, except for the little waves of the Mediterranean, gently lapping at the gravel strand.

Richard took the letter up and again read his mother's closing words:

> Above all, my son, I charge you to accept Berengaria as your wife in every sense of the word. Treat her with affection and respect, for she brings you a pure and loving heart, and is eager to do her duty as your queen and to be the mother of your children. I will not leave you until I am assured that your union is secure.

He knew his mother. As soon as she was ashore, she would start organizing the wedding; there would be no stopping her. By Easter he would be a married man.

Suddenly he struck his hand against his forehead. "But of course!" he said aloud. "Easter!" It was still Lent. How unseemly it would be to have feasts and all the other worldly entertainments that accompany a wedding, during the holy season! The ceremony would have to be postponed, perhaps until they reached Palestine.

Humming a tune, he walked back to the pier. Joanna, his youngest sister, stood there gazing to sea and absorbed in her own thoughts.

She had thrown back her hood and was enjoying the breeze as it caressed her face and played through her hair. Her expression was pensive; she was still sorrowful at the loss of her husband, King William of Sicily. She had loved him very much. It was restful to be with Richard, her favorite brother; they knew each other so well that she did not have to pretend a vivacity that she did not feel. She looked up at him with affection as he came near and he put his arm around her.

"You look almost cheerful, Richard. Have you decided to resign yourself to marriage?" Then she caught sight of the galley.

"There they come!" she exclaimed, as the red-and-white sail appeared and grew larger, and the banner on the mast was seen to be the royal colors of the Plantagenets. "Now at last I will see my mother, after all these years, and greet my new sister-in-law. Oh Richard, how wonderful it is to have something to look forward to again!"

"Speak for yourself, sister," Richard replied. Together they walked out onto the pier.

The vessel swept in gracefully, and the captain dropped the sail and ordered a maneuver by the oarsmen so that it glided gently to its resting place. Sailors rushed to secure it. Richard surveyed the passengers. Beside the familiar figure of his mother stood a slightly shorter woman in a long gray cloak, looking toward the shore with her hands on the rail. With the sun in his eyes, he could not see her face.

As soon as the galley was secure, the captain helped Eleanor step onto the pier, where Richard stood ready to offer his arm in support. She received his deferential kiss on her cheek, and he turned to help Berengaria. She too placed her hand on his arm, and for ten seconds his eyes held hers. She managed to keep her gaze steady, but she felt almost breathless. This tall, golden, incredibly handsome man was to be her husband, with whom she would spend the rest of her life!

At the sight of her so close to him, Richard took in her serene beauty, her composure. She was more comely than he had expected.

Perhaps this composure could be cracked, and she could give a man some sport.

However, he knew his mother was watching him closely and he would not give her the satisfaction of showing he was attracted. Still resentful of her interference in his life, he kept his voice courteous but cool.

"So we meet again, Princess Berengaria."

She looked at him gravely. "I was not sure you would remember your visit to Pamplona; it was so long ago."

"A man does not forget a tournament like that, or an adversary like your brother Sancho. He gave me more of a contest than I expected. And I remember that his little sister thought I had wounded him mortally!"

She smiled up at him, and her eyes met his trustfully. He glanced about. Joanna and her mother were embracing and talking animatedly. Impulsively, he leaned down and spoke so low that no one else could hear.

"You are very beautiful." He planted a quick kiss on her lips.

She blushed and to her relief he turned to introduce her to Joanna. "And look who is here to join in welcoming you to Messina." He was impersonal again.

Berengaria saw a woman of about her own height and age with a thin, plain, sober face. But when she smiled, her brown eyes sparkled and she looked almost pretty.

"Joanna, this is Princess Berengaria of Navarre."

Joanna moved quickly to take Berengaria's hand. "I have heard all about you from your brother, Prince Sancho, when he and your father visited us once in Limoges. Sancho said you were as good a sister as any man could hope to have. And now at last we meet! I am so glad." Her words bubbled out like the chirping of a wren — a bird she rather resembled. "And how very glad I am to know that we are to be sisters-in-law!" They stood smiling at each other, friends at once.

"And you are so pretty, too! My brother Richard is a lucky man indeed!"

Berengaria was touched, and amazed that this daughter of Eleanor's was so different from her cold mother. "I have heard of you too, Joanna, from my brother and also my father." She did not add that her father had once remarked that this Plantagenet princess seemed the only sane and sensible member of the family. Her mother, father and brothers were perpetually squabbling with each other or worse. "And I am truly sorry about the loss of your husband, King William."

Joanna's merry face became grave again. "It was very sudden and very sad, for he was not an old man. But I am thankful that we did have fifteen happy years together. And I am thankful that my bold brother is here to see that I get justice as his widow." She brightened. "But we will have plenty of time later to talk of all this. Did you know, Berengaria, that I am to go with you to Palestine, after your wedding?"

"I did not," said Berengaria. "But after five minutes in your company, I am overjoyed to hear it."

Richard and Eleanor had been conferring with the captain and the crew about unloading the galley. Eleanor and her ladies mounted their horses and left for the city. Richard rejoined the two women. He glanced at Berengaria, then spoke to his sister.

"Joanna, will you take Berengaria to the palace and help her get settled? I have many things to take care of here at the camp, so I will bid you good day, until tomorrow." He was off without another word.

What a strange, what a cool reception — except for that kiss! Had he really kissed her? It had happened so quickly. Berengaria was puzzled, but she told herself that no doubt before long Richard would start acting like a proper bridegroom.

Joanna's cheerful chatter was welcome as they rode side by side up the broad road. Seen close up the city was not quite as beautiful as it had appeared from the sea. Many of the houses were humble, even dilapidated, and the roads were rutted and dusty. But the townsfolk she saw had a happy-go-lucky air, unlike the sober, preoccupied residents of the cramped cities she was used to. Olive groves and vineyards were interspersed with homes, shops, churches and mosques, all drowsing in the late afternoon sun.

Then there was the palace. "How beautiful, Joanna!" she exclaimed as they rode up a long avenue lined with palms and bordered by gardens. "It is like no palace I have ever seen." It was of a dazzling whiteness, graced with arched windows and arcades that gave onto terraces and gardens in exuberant bloom.

"The Muslims built it long ago when they held this land," Joanna told her. "They did not need spiked walls or guard towers, only a pleasure palace. When our Norman armies conquered Sicily, thank goodness they did not destroy it. It was one of my husband's favorite residences."

"All my life I have dreamed of seeing sights like this," breathed Berengaria. They dismounted and she stared around her at the brilliant purple bougainvillea, the burbling streams and the fountains, the tall palms with their luxuriant fronds undulating gently in the warm wind.

"I could almost wish to stay here forever," she said. Joanna laughed.

"I know exactly what you mean, but don't get too fond of it. If I know my brother, the minute you two are married he will hustle everybody into the ships and we will be off. Richard does not let anything stand in his way when he has his mind set on something and he has thought about nothing but this Crusade for a year."

Berengaria thought this over and decided it explained Richard's aloofness. If he was so single-minded and worried about getting ready to leave, of course he would not have attention to spare for her. Later, when they were man and wife and sailing to Palestine, there would be plenty of time to get to know each other.

She took Joanna's hand. "Let us go in, and you will show me what a proper palace is like."

"N o, mother, it will not do."

It was the next morning. Eleanor and Richard stood facing each other, arguing. They were on the first floor of the tall, ungraceful wooden structure Richard had built between the Crusaders' camp and the town. He was proud of his new portable assault tower, and had insisted on showing it to his mother. He called it Matagriffon ("Death to the Greeks"). Richard and his men had fallen out with the local Greeks and Muslims soon after landing in Sicily. Richard had erected this fortress to put the fear of the English into their hearts.

Eleanor had politely said she would be glad to inspect it, but almost as soon as she got inside she brought up the subject of Richard's marriage to Berengaria and he began to talk of postponement. She was irritated, and the drafts that gusted through the cracks in Matagriffon's walls made her even crosser. It was too cold to sit down, and besides, there was no place to sit.

"It will not do to have the wedding now," he went on, "because we are well into Lent. How would it look to the world if the King of England defied the strictures of the Church? We are supposed to be sober and prayerful during Lent. All the festivities would be an insult to godfearing men."

"But I have come all this way only to see you wed, Richard. And I must return before the week is out. Surely one of your chaplains could perform a simple ceremony without offense to anyone." Eleanor was tired and feeling her years and the effects of her long journey. For once her words lacked conviction. She had, at least, secured his agreement to the marriage. Now that she had delivered the bride, let someone else take over.

Richard was more than ready to take over. Was he not king, the man who made the rules?

"I have enough sins on my head already, without adding one more by holding a royal wedding during Lent. It will have to wait. I cannot possibly stay here in Sicily until Easter, now that Philip has left for Palestine and the weather is propitious for sailing. But I promise you, mother, that as soon as we are safely ashore in the Holy Land, I will marry your Basque princess. Bishop John of Evreux is still here — I will ask him to come with us, so that all shall be done properly."

Eleanor heard the new firmness in his voice. This was not the obedient boy who had always looked to her for guidance. Since King Henry had died and Richard had assumed the throne two years ago, she felt he had distanced himself from her. Yet he was still the son she loved the most. And in this confrontation, he was the clear victor.

"So be it," she said. "I will have to believe that you will keep your word. And I suppose I should feel grateful that I will not have to organize a state wedding in this strange land." For a minute her shoulders drooped and Richard felt a very small pang of compunction. Then she stood straight again — once more Eleanor the High and Mighty, as Berengaria and her maid Cristina had privately called her.

"Now, my son," she said as he helped her down the rickety steps of the fortress, "will you please arrange some transport for me? I wish to get to Rome as soon as possible to see the Pope, before starting back to Poitiers."

"Of course, since you are determined to leave. The galley you came in is still here and if you like you may sail with the morning tide." So, her duty done, Queen Eleanor departed.

For the next four days Berengaria hardly saw Richard. The port was like a noisy anthill, with men running about bearing stores to load on the galleys, then running back for more; men-at-arms lugging broadswords, lances, clanking suits of armor and all their battle gear; and still more men urging reluctant horses and mules onto the boats.

Richard's major preoccupation was the dismantling of Matagriffon so he could load the parts on the boats and take it to Palestine. It proved much more difficult to take apart than it had been to erect.

"Sometimes I think my brother should have been called Hercules, because of the labors he takes on," said Joanna. She and Berengaria, attended by two armed retainers, had walked down to the harbor to see how things were going, but they were bewildered by the noise and confusion and went back to the relative calm of the cathedral square. There was commotion here too, but of a more familiar kind — hawkers of sweetmeats, jugglers hoping for a coin, boys and girls joining hands for an impromptu dance; and of course, beggars and probably thieves.

"I am afraid this city is infamous for its wicked men of every description," Joanna said apologetically; Berengaria had been surprised at their need for armed attendants. "My husband would never let me walk about here without guards."

They strolled slowly past the cathedral, and Joanna took Berengaria's arm and squeezed it.

"I am so glad you are here!" she exclaimed. "I have had no one to talk to for so long. It has been better since Richard came, but he is so busy."

Berengaria was glad the conversation had returned to Richard. "I can see that he is very serious about his preparations for the Crusade," she said. "I had hoped to see more of him while we were here, but I have not exchanged fifty words with him since I arrived. What do you think, Joanna? Is he glad to see me, or not? Does he really want to marry me?" It was hard to ask the question, but she had to. Joanna must have some inkling of Richard's feelings.

"I cannot speak for Richard." Joanna hesitated and looked down at the paving, as though seeking an answer in the patterns on the tiles. She remembered Richard's fiery face and shout of outrage, when he received his mother's letter telling him of the impending marriage. She could not even hint of that to Berengaria. She tried to think of an encouraging word. "But I am sure when he gets to know you better he will learn to love you." That sounded lame. "And besides, you are one of his oldest friends. He's often talked of the good times he had with you and your brother in Navarre."

"Of course we were friends then, as children are," said Berengaria. "But that was years ago! What of now? Sometimes I wonder, Joanna, how I happen to be here, and whether I should be

- 17 -

here at all." Her voice broke and Joanna could see how near to tears she was.

"Of course you should." She smiled her infectious little crooked smile. "And you are going to have a happy wedding, as soon as we get to Palestine. And while all the warriors are marching about and setting up their battering rams, you and I will be lady Crusaders, and we will use our feminine wiles and entice Saladin and his infidels out of Jerusalem, and Richard will be eternally grateful, and we'll go down in history!"

Berengaria could not help catching her mood. "And then we will come home, and you will fall in love with some handsome Norman noble, and we will all settle down in our neighboring castles and live happily ever after." Their laughter rang out over the sunlit square.

Just then Richard came up from the harbor, all sweaty and tired and not in the best of humor. He felt burdened by his responsibilities and found their levity quite unsuitable. "Excuse me for interrupting, but it now appears that we will be ready to sail at six tomorrow morning; so it would be well for you to gather your effects and come aboard tonight."

Like two little girls caught out, they looked at each other with complicity, composed their faces, and did as they were told. By ten that night, with the help of Cristina and also of Joanna's maid, they had settled into their seagoing quarters.

But Berengaria's hopes that she and Richard would become closer during the voyage were dashed. They would not sail together. He would be aboard the largest, swiftest galley, leading the way for the whole fleet. It was a warship, with no room for the comforts suitable for royal ladies.

So much for her vision of standing beside him on deck, sharing the joy of their swift passage over the waves, as they sailed ever eastward to their wedding day.

hat first night aboard was peaceful and Berengaria slept deeply, undisturbed by the gentle rocking of the boat and the squeaks of the rigging. However, the next morning she and Joanna were awakened by bumps and thumps, running and shouting overhead. They hurried to get dressed and climbed the steep, short stair from their cramped quarters to the deck, to find it aswarm with seamen. The crew had just weighed anchor and the captain stood at the tiller, barking orders. The two women stood astern, trying not to get in the way of the men toiling to hoist the mainsail.

"So this is a dromond," said Berengaria.

Joanna had told her that was what their vessel was called; she knew because she had sailed in a dromond from St. Gilles in France to Sicily when she came to marry William. "I was seasick the entire time. I would not want to repeat that voyage. But since then I have sailed many times from Palermo to Messina, and I am sure I have a stronger stomach for the sea now."

As they got underway, they could see the dozens of galleys that would carry Richard and his men still loading in the harbor. The galleys were more slender and graceful than the rather dumpy dromond.

"Why do you suppose we are the first to leave?" Berengaria wondered. "I hope we will not get too far ahead of the others."

"No danger of that; we're much slower. Richard told me that this ship is the safest in the fleet, and the pokiest. So we need a headstart. But he said that once we're all out at sea, he will make sure he is always close by."

Now they could see, one by one, the galleys moving out of the harbor, led by Richard's brave galleon, Trenk-Mer ("Slice-the Sea"). Behind them came the laden transports. It was an enormous fleet. Berengaria felt a little shiver of apprehension, and hoped there was safety in numbers. To set out on the trackless ocean, to be out of sight of land, to have no guide but the sun and stars — what kind of mad adventure were they embarking on?

"Do you know, I am a little afraid," she admitted to Joanna.

"Don't be," Joanna reassured her. "Just think of all the others who have made this voyage and come to no harm. My mother, for instance; she went to the Holy Land too, when she was even younger than we are, with her first husband, King Louis. She has certainly lived to tell the tale!"

Mention of Queen Eleanor was a bitter reminder to Berengaria of the last words she had heard her future mother-in-law utter before leaving Messina. It had been the morning when Eleanor left. Berengaria had gone down to watch the activity in the harbor. She was fascinated by the loading of the transports — the most capacious vessels of the fleet. She was amazed at the vast amounts of supplies that had to be loaded aboard, from casks of wine to hogsheads of salt pork. Beside her towered a tall stack of bales of hay, which would serve as fodder for the horses.

Suddenly, she had heard Eleanor's sharp, carrying voice on the other side of the stack.

"Now Richard, after I leave, remember what I have told you. I will be waiting to hear from you: first, that you are properly wed and second, that you have got your wife with child." Richard muttered in reply, his voice surly, "All right, all right. I know I must have a son, you have told me often enough. Now you have forced me into this marriage to …"

Berengaria could not make out the rest because of a noisy quarrel that had broken out among the toilers on the pier.

Her face burned with anger at this reminder that Eleanor thought of her only as breeding stock — and so apparently did Richard. She fought off hot tears and a sob caught in her throat. Terrified that she might be seen by Eleanor and Richard, she shook the shoulder of her dozing servant, who was sitting with his back against a bale of hay, eyes closed and mouth open but hand clenched firmly on the short sword in his belt. He jumped to his feet and she escaped, almost running up the hill to the palace.

I will not let this hurt me, I will not, she told herself. I will pretend I never heard them. Somehow I will make Richard love me for myself. Eleanor told me I could if I tried. But how?

She moaned softly and the servant wondered, "This poor lady, why is she so unhappy?"

By the time she reached the palace she was calmer. She must simply try to bury the painful memory.

Now at sea, surrounded by serenity, it was easier to thrust down the resentments and fears and to dwell on the voyage. With Joanna she stood at the rail, watching as the lighthouse at the end of the hook became just a white dot in the distance. They could see the other ships swiftly overtaking their dromond. Richard's crimson and gold banner flew from the prow of the leading galleon.

Though the sun was shining bravely on this April morning, as they sailed on so swiftly the breeze was more of a buffet than a caress. They pulled their cloaks around them and stood silently, both wrapped in their thoughts.

"I have spent the happiest years of my life on that island," Joanna mused. "To think that I was Queen of Sicily! But more than that, I was the wife of a kind and loving man. I wonder, will I ever sail again into that familiar harbor?" Her face was drawn, and she brushed at her eyes with a fold of her cloak.

Berengaria was thinking about what was to come. "And I wonder what it will be like, over there in Outremer — the land beyond the seas." Then she laughed. "What a silly question! There's no point in wondering — we will just have to wait and see. I am tired of worrying about the future." She was persuading herself as well as trying to cheer her companion.

"Let us simply enjoy ourselves on this grand sunny day. Do you know, Joanna, until I boarded the galley at Reggio to come across the strait to Messina, I had never been off dry land in my life? I don't count the little boats on the Ebro River in Tudela."

She looked up at the sails, tautly stretched to catch the wind, and down at the oarsmen on the lower deck, pulling lustily away as the vessel sped over the waves. "What a fine ship this is! At this rate we will be in Palestine all too soon!"

She took Joanna's arm. "But come, sister, let us go below decks — see how quickly I am learning to talk like a seafarer. We can see if the maids have unpacked our bags and made our little cabin all snug. Cristina should be very good at it by now, after all those weeks with me on the road. And your Elizabeth seems willing and competent."

"But I doubt if either has ever had to fit so many possessions into such a small space," Joanna said.

Just then they were approached by a burly, sunbronzed giant of a Norman with a head of thick black hair, a flowing black beard to match and a great deal to say. His booming voice preceded him.

"Ah, ladies, there you are. Now that we are well underway, I can bid you welcome properly. I am Sir Robert of Tornham, and I will be your guardian all the way to Palestine. The captain and I are honored to have you on our ship, and I trust our voyage will be calm and peaceful. But one never knows at this time of year. King Richard has instructed me to watch over my charges — that's you, ladies — like a mother hen with her chicks, and that will I do, that will I do. Are you content with your quarters? I know they are small. But mine are even smaller, if that's any comfort. And one of me is even larger than the two of you, ha ha!"

Even his laugh was outsize, and they were caught up by his infectious good humor. Before either could say a word in reply, he went on.

"Whatever we can do to make you easy, we will. You have but to ask. Now I must go discuss the rigging with our captain; the wind is freshening and he may need a hand. At your service, ladies." He sketched a sort of bow, and was off before they could even thank him for his solicitude.

Both felt vastly reassured — this Sir Robert of Tornham was obviously a man they could trust to see them safely and happily through any misadventure.

They went below, to find all shipshape. The maids had crammed as much of their clothing as they could into two big chests which did double duty as seats.

"But we could not get everything in," said Cristina, "and that nice Sir Robert brought us another big box for the rest and said he would find a safe place for it."

"It is a very small room," said Elizabeth. "But we have done our best."

The beds — little more than cots — were neatly made up with soft dove-gray coverlets and goose down pillows. Two wooden chairs were drawn up to a square table. Every stick of furniture was bolted securely to the floor.

"Yes, it seems even smaller than it did last night," said Joanna, looking about doubtfully. "But in this fine weather we'll probably be on deck most of the time so all we need is a place to sleep and eat."

Alas, not even the doughty Sir Robert or the capable captain could do anything about the terrible storm that struck, three days out of Messina. Neither oarsmen nor sails were any match for the fierce winds that blew the ship about like a cork on the heaving seas. For ten days Berengaria, Joanna and the two maids stayed huddled in their cabins, jounced from side to side, with only brief forays on deck to get a breath of fresh air and return in fright to their haven. Food and drink were brought to them by harassed-looking seamen, but they had no appetite. The soup was cold, the bread grew harder to chew every day, and the wine ran out so their only drink was brackish water from the casks in the hold. They could only pray that God would either put them out of their misery at once, or take mercy and cause the tempest to abate.

On the eleventh day they awoke to a strange calm. The floor stayed level, and it was actually possible to walk across the cabin without being tossed against the wall. They ventured on deck, to find the captain scanning the wide, flat sea with his glass. Sir Robert stood at his side. He looked haggard, and his beard was unkempt, his fine clothing salt-caked and rumpled. But he had not forgotten his responsibilities though his voice was hoarse and he sounded weary.

"Ladies, I am glad to see you unharmed and I am only sorry I could not personally attend to your comfort during this little blow. But I trust our seamen took proper care of you."

"They did indeed, and we are grateful," said Berengaria. "What a time you must have had, navigating through such a tempest! Is everybody all right?"

"All the men, yes. But I will tell you straightaway — no point in beating about the mulberry bush — your big chest that was lashed down on deck got away from us; it was washed overboard and I am afraid it is at the bottom of the sea."

"If that is all we have lost, God has been good to us," said Joanna.

"That's very well for you to say, sister. But my trousseau was in that chest. Well, Richard will just have to marry a ragamuffin!" Then she looked around in dismay.

"But where is Richard, Sir Robert? Where are the other ships?" They were all alone in an empty sea. Before the storm they had seen the rest of the fleet all around them, and Richard's galleon directly ahead.

"I am asking myself the same thing. But it would serve no purpose to go chasing about looking for them. Especially since we are in need of a safe harbor where we can do repairs and lay in supplies. And if I am not mistaken, we are not far from such a port."

They looked where he was pointing, and saw a smudge on the horizon. Slowly, as the ship forged on, the smudge took on shape and color. They could see the green of pines and cypresses clothing the mountains of a great island, with a cluster of brilliant white stone buildings on the shore.

"What land is that?" asked Joanna.

"Cyprus, I trust. We shall shelter in the harbor of Limassol, before nightfall." His voice was stronger.

Cyprus? Berengaria, who had seen maps of the Mediterranean, could hardly believe they had come so far. And where was Richard, where were the other ships?

Joanna felt even more misgivings. She had heard from her husband something of Cyprus and its "emperor," the usurper Isaac. Not only was he a collaborator with Saladin and the infidels, hence an enemy to the Crusaders, he had also been known to seize victims of shipwreck on the island's shores and hold them for ransom. Would that be their fate?

It very nearly was.

They anchored well out from the city at dusk. Sir Robert ordered a landing party to get ready to go ashore for supplies. But before they could set out, a small boat was seen approaching. As it drew alongside their vessel, a portly man wrapped in a fur cloak stood up and hailed the party on the deck. Folds of fat hung below his stubbled chin so it looked as though he had no neck. Beneath his big beaked nose his wide thin lips were stretched into an ingratiating smile.

"Greeting from the Emperor Isaac, Lord of Cyprus. He has seen from your pennant that you are part of King Richard's fleet of Crusaders, and from the state of your sails and your vessel that you have been beset by storm. He asked me to tell you that he regrets your misfortune, but he welcomes you to Limassol. And as token of his good intentions, he sends these hampers" — he pointed to three big wicker boxes at his feet — "filled with fresh bread and meat and our good Cyprus wine, for you and your weary crew. He begs any ladies on board to come ashore with us, and promises to extend to them his generous hospitality."

Joanna glanced at Sir Robert in alarm; she suspected treachery behind this seemingly courteous invitation. So did Sir Robert. His sharp eyes had made out a party of armed men drawn up in readiness on the beach. He acted at once. Without a word of reply to the emissary, he brusquely instructed the women to go below, and asked the captain to hoist sail. The oarsmen fell to, and within five minutes the ship was heading out to sea. Isaac's man in the small boat could only shake his fist in anger at the dromond as it sped away, and go ashore to tell his master that his plot had failed.

5

hile the hapless dromond was being tossed about the Mediterranean, so were the rest of the Crusader vessels. It was a dreadful time, even for the experienced sailors. For the main body of men, most of whom had never been to sea, it seemed the end of the world. Some were deathly sick. Some spent days and nights on their knees praying for deliverance. Some were lost overboard when giant waves broke over the boats and the raging winds snatched away the wretched men's cries of terror.

Richard and his captain managed to keep most of the vessels in sight during the storm, but they were blown so far off course that when the seas abated they were amazed to find themselves off the coast of Galatia, approaching an island that Spiros the captain declared to be Rhodes.

"I have heard it described," he told Richard, "and there, sure enough, is the long ridge the length of the island, and that tall peak they call Ataviros." Half Greek and half Sicilian, grizzled old Spiros had been specially chosen by Richard because he knew the Mediterranean waters better than any other seaman in Sicily.

Yet even Spiros was bewildered now. "How have we come so far north and so far east? Only the gods of the winds and the sea know. Mayhap we should have offered a sacrifice to old Poseidon before we set sail from Messina." Then he crossed himself guiltily, abashed that he had made such a pagan suggestion.

But Richard had not noticed. He was peering ahead to where the crags parted to reveal passage to a protected little bay. As the oarsmen propelled them, ship by ship, into this long-awaited safe harbor, every man breathed a prayer of thanks. The sapphire-blue waters reflected the ancient temple on the peak, and old Spiros sent a special private thank-you to the goddess who once was honored there, Pallas Athene.

The fleet spent a few days taking stock of their losses, repairing sails and rigging and filling their water barrels. When the men went ashore the villagers of Lindos laughed at how they staggered until they got their land legs back. Nevertheless, they were generous with meat and bread and grain.

Richard sent galleys out to scour the seas — now placid, as though they had never seen a storm — in search of the rest of the fleet. Some twenty-five vessels were unaccounted for. Not only was the dromond with the ladies missing; so was the ship bearing Richard's treasure, without which his Crusade could not last more than two days in Palestine.

There was no sign of the others. Richard gave the order to sail on an easterly heading, keeping the Turkish coast in sight, while scanning the ocean and the shore for the missing ships.

At last, out of the featureless sea, the mountains of Cyprus came in view, just visible above the horizon. Richard conferred with Spiros.

"No point in making a landfall on the north coast," said the captain. "But if we head for Limassol, around the cape there, we may be able to learn something. Ships sailing to and from the Levant stop in that harbor, and we may find someone who has seen or heard about our lost comrades."

As they rounded Cape Gata, to the west of Limassol, the lookout shouted lustily from his perch on the mast, "Ship in sight, I think it is the dromond!" He slid down and breathlessly described to Richard the large vessel he had seen outside the harbor. "I spied a pair of beached galleys too — they looked like some of ours, sire, but I saw no people."

Sure enough, there was the dromond. Since escaping from Isaac the day before, the ungainly vessel had been sailing back and forth just outside the harbor while Sir Robert glumly watched the activity on shore and tried to assess Isaac's forces. On catching sight of Richard's tattered standard, he let out a whoop of surprise and ordered the helmsman to make for the galleon. When the two vessels were a few feet apart, Richard leaped over the side and onto the dromond's deck. He strode to clasp Sir Robert's hand, smiling broadly.

"My faithful friend, God has been good. We meet again! I see that you have safely brought your ship through the storm. Are your passengers safe and sound?"

"As sound as can be, considering how they have been all topsy-turvy. There you see them, eager to greet you." Richard glanced quickly at Berengaria and Joanna and their maids, who stood aft waiting to be noticed, and raised a hand in greeting. Then he made his face stern as he spoke again to Robert.

"But I am disappointed in you. How did you come to lose yourself so completely?" Sir Robert, taken aback at the rebuke, stared and his bushy eyebrows bristled. Then he saw it as the jest it was.

"Nay, my lord, we knew where we were; we only wondered how you and the rest of the fleet had strayed so far from us." Both men laughed, and Richard embraced the burly Norman.

Berengaria thought she had never seen Richard show his generous nature so clearly. I have not seen this Richard before, she thought. He looks so weary. What a terrible responsibility he has, for thousands of men and hundreds of ships! A surge of love for this man she hardly knew surprised her. She waited eagerly for his greeting.

He was cool as ever. He clapped both women on the shoulder as though they were knights in his service. "So you have come through this little blow with no ill effects?"

Joanna threw herself into his arms. "Oh Richard, we are so glad to see you! We thought you were lost, we thought we were going to the bottom of the sea. And now we are together again, thanks be to God!" She was almost sobbing, and Richard patted her back. His eyes met Berengaria's, but she could not read them. The intense blue gaze told her nothing. He turned back to Sir Robert.

Richard, now that he knew they were safe and the ship was not seriously damaged, was all business. His first concern was the missing ships.

"We've seen not a glimmer of them," Sir Robert said, "but we think some came to grief along the coast there to the west — we made out a couple of vessels lying all downside-up. And then last night one of my men slipped ashore to snoop about, and came back to report that that misbegotten Isaac who calls himself emperor had captured a dozen of our shipwrecked knights and thrown them into prison." He glowered. Then he told Richard how Isaac had tried to lure Berengaria and Joanna ashore with false promises.

Richard was furious. Within half an hour, he had mobilized his fighting men and launched an assault on Isaac's forces.

As soon as the dromond had been moved to a new anchorage, well behind the war vessels, Sir Robert made off to join the attack party. From the deck, Berengaria and Joanna watched the drama. Neither had ever seen a battle. If they had not been so fearful, they might have enjoyed it as spectacle. They could plainly see the shore, where soldiers were dragging all kinds of objects down to the beach to pile up in a barricade: benches, casks, planks, debris from shipwrecks. Behind this higgledy-piggledy wall Isaac's troops were assembling. Still farther back lay the town, crowned by a castle on a thickly wooded hill.

"Look, there come some more!" cried Joanna. She had a vantage point in the bow. Another company of "griffons," as the Crusaders called the Greek defenders of the island, had just arrived on the shore, to join the hundred already assembled there. Standing in rows at attention, they looked from afar like toy soldiers — but they carried sharp-tipped lances and deadly crossbows.

For five minutes nothing happened.

"Why doesn't Richard bring his men ashore? Is he going to leave those villains unpunished?" Joanna was almost crying.

Berengaria, who had a better view from her spot on the port side, called out excitedly, "Here they come, Joanna! All the boats are leaving the ships now, full of soldiers. How they bob about on the water! I pray God they do not sink — so many big men in each little boat. Come quickly, you will see it all."

Sure enough, dozens of small boats, little more than cockleshells, were now approaching the shore. As the boats drew near, the defenders loosed a volley of arrows but their targets were moving too fast and too erratically and no arrow found its mark. Almost simultaneously, and while the Cypriots were hurrying to place new arrows in their bows, the Crusaders' archers leaped out of their boats, splashed through the water and sent a deadly shower toward the griffons, even before stepping on dry land. The defenders, whose hearts were perhaps not in this battle, wavered.

Many fell. From the rear of their ranks, two horsemen galloped away to disappear in the wooded ravines above the city.

"They must be going for reinforcements — but I am afraid Richard could not see them. Now, Richard! Attack!" Joanna was screaming as though she could be heard on shore. But Richard needed no urging. Before the Cypriot commanders could decide what orders to give, the Crusader swordsmen, with Richard in the forefront, swarmed up the beach, bounded over the makeshift barricade and rushed the griffons. The battle was over almost before it began, as the defenders fled. Some scattered through the town, not even taking time to mount their horses. Others leaped on their waiting steeds and galloped up into the forest.

"After them!" cried Richard and his men hurried to mount the horses the fleeing defenders had left behind. They rode pellmell through the town, then were lost to sight. They were anxious to take Isaac — it was he whom the two watching women had seen fleeing when he saw the battle was going against him, and Richard's sharp eye had spied him too.

Some time after the pursuers had disappeared and the dust of their galloping horses had subsided, a few townspeople came out to see to the wounded who still lay where they had fallen. Then the beach was deserted, nothing bearing witness to the battle except the tumbled disorder of the rubble barricade.

It was clear that the Crusaders had won the day. Berengaria and Joanna hugged each other in their relief. Cristina and Elizabeth had been as fearful and fascinated as their mistresses. While the four women excitedly compared notes on what they had seen, all talking at once, Sir Robert's head appeared over the rail. He was climbing the rope ladder from his boat onto the ship, puffing and wheezing but grinning from ear to ear.

"Did you get a good look, ladies? That Isaac will think twice before he tries to outsmart our king again. The old coward deserted his men when the going got rough. Probably holing up now in a cave in the hills. No business on this island in the first place. And soon he'll be sorry he ever called himself emperor, mark my words."

On deck now and still out of breath from his exertions, he paused and Berengaria managed to interrupt. "It was a glorious battle, and we saw you in the midst of it. But where has Richard gone? We quite lost sight of him. Is he…"

Sir Robert went on as though she had not spoken.

"Yes, King Richard will smoke him out soon enough. He's hot on the trail — halfway to the top of the island by now, I dare say. He sent me back so I could see to your safety until he returns. Which may be tonight or may be tomorrow, but no later if I know my king. Now if you'll excuse me, my orders are to get you ashore as soon as can be. You're to lodge in the home of one of the merchants. I thought I might have to show him the tip of my sword to get him to agree, but he said yes right away. I have a notion none of these griffons have cared much for old Isaac and his highhanded ways; good riddance, they're saying."

"Bravo, Sir Robert," said Joanna. "It will be heavenly to set foot on land again."

"And will the hospitable merchant feed us, too?" Berengaria asked. "After all these days with dry biscuits and stale cheese, we are ready for proper food."

"And so am I, my lady, so are we all," replied the knight. "My first act will be to see if these lazy Greeks can cook us a meal. How does roast lamb sound to you, and fresh-baked bread, and a pudding with cream?" His eyes lit up at the thought and his black beard quivered as he smacked his lips.

They assured him it sounded very good. "And Sir Knight, don't forget some of that famous Cypriot wine that Isaac tried to give us," Berengaria said gravely. "A thimbleful or two should go very well with the lamb."

He looked at her suspiciously, then caught her half-suppressed smile and gave a bellow of laughter. "Right you are, princess. I'll send out for the wine and the biggest thimbles in Limassol!" As he went aft to order the boats, his receding chuckles sounded like the sputtering-out of a distant thunderstorm.

wo days passed before Berengaria saw Richard again.

There was a great to-do in the town the evening of the second day. Guy de Lusignan, King of Jerusalem, had sailed into the harbor with a company of knights and nobles. Ever since Saladin had recaptured Jerusalem in 1187, Guy had been a king without a kingdom. When he heard that Richard and his army were on their way, he came to greet them at Cyprus, to tell Richard about his plight and make sure of his support.

Guy and his men had just disembarked when Richard and his weary troops came riding down the hill road after their two-day search for Isaac. They were hot and dusty but not dispirited. Guy hurried up through the town to meet them.

"Greetings, Sir Guy," called Richard. He dismounted and stretched and turned his horse over to a groom. "What brings you to Cyprus?" He was not fond of the short, rather fat Guy, who was one of his principal vassals in France. Richard thought him too conniving and unctuous. But he was a good man to have on one's side — especially if subterfuge and intrigue were called for — and he always knew all the gossip.

They walked along together toward the town.

"In any case, you are just in time to join us for the final act," Richard went on. "We have tracked the villainous Isaac down, and it only remains to take him — one way or another."

"By which you mean dead or alive, no doubt," replied Guy. "And if the latter, put him away somewhere so he'll have no more chance to make mischief."

They walked on to the shore. Richard made a quick survey to make sure that all his ships were riding safely at anchor. Guy was still talking.

"And speaking of mischief, the sooner you get to Palestine the better. King Philip is stirring up trouble and trying to force me out of my kingship of Jerusalem. As soon as we have taken care of this upstart emperor, I hope we can sail."

"Not quite that soon," replied Richard. "First we must not only find Isaac, but round up his army, too. They've had time to find hideouts all over Cyprus by now." He gestured up toward the wild, pathless, forested hills behind the town.

"And there is another reason for a slight delay. You must stay for my wedding."

The idea of a Cyprus wedding had come to Richard as he had ridden down from the mountains. The more he thought about it, the wiser it seemed. The festivities would be a welcome change for his weary men after weeks of grueling battles with the sea. It could be as grand an affair as Cyprus had seen in a century. Richard was vain, and the prospect of dressing in his finest and receiving the plaudits of the populace for ridding them of the hated Isaac was tempting. He had no doubt that it was only a matter of days before he would take his quarry.

"Your wedding? What, are you to be married?" Guy asked in astonishment.

"I am, for my mother has ordered it. Berengaria, daughter of King Sancho of Navarre, is with us, and we had planned to have the wedding in Palestine. But I think now that it might be well to hold it here instead. God knows, once we arrive in the Holy Land, we'll have to get about our business at once and there'll be little time for weddings. And besides, with you and all your company here to help us fill the church, it could be quite a celebration."

"True enough. None of us have had much to celebrate lately. Besides which, there's nothing like a pompous great show to impress the locals — keep them on our side when we go after Isaac." His crafty face broke into a deferential smile. "After the ceremony, my king, if you have little taste for the wedding bed, I know of more than one lad in my company who can amuse you."

Richard stared at him coldly. "Unseemly talk, Sir Guy. You are here to consult with me on our military plans, not to advise me on my personal life."

With one last steely glare, he mounted his horse and rode off toward the hilltop castle that had been Isaac's and that he intended to make his headquarters. He could almost hear his mother saying, "Well done, Richard. You know where your duty lies, and why you are marrying. Pay no attention to that lewd Norman."

Enjoying a rare sense of virtue, he made his way to the castle. As he washed off the grime and donned a fresh tunic, he found himself thinking about Berengaria. He had to admit that the princess was desirable. Her decorum, to be sure, was something of a challenge. He was not used to virtuous women, and it might be amusing to woo this one a bit. Perhaps if he flattered and teased her in advance, he could penetrate that reserve enough to arouse her. He was quite sure that she was attracted to him. Indeed, this sober Basque princess might provide some good sport on the bridal couch! The game would have to be played just so — but Richard was never one to refuse a challenge.

He called for Sir Robert of Tornham and told him to see to the preparations and to send the Bishop of Evreux to him in an hour. Then he left to seek out his promised one, to tell her that on the day after the morrow she would become his queen.

Berengaria, Joanna and their hostess Philomena — wife to the merchant in whose house they were lodged — were sitting in her courtyard, a bower where purple-blossomed bougainvillea bushes were trellised against honey-colored walls. It was after dinner, which had featured roast lamb as anticipated, and they were getting acquainted. The hospitable woman was proud to have as guests such exotic visitors as these, but the language barrier made communication difficult. She knew only a few words in French, and their Greek was even worse. Still, with gestures and goodwill they did not do too badly. Philomena was trying to tell them about the old Roman city that lay just to the east of Limassol, and offering to take them there.

Berengaria was in favor of the expedition, not only out of curiosity about the Roman ruins, but also in hopes it might distract her from her distress at Richard's indifference. Not a word or gesture of warmth since that surprising kiss on the pier in Messina. Perhaps he did not intend to marry her at all. Then what would she do? If only he would say something, reassure her!

As though on cue, Richard appeared.

"Good evening, ladies! May I join you for a moment?" he said cheerfully. This was not the unsociable, remote king but a comradely friend, dropping by to pass the time of day. Berengaria, startled, smiled in spontaneous pleasure, then tried to compose her face in the polite reserve that she thought he merited. But Richard's keen glance had noted her first reaction.

Joanna introduced him to their hostess, who was flustered at entertaining still more royalty — the King of England no less! She said she would go at once to order some refreshments, indicating her intention by miming the raising of a cup to her lips and sipping, then looked inquiringly at Richard. He nodded encouragingly and so did the others, and she hurried into the house.

"Very warm for May," he remarked as he sank into a chair and mopped his brow with the loose sleeve of his tunic. "And how have you two been occupying yourselves, while we were busy chasing the enemy out of town and making it safe for you?"

Joanna sniffed and looked at him with sisterly reproach. "Better for us to ask what you have been up to. You have certainly not bothered to let us know. Have you found Isaac? Are there more battles to come? And when do we sail away to Palestine, so we can have a wedding?"

Berengaria, trying to maintain her aloofness, anxiously awaited his answers.

Richard told them he had a very good idea of where Isaac was hiding, and that he planned a major operation to take him in a few days.

"But first, as to that wedding: I have decided that it should be held here and now, or at least the day after tomorrow. Can you be ready?"

For the first time he looked directly at Berengaria. She felt astonishment, then vast relief, then just a touch of resentment. This, apparently, was as much of a marriage proposal as she was likely to get, and she thought it lacked something in ardor.

Before she could reply, Joanna jumped to her feet. "Joyful news! I will go ask Philomena to bring her best wine, so we can celebrate!" She tactfully left the happy couple alone at this important moment.

Richard and Berengaria looked at each other — she still trying to control her feelings, but blushing under his gaze of frank invitation. This was a Richard she did not recognize. He rose, sat beside her, and ran his hand over her long brown hair, then let it rest on her shoulder. He felt her shiver at his touch.

"At last, my beautiful princess, we will be wed. Are you glad?"

Now she could speak her heart. "Oh Richard, yes I am glad! I have waited so long to hear these words from you." She looked up at him and her green eyes shone, telling him all.

"So may I kiss you?" His voice was low and urgent. Without waiting for an answer, he gently put his arm around her and kissed her softly on the lips. She did not resist. She felt his warmth, his strength. She wished the moment would never end.

He drew back and tilted her chin up so she could not help looking into his eyes. "Oh, Berengaria," he whispered, "you have the most beautiful eyes in the world." He let his fingers stray softly over her cheek, then traced the outline of her lips. Clasping her in his arms, he pressed her to him, then kissed her again — a long, lingering kiss.

Berengaria pulled away, confused by his ardor and her own turbulent emotions. She felt as though her lips were on fire. She could not speak. She looked down, blushing furiously, then up and into his eyes again. Now they were teasing her.

"I think we need to get to know each other better," he said, so softly that she could hardly hear. "But soon we will be properly married and we will know each other very well indeed. I hope we will please each other. Will you try to please me?"

Before she could answer Joanna and Philomena came back. She sat decorously with downcast eyes, but Richard's arm was still around her waist and she was acutely aware of his closeness. Philomena smiled broadly at them, set down her tray and filled goblets with the ruby-red wine.

"Now we must drink to this happy news!" said Joanna. "And Richard, where will the wedding be, and who will marry you?" It was time to get practical.

Richard told them of the chapel in Limassol Castle, and said he was meeting Bishop John of Evreux shortly to discuss the ceremony.

Joanna's agile mind was hard at work. "We must think at once, Berengaria, of your gown. What will you wear?"

Berengaria, on a cloud of happiness, came to earth with a thud. She looked down with distaste at her well-worn gown, an indeterminate gray. The Princess of Navarre could not marry the King of England in such a garment, but she had little else. "I don't know. I have absolutely nothing that will do. Remember, the chest with my wedding finery was lost overboard during the storm."

Philomena had been watching and seemed to understand the problem. She jumped up and pointed to her own dress, outlined the shape of a woman's figure with her hands, then pointed to Berengaria. She clasped her hands and looked ecstatically up as though in speechless admiration, then pointed toward her house. The meaning was crystal clear: she could provide just the dress for a wedding.

Richard laughed with the others, drained his goblet and stood up. "I must not keep Bishop John waiting," he said. He bent over Berengaria's hand and pressed his lips to it, looking up into her eyes. "Until the day after tomorrow, my sweeting." He patted Joanna on the shoulder, smiled at Philomena and left.

The courtship was over.

Berengaria sat a while in the garden, going over everything that had happened on this amazing afternoon. Again and again she relived the precious moment when Richard had kissed her and she had read the desire in his eyes. She was swimming in a pool of happiness.

Only later that night did it come to her that Richard had not spoken one word of love.

7

And in the morning was the damozel wed and crowned at Limassol. The fair maid with the bright countenance, the wisest lady in all truth that might anywhere be found. Now was the king in his glory and in great joy over his victory and over his marriage with her to whom he had pledged his faith.

Roger Howden, chronicler of the Third Crusade

rumpets blared a stirring fanfare as Richard strode into the chapel, like the rising sun that dazzles the waiting world with its radiance. The guests stared in awe at the regal figure, his lustrous tunic the color of rose petals, topped by an ermine-edged cape embroidered in gold. His hand rested on the gold hilt of his sword in its jeweled scabbard. He held his head high, as though the massive gold crown weighed no more than a feather. He walked toward the altar in measured strides, his face solemn. This was indeed a king in his glory.

Berengaria followed, on the arm of Robert of Tornham. Necks were craned — this was the first time many in the chapel had seen the princess who had come so far to wed their king. They were not disappointed. The resourceful Philomena had done her best. Seamstresses had been working a day and a night to alter a long-sleeved white linen gown to fit Berengaria's slender figure. Her sleeveless coat of blue silk was embroidered with golden fleur-de-lys. Her waist was encircled with a gold-mesh girdle. Her brown hair with its glints of chestnut hung loose, confined only by a pearl-studded gold circlet from which floated an almost transparent white wedding veil.

Like Richard she paced slowly, with dignity. After one quick look around the chapel, crowded with Richard's and Guy's most illustrious knights, she looked straight ahead, containing her emotion. Not Sir Robert: his face shone with pride and scrubbing. Even his black beard and eyebrows looked polished. Beaming with importance in his role as surrogate guardian, he relinquished Berengaria when they reached the altar.

Side by side stood bride and groom. The bishop of Evreux, attended by Richard's chaplain, Nicolas, performed the solemn wedding ceremony. Afterwards, when Berengaria tried to recall those moments, all she remembered was a blaze of candles, a drone of Latin by bishop and chaplain and a blur of the churchmen's brilliant vestments. She remembered how at the end Richard raised her veil. Looking straight into her eyes, he murmured, "Now you are mine."

Next came the crowning of the new queen. The bishop carefully removed the golden circlet from her head, and she knelt. Richard took from the altar a crown, shining with rubies and pearls, and handed it to the bishop, who placed it reverently on Berengaria's head. His sonorous words rang out through the chapel: "By the grace of God, we now declare you to be Queen of England, with all the rights, privileges and responsibilities pertaining thereto. May you be a wise and good sovereign to your subjects and helpmeet to Richard your king, and may God's mercy be with you to the end of your days." He gave her his hand and she rose — suddenly a queen, with hardly time to realize what was happening.

The crown was heavy, and so would be the responsibilities the bishop had impressed her with. "But," she thought, "Richard is used to ruling, and I will simply try to help him every way I can." She looked up at him, wondering about this totally new life. He was staring at her and though his face was suitably solemn, his eyes were not. She could read their secret invitation.

"Well done, Queen Berenguelita," he said sotto voce. He had never used that diminutive of her name before — nobody had except her family. He must have remembered it from long long ago, when he had come to Pamplona for the tournament, when she was only six. She was deeply moved, and torn between sudden home-sickness for the sheltered, familiar life she had left behind, and joyful hope for the future, at the side of her dearly beloved.

The ceremonies were not yet over. Now they were escorted onto a balcony overlooking the castle courtyard, where the townspeople of Limassol had gathered, noisily expressing their support for this liberator from the west who was about to unseat their oppressive emperor. The crowd cheered when the royal couple appeared on the balcony. Richard was now their hero, his queen their heroine. Besides, there was sure to be a great feast for all.

And feasting there was, until far into the night. Tables laden with roasted meats and jugs of wine were set up in the town square, while within the castle a more elaborate repast was laid out for the royalty, the lords of the Church, the Crusaders and a few select Cypriots and their ladies. Almost all the food and drink had been taken from Isaac's private stores, and more than one derisive toast was drunk to their absent and unwitting host.

At table, Richard immediately began talking to Guy de Lusignan on his right. Berengaria, on his left, had nothing to say but took it all in. They were discussing plans for taking Isaac and defeating his army for once and all. Guy's knights and Richard's joined in noisily, growing more belligerent with every gulp of wine.

"I say we should hang him by the heels as soon as we smoke him out."

"But don't forget that pretty little lass, his daughter — we must get him to tell us where she is, before we knock him senseless."

"They say he's hidden his gold under the floor of the monastery at the top of the mountain. We'll soon see how brave those prissy Greek monks are, when King Richard comes to collect it!"

Richard heard this and let out a roar of laughter, banging his flagon down on the table so drops of wine flew. "By our Lady, that will be a sight! They'll go flying down the mountainside like a flock of crows with their black robes flapping behind them!"

Berengaria was bewildered by this loud and uninhibited company, so unlike any banquet at her father's more decorous court. Only once did Richard turn to her. Already well into his cups, he threw his arm around her shoulder, pushed his face into hers and said, "Do you just be patient, my pretty queen. Bear with this a little longer, then you and I will steal away and seek gentler sport." She did not know what to say, but it did not matter, for he turned to respond to a shouted question from farther down the table. In any case conversation was impossible.

She wanted only to escape. It had been a day more filled with ceremony and strain than any in her life up to then. Yet beneath the fatigue coursed a current of anticipation — half fearful, half impatient — as she wondered about the night to come.

Joanna, on her other side, was resting her head on her hand, her eyes closed. Berengaria nudged her. "Do you think anyone would notice if we got up and left, Joanna? My head is about to burst, Richard is too busy thinking about battles to pay us any attention, and I cannot stomach another morsel of food or sip of wine."

Joanna lifted her head and agreed. "Yes, let us leave. But I doubt if we can slip out without being noticed. After all, this is your wedding feast, and the company will soon remember that when we rise to go. Just hold your head high and remember that you are a queen!"

It was good advice. Ribald remarks rang out as they made their way from the head table toward the door. Berengaria was glad she could not make out most of them.

Richard, at last noticing their departure, bounded down the steps after them and shouted, "Leaving so soon, my lady?" In front of everyone he pulled her against him and planted a kiss full on her lips. He reeked of wine and, hot with embarrassment, she tried to pull away. But he held her so close that she almost lost her breath. He added in a hiccupy whisper, "Wait for me. I will join you soon, and you will learn what manner of man your husband is."

To her amazement, as his body still pressed against hers, she felt a surge of excitement that spread from between her legs up to her breasts and through her whole being. He released her. "Wait for me," he said again in a slurred mumble. Then he rejoined the company.

Face flaming but head still high, she left.

And wait she did, for what seemed hours. After Cristina helped her undress and put on a white silk nightdress — another loan from Philomena — she dismissed the maid and lay down on the canopied bed, wide-eyed. From below came sounds of laughter, loud talk and the occasional crash. A knight falling off his chair? A platter dropped by a servant? Richard pounding his flagon on the table? For a long time she lay, hoping at every moment to hear Richard's step, imagining how it would be when he came to her and gently, oh so gently, kissed her and caressed her, and how gladly she would give herself to him.

Gradually the noise subsided, and worn out with waiting, she fell asleep.

The next thing she knew the door was flung open and Richard was standing beside the bed, holding a candle, staring at her. His face was flushed, his eyes were like slits as he squinted at her and his lips were curled in a caricature of a smile. He put the candle down. With one hand he pulled at her gown, tearing the fragile silk until it ripped from neck to hem. With the other he fumbled at his own garments. No word was spoken. For a moment he surveyed her naked, vulnerable body without a glance at her terrified face. He was too far gone in wine to remember his notion of gently enticing his bride, of disporting himself with her while teaching her the joys of love. He fell on her and brutally, swiftly entered her. She felt only a searing pain, then the terrible weight of his body as he pushed repeatedly against her. Within minutes he had his way with her, then with a groan he fell to her side and was asleep in an instant.

But Berengaria did not sleep again that night.

he had no idea how long she lay there, face to the wall, staring into the dark. Beside her, Richard was dead to the world, except for the occasional snort and moan of a man who has drunk too much. Worn out with sobbing, she huddled under the covers until dawn sent pale exploratory shafts of light into the blackness. Then she heard Richard rise and dress. Would he, by some word or touch, show her he was aware that he had wounded her in heart as well as body? She heard nothing, and thought he had left. Then he spoke.

"Berengaria."

She turned on her back to see him standing by the bed. He did not look like a man filled with regrets. She waited.

"Berengaria. That was not the wedding night I had intended. I can only blame the wine." His voice was not warm, not cold — rather as though he were reciting a speech.

He is not used to apologizing, she thought bitterly. Blame the wine? Of course that is the easiest way out. But still she did not speak, only lay there looking up at him.

He had expected an angry outburst and was relieved at her silence. He assumed she had accepted what he considered an apology. He went on: "I cannot stay. We must begin the search of the mountains for Isaac. But I will ride more cheerfully if I hear you say you have forgiven me."

Berengaria sat straight up in the bed, wrapping herself in her torn, blood-spattered nightdress and the rumpled coverlet. "How can I forgive you, when you have not even said you were sorry?" She did not raise her voice, but every word was charged with her pent-up hurt and outrage. Her eyes, puffy with weeping, overflowed again with angry tears. "You told me to wait for you and you would show me what manner of man I had married. Well, I waited, and you did indeed show me."

Anger gave way to a terrible sorrow. She buried her face in her hands and he could hardly hear the muffled words. "Richard, is this what my life with you is to be? I loved you, and I thought you loved me — or wished to learn to do so. Am I to be just another of your strumpets, to be used and tossed aside whenever it pleases you?"

He was still silent. She could not read his face. Again her wounded pride overcame her. "I do not think that is what my father — or your mother — expected from our marriage! I would rather go back to the monastery in Navarre for the rest of my days than stay with a man so vile, no matter how great a king!"

Now Richard was alarmed. He could imagine Eleanor's reaction if she heard that the marriage had failed on its second day. He would have to mend his fences. He sat down beside her and put his arm around her shoulders, but she still sat stiffly upright.

"Of course I am sorry, and now I am sorry I did not say I was sorry! There, two apologies for my Berenguelita. And I promise you that the next time we share a bed you will find me as loving and kind as last night I was hasty and thoughtless." He kissed her on the brow and rose. "Now I must be off on my warrior's business. Am I to ride cheerfully, with your forgiveness?"

She did not know what to think. She wanted desperately to believe in his repentance and his promises. She searched his face for some reassurance beyond his words, but she found none. She had no choice but to believe him.

"Very well. Go now, go fight your fight."

Relieved, he bent to kiss her again quickly, then hurried out the door. Slowly, Berengaria got out of bed, put on a loose robe, and called Cristina to come help her wash and dress.

"He said he would be a loving husband the next time we share a bed," she thought, tiredly. "Well, we will see."

By land and sea, Richard and Guy and their troops pursued Isaac, but the search took longer than they expected. From Famagusta on the coast he escaped inland to Nicosia, where he eluded them again, fleeing on horseback and leaving his men to be captured or slain. Finally, while Richard was taking possession of Nicosia, Guy trapped their prey in his castle at Kyrenia, and took not only Isaac but also his young and nubile daughter, Maria.

The one spark of humanity in Isaac's dark nature was his love for his only child, and he begged his captors to spare her and treat her gently. Richard promised to do so: "I will give her as much love and care as though she were my own sister."

But as for Isaac, he was cast in a specially made set of silver chains (a cruel joke — he had implored not to be placed in irons), and dispatched to prison in Syria.

Richard returned in triumph to Limassol, declared himself king of the island and confiscated Isaac's treasure. The Cypriots rejoiced at the capture of their despised emperor, but were not quite so happy when Richard levied a stiff tax on his new subjects, and ordered them to send regular shipments of corn and wine to the Christian forces in the Holy Land.

Gradually, all but two of the ships that had gone astray during the storm had straggled into Limassol Harbor, among them the one bearing Richard's treasure. Now there was nothing to keep the Crusaders in Cyprus. The last few weeks in Limassol were almost a repetition of the last few days in Sicily. Richard, single-minded, was far too busy preparing for the journey to pay attention to Berengaria. He still lodged in Limassol Castle with his lieutenants, she and Joanna in the town. If she had hoped that his repentance was real and he would begin to act more like a husband, she saw no sign.

The arrival of Isaac's daughter was a welcome diversion. Guy de Lusignan brought her to Joanna, relaying Richard's request that she be accepted as though she were a sister. "For it is not her fault that her father was such an evil old bastard," said Guy, perhaps thinking the girl did not understand French — or perhaps not caring if she did.

However, she had been well educated, and understood very well. She paled and turned her face aside as he left.

Joanna looked with compassion at the confused and frightened girl. Though not quite sixteen, she was on the way to being a beauty with her olive-skinned oval face and her long black hair tied back with a scarlet ribbon. She was young, ingenuous and trusting, but Guy's words had clearly wounded her. Joanna put her arms around her and comforted her.

"Pay no attention to that foolish man," she said. "You are welcome here and my brother spoke truly. From now on, you will be my little sister, and also sister to Richard's queen Berengaria — who, if I am not mistaken, is about to join us."

Indeed, Berengaria had just entered the room, having been told by Guy on his way out that "Isaac's little wench has arrived, and Richard says you're to take care of her and let no man near her." ("Except himself, no doubt," he added in a spiteful mutter, but Berengaria did not hear that.)

Like Joanna, she was touched by the girl's tragic story and sensed her need of reassurance. She held out her hand, and Maria clasped it. Thus was a friendship forged.

Sometimes during the days of waiting for departure Berengaria passed the time by riding out to visit the ruined Roman city that Philomena had told her about. Testing her Latin, she tried to decipher the worn inscriptions in the temple, where marble statues of now-forgotten Roman heroes, some missing heads or arms, stood stoically, unmindful of what the centuries brought. "They are a lesson in patience," she told herself. "I too must learn more patience."

One warm afternoon, returning from such an expedition, she gave her horse its head as they rode back along the Roman road. The steed trotted from bright sunlight into the deep shade of one of Limassol's narrow streets and nearly ran over a pair of men who had just rounded a corner. Both men jumped, and she saw that one of them was Richard. He looked up, startled and ready to rebuke this careless rider, then laughed.

"So it is you, my lady queen," he said, as casually as though they had parted that morning. "I trust it was your horse, not you, so set on running us down. Perhaps we will have to find you a gentler mount."

"I am sorry; I did not see you in time to pull him up. The sun had nearly blinded me."

"No matter, no matter," Richard said. "No harm done." He turned to continue down the street. Berengaria kept her horse standing for a minute and looked after him, wishing for the hundredth time that she were not so easily hurt by Richard's indifference.

As she watched, she saw him talking persuasively to his companion, a flaxen-haired young man Berengaria had never seen before. Richard pointed toward the harbor. The young man smiled back and said something that must have pleased Richard, who brushed the lad's cheeks with his lips, clapped him on the buttocks and walked jauntily off, whistling.

Berengaria had not forgotten Eleanor's puzzling warnings about Richard's tastes for "unsuitable" companions. Now she understood: the Cypriot lad had taken Richard's fancy, and was being recruited to join the Crusaders, so he would be handy.

She rode on toward Philomena's house, her heart a dull weight in her breast. She had thought, after her wedding night, that it was bad enough that Richard could be cruel to his bride. Was his liking for young boys to be another threat to her marriage? Still, she thought she could deal with that more easily than with his neglect of herself. "But I will not give up," she told herself stubbornly. "I will try to understand, I will try to be forgiving, I will love and obey even if I cannot always honor."

A week later Richard appeared briefly when she and Joanna were just entering their house after a walk in the town.

"Will you not come in, brother?" Joanna asked. "Philomena would be glad. So would we."

"Yes, Richard, do stay," said Berengaria. "You are quite the stranger." She meant it as a gentle rebuke, but Richard seemed not to have heard. "Will you have some refreshment?" she asked politely.

"No, I am here only for a moment," he said brusquely. He was not wearing armor or kingly garb, but a rough homespun tunic and heavy boots, like any laborer. It was plain that he was working as hard as his men to gather supplies and load boats.

"I have come only to ask about Isaac's daughter. Is she content here with you? I hope she is not a burden."

"I was wondering when you would remember to inquire about her," his sister rejoined tartly. "She is your ward, after all. But she is no burden and we are glad to have her with us, even though she arrived so suddenly and with no notice."

Berengaria, still trying to be more understanding, saw how tired Richard looked, and wished Joanna had not sounded so cross. "How can he think of wives and sisters and wards, when he is responsible for ships and stores and the Crusade itself?" She longed to comfort him, but he did not look at her. Satisfied with Maria's welfare, he walked quickly out.

It was true that Maria was no burden. Eager to please, bright and curious, she soon found her way into Joanna's and Berengaria's hearts. Only Robert of Tornham grumbled, if unconvincingly, at the new state of affairs. He was still in charge of the royal ladies, and pretended to resent the addition to his responsibilities.

"Here I am, a king's captain, and never thought I'd be a nursemaid at my time of life," he protested, when Berengaria and Joanna explained to him that room would have to be made for another passenger on the dromond when they sailed for Palestine. "Glad I've been to do my monarch's bidding and keep you two ladies safe from harm all these months, and what's more walked down the aisle with one of you to give her over to the arm of her king and husband, which was a wonderful marriage if ever I saw one." At the memory of that splendid and moving occasion his booming voice sank to a subdued roar, but soon gathered force. "But with all due respect, ladies, this is something else again."

They had learned by now how impossible it was to deflect Sir Robert as his words came rolling out; but they still tried. "Why so, Sir Robert?" Berengaria managed to ask, as he drew breath. "Surely one more person will not make that much difference."

"This is something else again, because once more with all due respect, you two are old enough to take care of yourselves, but here we are with a young and hardly grown lady, a temptation to every lusty knight in the army begging your pardon, and what's more not even English which if she were might gain her a bit more respect, but as she isn't, and as I can't be everywhere at once, who's going to keep her out of harm, as King Richard says we must do?"

"Why we will, Sir Robert," Berengaria replied. "Do you sail your ship, straight for Palestine this time with no stops at unfriendly islands. Queen Berengaria and Queen Joanna will take full responsibility for Princess Maria."

Appeased, Sir Robert left. As Berengaria's words sank in, they heard his belated appreciation. "No stops at unfriendly islands, that's a good one." Barking with laughter, he went out into the street, and Joanna and Berengaria smiled at each other.

ichard and Guy de Lusignan, by now serving as self-appointed chief counselor, were reviewing the sailing plan with all the ships' captains, in their makeshift headquarters in a shed by the harbor.

A seaman ran in, shouting, "A big ship coming from the southeast!"

Three dozen men tumbled out of the shed and ran to the strand. It was indeed a big ship, and it bore the Plantagenet standard. Richard was as mystified as the rest. Was this some subterfuge by an enemy? But as the vessel approached the pier and he saw several women on the deck, in company with four men who were obviously not seamen, he remembered. His mother had promised to send ladies to accompany her daughter and daughter-in-law to the Holy Land.

"It is not seemly," she had said, just before leaving Messina, "for those two highborn women to have no company except their maids. When I get to Naples and find a ship" (for Richard had commandeered all the Sicilian ships), "I will send two of my own ladies-in-waiting and four of my retainers."

Richard had been so busy getting ready to sail that he had not paid much attention. But here they were, as promised. Though they had escaped the great storm, having sailed later than the Crusader fleet, they were thoroughly sick of the sea and looking forward to a spell on dry land.

They were disappointed. All was in readiness for departure and the tide was high and outgoing. The ship's captain was given only enough time to fill his water barrels, then it was off to sea again for the Christian fleet.

Berengaria and Joanna, who were quite at home on the dromond by now, took pleasure in showing Maria about the ship and helping her settle into her tiny cabin. Sir Robert had ingeniously created it by partitioning the already small one that Cristina and Elizabeth shared. Elizabeth grumbled at this, but not the philosophical Cristina.

"I have stayed in much worse and smaller quarters than this, since leaving my Basque homeland to serve my lady. And you can stand it for three days, surely — that is how long Sir Robert says we will be at sea."

Besides, Maria was so grateful for any kindness that nobody could resent her. Joanna, who had never had a little sister, took her under her wing, heard her confidences and tried to assuage her homesickness.

Berengaria thought they should find a way to occupy her to keep her from brooding about her fate. So, on their first day at sea, she somewhat diffidently asked Maria to help her learn Greek. Though Maria knew Norman French, the lingua franca of the Mediterranean world, her native tongue was Greek and she spoke and wrote it faultlessly. She was flattered at Berengaria's request.

"Now finally there is something I can do for you, after all you have done for me."

"And you must be a strict teacher, you know," said Berengaria. "I was used to strict teachers back in the monastery. They always told me when I made a mistake, and made me repeat, repeat, repeat."

Sixteen-year-old Maria giggled at the thought of being any kind of teacher, much less a strict one, for this practically middle-aged lady — a good ten years older than she was. "I doubt if you will make any mistakes," she said, as gravely as she could. "But if you do, I too will make you repeat, repeat, repeat. When shall we start, Berengaria?"

"Why not now?"

So they brought stools on deck and set up their classroom in the shade of the big triangular sail, with the friendly blue sea all around and the blue sky overhead. They were at the very center of the fleet, and wherever they looked, they saw the other vessels, all coursing swiftly toward the east like a pack of hounds after a hare. Joanna had brought her embroidery and sat near the pupil and teacher, keeping her ears open — maybe she would learn a few words too.

The seamen, at first annoyed at having to go around the little party, presently decided the novelty of having three such pretty passengers made up for any minor inconvenience. Sir Robert, too, looked benevolently on his three "chicks," and was glad to hear their laughter and chatter, such a contrast to the groans and misery of the first leg of the voyage.

On the evening of the third day the shores of Syria came in sight, but night fell before they could get a good look at this strange, bare, seemingly uninhabited land. The fleet rode at anchor offshore. Many a man lay awake that night, thinking of the long passage that had taken him so far from home and family, but eager to begin the great adventure. Everything up to now had been prelude. Now for the Holy Crusade.

Berengaria too lay awake, reflecting on the strange course her life had taken in the past six months, since Eleanor had come to pluck her away from her settled life at the monastery of Leyre. She had always been curious about foreign lands and pored over the accounts of men like Benjamin of Tudela, who had traveled farther than any westerner, into the *terra incognita* of Asia. Now she herself was going to those unknown lands, and was as eager as any explorer for the discoveries ahead. But as always as she lay waiting for sleep, her thoughts circled back to Richard. She went over and over their every encounter — there had been precious few of them! The times when he seemed ardent and loving; the agonizing wedding night; all the times when he showed nothing but indifference; and now, the disturbing realization that he had a liking for young boys. Ay me! she thought. Who is this man I have married?

At midnight, still wide awake, she got up quietly, put on her cloak and went on deck. The sky was a velvet black studded with stars. The sea was perfectly calm. Not a breath of wind blew. All around she could see the faint shapes of the other ships and closest to shore the largest, with one bright light on the mast, signaling that it was Richard's galleon. She heard no sound but the slap of waves against the dromond's wooden hull. She stood still, looking up at the sky. She could not remember ever seeing so many stars, so bright. For the first time in weeks she felt at peace — and closer to God than to earth.

Berengaria's faith had always run strong and deep, and she never doubted that her God was directing her life as He thought best. She seldom thought it necessary to beg Him to grant her any special treatment. Her prayers were more often of gratitude than of pleading. Yet of late, she had felt more tormented than grateful. Now, all alone with the sea and the sky, she was momentarily cleansed of her discontent. She folded her hands and, looking at the heavens, said a silent prayer.

Thank you, Lord, for this beautiful night. Thank you for showing me your handiwork and opening my eyes to its perfection. Thank you for friends, for health and for this journey to your Holy Land. Thank you for the trust in your goodness and mercy that I learned from my blessed mother. And thank you for giving me strength to accept your will. Let me avoid complaint and self-pity, and wait with patience as your plan for my life unfolds. Amen.

She closed her eyes and took a deep breath, trying to preserve the transcendent moment of communion.

And please, Lord God, if in days and years to come I feel despair or discontent, let me remember and relive this time and place.

She crept back down to her little room and into her bed, where she lay for a few minutes cherishing the rare freedom from her nagging worries, then fell into a dreamless sleep.

The fleet stopped briefly at Marqab in Syria, and everybody admired from a distance the imposing castle of the Knights of St. John on the height, built by Crusaders who had been there in the last century. However, their business was not here, rather at St. Jean-d'Acre, a day's run to the south. They sailed on down the bleak Syrian coast, arriving at Acre on June 8, 1191.

As ship after ship came into harbor, the weary Crusaders rushed to the decks to hail the city with shouts of joy. They had come so far and endured so much, just to reach this famous port, gateway to Palestine and the Holy City. They could see the sprawling camp of their fellow Christians, the armies of King Philip of France and King Leopold of Austria. Tents crowded around the walls of Acre, which Philip had been besieging for six weeks.

Clapping each other on the back, the jubilant newcomers raised clenched fists and shouted their battle cries: "Down with the infidels! Knock down the walls! Acre today, Jerusalem tomorrow!"

The chronicler Ralph of Diceto described the sight that met the Christian fleet.

The shore resounded to clarion calls, the braying of trumpets and the fearful din of horns, exciting the Christians to the fight and striking terror into the hearts of the besieged Saracens, announcing the arrival of a great prince.

Berengaria observed the city with interest while they waited their turn to land. It lay at the end of a promontory, clearly visible from the dromond's deck. She could see strong walls and fortified towers, flying the pennants of Islam with the golden crescent on a field of blue. What she could make out of the city within the walls seemed squalid, all mud-colored with none of the brilliant white and pleasing colors of the towns they had seen so often along the shores of Italy and Turkey.

"It is not nearly as impressive as I expected," she said to Joanna. "After all we have heard, I was prepared for golden domes and walls of marble. But this grimy little town can't hold a candle to your Messina, or even Limassol."

Joanna agreed and she was dubious about their immediate future. "What do you think, sister?" she asked. "Can we endure it here?"

It looked unlikely. By now they were quite close to land. The oarsmen had paused and the seamen were furling the sails as the dromond approached the shore. The watchers on deck could clearly see the narrow plain on the landward side of the city, crowded with the Crusaders' tents and makeshift shelters. From this disorderly camp men rushed to the shore to greet the new arrivals. More than one shabbily dressed, blowsy-looking woman could be seen in the throng. The soldiers looked almost as disreputable.

"Those must be the men of Philip of France," said Joanna.

"Ay me, so they are, madame," growled Sir Robert, who had joined them at the rail. "And the army of King Leopold too. Did you ever see a sorrier-looking scraggy mob? No wonder they're so wild to welcome a real king and a real army. Philip and that Leopold are like babes and ninnies when it comes to making war. Why, I heard they sent a hundred of their men to scale the walls on the land side of the city, and Saladin had been watching the whole thing from up there on the hill, laughing his head off no doubt."

He pointed toward the slopes behind the town and now the women could see, above the plain and stretching to the crests of the enveloping hills, encampments (more orderly than those of the Christians) with the crescent flying proudly from the tentpoles.

"Is Saladin there now, do you think?" asked Maria, fearfully. She had not yet learned how hard it was to turn Sir Robert from his train of thought. He had not finished his story.

"Well," he went on, "before the troops had so much as a ladder up the wall, Saladin sent a few of his soldiers down to nip at their heels, and that was the end of that. But now that King Richard's here, we'll see a different kind of battle, mark my words. There's no one in Christendom knows more about the proper way to besiege a city than our king. He'll knock down those walls in no time, before the Turks have lobbed a single stone at us." He went aft, harrumphing, to see about the landing.

A siege? Knocked-down walls? Flying stones? Berengaria knew even less than Joanna of actual warfare. As a girl she had often said goodbye to her father and her brother as they went off to battle, but where and how the battles took place she never quite knew. The engagement they had witnessed on Cyprus hardly counted, it was so brief and one-sided. Now they were going to find themselves in the midst of a serious fray.

"Richard told me that once he has taken Acre he will find us suitable lodgings and leave us while he goes on to capture Jerusalem," said Joanna. "But meantime will we have to stay in that dreadful-looking camp?"

"I suppose so," replied Berengaria. She wrinkled her nose. "I swear I can smell the stench from here!" Maria, whose eyes had been darting over the confused scene on the shore, cried out, "Look, Richard is already on the beach, and he is beckoning our ship to come next."

The dromond nosed its way toward the sloping, sandy shore and Sir Robert helped his three royal charges down from the vessel and into the small boats that bore them to the pier — which looked decidedly bumpy. It was merely a long pile of rocks, nothing like the sturdy, flat-surfaced stone piers they were used to.

A short, richly dressed, dark-complexioned man whom Berengaria had never seen was waiting. He took off his plumed hat with a flourish and held her arm to assist her and steady her as she found her footing on the uneven rocks. Bending over her hand, he said suavely, "Philip Augustus at your service, Madame." He helped the others onto the pier, then repeated his greeting to Joanna. At sight of Maria, he looked inquiringly at Berengaria.

"This is our ward, Princess Maria of Cyprus. And we all thank you for this courteous welcome."

Maria, too, received a quick appraisal and a bow from the king of France.

"I told King Richard that since he would be so occupied with disembarking his troops, I would see you safely ashore and show you to your lodgings. Before your arrival, I took the liberty of preparing tents for you and your attendants. They are well away from the soldiers' camp and are as comfortable and secure as we can manage in this benighted place."

He summoned two knights who had been standing nearby, and told them to conduct the ladies to their tents. He bowed again in a general farewell to all, and left.

Berengaria, who had never lived in a tent and was expecting the worst, was agreeably surprised when they reached their little camp. A rainbow of color met her eyes as a servant pulled the curtain aside. Her new home was some twelve feet square. An exquisite, intricately patterned carpet covered the wooden floor. With its deep blue scrollwork on a field of lighter blue, it reminded her of the graceful calligraphy of the Arabic manuscripts she had studied with such delight in the monastery. Tapestries softened the sober gray of the thick woolen walls. On the low couch were an azure coverlet and four enormous square pillows, two of scarlet and two of royal purple. Tall iron candlesticks held white tapers, ready to light. The exotic, lush eastern flavor of the ménage enraptured her. She had never seen anything like it in her life.

"This is not impossible!" she exclaimed to Joanna and Maria, after each emerged from a quick inspection of her tent. The two new ladies-in-waiting, who had just arrived, agreed that the tent lodgings would do, though they were nothing like what they had been used to at Queen Eleanor's court.

But Joanna had something else on her mind. "What did you think of Philip Augustus?" she asked Berengaria.

"Why, I thought him polite enough and he has certainly gone to great lengths to make us comfortable here. Why?"

"Because the last time I saw him, he was livid with anger at Richard for jilting his sister Alice, so that he could marry you. On the very morning you arrived in Sicily he packed up in a dreadful hurry and sailed away — we all thought it was because he could not bear the thought of facing you; after all, you were his sister's successful rival. Yet now he greets you like an honored friend."

Berengaria remembered hearing something about this Alice: her father had told her how King Henry, Richard's father, and King Philip had agreed to the marriage years ago, for political reasons. Then there was some scandal about the girl — a child born out of wedlock — and Richard had repudiated her. She had thought it was over and done with. If King Philip held a grudge against her why was his welcome so cordial? It was strange.

Maria, who was proving as much a romantic as Berengaria's sister Blanche, had a theory. "I know!" she cried, full of glee. "He has his eye on you, Joanna — a beautiful young widow. So he is making this show of gallantry to all of us, to impress you."

"Hardly likely. His wife died but three months ago and he was devoted to her. I doubt he would be seeking a replacement so soon. And no matter what they say about Philip, they do not say he is a womanizer."

Maria was unconvinced. "From what I have seen," she said, "none of your Frankish men care much for faithfulness. Why should a king be any different?"

"Pooh," said Joanna, who felt the conversation was hitting too close to home for Berengaria. "Here comes our baggage. Let us help with the unpacking, and see how snug we can make these tents. We may have to stay here a long time."

hilip's public display of consideration to the ladies was all the more noticeable in view of Richard's inattention. They had not seen him since coming ashore. However, Philip's motives were more devious than Maria's theory — if less interesting. He was intensely jealous of Richard's good looks, his bravery, his skill at warfare, his popularity with the troops. He resented his arriving like a conquering hero, when it was Philip who had commanded the Crusaders for months in Acre while Richard played at war on Cyprus. Besides — Philip told himself — though Richard is monarch in England, he is my vassal for all his lands on the continent, and has publicly sworn allegiance to me for them. I am no man's vassal. And no man's fool.

Brooding on his wrongs, he hit on a way to get the recognition he craved. He would, in full view of all the armies, ostentatiously take Richard's consort and his sister under his protection. He would provide them with living quarters as close to luxurious as conditions permitted. It was the kind of gesture a generous king could make to his vassal. Not only would it show Richard and all the world that he, Philip, was so magnanimous that he held no grudge about the Alice affair; it would perhaps encourage his own troops to stay loyal to him. He knew well enough they did not have much respect for his military prowess.

Unfortunately, nobody but the ladies seemed impressed with his generosity. Nor were his troops any more loyal. Richard simply sent out the word to the French and Austrian armies: "If any man cares to fight under my banner, I will raise his pay by one quarter." Many of Philip's men jumped at the chance.

Four days after their arrival, Richard finally paid the women's camp a visit. Striding into the little courtyard onto which their half-dozen or so tents faced, he found them seated at a table, sipping

- 57 -

cool drinks and hoping for a breeze. They wore their loosest, lightest gowns and plied their fans assiduously. The ladies in waiting sat a little apart, feeling sorry for themselves. In France the heat was never this bad. Richard, despite leather jerkin and leggings, seemed impervious.

At his sudden appearance Berengaria felt the familiar agitation, as though some force had compressed her heart and then as quickly released it. Yet she had learned control and none of her inner turmoil showed. She even managed a welcoming smile, looking up at her husband.

As always, he greeted her with detached courtesy.

"I am glad to see you looking so well, my lady queen. I trust you are being properly cared for."

"Indeed we are, my lord," replied Berengaria smoothly. She could play this game as well as he. "And since King Philip has lent us his personal cook and serving man, and since nobody can do anything about the heat, we are as content as can be."

"But we miss Sir Robert," said Joanna. "What has become of our big bold nursemaid?"

Richard laughed. "Why, he's chief nursemaid for one of the siege engines, and doing a manful job of it too. He has gathered a huge pile of fearsome stones ready to catapult over the walls. He's even given his big toy a name: 'God's Own Sling.' I felt he had earned the right to join his fellow soldiers, and so did he. He will have a chance to test his aim tomorrow, when we begin the assault."

Then he turned to Maria. Joanna, who was watching, thought she recognized the quick look he gave the girl — like a hungry cat that has just caught sight of a bird. But all he said was, "And how is our Cypriot princess? Flourishing I should say, and even prettier than before. Are you lonesome, are you well occupied?"

Maria, intimidated by this attention from the great king, blushed and lowered her eyes. "Thank you, my lord. I am lonesome for Cyprus and I miss my father, of course. But I am indeed well occupied, thanks to my two friends. They are very, very kind." She paused, then looked up at him shyly. This was sure to please him. "Did you know that I am helping Berengaria to learn Greek?"

Richard did not know and did not care. "Good, good," he said, and turned to go. Joanna saw him cast another penetrating look at

- 58 -

Maria, and the girl's timid black eyes met his searching gaze for a second. She blushed and turned her head aside.

The next day the actual siege began and it was quite clear who was in charge. Richard had reassembled his wooden fort, Matagriffon, that he had brought in pieces all the way from Sicily. It was a tremendous success: so high that his besieging forces could see from its top right into the cowering city, and launch showers of arrows. At the same time the fearful siege engines lobbed huge rocks over the walls to smash houses, defenders, innocent towns-people, and whatever happened to be in their way.

On July 12, 1199, less than a month after the first assault, Acre fell.

Then Philip launched his own projectile. Surprising Richard and all the host, he announced that he was going back to France. Richard tried to dissuade him. No matter what their personal animosities might be, Philip and his thousands of men were important to the Crusaders' cause.

"Why leave now, when we are on the brink of a triumphant push south and toward Jerusalem?" Richard asked testily. They were in his tent, along with several advisors of each. Everybody was tired and dirty, yet feeling the euphoria of the victor in a righteous battle. Richard sprawled on a couch, and his annoyance was about to turn into anger. Philip, sitting stiffly on a stool, betrayed nothing beyond a stony obduracy.

"I must leave for two reasons. One, I am not well. What with this terrible heat and the flies and the miserable filthy camp, I have suffered with dysentery ever since I came. You would not like me to become so ill that I would be a burden, I am sure."

"Every man here suffers from the same hardships. Do you not think it important to show your troops that you share their troubles — and their fortitude?"

Philip went on without noticing how his lieutenants winced, embarrassed at their king's unmanliness. "Most important, Richard, is the news I have received from France. The count of Flanders has died and left me his lands. If I am not there to defend my rights, I will lose all Artois."

"So." Richard's voice dripped with derision. "You care more for a paltry bit of France than for your sacred promise to drive the infidel from our holy Jerusalem." His face was flushed and he rose to leave the tent.

Philip addressed his back. "However, you have my word that you need not worry about your Angevin lands; I shall not take advantage of your absence to attack them." Richard merely cast him a look of contempt and stamped out. Still, the promise had been made in the presence of the French and English knights, and might be expected to have some value.

In spite of Philip's promise, after he sailed Richard sent word to his friend, ally and brother-in-law, young Prince Sancho of Navarre: "Philip of France is abandoning the Crusade and returning to Paris. Be watchful. In spite of his agreement with me, he may try to make mischief in Aquitaine. I count on you to protect our interests."

To make matters worse, Leopold of Austria also sailed home, resentful of Richard's highhanded ways. The Crusaders' forces were seriously depleted. Nevertheless, at least Richard was now in sole, undisputed command. He had a zealous army of some 5,000 men, eager for more victories. It only remained to prepare appropriate accommodations for the ladies and servants in Acre, before he rode south to take Jaffa — and then, Jerusalem!

Richard ordered that the Tower of the Chevaliers in Acre, a gloomy fortress, be turned into a makeshift palace. It had never been meant as a dwelling but with its thick stone walls, it was preferable to the hot tents in the field. The women were able to bring their rugs and divans and comfortable furnishings, but not their French cook, who had gone home with his master.

"Still," said Joanna, "I would far rather have a good night's sleep in a cool room than an almond tart in the heat of the sun."

Queen Eleanor's ladies also took the opportunity to go home with the French fleet. They did not like the heat, the confinement or the boredom. With unlimited time to gossip, they had nothing to gossip about, and the royal ladies they were supposed to attend did not seek their companionship. They were not particularly missed.

Two new guardians were assigned to the palace. Robert of Tornham, who would be marching with the Crusaders, brought them around to meet their charges.

"You see ladies, it takes two men to fill the job your Robert used to handle all alone. But they're good lads, I've known them for years and so has King Richard, they've served him all over Maine and Anjou. And if they don't keep you safe from harm while we're off chasing those cursed unbelievers, they know who they'll have to answer to!" He glared at the unfortunate pair, his eyes flashing at the thought of the punishment he would mete out if he had to. Then, an instant before Berengaria could remind him, he realized he had not introduced them.

"This stout fellow is Bertrand de Verdun, and this not-quite-so-stout one is Etienne de Longchamps."

Bertrand was a flaming redhead, tall and robust. Etienne was short and thin and nearly bald. ("At least we'll have no trouble telling them apart!" Berengaria thought.) Both were amiable of countenance and apparently used to Sir Robert's blustery ways. They were above middle age and though hardly fatherly in appearance, might be thought of as uncles at least.

"They'll be lodged right down below, so nobody gets in or out without their say-so. Now that's that, and if you'll excuse me I'll be off because King Richard says we're to march in the morning. Oh, one more thing. He asked me to tell you he probably won't be able to come around to say goodbye, what with the packing up, and making sure all the captains have their mounted troops well briefed, and the foot soldiers know the line of march and all that. But he'll send messengers every three days to the garrison here, so you'll know where we are and how many Muslims we've taken."

Berengaria heard this news without revealing her hurt that Richard did not care to bid his queen farewell. Joanna's disappointment showed on her face. She would have liked to wish her brother godspeed. Nobody noticed the shadow that passed over Maria's face at the word that they would not see Richard before he left.

Sir Robert was about to go when both Berengaria and Joanna ran up and put their arms around him in a confusion of hugs.

"We'll miss you sorely, Sir Robert. Take care of yourself, and watch over Richard for us," said Joanna.

"We'll pray to God to bring you safely back to us," said Berengaria with a catch in her voice. It was hard to say goodbye to this gruff but steadfast friend.

For once Sir Robert was at a loss for words. Patting them both on the back, he made his escape. But when he was out of sight, he wiped a tear from his eye.

cre is not a very amusing city." Berengaria stood by the barred window of the palace hall, frowning at the grimy old buildings across the way and, just visible over the city wall, the hills that rose row after row into the hazy distance.

She turned quickly and paced up and down, twisting her fingers together. "And this is not a very amusing palace." She looked with distaste around the dark, nearly airless room. In spite of the carpets, hangings and cushions the women had brought from their tents, this dank cavernous dwelling refused to look or feel cheerful or comfortable.

Joanna looked up from her embroidery. "Why sister," she said, "you who usually set the rest of us a good example by not complaining, whatever is the matter?"

"I'm sorry. Of course I'm not the only one cooped up here. None of us like it. But how I wish that just once I could get out of the city and go riding up into those hills!"

"So do I. And I wish that when we do go out, we would not have to be accompanied by a dozen soldiers and the people we see on the streets would not look at us as though we were the ones who had smashed their houses and killed their husbands and their brothers. But how can I tell them I am sorry?"

Berengaria had stopped pacing. She too felt pity for the townspeople; but that was war and apparently men felt war was necessary, especially a holy war like this one. She sighed.

Joanna broke the silence. "Well, while we are wishing we might as well aim even higher than those hills." She smiled impishly. "Why not wish that we might hear that Richard had defeated Saladin, and taken Jerusalem, and we could all go home?"

Maria came in while Joanna was speaking and heard only the last part. "Has a messenger come, has there been a battle?" She spoke quickly, almost breathlessly. She had not tied back her hair but wore it loose, so that two smooth black wings framed the perfect oval of her face.

"What a striking girl!" Berengaria thought. "And she seems more herself." She and Joanna had been worrying about how listless and withdrawn Maria had seemed for the past few weeks, ever since the Crusaders had left. "But she is only sixteen," they told each other, "and moodiness is only natural at that age."

Joanna had to tell her that they had been only wishing.

"Oh how I wish, too, that we could hear some good news from the army," Maria said. "All we know is that they reached Jaffa, and took it with hardly a battle. So what are they doing now, aren't they going to hunt Saladin down and chase him out of Jerusalem? And if they hold Jaffa, why can't we leave this prison, and go there to be closer to them?"

"I don't know," said Joanna, "but you can be sure that my brother has his reasons. Maybe he expects Saladin to try to retake Jaffa. Maybe it is in ruins; the last messenger did tell us that the army had to camp outside the walls, not inside the city. Anyway, there is not much point in our getting all worked up. There is nothing we can do but wait for more word."

Berengaria went over to Maria and gently took her hand.

"She is right, you know, Maria. There is nothing we can do, so let us try to occupy ourselves here, and in time, we will be released from our prison."

The very next day the release came. Their rotund guardian, Bertrand de Verdun, brought a tired, perspiring messenger into the dreary hall where the ladies were sitting after breakfast, trying to make some progress on their embroidery.

The man relayed King Richard's message, with no elaboration.

"He wishes you to come to Jaffa at once. He says that these may be the last peaceful days for some time because the Crusaders will soon make their assault on Jerusalem. He knows you have been lonely in Acre. He has sent knights to escort you."

This did not seem like warrior Richard. Why bother with his dependent women, when he should be concentrating on an assault on the Holy City? But they eagerly prepared to leave. Each of the three was to learn, in her own time, a different reason for the summons.

With the fast horses Richard had sent, a contingent of knights, and no harassment from the Turks, they arrived at Jaffa in far less time than it had taken the heavily laden army a month before; but it was a tiresome journey. The countryside they rode through was parched and brown and the reflection of the pitiless sun from the dusty white road was almost blinding. Sometimes the pewter-colored expanse of the Mediterranean came into view to the west but it offered no relief to their tired eyes; even the sea looked pale and hot.

At last the sere, barren fields gave way to olive groves, palms and orchards of fig and almond trees. They all brightened. It was still fearfully hot, but the greenery gave the illusion of coolness.

"This is more like it," said Joanna. "It reminds me a little of Sicily."

When they saw Jaffa itself, though, they pulled up their horses and looked at it with misgivings. Its walls were hardly more than piles of rubble enclosing tumbledown buildings. Saladin had destroyed as much as he could before yielding it to the Crusaders, to keep them from using it as a defensive position.

A large knight on a large horse approached from the city. "Never mind, my ladies. You won't have to camp in the fields this time." It was their old friend, Sir Robert, booming out his greeting.

"King Richard sent me out to meet you, and we'll go now to your lodging. You'll be cozy enough, I warrant; things inside the town aren't nearly as bad as they look."

He conducted them to one of the undamaged houses, well inside the city, and large enough so each had her own room. With relief, they shed their dusty garments and washed the grime of the journey off their faces. It was a blessed feeling to be cool and almost clean again.

They dined with the king that night, along with Sir Guy, Sir Robert and a half-dozen other knights. Berengaria sat next to Richard but he hardly spoke to her until the removal of the platters of greasy bones and the bringing of date cakes and sweet wine. Then he became suspiciously attentive. He asked particularly about her health. "No strange humors, no faintness from the heat? Are you enjoying your usual good appetite?" All at once she realized where this was leading. She was annoyed at his deviousness.

"I assure you, Richard, I am feeling very well. And if you wonder, as I believe you do, if I am bearing your child, the answer is no." And glad I am, she thought. If I had conceived a child that dreadful night, could I ever have loved it?

For a moment he was taken aback by her vehemence and the fire in her eye, but he went on quickly. "Why then, we shall have to do something about that." He looked into his queen's eyes with a gaze so penetrating that it seemed to bore into her very soul. She felt captured by the intensity of those blue eyes and was as helpless as a butterfly on a pin. For that transfixed moment, it was as though they were the only two people in the world. Her anger of two minutes ago had melted, and in spite of herself she felt a flutter of excitement. Could it be, could it possibly be, that Richard did indeed care for her? She longed to believe it.

"If you will have me, I will come to your chamber after dinner," he said in a low voice. "I promise you it will be different from last time." He knew how to charm; and try as she might, Berengaria could not resist the charm, could not smother her hopes of requited love. She smiled and raised her glass. "I will await you, my king."

What she did not know was that Richard had received a letter that morning from Eleanor, engineer of their marriage. A thousand miles away she was waiting impatiently for it to bear fruit.

"Is Berengaria pregnant yet?" she had written her son. "And if not, why not? Are you doing your husbandly duty? Have you forgotten why you brought her with you to Palestine? Not for love of her, anybody could see that. But I did hope that with her by your side, and at your service, you would be less tempted to stray from the conjugal bed. Reassure me!"

So Richard had to give his mother reason for reassurance.

That night, as once before, Berengaria lay on her bed, waiting. Again, the door opened and her husband stood there. This time he was perfectly sober, and in fact the whole encounter was sober and passionless. He knew exactly what he was doing: planting the seed of an heir. He seemed to take little enjoyment in the act of love, if such it could be called, so cold and calculated it was. And he did not care if she enjoyed it or not. Only at the end, when he was rapidly probing deeper and deeper, did she feel a throb of desire and excitement. But before it could be fulfilled he had withdrawn. Neither had spoken a word. There were none of the endearments, the intimacies that she had looked forward to. He left and she lay in an agony of arousal, despair and confusion. So his words of enticement at the dinner table had been only words; he had been toying with her. She remembered what Eleanor had said. "It will be up to you to make him want to lie with you." But how?

Richard went the next night to the bed of the Cypriot princess. Maria had half hoped, half feared that he would. It was the second time they had lain together. That night in Acre when he had visited their encampment, he had returned an hour later, slipped into her tent, and overcome her protests — for she had adored this tall, godlike, golden man from the first moment she saw him. He told her that she owed him obedience because he had conquered her country; that Berengaria need never know; and that she was so lovely that he could not wait another minute. She resisted. He renewed his pleas and caressed her gently, then urgently. She submitted. She was enraptured.

Now, after a month of separation, he was curious to see if she had strengthened her resistance, and would need to be won again. She did not. All her scruples had been swept away by the blind force of a young girl's first love. She welcomed him eagerly.

Alas for Maria. For Richard, when the conquest was over, the game held no more interest. He was bored and annoyed by women — or men — who clung to him. Promiscuous as he was, his enduring, unflagging interest was in war and the prizes of war. Amorous escapades were only an amusement and this one had ceased to amuse. He left Maria's bed, his mind already on the coming confrontation with Saladin.

For ten days, the women were left to themselves, with no notion of what Richard was up to.

He had never encountered an enemy like the Turkish commander. Tales of his rise to power and his military exploits had spread all over the Middle East and into Europe. Richard had learned everything he could about his foe. He was the nephew of a Kurdistan chieftain and he had risen through the ranks to become sultan of a vast area stretching from Turkey to Egypt. He was a devout Muslim who had publicly and frequently vowed to drive the Christian unbelievers out of the Holy Land. His armies were described as numerous as the grains of sand in the desert.

Though often rash and impetuous in the heat of battle, Richard was a realistic strategist when planning his attacks, and he was now having second thoughts about an immediate assault on Jerusalem. He called his counselors to a parley in front of his tent, on the edge of the olive grove where the Crusaders were camped. A dozen men sat or stood on the dusty earth, where a few discouraged blades of grass survived, evidence that before the Christians arrived this had been a flourishing meadow. Not a breath of air stirred and the red-and-gold Plantagenet pennant on Richard's tentpole hung limply.

Richard spoke bluntly. "My comrades, we must decide whether to launch an attack on Jerusalem this fall. I can see some reasons for, some against; but I wish to know your views."

One of the older generals, Edward of Joinville, a veteran in Richard's service, spoke first. "I think the sooner we leave Jaffa the better, whether to Jerusalem or wherever. The men are feeling the lack of discipline and getting soft. They need to be reminded why we're here. Some of them are even deserting."

Another warrior agreed. "Right, Sir Edward. And the quarrels in the ranks are getting worse — some men are even coming to blows with their fellows. It's those pesky men from Pisa and Genoa who are at the root of it; they're always squabbling with each other, and it spreads to the rest."

Sir Edward nodded and added dourly, "And the French are even worse — the best of them went home with King Philip, and the ones that stayed are the dregs. They can't get along with anybody."

Richard's jaws tightened and his face darkened with the anger they all knew too well. "Then, Sir Edward, why have you not done your duty and found a way to stop their mischief, instead of wasting our time with your complaints? Now who has something to say in answer to my question about an attack on Jerusalem?"

A young captain with a doughy face and a body going to flesh stood up. "My liege, I'm for overwintering here. Starting this late, we could find ourselves held up by a storm, in the middle of nowhere without food long before we reached Jerusalem."

One of his companions jeered in a low voice to his neighbor, "We all know why he wants to stay at Jaffa. He's gotten too fond of the lasses who come out of the city to sell their comforts to the highest bidder. And the wine they make hereabouts is none too bad either, eh? Women and wine — that's what he'd miss if we went out to battle."

If Richard heard this, he gave no sign. His face was still stern and his tone was deadly serious. "Though I do not agree with all your reasons for postponement, there is another consideration that I would put before you. My spies have just come back from an investigation of the route from here to Jerusalem. They report that we are far outnumbered by Saladin's forces, perhaps two or three to one. A siege of Jerusalem would be chancy at best, even if we got there without losing many men through desertion or illness."

He stopped a minute as though to emphasize his next words.

"So far, we have made no effort to treat with the Turks. I believe the time has come; certainly nothing would be lost, and if we fail, we will simply resume hostilities."

The men murmured, but nobody openly disagreed. So Richard began his try at diplomacy. He had been thinking for some time of the best way to appeal to Saladin.

He sent a purposely brazen message.

Since continued fighting can only result in further losses for both our armies and in destruction of ever more cities, I propose that we call a halt and that you yield to us Jerusalem, which is so holy to the Christians. We also request that you return the piece of the True Cross that you hold. For you, it is nothing but a scrap of wood. But for the Christians it is a sacred relic. What does it profit you to hold it?

Saladin's reply was as firm.

Jerusalem is just as holy to the Muslims as to the Christians. From here our Prophet ascended into heaven.

And the Kingdom of Jerusalem belonged to the Muslims long before your armies stole it from us less than a hundred years ago. Now that we have regained it, we will not give it up.

Richard had not expected anything else. But he had more tricks up his sleeve. He sent a request for an in-person interview.

"What will this brash young man suggest next?" Saladin asked his younger brother Safadin. Partly out of curiosity he agreed to Richard's request and delegated Safadin to represent the Turks.

The meeting was on neutral ground, in a sumptuously appointed tent provided by Safadin and set up on the plain just beyond the Christian camp. Both sides displayed extreme politeness. To lay the groundwork, Richard had sent Safadin a gift of a superb horse.

The two men liked each other at once — under other circumstances they might have become fast friends. Richard had never met a Turk except on the battlefield and was impressed with Safadin's civility and poise, and with his leisurely approach to the business at hand. Seated at his ease in the luxuriously comfortable tent — so unlike his own wartime quarters — Richard assessed his host. Safadin was clad in loose, flowing white. The cloth of fine white wool that covered his head was confined with a jeweled circlet. Even in repose he had an air of restrained energy — like a coiled spring.

"I could learn something from this fellow," Richard said to himself, savoring the sweetmeats and honeyed tea his host offered him, and surveying the inscrutable, hawk-nosed, bronzed face.

Presently they plunged into bargaining. Richard made his startling proposal in all seriousness: Saladin was to give Palestine to his brother Safadin. Richard would in turn permit his sister Joanna to marry Safadin. Together, the couple would reign over Jerusalem and the coastal towns Richard had conquered, which would be Joanna's dowry. Christians and Muslims alike would have access to Jerusalem, to worship in their holy places.

Safadin's deepset eyes did not even blink at this but his mouth twitched slightly in amusement.

"It is a novel idea, to say the least. I will report your words exactly to my brother. You will hear from us shortly as to our next meeting. Now let me call the escort to see you back to your camp." They parted on the best of terms.

When Saladin heard Richard's proposal, at first he smiled, then hooted with laughter. It was so outrageous! But he did not dismiss it out of hand. "It does have some merit," he told his brother. "It would be an honorable way to halt this awful war."

As for Safadin, it was a tempting prospect: marriage to a presumably beautiful Christian woman — how could she be otherwise, since she was sister to the dashing and handsome Richard? Her eventual conversion to his faith he took as a matter of course.

Saladin told Safadin to indicate tentative agreement: "We'll see how serious the Lionheart is." Then he waited.

Back in Jaffa, Richard belatedly thought perhaps he should consult Joanna. She was outraged. "Marry a Muslim? Not for all the holy places in Jerusalem! You are my dear brother, Richard, but sometimes I wonder if you have any idea how women feel. This is more than any sister could agree to. Marry a heathen indeed!"

Richard had to go back to tell Safadin that his sister had regretfully declined the honor. However, he suggested an alternative. They could still marry, and Safadin could embrace the Christian faith.

Fortunately, before Joanna heard about this new proposal the Turkish lords said that would not do at all. It was an impasse. Once again, the two negotiators parted again in friendly fashion, enjoying one last diplomatic dinner and exchanging gifts — a magnificent saddle for Richard, a crimson cape of the finest English wool for Safadin.

The war resumed. The ladies were sent back to Acre. Each now knew why she had been summoned.

or the next seven months the war seesawed back and forth. The Crusaders marched about Palestine, taking a city here and winning a battle there, but never coming in sight of their goal, the Holy City of Jerusalem.

Life back in Acre was still dull, but all three women were more glad than not to be away from the unsettling presence of Richard. Furthermore, now that the heat of summer was past and fires could be lit in the palace, they were drier and more comfortable.

Berengaria and Joanna passed the time with embroidery, though neither was very adept. One day they decided to embark on an ambitious project. It was Berengaria's idea. They would create a long and beautiful tapestry, depicting the Crusaders on the march, dealing death and destruction to the Turks.

"It will be a tribute to my father," said Berengaria. "When I was a little girl, he asked the monks of Calahorra to create an illustrated Bible. It was to have three hundred pictures, telling the whole story from the Creation to the Resurrection. When I left for the monastery at Leyre, it was only half done, but I had seen some of those pictures, and they were so beautiful, Joanna! My father told me that even if it took the whole lifetime of the monks, it would be worth it. It would be a gift that God would receive with joy."

Joanna looked doubtful. "I do not plan to spend a lifetime on our tapestry, Berengaria, no matter how pleasing to God it proves."

Her sister-in-law coaxed her. "Nor do I. But it will be something to occupy us. Let us make a beginning, and take each day as it comes."

So they set to it. After two weeks they felt ready to show their work to Bertrand and Etienne.

"Does it look right? Are the horses properly garbed? Do the knights' suits of armor have all the essential elements?"

Maria joined the two "uncles," and the three critics inspected the tapestry, which so far presented two mounted knights and a palm tree, all in a row. Bertrand and Etienne seemed unwilling to hazard a comment, but Maria laughed almost until the tears came, then managed to speak.

"With all due respect, ladies (as Sir Robert would say), they don't look so much like knights on horseback as porcupines riding on goats." Bertrand and Etienne, who had been wondering how to be tactful and noncommital, were relieved. Their repressed grins became guffaws. At first the two artists pretended to be offended, but on looking at their work more objectively, they were laughing too. Wisely, they decided to abandon the tapestry and go back to simpler work like diamond-patterned pillow covers.

The Greek lessons went on. Berengaria had learned to say such useful things as "May I purchase a bunch of grapes?" and "The sea is beautiful today." She had made enough progress in writing the language to try translating some of the prayers in her psalter from Latin to Greek. Maybe she would then send copies to Brother Anselmo at the Monastery of Leyre. She could see his saturnine face cracking into a smile at this evidence of his pupil's progress.

One wintry afternoon, Berengaria and Maria were working in the hall. The sun streamed through the barred window, making an interesting shadow pattern on the floor but not providing much warmth. Teacher and pupil wore woolen mantles over their dresses. They were glad of the brazier at their feet and the fire on the hearth. Berengaria was scratching out her translation on a long wax tablet. Parchment was hard to come by in Acre, and besides it was easy to rub out a mistake on the wax and start over. She had just written "Forgive me, Lord, for my transgressions, for I knew not what I was doing," and asked Maria if it was correct. The girl stared at the words, then looked wildly at Berengaria and jumped up and ran from the room.

Berengaria dropped the tablet and ran after her. "What is it, dear girl?" she asked, putting her arms around Maria's shoulders, which were shaking with her sobs. Maria tried to stifle her crying and Berengaria led her back to their table. Head lowered and not daring to look her friend in the face, Maria stammered through her weeping.

"O Berengaria, I am the one who needs forgiveness. How could I have let it happen, when I love you so much? You and Joanna are the best and kindest women I have ever known. How could I betray you?"

Berengaria was mystified. What was the girl talking about?

Maria looked up.

"I must tell you, I have wanted to tell you for so long! When Richard came to my tent that night, he told me that no harm would be done, that no one would know, and that we two were meant to be lovers — that he had wanted me from the day he saw me on Cyprus. And heaven forgive me, I was persuaded and I yielded. For already I loved him!"

Before Berengaria could take this in Maria went on. "Then when we were in Jaffa, he came to me again. And again I let him have me. How could I, how could I? But he was so strong, so beautiful, and I did love him so!" She buried her face in her hands.

Almost automatically Berengaria's arms went around her, while she struggled with her emotions: outrage, pain, jealousy — and yes, sympathy. She knew what it was to love this man helplessly.

So they stood for two or three minutes, Berengaria murmuring and smoothing Maria's back while she herself tried to regain her calm. The girl's sobs subsided and she raised her head and looked piteously into Berengaria's face. "Can you forgive me? Can you believe that it is all finished now, and that I repent sincerely? Oh how I have longed to confess! And this afternoon when we were writing that prayer about admitting one's faults I knew I had to speak."

"Of course I forgive you. Richard took advantage of your youth and trust. He is far more to blame than you." Yes, she thought sadly. I will forgive you, and soon you will forget the whole affair. And for me, it is just one more wound to a heart already sore beset. Oh Richard, Richard, how can you still have the power to hurt me so?

The lessons were over for that day. When they resumed, neither of the two spoke of the matter again.

However, Maria's confession had stirred Berengaria's own emotional turmoil, which she had tried so hard to keep tamped down. The next day Joanna came into the room where Berengaria was working at the same translation, the one about transgressions. She pushed the tablet aside and looked at her friend. She spoke with as much control as she could.

"Joanna, I think you can tell that I have been very unhappy. I don't know what to do and I have no one but you to talk to." She paused to get a grip on herself. Joanna sat down beside her and put a comforting arm around Berengaria's shoulders. "I know, sister, I know. It is Richard, isn't it?"

"Yes, of course it is Richard. Your brother, whom you love. And so do I, in spite of everything. But Joanna, what am I to do? When we were in Jaffa he pretended for a few hours to be my husband, yet he was so cold and unloving that I felt like an object, not a woman. But I cannot, God help me, stop hoping that he will show me some affection or at least some consideration — I do not even ask for love, now." Looking down at the work on the table, she said tonelessly, "Sometimes I think the only thing to do is leave here, give up pretending to be Richard's queen, and go back to the monastery at Leyre. At least there I knew who I was."

Joanna listened, frowning in her concern.

Berengaria continued. "I might as well tell you the rest. Maria has confessed to me that Richard has been twice to her bed, the last time while we were all in Jaffa. She had been adoring him from a distance, and could not resist when he came to seduce her. Of course the poor girl is overcome with remorse. I have told her I forgive her and blame Richard."

Joanna was silent for half a minute, thinking what to say.

When she spoke it was hesitantly. "I do believe the trouble with Richard is that he does not think women are really human. He doesn't realize they have feelings, that they can be hurt and offended, just as a man can. Otherwise how could he have tried to marry me off to that odious Turk? And made all the arrangements without even asking me? And how could he have played such a heartless game with poor little Maria?"

"And when we were at Jaffa, how could he have been so callous as to pretend to me that he was a dutiful husband, knowing well that he was about to seek his real pleasure elsewhere?"

"Yes," said Joanna. "I was coming to that. The worst of all. I hoped that when Richard was married to someone so good, so beautiful, of such noble birth as you, he would mend his ways. After all, he is thirty-four years old. How long can he go on so irresponsibly, not caring whom he hurts?" She put up a hand to forestall Berengaria, who was about to interrupt. "Yet he is my brother and we care for each other. I have tried to talk to him. Just before we left Jaffa, after I had gotten over my fury at him for that Safadin affair, I told him I thought he was treating you shamefully, and pled with him to show you more consideration. Richard and I are still good friends, thank God, in spite of all the quarrels that have split our family apart."

"And what did he answer?"

"Why, he said that he is far too busy doing the Lord's work, trying to recover Jerusalem, to worry about anything else. He said that perhaps he has not been as good a Christian in his personal life as he has been on the battlefield, but that one of these days he will do penance and God will forgive him."

"I see," said Berengaria, her voice expressionless. "He accepts no blame, he does not see why he should act as though he had a wife. Your mother tried to warn me of this, but she made me think perhaps I could tame him. Either she did not know her son as well as she pretended, or she was simply trying to mollify me, to make me want to turn Richard into a faithful husband. And father."

"Still," said Joanna, "people do change, you know. Maybe Richard will. When he has had a great victory, and we can leave this dreadful land, he may become a new person." Neither spoke. There was nothing to say. Berengaria was a portrait in dejection. Hands clasped in her lap, shoulders drooping, she stared unseeingly at the brilliant red, green and gold of the open pages of the psalter. Joanna looked at it too. The Transgressor's Prayer was on the right; on the left was an armed and mounted knight, approaching the Holy Sepulchre in Jerusalem.

"Berengaria!" she exclaimed. "Look at your knight before Jerusalem! We should have just copied from your psalter, instead of trying to imagine it all. Then if anyone criticized, we could have told them it was the illustrator's fault, not ours. Shall we try again?"

"Not I. I have lost all my enthusiasm for the tiresome tapestry. But speaking of Jerusalem — shall we go ask Etienne and Bertrand if there is any news from the army? A messenger must have come this morning. How wonderful it would be to hear of a victory. Then we could begin to think of going home."

Her only hope now was that back in France, perhaps she and Richard could start over.

he bitter winter passed. Spring of 1192 brought green hillsides and fields gaily sprinkled with anemones. The orchards were briefly clothed in a froth of tender pink and virginal white. Summer, with its parching heat and scarcity of water for Crusaders and Muslims alike, reached its zenith. Yet still no word came to Acre from the Crusaders' army.

The last messenger, in early June, had brought the news that Richard was about to launch the long-awaited assault on Jerusalem. The stay-at-homes in Acre rejoiced.

"Surely this is the beginning of the end," Berengaria said to Joanna. Every day they climbed the steep steps to the walkway on the city wall, to scan the southern road in hopes of seeing a messenger galloping to bring them news. In vain.

What with the uncertainty and the heat, everybody was on edge. One day Berengaria heard the cook snap at the potboy and threaten him with a cleaver because he had forgotten to bring a pail of water to the kitchen.

Something had to be done. She asked the two guardians if they could send a man south for news. Bertrand ran a hand through his bushy red hair and looked embarrassed.

"We would be overstepping our authority if we did that, madame. We are under orders from King Richard, and unless he tells us himself or sends someone with the order, we cannot send any of our men out on such an errand."

At first she thought he was joking, though he had never joked before. "You mean, Sir Bertrand, that we cannot send a messenger until Richard sends a messenger to us to tell us that we may send a messenger?"

When he had taken this in, his embarrassment only increased. "When you put it that way, it does sound foolish. But I have been in King Richard's service for thirty years, and I must go by the rules as I always have."

She looked at him fixedly, feeling first frustration and then an unwonted anger. Perhaps it was the anger that spurred her resolve. In a flash she saw what she must do.

"Sir Bertrand, will you please ask Sir Etienne, the captain of the guard and two of his men to meet us here in half an hour? I will call Joanna and Maria and we will hold a council."

Still inflamed by her exasperation, she asked Cristina to find the crown she had last worn in Cyprus. When the others came into the hall, they saw her sitting at the head of the table, chin high, her crown placed squarely and firmly on her smoothly brushed hair. This was a Berengaria they had not seen before: a woman openly exercising her royal authority.

"My friends," she said, "I am Richard's queen. In his absence, I have not only the right but the duty to act for him, as I believe he would act. I assume you accept this."

Silence. Then Joanna spoke. "Of course, Berengaria. That is exactly what Richard would want you to do." Nobody disagreed.

"Very well. I have asked you to come here because we are all wondering why no word comes from Richard and the army. I know that all of us keep imagining the worst. So I propose that we send someone south to seek them, wherever they may be, and learn why we have not heard for so long. What do you think?"

Bertrand, the man who played by the rules, spoke first. It had not taken him long to adapt to the new ones.

"Your Majesty, it is an excellent suggestion. We should send someone. But…"

As he paused, Etienne de Longchamps broke in. "Yes, anything would be better than this uncertainty. But who could go? We have no messengers here, and none of the garrison has ever been to Jaffa, much less Jerusalem — am I right, captain?" The officer nodded. "It needs somebody familiar with the country," Etienne concluded. He mopped his bald head and looked around the table.

Berengaria answered at once. "But you know the country, Sir Knight. So does your comrade there, Sir Bertrand. Each of you has been to Jaffa at least once during the past year, to report to the king. Surely one of you could be spared for a time?"

Bertrand looked disapproving. "Our orders from King Richard are to guard the royal ladies. What if one of us were gone and some emergency arose?" He liked the duty in Acre, with few chores and plenty of naptime.

"You are both such competent knights," Berengaria said, "that I am sure either of you could perform on his own very well in any emergency here. Besides, the citizens in Acre have calmed down, all the Turks have long since gone, and we are in no danger. And we have a ten-man garrison." She addressed tall portly Bertrand, and short slight Etienne. "Now, which one of you will it be?"

They looked at each other. Bertrand was the larger and the senior, and he outstared Etienne. So it was decided that Etienne de Longchamps would leave on a fast horse the next day for Jaffa and, if necessary, Jerusalem.

Berengaria found herself oddly pleased with this, her first foray into royal power.

In three weeks Etienne was back, with three other knights. They were an alarming sight. Etienne's left arm, bound with blood-stained cloths, was in a sling. He limped, and his eyes were bloodshot. When he took off his hat, his poor hairless head was seen to be bandaged too. The others were in similar shape. But before he could be tended to, Etienne insisted on giving his report to Berengaria.

The same little group who had seen him off gathered in the hall, shocked at Etienne's condition and at the news he brought.

He had arrived in Jaffa just as the army returned from an abortive assault on Jerusalem. He learned that they had gotten very close, even reached Montjoie, the hill so named by pilgrims for the joy they felt at their first sight of the Holy City. Here Richard had paused to confer with his advisors, and with the greatest sorrow and reluctance they had decided not to continue.

"Why on earth not," cried Berengaria, "when they were so close?"

Etienne's face became even more grim. "Believe me, my queen, the reasons were powerful. For one thing, Richard's spies told him Saladin had three times as large a defending army in

Jerusalem as Richard had in his assault forces. And there was the matter of supplies — nothing to forage for in that barren countryside, and a fearfully long way they were from their stores on the coast. But the worst problem was water. Saladin's a sly one; he'd poisoned the wells for ten miles around Jerusalem."

His listeners looked at him and at each other in dismay. Then Bertrand spoke. "You must go and have your wounds tended to, my friend. But first tell us quickly how you came to this state."

"Yes, I was coming to that," Etienne said. His voice was weakening and his face was white. Doggedly, he went on. "I got to Jaffa on a Monday, the army came back on the Tuesday, and on Wednesday a mighty force of Turks came out of the blue and fell on us. It was the worst fighting I've seen in a lifetime of battles; they are beastly, cruel warriors. But we gave as good as we got, and finally pushed them off. After we'd licked our wounds a bit, King Richard told me to come back here if I was up to it, and tell you what I've just told you. And he said to tell you in spite of all our wounded, our army is more or less intact; and things could be worse."

"I don't see how," murmured Joanna. Etienne limped out with Bertrand helping him, and the others, downcast, straggled from the room.

The next day they learned how much worse things could be. A messenger arrived with the news that the king had fallen grievously ill, apparently the very day after Etienne had left. His doctor sent word that if Berengaria and Joanna wished to see him alive, they would do well to come at once. The messenger had left Jaffa three days ago — who knew what might have happened in those three days?

"He has always been subject to these fevers," Joanna said, tense with anxiety. "But he has always managed to pull himself out of them. Come, let us get ready to go to Jaffa." She took Berengaria's hand and they hurried out of the room. "I must be with him, he is my dear brother."

"And my husband," said Berengaria. She forgot all her resentments and grievances in her anxiety to go to Richard.

But before they were out of the Acre gates, with Bertrand as their guide, another messenger came pounding up.

"He is better, he is going to live to fight many another battle! He asks you to stay here and wait for him, for he expects to join you shortly."

"Thank God!" said Joanna. "The Lord be praised!" said Berengaria.

Bertrand let out a great shout of joy. "Ha!" he bellowed. "I knew our lionhearted king wasn't ready to give up yet!"

On their way back to the palace they began to wonder. "Now what can he mean, telling us to wait here for him?" Berengaria asked. "Why would he come back to Acre, which is certainly in no danger, instead of staying there in Jaffa where Saladin could attack again at any time?"

Bertrand galloped to overtake them, his red hair flying, his jowly face puffed up with self-importance. He had been talking to the messenger. "Richard expects to come to Acre as soon as he finishes treating with Saladin on the terms of the truce."

"Truce!" exclaimed Berengaria. "Is he giving up the Crusade then — with Jerusalem still held by the infidels?"

"Perhaps he has not really recovered after all?" Joanna wondered. Unfortunately, Bertrand had told them all he knew.

Bits of news dribbled in for the next few weeks but not until the middle of September did they learn the whole story. Along the coast road came the vanguard of the Crusaders' army, marching still in disciplined formation but with a little more looseness in the gait, a little more banter back and forth than when they had set out on their great adventure a year before. The towering figure of Robert of Tornham could be made out, mounted on a suitably enormous horse, as black as his rider's hair.

While most of the army went on to the camping ground outside the city, Sir Robert made for the small town square on which the palace fronted. "Let me just sit down in the shade here, lad, and get my breath before I go in to see the ladies," he said to Bertrand, who was eager to take him into the palace.

His audience came to him instead. Berengaria, Joanna, Maria, their two guardians, their servants and most of the garrison crowded around him, pelting him with questions. Sir Robert was in good voice and equal to the occasion.

"Eh now, ladies, I'm right glad to see you, and I can tell you are a bit pleased at the sight of your old nursemaid, right? Now you want to know where is King Richard and why wasn't he at the head of the column where he belongs, and is he all right? Yes, he is, and should be here within the hour, but he's riding on a litter for this last hot stretch, being still somewhat weak from his fever. And I'll thank you for another cup, lass, if you'll be so good." Cristina had handed him a goblet of cool water from the well as soon as he sat down.

"And you want to know what happened and why we're all marching back here. Well, I'll tell you what happened."

While he took a deep draught from his cup, Joanna interjected, "Just tell us first of all, is the war really over? Are we going home?"

"What happened is, King Richard and that slippery old sultan have agreed to stop the fighting for three years at least. So Richard can go home and take care of the troubles in England and France. King Philip and Richard's wicked brother John are about to move into every castle he's lord of, from what Queen Eleanor writes, unless he comes at once."

"But to give up the Holy Crusade! If the greatest warrior in the world gives in to the infidels, who will stop them?" Berengaria's face fell and her eyes were wide with shock. She looked at Joanna and she knew they were thinking the same thing: Richard must indeed be more ill than anybody had acknowledged.

"I won't deny, my lady, there's plenty who grumble about turning tail when the Holy City was so close to being ours. But if Richard goes home for a year or so and shores things up, then he'll be able to come back and finish the job here once and for all. And remember this" — his tone hardened and he looked fiercely around as though daring any renegade to disagree with him — "remember this, he was deserted by Leopold of Austria and Philip of France too, along with two thousand of their men and their ships. They're the ones who've betrayed the Crusade, not Richard and those who stayed loyal to him!"

He paused and drank, as though to drown his anger with the cool water, and turned to Berengaria and Joanna. "And you're among those who have been loyal, ladies," he added gallantly, his eyebrows rising in a salute. "You have not had an easy time of it, cooped up here and wondering what was going on. Now you've had enough of old Sir Robert. I'll be off to some quiet little corner where I can take off this heavy armor and lie down on a real bed instead of the stony ground."

Two hours later Richard arrived. He stepped unsteadily from the litter. Joanna ran up to him and hugged him. Berengaria, uncertain, took his hand and pressed it, looking at him with dismay. They were appalled at his appearance: not only did he seem unnaturally subdued, he was drawn, gaunt and sallow. His golden hair was bleached almost white. His eyes were sunken and he had trouble keeping them open.

He sat on a couch and let his head fall back to rest against the wall, his eyes closed.

He opened his eyes and looked first at his wife, then his sister, and smiled wanly. "It took this spot of sickness to make my two girls forgive me for my misdeeds? Maybe the first misdeed was bringing you to this cursed country, where so little has turned out as we hoped."

Berengaria spoke gently. "Richard, all we care about now is your health."

"I will get better, the doctors say so." He did not sound as though he believed it.

Joanna asked, "Can you tell us any more about the truce? Sir Robert said only that it was for three years. What did you gain, what did you give up?"

Richard sat up straighter and his eyes almost flashed with the familiar fire. "More of the former than the latter, to my way of thinking." He explained the terms.

"First of all, there's the coastal strip from Tyre which is north of here, all the way down to Jaffa. All that, which we fought so hard to take, will remain in Christian hands. Then there's Ascalon, on to the south. It's not so much of a city now because Saladin knocked its walls down, just the way he did Jaffa's. But it's still important because it's right on the way to Egypt. We agreed it will be an open city."

"But what about Jerusalem?" Berengaria asked. "The most important city of all. Surely this cannot be a good truce if Saladin keeps it."

"That's the best part of our agreement. Pilgrims from all Christendom will be able to visit the city freely, and pray at all our holy places, with no hindrance from the Muslims."

Berengaria felt more cheerful. "Why, that is all we really need — safety for the faithful who wish to make pilgrimage to Jerusalem and Bethlehem. What does it matter whose soldiers are on the ramparts, if good Christians are free to come, to worship and go safely home again?"

"You are too trusting, Berengaria," Richard said. "If only it were that simple. As long as Saladin lives the truce will hold and all its provisions will be honored. He has always been a man of his word to me. But he is not young and he is becoming very tired. Nobody knows what will happen if he dies before the three years are up."

His voice became more impassioned, and he pounded his knee with his fist. "If only I had the men and the time to stay and see the fight to the end! If only John and Philip weren't tearing around France, dividing up my lands between them! If only..." He did not finish the sentence and slumped against the wall once more.

Presently he rose heavily. "I must rest, if I am to get over this cursed fever. Thank you for letting me unburden myself. We will talk tomorrow about the journey home."

That night Berengaria lay awake a long time, pondering. Then it came to her. There are many Richards, she thought. There is the Richard I first saw in Pamplona when I was six and who charmed me, then threw away my gift to him. There is the Richard who married me to please his mother and who broke my heart and did not care. There is the Richard who seeks his momentary pleasure with any lad or girl he fancies. There is the Richard who is a lion in battle, whose men would follow him anywhere — I have not seen that one but I know of his fame. And there is this king, this proud and powerful king, who finds himself forced to give up before the battle is won, and who suffers.

For an instant she had a glimmering vision of how she could serve as the queen of this last Richard: to forgive him his excesses, to be loyal in his adversities, to always show a calm and dignified face to the world, even if Richard wounded her. She had been brought up to accept that kings and queens had a unique and difficult role to play, and this role would never be easy. But she believed she could play it, with God's help.

Perhaps... if there were children... she might discover still another Richard.

s before, the women were dispatched first in their lumbering dromond. Richard would rest a few days and see to dismantling of the camp before embarking. He was still not his vigorous self. When they said goodbye he was as subdued as when he had arrived from Jaffa.

First he kissed Joanna, then took Maria's hand and wished her a safe journey.

"My mother will take care of you. I have sent word to her." She thanked him but could not bring herself to look at him. The memory of how he had captured her heart and tossed her aside was still vivid. He had long since forgotten.

Finally he took Berengaria's arm and led her to one side.

"Now we say goodbye again for a time. You have been patient and forebearing during all this difficult year, Berengaria." He put his arms around her and rested his cheek on the top of her brown head.

She did not move or speak, giving herself to the embrace of those strong yet gentle encircling arms, wondering whether she dared believe in his sincerity. Was this still another Richard? Had be been so frightened by his near-fatal illness that he had become penitent enough to atone for his misdeeds? Or was it Eleanor speaking through her son?

He released her and looked into her face, then kissed her lightly. Though it was more the kiss of a friend than a lover, the touch of his lips on hers filled her with the familiar tremors of hope.

"Goodbye, Richard. I will think of you and pray for you until we meet again."

"That will be at my mother's palace in Poitiers. I will come there before I go to England to thank my subjects for their support of my Crusade. Until Poitiers, Berengaria, in three months at most. Then I hope we can start again on our marriage."

"That is my hope too. And I hope I may come with you to England. The English are my people now, and I think I should get to know them."

"And so you shall, my green-eyed queen. But now, goodbye, and a safe voyage."

Did he mean it? The green eyes were misted with tears as she turned to be rowed out to the dromond.

In three months neither Berengaria nor Richard was in Poitiers.

Berengaria was in Rome. The three women and their party had planned to rest there a few days after the tedious sea voyage from Acre. However, Pope Celestine, whose minions were everywhere and kept him informed of all important visitors arriving, had sent an emissary to meet them on the road and urge a longer stay.

The foppish young messenger wore the sober black livery of the church but had spiced it up with a high fur collar and a hat with an enormous white plume. Clearly unimpressed with this bedraggled group of travelers, he doffed his hat, inclined his head a trifle and recited his message.

"His Holiness, Pope Celestine the Third, invites you to be his guests and to wait in Rome for better weather and safer travel. I will conduct you to your rooms in his palace. His Holiness will receive you in his audience chamber this afternoon."

They gladly followed him. Berengaria was relieved at the prospect of a respite from the hard riding since they had come ashore at Brindisi. Joanna was not good company. She had been seasick, and still felt weak and listless, slumping in her saddle and talking little. Etienne de Longchamps, their official escort, was not nearly the forceful, effective man Sir Robert was. As often as not it was up to Berengaria to decide where they would spend the night and to seek out a local lord or churchman who could be persuaded to put them up.

Now, though, to be lodged in the Pope's own palace — that sounded like luxury. The whole party took heart as their horses trotted along the wide, stone-paved Roman road by the Tiber River. Across the water they glimpsed marble monuments and pillared temples, and ahead, the Castle of St. Angelo topped a hill. Even Joanna perked up, sat erect and looked around her.

"My mother has been to Rome many times, but this is my first visit. And I have never met a pope. Have you, Berengaria?"

"Never," replied Berengaria, "though my father corresponded with Pope Alexander the Third; he greatly admired him. But that one has been dead for some time, and I don't know anything about this Pope Celestine."

Their apartments were even more sumptuous than they had imagined. Berengaria looked in amazement at the plum-colored silk curtains, the gold ewers and silver candlesticks, the ivory figurines on a polished ebony table. The huge bed was enveloped in velvety purple hangings. What wealth the Pope must command, to give his guests such royal treatment!

When they were summoned to meet him they were even more dazzled. His audience chamber, at the top of one of the palace's four slender towers, was like a little jewel box. It glittered with the riches the Church had acquired over the centuries. He received them seated on a golden throne, and his vestments, white as alabaster, were embroidered with so much silver that they could almost have stood alone.

Despite the splendor, their eyes were fastened on the Pope's lined, somber face. The eighty-five-year-old pontiff, only recently elevated to the throne of St. Peter, had spent a lifetime in the service of the Church and had seen all that the world could produce in the way of good and evil. If one had not been taught that the Church's message was one of hope, one would say this was the face of a deeply disillusioned man. First Berengaria, then Joanna, advanced and knelt to kiss his ruby ring, then stood respectfully before him.

"Welcome to Rome, my daughters." His voice was thin and reedy and he spoke slowly, but with precision. "I know you have had a long and tiring voyage, after your sojourn in the Holy Land. I know too that your husband the King, madame," he looked at Berengaria, "did great service to Holy Church, and has vowed to go back soon and finish the recovery of Jerusalem."

"So he intends, as soon as he has dealt with various matters in his kingdoms," Berengaria answered.

"If he could advise you now, I am sure he would urge you to stay in Rome for a time, rather than hurry off in the dead of winter. It would be most unwise for you to resume your journey now, when the weather is unpredictable and travel can be so difficult... so difficult." His voice became faint, then regained strength.

"But more than that, it would not be safe. Even with your armed escort, you might be overwhelmed by brigands. They are swarming over the countryside nowadays. We may sympathize but we cannot condone. Most are mercenaries or soldiers who find themselves idle and unemployed, because, through God's grace, no cruel wars are now demanding their services. Peace has its price, does it not?" A faraway look came to his faded blue eyes as though he were conversing with God, which was just as well since they could think of no response.

"So," he resumed, his thoughts returning from wherever they had been, "please accept our hospitality for as long as you wish. My people will do all they can to make your stay comfortable." They sensed that he had ceased to see them, and they respectfully withdrew.

He was right, they agreed. So Rome it was. In spite of the stormy weather, they tried to see the sights, though it was hard to appreciate the classic grandeurs of the Forum when the rain was in one's eyes and the wind whipped one's cloak around like a sail. Still, it was awesome. Berengaria realized that the Roman ruins she had seen in Limassol were only a faint foretaste of the glorious relics of Rome — many still miraculously preserved, as though the toga-clad Romans had just gone home to lunch.

Before long, they had more serious things on their minds than sightseeing.

A messenger from the papal legate in Vienna brought blunt news to the Pope: "King Richard of England is a prisoner in Germany."

The Pope called at once for Berengaria and Joanna to be present while the man gave the rest of his message. They listened in disbelief and dismay.

Richard had, for some unknown reason — perhaps the onset of winter and its storms — left his vessel at the head of the Adriatic Sea to continue his journey by land. Before he got far he had been captured by Leopold of Austria, who still bitterly resented the slights Richard had inflicted on him when they shared the command of the crusading forces. Leopold had soon "sold" his royal captive to his own overlord, Emperor Henry of Germany. Now Henry was demanding an enormous ransom — two million marks.

There matters stood. Richard was imprisoned somewhere in Germany. At the end of the report, Berengaria and Joanna looked at each other in alarm, then at the Pope.

Celestine's first reaction was surprise at the amount of the ransom demand. "Two million marks!" he exclaimed. "But I suppose Henry asks so much because such a valuable prize is not likely to come his way again." Then, seeing their distress, he remembered his Christian duty and tried to comfort them. "I have some influence with Henry of Germany — he is emperor only because I anointed him. I will begin at once to try to persuade him to release Richard, or at least to moderate his ransom demands. Meantime, perhaps the next news will be more cheerful."

But no more word of any kind arrived. When the days lengthened and the weather was better, Joanna was eager to be off.

"You may be sure," she said to Berengaria, "if anybody has news of Richard, it will be my mother. So the sooner we get to Poitiers, the better." At the prospect of action, she was again like the little wren Berengaria had first thought she resembled, bustling about and chirping encouragement to the others. Maria was glad enough to resume the journey — being still young enough to be bored by inaction and hopeful of adventure. Berengaria thought they should stay a little longer.

"The Pope has been so helpful, and he has his ways of knowing what is going on — should we not stay at least a week or so, in case we can learn more?"

Sir Etienne was all for moving on. He had a young wife in Normandy whom he had not seen for two years, and was increasingly anxious to get home. The more anxious he became, the greater his energy. The little man became brisk and efficient, and busied himself with organizing their departure. He reassured Berengaria.

"I have spoken to the chief officer of the Pope's messenger force, and he assures me that word will be sent to us at once by the swiftest means, if any more news of Richard comes. And the Pope has promised to send six armed men to ride with us until we are in Poitou."

So Berengaria was persuaded, and they set off again.

After a night in Avignon, halfway to Poitiers, they left the city and neared the bridge across the Rhone. It was a bright March day, and the wind ruffled the sunlit waters of the river and set the greening branches of the trees by the road to dancing.

For a moment Berengaria was distracted from her cares, and her heart lifted. She drew in her horse and called to Joanna, "Stop a minute, sister, and look at this beautiful sight. I always thought our bridge at Puenta la Reina was the finest in the world, but this is ten times grander. See how graceful the arches are! And so many of them, reaching all the way across this wide river."

Joanna counted. "There are twenty. Now I remember that when I came here, on my way to Sicily to marry William, they were just starting to build the bridge; I do know that we had to go across the Rhone in a boat."

Berengaria was thinking back. "Well, I suppose I should remember it from when I came this way with your mother. But it must have been one of those dark wet days when we huddled in our cloaks and hardly looked to one side or the other." She shivered, recalling that dismal journey.

A sound of galloping hooves brought them back to the present. They turned to see a party of armed men clattering up from the city. Sir Etienne and the guards wheeled their horses and drew their swords, but the newcomers' leader called out, "Stay, put back your swords, we are friends! I have come only to offer my services to these royal ladies. I am Raymond, son of Count Raymond of Toulouse."

He turned to Berengaria and proffered his hand. She removed her glove and reached out to take it.

He bowed and said, "You must be Richard of England's queen. And this is Joanna Plantagenet, if I am not mistaken?"

"You have it right," Berengaria said. "And this other lady is our ward, Princess Maria of Cyprus; and this is our guardian, Sir Etienne de Longchamps." Berengaria assessed Raymond. She saw a good-looking young man with black hair cropped short, sporting a small pointed beard. He sat tall in his saddle, and seemed manly, open and polite — nothing like what she had heard of his father,

Count Raymond the Fifth, whom her father called the most unscrupulous man in France.

"How do you propose to serve us, Sir Raymond?" she asked.

"I suggest that you permit me and my men to ride with you to Poitiers, since we are going that way too," he replied, looking around to appraise their party, now all crowded together on the bridge. "With my four men and your eight, we should be able to stand off any troublemakers. And there are plenty of them on the roads these days."

"So we have been told," said Sir Etienne. "I for one would be glad of a few more strong arms."

So they accepted, though Joanna was suspicious of Raymond's motives. When the party was on the road again, she said in a low voice to Berengaria, "He seems rather brash to me; why should our safety be so important to him? Don't forget, Berengaria, his father has always been one of my family's worst enemies. I would not be surprised if he has sent the son on some devious errand," she said darkly.

"Still, we might as well take advantage of the offer," Berengaria protested. "After all, there are more of us than of them, and we will tell Sir Etienne to watch carefully."

Somewhat unexpectedly, the young count was solicitous of their comfort all the way, and they soon got used to his presence. Instead of craft and shiftiness his face spoke of friendship and a wish to please. Yet Berengaria shared some of Joanna's misgivings. There was something not quite right, she thought; he was almost too handsome, too courteous.

They traveled northward beside the banks of the broad, smoothly flowing Rhone, then struck off westward, making their way along narrow tracks through forests of ancient oaks. First rode Raymond and the other knights, wearing their swords but freed of their cumbersome armor — to make them more mobile in case of attack. Then came the women and their serving people; then the squires; and finally the pack animals. A noisy clanking sounded from the mules that bore the discarded armor. It was no wonder that when the party passed through the tiny villages, men, women and children turned out to stare. Some, in ragged clothing and extending thin scrawny arms, came out to beg. It had been a hard winter, and it was months before the new crops would bring nourishment.

Berengaria tossed what coins she could find down into the outstretched hands; but she noticed that Raymond did not — he only stared straight ahead, as though not seeing the misery.

Finally, in late April, the weary travelers saw the city of Poitiers with its cathedral and palace crowning its hill. For Berengaria, it was the place where she hoped to be reunited with Richard; where, when he was freed, he would surely come. For Joanna, it was coming home. For Maria, it was all strange, new and exciting.

In the palace forecourt all dismounted and Raymond gallantly bowed over the hand of each of the three ladies.

"Thank you, my lovely charges, for the pleasure of your company."

He smiled and his black eyes surveyed them in turn, resting for just a split second on Joanna. "I will hope to repeat the pleasure some day." Then he leaped into the saddle, wheeled his horse and galloped off, before they could return his thanks. His departure was as abrupt as his arrival had been, back in Avignon.

Maria could hardly wait to comment. Even curiosity about the palace, and eagerness to learn in which of its towers she would be lodged, could not keep her from wondering aloud about Raymond. Ever since she had had to give up the idea of Philip Augustus as a suitor for Joanna, she had been hoping another would come along. Raymond seemed perfect for the role.

As they mounted the broad stone steps, she demanded, "Now Berengaria, did not the handsome count hold Joanna's hand a trifle longer than yours or mine? And did you see the look he gave her, just as he left?"

But Berengaria was too tired to talk about it, and Joanna was already inside.

They had expected to be greeted by Eleanor but she was not there; she had left for England the previous month to raise Richard's ransom, according to her seneschal. This dignitary, full of his own importance, summoned the three women to Eleanor's spacious audience chamber. As her representative, he saw fit to seat himself on her throne. But to the women he seemed more ridiculous than commanding. He was short and fat with a perfectly round head. Through a fuzz of white hair his pink bald pate gleamed.

"Welcome to Poitiers," he greeted them, waving them toward seats with his plump hand. "My gracious sovereign has asked me to tell you what plans she has made for you."

Berengaria thought, "How in character — still running my life!" But when she heard what Eleanor had proposed for her it did not sound too bad.

"Queen Eleanor has ordered that a small castle in Anjou, Beaufort-en-Vallée, is to be prepared for Berengaria. Our queen believes that it will be quite suitable for Berengaria to occupy while waiting for Richard's release."

Joanna, Eleanor had added, could go there too, if she liked.

"But what of Maria?" Joanna asked. The Cypriot girl's eyes were fixed intently on the seneschal's face as she waited tensely to hear what her fate was.

"She is to remain at the palace in Poitiers, in the care of Eleanor's ladies."

Maria looked uncertainly at her two friends and said hesitantly, "Please Sir Seneschal, may I not go with them to the castle at Beaufort? It will be very hard to part with them, after all this time."

"No, you must stay here," the seneschal said. (Even his voice is fat, Berengaria thought.) "Queen Eleanor especially instructed me as to that. You are King Richard's ward, and in his absence his mother is responsible for you."

"Never mind, Maria," Berengaria comforted her. "We will not be far away. You will come, will you not, Joanna?"

Joanna declined, at least for now. For her, Poitiers was home, and she wanted only to settle down for a while. But for Berengaria, it was too filled with the presence of Eleanor, and she was anxious to leave. She could not help thinking that at any moment her formidable mother-in-law would appear from around some corner, with a curt word or two or — more likely — no word at all, just a reproving look.

She looked around Eleanor's elegant reception hall, marble-floored, with cushioned benches around the walls and bright-hued frescoes depicting scenes from the Old Testament. It was certainly a suitable setting for its illustrious chatelaine. Surveying the grandeur, Berengaria tried to picture her "small castle" at Beaufort. No matter how humble it proved, she was sure it would be quite appropriate; her tastes were simple.

But just before her departure from Poitiers a messenger from Eleanor brought great news. That indomitable queen had, by appeals and demands to monasteries, bishops, nobles and merchants, squeezed the ransom money out of the English citizenry and was on her way to Germany to retrieve her imprisoned son.

Berengaria wondered: should she remain here, for surely Eleanor and Richard would make Poitiers their first stop after he was freed? But she decided to hold with her plan to go to Beaufort, and begin establishing a home where she could await her husband.

t took Berengaria and her party just three days to travel from Poitiers to Beaufort-en-Vallée. She was accompanied by three knights from the court to act as guides and guards; a cook; a housekeeper; and a young boy to serve as lad-of-all-work. In addition, there was Lady Héloise Mainteville, delegated by Eleanor to serve as her lady-in-waiting. The two women did not converse much on the journey. Berengaria was suspicious of anyone associated with Eleanor, and Lady Héloise seemed content to ride in silence.

Everybody was looking forward to the end of the journey and the "small castle" promised by Eleanor — which sounded like a snug haven, just right for their small party. After a final passage through well-tended, prosperous pastures, at last the village came in view.

"Well! It is a good thing I did not have great expectations," Berengaria said to Lady Héloise. They saw a modest hamlet in the valley of the Authion, a river equally modest, a tributary of the Loire. The unprepossessing village had grown up around the feet of a castle, which stood on a low, conical hill above the river — a site obviously chosen for its defensive position. They walked their horses along the narrow street, looking up dubiously toward the castle. It was indeed small as promised. It gained little in attraction as they rode up the track that wound around the hill.

The moat was dry and empty. They crossed it by a shaky wooden bridge and passed through a gateway in a crumbling wall. They emerged into a circular courtyard, enclosed by the wall and three equidistant towers, two of which had been decapitated in some long-ago siege. The towers were connected to each other by low stone buildings built against the wall. The open space where they sat their horses — the old bailey — held a few wooden sheds and a dovecote, around what once might have been a garden with a scattering of emaciated fruit trees.

They dismounted in silence, looking around them in dismay. "Maybe it will look better inside," said Héloise hopefully. It did not. The preparations Eleanor had ordered consisted of clearing out the lower floor of the one tower that was in reasonable repair, to serve as main hall; the room above it for Berengaria's chamber; and three or four rooms in the connecting buildings. There were a minimum of furnishings — beds, tables and chests. Dust covered everything.

"We will have our hands full, making this liveable," Berengaria said, trying not to sound discouraged.

"We will indeed, but I think we are up to it, my lady." Héloise spoke firmly and Berengaria's spirits rose a little. Maybe this one would be different from the two ladies-in-waiting Eleanor had sent to Palestine. Héloise did not seem to flinch from an adventure.

Some ten or fifteen years older than Berengaria, Héloise had seen a good deal of the world while in Eleanor's service. But for a year she had not budged from Poitiers, with nothing to do but dance attendance on Eleanor. She had been getting just a little bored. Small chance of that here, she thought, with all this work to be done!

"I am glad you feel so confident," Berengaria told her. "It will be a challenge, but it will keep our minds off our troubles."

Héloise wondered what that meant but did not ask. Both women were appraising each other — both knew that they would have to depend on each other for company in this godforsaken corner of Anjou. Héloise knew only what Eleanor had told her — that Berengaria was waiting for her husband, Richard, to rejoin her when he was freed from imprisonment in Germany. She admired the queen's composure, her kindness and intelligence — as well as her beauty, of which she seemed unaware. She did not expect any quick confidences — not until they knew each other much better. But that was all right with Héloise.

For her part, Berengaria sensed a kindred spirit in her new companion. She maintained a calm, unruffled demeanor, remindful of Berengaria's mother, Queen Sancha. But in appearance she was unique: tall, long-legged and so thin as to be almost angular, something like a stork. But she had come to terms with her ungainly body and moved without hurry and with surprising grace. Her face too was thin, with a prominent Roman nose and a wide, generous mouth — not a pretty face but one not soon forgotten. Her blond hair showed a few strands of gray; she wore it coiled in a knot at the back of her neck.

As it turned out, the two became a good team in the chore of making the neglected old castle more comfortable. Encouraged by their energy, the whole staff fell to, eager to bring order out of the chaos, but it was slow going. Then help arrived: to Berengaria's joy, one day as she was investigating the old dovecote and wondering if it could ever attract any doves, she saw her maid Cristina, and her new husband Carlos, riding through the gate.

Berengaria could not have been more surprised. "Did your father not tell you we were coming?" Cristina asked when she saw her mistress's confusion.

"He most certainly did not. I have not heard from him since I sent word that I was going to settle here at Beaufort."

Apparently, King Sancho had decided his daughter might need some dependable Basque hands in her new home, and had dispatched the couple. Here they were — quick, clever Cristina, so devoted to her mistress, and tall, taciturn Carlos, with his countryman's skills.

There was much catching up to do. Berengaria had not seen Cristina since they had parted at Avignon during the homeward journey from Rome. With Berengaria's blessing, Cristina had returned to Navarre, fearful that some other lass might have snapped up her sweetheart Carlos during her two years away; but he had been faithful to her.

"And now my little Cristina is married, and has left home again to serve me. You are both most welcome." She smiled warmly and clasped both their hands.

Before long, with the addition of a few servants from the village, they became quite the settled little household. Carlos, tireless and ingenious, drew on his knowledge of husbandry to restore the garden. Workmen from the village were recruited to repair a half-dozen of the empty rooms so everybody had adequate lodging. Héloise claimed the ground-floor apartment adjoining

Berengaria's tower, and Carlos and Cristina set up housekeeping next door. They had brought two mules loaded with Berengaria's effects as well as some welcome additions to her wardrobe, selected by her sister Blanche. Héloise had sent for more furnishings from Poitiers. Finally, the dilapidated, woebegone fortress began to look like a very liveable abode.

"You see, Berengaria, we have done it!" Héloise said, the day when Carlos and the lad-of-all-work had just settled a dozen doves in the repaired dovecote. It was the last step in restoring the establishment to what it once had been. The two women were walking through the recently planted garden, where lettuces were already pushing up their folded leaves and reaching toward the sun. The air was soft and warm, filled with the sound of the gentle cooing of doves. By now, Berengaria and Héloise enjoyed an easy friendship, nurtured not only by months of working together but also by their shared pleasure and pride in what they had accomplished. And though Berengaria had not told Héloise her whole story, the latter read between the lines and shrewdly guessed the reasons for Berengaria's reserve and occasional melancholy.

On this balmy spring day, though, nobody could be melancholic.

"Can you remember how this all looked when we first came?" Héloise flung her arms wide to take in the whole scene. "And we both said we were sure we could take on the task of restoring it — but if you had shown the least doubt, I think I would have gladly given it up and gone back to Poitiers."

Berengaria laughed. "That makes two of us! To tell you the truth, I was not as optimistic as I sounded, either. But I had no idea then of how energetic and clever you were; and of course we had good help from all our people."

"And what now, Berengaria?" Héloise asked seriously. "How shall we spend our time, now that we do not have to hem bed curtains, or supervise the bricklaying, or keep going down to the village to see if the carpenter has finished the tables, or decide where we want the rose garden?"

"Oh, I am not worried about that," Berengaria said, taking her friend's arm as they made their second turn around the gardens. "I have a great stack of manuscripts, just waiting for me to get at them and make copies. Some time ago I sent a message to my old friend Brother Anselmo at the monastery at Leyre — I have told you about my time there, have I not?"

Héloise nodded. "Yes, and I wondered mightily at your diligence in learning."

"Well, I have been far from diligent lately. But I asked Brother Anselmo to send me whatever he could that needed copying or translating. Which he did, almost by return messenger. I have been itching to get at them. And now that I have set up my work table by the window in my chamber, there is nothing to stop me, except finding the time." She looked doubtfully at Héloise. "You may be like everybody else I know, and scoff at this interest of mine in old parchments and writers nobody has ever heard of."

"Not at all," said Héloise brightly. "I applaud you, and I envy you. I wish I had something to absorb me so much. I have never risen above the level of reasonably competent knitter. Now I have a suggestion. Since I have no skills in copying and do not intend to acquire any, why not let me take over your responsibilities as chatelaine of our little ménage, so you can feel free to scratch away to your heart's content? That way we both will feel useful."

So they settled down to a division of labor that was agreeable to both. As spring of 1194 blossomed into summer, each plunged contentedly into the new regime; and Berengaria found to her relief that she could still make a creditable copy.

On a warm and cloudless day in June, a messenger toiled up the path toward the castle on the knoll. He had left his horse at the inn in the village to be watered and fed, and was finding the way up steeper than he had thought. Why did royal personages always insist on living on the highest point in the neighborhood? It made sense, of course, in places like Poitiers, where the enemy could appear at any moment. But here, in this insignificant little town? Who would want to take this lonely old castle?

Still, he couldn't complain. He was being paid well enough. "Take this letter and deliver it in person to the Lady Berengaria," they had told him in Poitiers. He had never heard of any Berengaria — probably some aged aunt of the Plantagenets, living out her life here in peace and quiet.

Puffing and redfaced, he passed through the gate and up the short slope into the bailey, hallooing as he came. (Perhaps the old woman was deaf.) As he entered, a lady and a manservant came out of separate doors, to see what all the noise was.

The lady, to his astonishment, was no wrinkled stooping crone, but a slender woman who stood surveying him questioningly. She was not young but she was so fair as to make a man catch his breath. A gauzy blue wimple covered her hair except for two wings of chestnut brown at the temples. He could not take his eyes off the smooth face, the serene brow, the steady gray-green eyes, the straight nose, the lips curving in amusement at his embarrassment.

Carlos was not so amused. "Here now, my man, what's all this shouting? Do you have something for Queen Berengaria? Give it to her at once, and I'll take you off and see if we can stop up that loud mouth with some bread and cheese and ale."

As they went, Berengaria called, "After he's rested a bit, Carlos, have him come back to see if I have an answer to send." She hurried into the hall, eagerly breaking the scroll's seal as she went. She had already recognized Joanna's bold handwriting on the superscripture. Perhaps she was sending news of Richard! It was a long time since she had seen Joanna, and the letter was welcome. She settled down on a windowseat and began to read.

Dear Sister,

Richard is free! But I have not seen him. He and my mother went down the Rhine and sailed for England, without stopping anywhere in Normandy, much less Poitou. And now word has just come that he was recrowned at Winchester Cathedral in March, so his English subjects could rejoice at his safe return and renew their allegiance. I hear there was much pomp and ceremony and my mother sat at Richard's side. My mother is back at the Abbey of Fontevrault now, and has sent me all this news.

A torrent of emotions swept over her. First, profound relief that Richard had been released. He was free, he was unharmed! Then a stab of hurt pierced her happiness. He had not come to see her or even sent a message before going to England. Finally, she was over-whelmed by searing anger and wounded pride. She had not been present at the coronation. She should have been crowned Queen of England when he was crowned King. She blamed Eleanor for that — though deep down, a buried thought rankled: if Richard had wanted her there, he could have sent for her.

She told herself that the important thing was that he was no longer a captive. But where was he? It was three months since the coronation. He must have come back across the Channel by now. Surely he would sooner or later remember that he had a wife. She had never forgotten his farewell at St. Jean d'Acre — "I will see you in Poitiers. And perhaps we can start again." She fought back tears. All these years, she had clung to the hope of starting again.

She read on.

> *And now for another surprise. Berengaria my dear, do you remember how kind and helpful young Count Raymond was, during the last part of our journey home? He stopped here a few weeks ago on his way to tend to some affairs in Nantes, and asked me to marry him. And I think I will.*

"Lord God, what is she thinking of!" Berengaria exclaimed, putting the scroll down. Why would Joanna marry into the family that had so often been an enemy to her own?

> *I know what you are saying — that my father and all my family have always said that Count Raymond of Toulouse was a bad man.*

Berengaria pictured her funny little friend as she made a face and emphasized the word "bad" with mock disapproval.

> *But that does not mean his son is the same; to me, he has shown nothing but courtesy and kindness. He will come back soon to have my answer. Then I expect I will travel to*

Fontevrault to see my mother, then go on to Toulouse for the wedding. Now my dear sister, why do you not come and see me before I leave? It has been so long, and we have so much to talk about.

Berengaria thought, why not? Eleanor would not be there, and they could have a proper visit. If Raymond arrived perhaps she would learn to like him better and feel more confident that Joanna was making the right move.

And another perhaps. Would it not be natural for Richard to come and wish his sister well? With a surge of hope, she called Carlos and asked him to summon the messenger. The latter, still abashed and the soul of deference, listened attentively and promised to deliver her message: "Tell Queen Joanna that Queen Berengaria will be at Poitiers in five or six days' time."

he day before Berengaria was to leave Beaufort for Poitiers a mendicant friar stopped at the castle. His travels had taken him from Amiens to Paris to Orléans, and he was now slowly urging his donkey southward, hoping to arrive in a warmer climate before autumn. The two of them were seen by Carlos, who was starting down to the village on an errand, just as they began negotiating the winding road up to the castle. Carlos turned to go back to tell Berengaria and the others. A visitor was always an event.

On fine summer days, Berengaria and Héloise took the main meal of the day in late afternoon, on the stone-paved terrace between Berengaria's tower and the garden. On this June afternoon, the sun shone through a gap in the broken western wall of the castle, its warmth reflecting off the paving. The table had just been prepared when Carlos presented their visitor to Berengaria.

"Please refresh yourself in the room Carlos will show you, then join us, Friar Johann," she urged, and the road-weary man was glad to accept.

At table, the friar downed his bowl of mutton stew before the two women had made a good start on theirs. They watched, admiring his appetite, as he made short work of a second bowl. Then he repressed a belch, patted his round stomach, and sat back before attacking the plate of roast beef and turnips that Cristina had placed before him. She and Carlos were hovering near the table, in expectation of hearing some news.

The friar knew that in return for his meal, and beds for himself and his patient beast, he was expected to provide any bits of information he could.

"As you are aware, Queen Berengaria, a wanderer like me picks up a lot of gossip as he travels. I have been trying to remember what I have heard about your husband, King Richard."

Berengaria knew she should urge him to finish his dinner but she was too anxious to hear what he had to say. "Please tell us what you can."

"Two weeks ago," he said, "when I was in Tours, I heard that King Richard came over from England in May, I think it was, and fell to battling Philip Augustus all over Normandy, up in the north, and getting the best of him for the most part. I don't pretend to know what's right and what's wrong in those grand people's affairs, that's up to the Lord God to decide. But it does seem to me it wasn't fair for the French king to seize so much of Richard's land, while the Lionheart was off there fighting his Holy Crusade, and while he was captive in Germany."

He paused, speared a turnip with his knife and stuffed it into his mouth, chewing ruminatively. He swallowed a mouthful of wine, then went on. "And let me see; yes, they said that after that he was not so far from here, besieging Loches. And he took it — bad luck for Philip Augustus." He stopped again, demolished a chunk of meat, and looked up. "And now that I think of it, they say Richard had some help there from troops sent by your brother, Sancho of Navarre."

Berengaria was surprised. She knew Young Sancho had helped to defend Richard's lands to the south while his brother-in-law was off on his Crusade; but what was he doing now, getting involved up here in the Touraine?

"But I have heard no word of Richard since then," Friar Johann concluded. Berengaria was left with the old uncertainties.

If Richard had been so close, why had he not come to Beaufort to see his wife — or at least to Poitiers to visit his sister?

Héloise had a question. "What of my lady, Queen Eleanor? Is she in Poitiers, or still in Fontevrault — have you heard?" The friar did not know.

They left him to finish his meal in peace, and went in to prepare for Berengaria's journey to Poitiers; Héloise would remain in charge of the domain in Beaufort.

Three days later, Joanna greeted Berengaria in her tower room of the palace in Poitiers. It was a joyful reunion. While they were still talking, interrupting and catching up, Maria appeared, and Berengaria hugged and and kissed her.

"Now we three veterans of the war are together again. And by my faith, you have grown into quite the young lady!" She stood back to get a better look. Maria's dark beauty, so striking in contrast to the paler, more delicate northern women, had blossomed, like a Mediterranean poppy among the lilies.

She happily described to Berengaria her life at court among so many fine ladies and gentlemen. "It is so different from Cyprus or Palestine!"

"And she has already had two offers of marriage, and can't decide which knight she likes better," Joanna whispered. "But of course my mother will have the final say on that."

Late in the morning the two of them walked out toward the church near the palace, and Berengaria tried to draw her friend out. She wondered if Joanna were really looking forward to her marriage. She looked tired and drawn.

It was warm and they had come without cloaks; but as befitted a widow and a married woman, they had covered their heads — Berengaria with a white silk scarf, Joanna with the hood of her plain gray gown. Berengaria, in her deep green dress with its silver sash, quite outshone her sister-in-law. After months of plain living and seeing few people at Beaufort, she welcomed the excuse to dress up a bit. "After all," she told herself, "it is important to keep up appearances. It is too easy for me to forget that I am queen of England. I should look the part when I am in such a public place as Poitiers."

They found a bench in the church garden and for a few minutes both sat quietly, soothed by the peace and warmth. Daisies and buttercups dotted the grass, and blackbirds hopped about. Just over the wall the sounds of a busy street could be heard: booted feet tramping on the cobblestones, a hawker offering oranges from Spain, shrill-voiced children at their games, a loud but off-key song bellowed by some citizen who had drunk too much ale. Berengaria thought how different this was from her customary life, where the quiet was broken only by the crowing of cocks, the humming of bees, the tap-tap of a hammer or rasp of a saw.

She broke the silence. "Joanna, I can see that something is amiss with you. Now tell me: do you look forward to your marriage to Raymond?"

"Ye-es," the other replied, drawing out the word. "I do. I cannot pretend that I am really in love with him, not yet. But when I married William I hardly knew him, yet we came to care for each other very much. Raymond has been thoughtful and considerate, and he promises that he will take care of me. And after all these years with no one, that is all I ask." Her voice trembled a little. Her dark brown eyes, usually so bright, were clouded and downcast. She clasped Berengaria's hand without looking at her. "I am not as strong as you are, Berengaria; I don't feel equipped to live my life alone."

She looked up, stricken. "Oh my dear, I know you don't choose to live your life without a husband. But surely that will change. I hope and pray that Richard will join you soon. But what do I have to look forward to? You know me well — surely you can understand that I need someone to take care of me?"

"Of course I can. I only want to be sure you are taking this step after careful thought. It is well known that Raymond has wed and discarded two wives already. Does it worry you that you might be the third?" It was a blunt question, but these two were always striaghtforward with each other.

"It is a chance I will have to take," said Joanna. "I do believe he cares for me, and by now he must be wishing for children. And there is this about it too: if I were to be cast aside, Raymond must know that Richard would be furious and would take some kind of terrible vengeance."

A strange foundation for marriage, Berengaria thought, but all she said was, "Very well then. We shall hope and pray for harmony and affection in the palace at Toulouse."

The church bell tolled twelve. They rose to stroll back to the palace. Berengaria was tempted to talk to Joanna about Richard. The mention of Raymond's rejection of his wives brought to the surface of her mind the question that had tormented her for months, unacknowledged but always there. It was almost on her lips: "Joanna, do you think Richard means to repudiate me?"

As she hesitated, Joanna spoke. "We don't talk about it, but I know you are always worried about Richard, wondering when he will come to you, or send for you to come to him. I have been thinking about this a great deal — I would like to see him, too! It is getting harder and harder to understand his strange neglect."

She stopped and put her hand on Berengaria's arm. "But you must remember that Richard is first of all a warrior. His only interest now is fighting King Philip to regain all the Angevin lands that Philip snatched while he was away. My mother once said that if Richard had to choose between family and foes, it would be foes every time — there is nothing he relishes more than a good battle. Of course he is to be blamed for not even sending you messages; but when he is at war he thinks of nothing else — not you, or me, or even his mother."

Berengaria remembered that back in Acre she had counted to herself the different kinds of man that Richard was. One had been the warrior, whose sole delight was to lead his men into battle. If she could keep that in mind and accept it, instead of wishing he were different, it might help — if not to forgive, at least to understand. She was grateful to Joanna. "I will try to be more patient," she said quietly. "Thank you, Joanna."

By unspoken consent they turned to less consequential matters as they walked on, such as Maria's suitors and a merchant who had promised to come in the afternoon with some silks just arrived from the east.

They had hardly reached the antechamber of the palace when Cristina came running. "Oh madame! A letter from Navarre has just been brought and I think it is from your sister Princess Blanche. I laid it on your table." Berengaria hurried to her room. Yes, it was from Blanche. It was short.

Dear Sister,

I grieve to be writing this. Our father died the day before yesterday. [The letter had been written three weeks ago.] *He had been unwell for some time — but we thought he was getting better. Our brother Sancho was here at the end; he had been in Gascony and I don't know where else, fighting on Richard's behalf; you know how he always looked forward to helping Richard wage his wars. But he came home when he heard our father was ill. He was buried in the cathedral at Pamplona, next to our mother's tomb.*

How I wish you could have been here! It is so long since I have seen you — how are you, dear sister? I am back in Estella, and I am so lonely. Sanchito stayed long enough to be crowned, then went back to his battles. Could you not come home for a visit? At least please write to me.

Berengaria cried as she read and reread Blanche's words. Her dear father — gone. He had always been like an anchor to her life and even though it was years since she had seen him, she had clung to the thought of him, strong and wise, someone to turn to if her world fell apart. And poor dear Blanche. Of course she was lonely.

Suddenly she thought, why couldn't Blanche come visit her? There was not much to keep her in Navarre now.

Then she saw a postscript to the letter. It seemed that Blanche had the same idea.

If you cannot come here to Estella, perhaps I will come to you in Beaufort. The Countess of Champagne has asked me to visit her. We met and became friends when she passed through Navarre on her way to pray at the tomb of Santiago for the soul of her husband, who died in the Holy Land. I would like to make the journey. Perhaps I could stop for a few weeks with you, before I go on to Troyes in Champagne?

Berengaria sat on, the midday meal forgotten. She was remembering her father, and trying to imagine Sanchito as King Sancho the Seventh. After a bit, she got up and found her little psalter, to look up a prayer for the dead, and recited it solemnly. She had no doubt that her father's soul would go straight to heaven, but perhaps she could speed it on the way.

Then her eye fell on Blanche's letter again. She must write to her at once and urge her to come. She loved Joanna, she was coming to love Héloise, but no one could take the place of her own, her only sister.

lanche arrived at Beaufort like a breath of spring, though it was October and the nip in the air hinted that winter was on its way. Berengaria heard the rat-a-tat of hoofbeats along the village road below and hurried out to the terrace to wait impatiently, hugging her shawl around her, until Blanche and her attendants appeared, riding up through the gate.

Blanche dismounted, almost tripping over her stirrups in her haste, and the sisters fell into each other's arms. It had been so long! Then they drew back, half laughing and half crying, to look at each other.

"My little Blanquita!" Berengaria exclaimed, surveying the golden-haired, rosy-cheeked young woman. "You haven't changed a particle. You could be a lass of Touraine rather than a daughter of our sober old Basque country! Can it really be that my little sister is twenty-four?"

But Blanche saw changes in Berengaria. She was still lovely. The hair that framed her calm face was still a shining russet-brown. But the face was that of one who has lived through and survived adversities. She was no longer the young, vulnerable woman Blanche had last seen. Her bearing was more queenly, and she seemed much more self-assured. Yet her dignity was tinged with an underlying, brooding sadness, and Blanche suspected that Richard was at the root of it. By now it was common knowledge, even in far-off Navarre, that Richard had as good as deserted his queen.

Lady Héloise had left for Saumur a few days before, to be present at the lying-in of her daughter-in-law; she would not be back for some weeks. So the sisters could give all their time to each other with no distractions. On their first evening together, in Berengaria's room above the hall, they settled down to exchange confidences, and it was just as though they were back in Estella. Blanche looked around appreciatively at the pleasant room, with the work table near the window to get the southern light.

"I see you are still at your scribbling," she teased, walking over to look at the manuscripts and pens and inkpots on the table.

Berengaria had to admit that she was. "It helps to pass the time," she said, looking affectionately at Blanche. Now after the first appraisal, she could sense, beneath the lightsome face Blanche presented to the world, a hint of — what? Weariness? Undoubtedly, during King Sancho's last years, he must have depended heavily on this one remaining daughter. It could not always have been easy.

"We are both older, aren't we, Blanche? One hates to admit it, but there it is. Do you think we are any wiser?"

"I doubt if I am, but you must be, after all your adventures." Blanche came back to her chair and sat down, clasping her hands together in her lap and looking expectantly at Berengaria. "Now, you must tell me everything, and perhaps I will be wiser. When did you last see or hear from that slippery husband of yours?"

There was no reason to try to put a good face on it. "I last saw him when we left Acre, two years and two months ago. And I have not heard directly from him since." She did not hold back but told Blanche the whole sorry tale of her indifferent king and her marriage that was not a marriage; and that Richard had been back in France for six months, but had not bothered to call on his queen to join him.

"It is not only for myself that I mind," she said, "though God knows that is enough in itself. I do mind, terribly. I can tell you, but no one else, that I have never been able to stop loving Richard, in spite of everything; and to hope that he will come back to me. You used to be so moved by tales of unrequited love — I always thought it was something that happened to other people, and never dreamed that I would live such a story."

Blanche was listening intently. "You did not deserve this."

"But almost as bad," Berengaria went on, "is the dishonor his neglect does to our family and our kingdom and the memory of our father. He urged me to marry Richard and told me he was an honorable man. What would he think now? It's true that I was publicly crowned queen of England at Cyprus, when we were married. But how does it look to the world when the king of England is recrowned at Winchester with all that show and circumstance, while his mother occupies the seat of honor, and his wife, his queen, is not... even... invited?" She bit the words off in her anger.

The next moment she drooped in defeat. "I have come to see that there is nothing to do but wait and see what God has in store for me."

Blanche, who had envisioned this marriage as the ultimate romance, was disheartened too. She could not immediately think of anything constructive to say, then it came to her.

"There may be something to do. We must tell Sanchito about this. If he is such a friend of Richard's he could speak to him. He would surely want to defend his sister's honor."

"No, not yet. Let me wait just a little longer. If I have not heard from Richard by Christmas, I will write to Sanchito."

She rubbed her forehead with her hand, as though to erase the angry frown. "But enough of me and my troubles. What of you, sister? Have the suitors kept hovering about you like moths drawn to a flame? How can it be that you have not yet chosen one of them?"

Blanche admitted that she had had plenty of wooers; but none who captured her heart. "And besides — it would have been very hard for our father if I had taken a notion to get married and leave him; though he never said so, and even encouraged me to look favorably on some of the young men."

"Any that I know?" asked Berengaria. "How about that foppish Count Emilio de Tafalla, the one who insisted on showing us how clever his hound was at catching a pig? I always thought you two were meant for each other!" They both laughed, remembering the pretentious young man.

"Now, of course, since Sanchito has become the king, it is different," said Blanche. "I am hardly needed at court because he is seldom in Navarre. He spends most of his time as he always did, off crusading against the Muslims in the south or battling for one thing or another. So I felt perfectly free to accept the Countess of Champagne's invitation to come visit her in Troyes." Then she burst out with the news she had been holding back. "Can you guess, Berenguelita, why she asked me?"

Berengaria could not, and had in fact been wondering.

"I think that though she has not actually said so, she believes I would be a proper bride for her son Thibaut. When she stayed with us in Estella, I could not help noticing that she was watching me very carefully. Apparently I passed the test!"

"But what of this Thibaut?" Berengaria asked. "What do you know of him?"

"Of course I have never met him. But she made a point of telling me that he will be there in Troyes when I arrive, and we shall see! I have heard that he is courtly and brave. Perhaps he will prove handsome as well!" It was just the kind of adventure of the heart that Blanche had always dreamed of.

"How wonderful, Blanquita!" Berengaria said. "Now one of us, at least, has something to look forward to. Somehow I feel this story will have a happy ending."

The next day the sisters plunged into sightseeing. Blanche had never been north of the Pyrenees and insisted that Berengaria take her out riding through the countryside. She was full of curiosity and enthusiasm and admired everything she saw, from the fine chateaux along the river, to the ancient oak forests where woodcutters were with great labor and skill felling trees for winter fuel and timbers to repair their houses. But most of all, she was impressed with Berengaria's little castle on its hill, snugly contained within its walls — dilapidated as those walls were, as Berengaria pointed out.

"I will say that my mother-in-law did me a service when she arranged for me to settle here," said Berengaria, "though her motive was doubtless simply to bury me in some out-of-the-way corner where I wouldn't make trouble."

The time came for Blanche to leave. From the gatehouse, Berengaria watched her and her servitors ride through the village and disappear into the wood, where patches of red and gold flamed amidst the green. "When will I see her again?" she wondered.

Héloise came back from Saumur, sorry to have missed Blanche but full of talk about her first grandson. Life in Beaufort resumed its familiar quiet pattern.

A few weeks later Berengaria again received vague, imprecise news of Richard — unsettling news. Carlos heard it from the innkeeper in the village, who had heard it from a band of mercenaries. Richard had again fallen prey to the fever that had nearly taken his life in Palestine.

Carlos reported to Berengaria: "The innkeeper says he also heard that the king recovered, but only after a long and painful siege of it. And the soldiers who told him about it were on their way to join up with Richard's army, so he must be back in the saddle."

Carlos hesitated, then added that some in the village said they had heard the soldiers joking with each other about a holy hermit who had met Richard while he was riding in the forest, gave him a round scolding and bade him live a more godly life. But nobody knew any more than that.

"Godly?" thought Berengaria. "If godliness means faithfulness to one's wife, what does Richard care about that?" She could sincerely pray for Richard's health. But otherwise there was nothing to do but wonder and wait. Somehow, she took comfort in the fact that she need do nothing until Christmas — the date she had told Blanche she would write to Sancho.

Then one December day, when Berengaria and Cristina were in the garden gathering herbs for the evening meal, a horse and rider came clattering up the hill and burst into the courtyard.

It was Richard.

Stunned and speechless, she put a hand to her heart and stared at the tall, robust man who had appeared as though someone from a dream. But it was no apparition. It was indeed Richard. Her heart pounded and she felt faint. Her basket fell from her hand.

Richard dismounted quickly and tossed back his shock of red-gold hair as he came toward her, hand outstretched.

"By my faith, Queen Berengaria, you look like one of God's angels surprised by the devil! But this is no minion of Satan, it is your own husband, come at last to see how you are faring and to spend Christmas with you." He grasped her hands in his and stared first at her, then around him, with growing admiration. "A beautiful queen in a fitting setting, I swear! You are as fair as ever, and you have made this old castle into a fine little abode. Although," he added, looking critically at the places in the walls where stones had tumbled out, leaving gaping holes, "it is as well we expect no enemies; your defenses leave something to be desired."

At last Berengaria found her voice. "You are welcome, more than welcome, Richard. But why did you not send me word that you were coming?" Despite her overwhelming joy, she could not help thinking how like him it was to act on impulse, unmindful that others might wish time to prepare. But he was here! That was the one indisputable fact. She looked up at him, all her love shining in her eyes.

He smiled down at her quizzically. Now she noticed that he looked older and more careworn; his face bore some of the same signs of strain and illness that she had last seen in Palestine, just before their parting. "Are you all right, Richard?" she asked anxiously. "We heard that you had suffered again from the fever."

"I did have another touch of it, but now I am quite well, I assure you. Or as well as anyone can be with a shifty enemy like Philip Augustus, popping up where least expected. He has kept me so busy that I could not even send a message to my queen. But now I am here, and I think perhaps you are not sorry. So shall we move on to more immediate matters?"

His eyes were teasing, his voice was as politely solemn as a little boy asking for a sweetmeat. "Please, may I stay for dinner? No bread or meat has passed my lips since I left Angers this morning, and then I had but a piece of cold bacon and an indifferent crust of ancient wheaten bread."

Berengaria laughed in her delight, still unable to believe he was here. But the pressure of his hands, still holding hers, told her this was no dream.

"Dinner will be ready very shortly, my lord. And I will personally see that something better than cold bacon is on the table, and the bread is fresh. Now, you will want to refresh yourself. I have kept a chamber ready for you ever since I moved to this castle. Carlos will show you the way and bring you a basin of water."

Cristina had already hurried in to tell the cook to do her best. Carlos, who had been standing in the doorway staring in awed admiration at this king he had heard so much about, came at his mistress's gesture to show Richard to his room, next to Berengaria's on the tower's second story.

They would be only two at table; Lady Héloise had tactfully insisted that she would take her meal in her own quarters. She could recognize a honeymoon when she saw one.

Berengaria ordered fresh candles for all the sconces, and a fire on the hearth; she herself saw to the laying of the table with her finest damask cloth, and set out polished pewter goblets and china plates.

"It is a table fit for a king, mistress," Cristina said.

"I think it is, Cristina." She laughed. "Or should we say, for a king and his queen?"

Cristina laughed too, happy to see her mistress as excited as a blushing girl of sixteen.

Dinner started gaily, with the flurry of servants bearing laden platters and flagons of wine. Richard raised his goblet, looking intently at his queen across the table. She met his gaze, her eyes shining in the candlelight. He spoke solemnly, but with the twitch of the lips that she loved, though she had so seldom seen it, betraying the barely hidden laughter.

"So, my queen. We meet again. To your health! Will you join me in a toast to our reunion?"

Berengaria raised her goblet and said, with a little catch in her throat, "With all my heart. It is a long time since we said goodbye in Acre, but to see you here at my table erases the lonely months."

They drank, still holding each other's eyes. Then Richard attacked his plate, and gradually his cheer deserted him. He made less effort to be charming. He became preoccupied, hardly noticing what he was eating but signaling Carlos for frequent refills of wine. She tried to make conversation, to talk about Joanna, her garden, his wars with Philip. He answered in monosyllables if at all. So she too fell silent and kept her eyes on her plate. Once in a while she looked up to see him staring at her but not seeing her; or he would be looking absently out the window. Evening had darkened into night, and the candles were burning low. The old despair was chilling her heart.

"What is it, Richard?" she asked at last. "Are you planning your next campaign against Philip? Your thoughts are certainly far from Beaufort."

He looked at her, startled, as though she had recalled him from some far place. All at once he was the cheerful Richard who had appeared at her door a few hours earlier. "I was thinking of a castle I must build, but that need not concern us now. And yes, I am planning my next campaign, but not against Philip. I have a more immediate and pleasurable conquest in mind."

He pushed back his chair, rose and took her by the hand. "So, my lady queen, unless you have another engagement, shall we retire to the bedchamber and see if we can improve on our past performances?"

He had drunk a good deal of wine, and Berengaria was fearful. She was determined not to be the submissive victim again. She tried to keep her voice light as she countered, "Indeed, let us retire. But have I your word that this will not be a repetition of one particular past performance?"

"You have my word, little one. Your husband has learned his lesson." With his arm around her waist, they ascended the stairs to her chamber.

erengaria stood at the narrow window, wearing only her long white shift. Her tousled hair fell loosely to her shoulders. She shivered a little. But though it was December — Christmas Day! — it was remarkably mild. The sun was barely risen. She leaned forward through the window embrasure in the thick wall to look out. She saw gauzy mists floating, dissolving and reforming over the green fields that had been carved out of the oak forest in the valley below.

Looking up, she saw a pair of hawks tracing graceful arcs against the pale blue sky. Berengaria felt weightless, as though she too could soar heavenward. For the first time in her life she knew what it was to feel fulfilled as a woman.

Behind her in the bed Richard stretched, yawned with a bray like a donkey and turned over as though to go back to sleep, then opened his eyes. He leaped up and walked across the room to stand beside her. He put an arm around her and with his other hand turned her face up to his. "Why did you never tell me you knew so well how to please a man?" he asked quite seriously.

Berengaria blushed. But with newborn confidence she replied as seriously, "Why did you never take the trouble to teach me how to love until now?"

For indeed, he had been nothing like the hasty, selfish lover of their wedding night or the cool, emotionless performer of the one other occasion he had come to her bed. No — he had lain beside her, guided her hands and her timid lips over his body while he explored every inch of hers. Then, as she held him tighter and her trembling grew, he had gently, slowly, slowly, brought them both to the moment of exquisite climax.

Remembering it now, Berengaria smiled a woman's secret smile and clung to him — her husband at last. But why was he looking so solemn?

"There is something I must talk to you about, Berengaria. You said last evening that you had heard I had been ill. I sensed that you also knew that I had been admonished by Brother Jerome for licentious behavior in the eyes of God and man."

So those vague tales of the hermit in the woods were true. She had not been surprised when she heard them and she was not surprised now. She had, she thought, come to terms with Richard's untrammeled lusts, his disregard for public opinion or disapproval by the church.

"Yes, I heard something of the sort," she said, uncomfortable with the subject and trying to dismiss it. "So the holy hermit came upon you in the forest and threatened you with God's vengeance unless you foreswore your evil companions? We need not talk about it if you do not wish to."

"I do wish to, I must. And you are very close to the mark. But Brother Jerome was even harsher than you suggest." He grimaced with distaste at the memory. "He told me sodomy was a grievous sin against God's design for the world. He described hellfire in horrible terms, not to mention the agonies of my death that would precede my descent to the inferno."

Berengaria shuddered and moved closer into his arms. Absently he stroked her hair. "So," she asked, "he ordered you to repent, and you have repented?"

"Yes, both publicly and now privately — last night."

Berengaria laughed. "That was repentance? Oh Richard, I thought it was lovemaking. But if you wish to call it repentance, why let us repent every night of our lives." She looked at him, her eyes full of love and mischief, searching for an answering gleam in his. But he did not return her look.

"There is more," he said. He seemed determined to tell all, and in a strange way she was not displeased — that is what a wife is for, she thought: to hear her husband's confidences, things he can tell no one else.

"Brother Jerome told me that not only must I give up my wicked habits; I must return to my queen and live with her as God intends man and wife to live, in order to produce the heir to the throne that the kingdom needs. When I told him that I had already done my best in that regard, to no avail, he told me that I had not done my best; that I must have failed to treat my wife with loving consideration, as we are told to do when we enter into holy matrimony."

I am beginning to like this Brother Jerome, Berengaria thought. He seems to have seen through Richard perfectly. But she said nothing.

"Then I fell ill of the fever, and came so close to death that I knew this was a sign from God of the truth of the hermit's lesson. I knew I must swear to do as he had bidden me and pray God to spare me. After my sacred oath, the fever began to leave me. Then when I told my mother of his admonitions, she too urged me to come back to you and try again to father a child; for her dearest wish is to see the succession secured."

For the first time Berengaria felt a twinge of uneasiness. She resented Eleanor's intrusion into this private drama. She already knew that her mother-in-law saw her only as a means of producing Richard's heir. But was that Richard's view too? She put the question aside. She was far too filled with her new state of bliss to let such silly possibilities bother her.

The next few days passed quickly, yet she knew she would always remember every minute. They were still blessedly alone; Lady Héloïse had suddenly remembered some urgent business in Angers. Richard was busy during the daylight hours seeing to repairs to the castle. Restoring it became an obsession.

"This castle has been in the Angevin fold for close to two centuries," he told Berengaria, "and I still remember my father telling me, when it came into my possession, that it was sadly in need of repair but that in years past it had performed nobly. He said we had the Romans to thank for it — they built here first, and had the sense to put their fortress on this hill, where they could see in all directions, and were close to the main road along the Loire."

They were still at table, finishing their evening meal. The sun was just going down. Richard sat with his back to the window, and Berengaria thought his head seemed to wear a golden halo. She loved listening to him when he was caught up in a subject like this; and she knew if there was anything the Lionheart understood, it was castles and fortifications. He had seen and studied the best and the worst, in Europe and the Holy Land.

She heard and agreed with him about Beaufort's virtues, but thought to herself that she had quite different reasons for liking the castle. It was less pretentious than the ducal palace at Poitiers, it had no associations with Eleanor, and it was her own.

Richard was still discoursing on history. "Then my own ancestor, Foulkes Nerra, was just as wise as the Romans, and built the first Angevin fort on top of the Roman ruins. I have dug down to his foundations and they are are as solid as they ever were. If Philip should take a notion to come after us down here, let him look out!"

So he plunged into the task of making Beaufort the fairest little citadel in the valley of the Loire. Berengaria was glad she had taken such pains to soften its walls with tapestries, to put cushions in the window embrasures and carpets on the cold stone floors. Though Richard professed to care little for such refinements, she could see that after a day of laboring on the moat and the parapets he was glad to come in to comfort and warmth.

For a while each night was a repetition of the first, with variations. Berengaria surprised herself and Richard with her growing adeptness in the arts of love. Now it was often she who tenderly, skillfully aroused Richard rather than the other way around. Every morning she woke in astonishment that the pleasures of the night had not been a dream.

However, after a time it seemed that Richard's lovemaking became more perfunctory, or he would fall into bed and instantly go to sleep. She tried to persuade herself she was imagining things, yet she agonized — had she ceased to please him so soon? He was more absent-minded at meals too.

Finally, with the help of Carlos and stonemasons from the village, he had completed the repairs to his satisfaction. That night he was especially tender to her and she told herself she was a fool to have worried so.

In the morning he rose quickly the moment he was fully awake, as was his custom. Berengaria lay in bed, lazily watching him as he dressed, admiring his long, strong limbs, his handsome, serious face — more serious than usual. And why was he putting on a leather doublet and a woolen cloak? Was he planning to go out before the morning meal?

Buckling his broad belt and swiftly placing his other garments in a capacious saddlebag, he looked around to see if he had forgotten anything. Berengaria felt frozen, unable to say a word or ask a question. At last he turned to her and spoke, not unkindly but matter-of-factly, as though remarking that he was going out to take a turn around the bailey to inspect the new ramparts.

"Now the time has come for me to leave, my little queen. My work here is finished. The castle is in good repair, and as for my other work — it too is finished. It has been as pleasant a task as any in my life. I thank you for proving such a willing partner. If we have not made a son, after these weeks of trying, the fault will not be mine."

Stunned but desperate, she sat up in bed, pulled the coverlet up to her chin and stared at him. She forced herself to speak, trying to keep her voice steady. "But where are you going? When will you return?"

"I am going north, into Normandy, where King Philip is likely to attack, and soon. I cannot delay in strengthening my defenses along the Seine. And I have it in mind to build a new fortress above the river, strong enough to withstand whatever he brings against it."

In spirit he had already left her, his thoughts leaping northward to a brave new castle a hundred leagues away.

"As for when I shall return — that will I gladly, as soon as you send word that you are with child."

Berengaria sat unbelieving, still clutching the coverlet. Hot tears filled her eyes as she watched while he gathered his belongings and strode toward the door. Too proud to beg, too hurt to speak, she could do nothing but watch him leave, without another word between them.

ith Richard's abrupt departure for Normandy, Berengaria's life entered its bleakest chapter yet. She could deceive herself no longer: Richard did not care for her as she had cared for him. But though her head realized this, her heart was slow to accept it. She went mechanically about her customary routine: rising, dressing, breakfasting; then perhaps sitting for an hour with Héloise at their embroidery while they exchanged only the briefest of remarks. If the weather permitted, she would walk in the garden and sit on the terrace, idly watching the doves flying in and out of their nests in the dovecote. What a carefree life they lead, she thought enviously.

In her chamber, she would look around at the familiar surroundings, but everything reminded her of Richard. Her manuscripts and copying materials were still spread out on her work table, but she hardly gave them a glance.

Sometimes she managed to rise out of her listlessness while Héloise tried to interest her in the tiny events of castle life. Perhaps the bees had swarmed. The butcher in the village had sent a haunch of venison, thanks to his huntsman's good luck. Héloise and Carlos had gone over the accounts, and all was in order. The cook had cut his hand grievously, so Cristina had volunteered to learn to cook.

Berengaria listened and tried to show interest, and repeatedly told Héloise how good she was to take charge of the castle's affairs.

Nights were the worst. In the bed where she had lain with Richard, sometimes she dreamed that she was resting in his arms after love, drowsy and contented. Then suddenly the picture would change. She would see him rise, dress and speak those words that were seared in her brain; "Now my work here is finished." She would awake with a start, half-expecting that his rude departure would prove to be only a bad dream. Then, fully awake, she faced another day of dull despair. She would berate herself: how could she have been so deceived, believing his affection was genuine and signaled a new Richard? Perhaps it was genuine as long as it lasted — which was only long enough to fulfill his vow to "return to his queen and treat her with loving consideration."

Richard, it seemed, could become another person as easily as he changed his boots — and change back again just as casually.

For a while she clung to one last desperate hope: that she would find herself with child. When she was sure this was not to be, her dejection was total. She sank into lethargy, hardly left her room, ate little, became thin and pale.

Héloise, more and more concerned, decided to ask the opinion of Cristina, the person who had known Berengaria the longest. She found her in the kitchen dealing powerful punches with her little fists to a ball of dough. Though the cook's hand had healed, Cristina had learned to like cooking and baking, and it kept her busy — Berengaria required little from her these days.

Héloise, who knew little of breadmaking, asked, "Can you leave that big lump you seem to be so cross at, Cristina, so I can talk to you? Or will it rise up and jump off the table?"

Cristina flashed her a look to see if she was serious, then grinned. "I have pounded it down now, and it will be quiet for an hour. So I may leave my baking for a while."

Héloise shepherded her out of the hot, steaming kitchen and into the hall, and came to the point at once.

"Our lady looks as though she might waste away before our eyes. You have served her for many years; what do you think?"

Cristina too had been worrying, but she had a basic belief in her mistress's resilience.

"I think that we must just wait. She is a Basque, after all, and we Basques have too much good sense to knuckle under when it looks like life is getting the best of us. Once before when my lady was very young she suffered a terrible loss. The man she loved was killed in battle."

Héloise had never heard of this. "How dreadful!" she exclaimed. "I had no idea she had been through anything like that."

"And we all watched and waited," Cristina went on, "and in time, sure enough, she pulled herself up out of her despair, and came back to us, bless her sensible heart."

So, Héloise said to herself, we must just watch and wait.

A letter came from Blanche, back in Pamplona after her visit to the Countess of Champagne in Troyes. Banquets, entertainments, jugglers and minstrels — Blanche wrote it was just the diversion she needed after her dull life in Navarre. But what of Thibaut, Berengaria wondered, the potential suitor? She read on:

> Thibaut was off campaigning for King Philip during all my six weeks there, except for two times when he could be spared to come home for a day or two. But, oh Berengaria, he is a man I could love. He made a point of sitting next to me at dinner and we got on very well; I could tell he liked me, and I think he was aware that I was not indifferent to him. But neither he nor the countess ever brought up the subject of a betrothal. I think perhaps there is another lady in the running. So here I sit, wondering whether to hope or forget.
>
> Sanchito is glad to have me back. He says while I was gone the whole palace went to pieces because he is no good at running a household, just an army. Do you think he will ever marry, Berengaria? He should! Some lady should take our big brother in hand and civilize him. Meantime I will do my best because it looks as though I would be here for a while.
>
> Should I tell Sanchito that his sister in Beaufort needs a champion against her errant husband? You said you wanted to wait until Christmas, but Christmas is long gone.
>
> He sends you his love, as do I.

After reading this, Berengaria sat for a long time, head bowed, wishing she could unburden herself to the sister with whom she could share everything. She wished, too, that she could give a good shake to that Countess of Champagne and her son. What ailed them, to keep the poor princess in uncertainty?

"Ay me," thought Berengaria. "We two daughters of King Sancho and Queen Sancha Maria have not brought much honor and glory to our family's escutcheon, have we? We will just have to depend on Sanchito for that!"

She raised her eyes and looked around her snug chamber, with virtually every comfort she could wish. Blanche's letter had jolted her out of her self-pity. What a fool I am, she thought. The world is full of people who have been unhappy in love and at least I know the truth now. But poor Blanche has to keep wondering where she stands — she's the one to be pitied.

That night, after an hour of fitful sleep, Berengaria awoke to a room filled with moonlight. Something impelled her to rise, throw on a cloak and walk downstairs and out into the courtyard. Seating herself on a bench she looked around as though seeing everything for the first time. It was a world of blacks and whites. Beneath the plum and apple trees the shadows were impenetrable and mysterious. The neat rows of turnips and lettuces looked as though carved in ice, each leaf brilliantly reflecting the bright white rays of the full moon.

Suddenly the memory of another night came to Berengaria — a night not of moonlight but of starlight, when she stood on the deck of a ship, wondering what her future held. She remembered the prayer she had said, asking God to give her strength and wisdom to accept whatever life brought her. Perhaps she had had a premonition then that her life would bring a deep love — then a devastating loss of love.

God had been waiting, all this time, for her to remember that He offered comfort to the bereft and invited them to forget self in service to Him. She felt as though an immense weight were being lifted from her heart.

How could I have thought only of my own concerns all these months? she asked herself in wonderment. How could I have forgotten that God has a plan for each of His children, and that I need not understand it, only accept what comes, as God's will?

She clasped her hands and bowed her head. "Oh my Lord, I have forgotten You but You have not forsaken me. Help me now to learn to forgive Richard. Help me to find meaning for my life again and to keep You in my heart. Amen."

For another quarter of an hour she sat there, feeling peace creep back into her soul like a cooling stream, washing away the hurt and bitterness. Tomorrow, she told herself, I will get out those last two manuscripts that Brother Anselmo sent, which I have barely glanced at. I will write him that I will gladly try my hand at translating them. And though one is only a medical treatise and the other is an Arabic love poem, I think God will be pleased that once again I am using the brains He gave me.

Her fragile new strength was almost shattered when a message came from Richard, three months after his departure.

> *To Queen Berengaria, greetings.*
>
> *My brave castle is rising daily to lord it over the River Seine. She is like a daughter to me, and I watch her wax stronger and more beautiful with each day. If I were to learn from you that I will also be blessed with other issue, I would be the happiest of fathers. The messenger who brings this will bear your reply.*

She sent no reply. Richard's cruel callousness had finally finished what his indifference had begun. He had killed her love.

Little by little, she set out to rebuild her life and restore the independence of her heart. She threw herself into her Arabic studies and her translating, while Brother Anselmo encouraged her from afar. She journeyed to Tours, to meet a group of copyists at the Basilica of Saint-Martin, who had sent a request for her advice about a matter of translation. When she returned, Héloise hurried to greet her. She was delighted to see her lady almost beaming.

"Just think, Héloise, you are looking at a scholar. That is what they called me in Tours. They did not care whether I was queen or commoner, only that I had enough knowledge of Arabic to get them through a paragraph that had puzzled the wisest of them." She was doing her best to look modest.

Héloise, with as solemn a face as she could muster, dropped a deep curtsey. "My humble obeisance to the queenly scholar, and my congratulations to the astute scribes in Tours, for their recognition of her abilities."

Berengaria let out a peal of laughter, and for a moment Héloise saw how she must have looked before her troubled marriage.

"Oh Héloise, you are so good for me! If I were ever in danger of being puffed up with pride, you would burst the bubble!" More seriously, she added, "I am very aware of my good fortune in having you for a companion, and I do not tell you so often enough. I hope you realize it nevertheless."

Héloise, whose emotions were seldom near the surface, to her surprise felt a prick of tears and said gruffly, "Well, I am fortunate too to have such a lady as you to serve; and especially now that I have heard you laugh for the first time in months."

There was a sudden commotion in the courtyard — the clatter of hooves, the snorting of a horse and footsteps running. In a moment Carlos knocked.

"It is a messenger from King Sancho, your brother, my lady. He is nearby, in Angers, and is on his way to Beaufort."

Berengaria and Héloise looked at each other in alarm. If Sancho were coming in person, it must be bad news.

20

"N o, it is not bad news," Sancho said to Berengaria's anxious question, while he was dismounting. Once on the ground, he towered over her by a good two feet.

"Sanchito!" she cried. "Don't tell me you have grown still more!" She remembered her brother as a very tall young man when she last saw him some ten years ago; but this was nearly a giant.

"Never mind, I can lean far enough down to hug my little sister."

After the powerful squeeze of his massive arms she caught her breath and laughed up at him. "I hear they are already calling you Sancho the Strong, and I can see why. Now, come in and give me all the news," she urged, and led him by the hand into the hall of her tower.

He let her settle him in the largest chair in the room, which groaned as he lowered his burly body into it. She sat next to him, still holding his hand. He looked appreciatively around him at the handsomely furnished chamber, and poured himself a goblet of wine from the pitcher on the table at his side. Then he turned his keen gaze on her.

"You are older, I know, sister, you must be thirty-two by now for I am thirty-seven; but how have you stayed so fair?" he asked, assessing her. "Not a wrinkle on that pretty face and you are slim as ever. While I, as you see, am somewhat heavier and a wee bit balder and a great deal more worn, all due to time and the wars."

"But Sanchito, you like nothing better than going into battle," she teased him. "Why should the wars age you?"

"You remember me as a prince who fought at the side of his father the king; it was all adventure then. But now, it is up to me alone to protect our kingdom. Poor Navarre! I wonder if you have heard how King Alfonso of Castile and King Alfonso of Aragon, one on each side, have been pressing us like a nut caught in the pincers. God save us from all Alfonsos." He sighed.

"I have heard only rumors. But if things are so desperate at home, what are you doing here?"

Sancho had kicked off his huge boots and was wriggling his toes, one of which had popped through a hole in his rather grimy gray hose. Berengaria thought perhaps she should offer some washing and mending while he was here.

"What indeed?" he said, sipping from his goblet. "Well, for one thing, we have just come to a sort of truce with Castile and Aragon. It took a good deal of nudging from the Pope, but it should last for a few years. So during the calm in the storm, I thought I would come see how my little sister was getting on. Blanche says you are bearing up quite well, considering." He cast her a shrewd look from the brown eyes under the beetling brows.

From this, Berengaria gathered that he had at least some idea of her marital problems. She waited for him to go on.

"But as I am sure you have guessed, I'm also here on behalf of my brother-in-law. I didn't really expect to find him at Beaufort, but I hoped you would be able to tell me where he is."

"As far as I know, he is still at Les Andelys in Normandy, building a castle. Why do you ask?"

"It is a longish story. We promised each other, when you married him, to protect each other's interests in the south. So far, I have done most of the protecting, while Richard was off on Crusade. And now he is being threatened again. I have learned that a certain Ademar, a noble of Angoulême and technically one of Richard's vassals, has been on a rampage. He has captured some of his neighbors' castles and declared his allegiance to King Philip. He's a hothead and possibly a madman, but he may manage to persuade others to join his revolt. I am honor-bound to tell Richard what I know of this, and get his views on our strategy."

He stopped to drink again from his goblet. "Les Andelys, you say? That is nearly as far as Rouen."

"Yes, that is where he is building his mighty fortress on the Seine; he thinks he needs it to defend Normandy against Philip. He left here to begin the work nearly two years ago but I have not heard from him for a year and a half. They say he calls it Chateau Gaillard — his 'Saucy Castle.' That's to taunt King Philip, I suppose." To her surprise, she was able to speak without a qualm of Richard and the castle that had taken him away from her. She felt no anger, no longing — she felt nothing.

Sancho was silent. Then, "This Saucy Castle is a good ten days' journey from here, as I reckon. A long way to travel to offer assistance to a brother-in-law who seems to have repudiated my sister."

So — he did know about Richard's desertion. For the first time in two years she did not feel totally alone and defenseless.

Sancho could read all this in her face. "Yes, Berenguelita, Blanche told me as much as she knew and now you tell me that you have not heard from Richard for a year and a half. I do believe if our wise father were here to counsel us, he would advise me not to go to Normandy, but simply to send a message to Richard about Ademar's maneuverings. Then he would tell me to go back to Navarre, where real enemies are on our doorstep. And finally he would advise me to urge my little sister to remain steadfast and to remember that after all, she is not only a princess of Navarre, but also the queen of England." He emphasized the last words.

"I know I am queen of England, I remind myself of it every day," she said, a little nettled. She felt he was reproaching her for some weakness of character. "But what good does that do me? It is a meaningless title, as long as the dowager Queen Eleanor lives and rules her son's life."

"Leaving that aside for the moment, has she, or Richard, made adequate provision for your livelihood? I must say," he said, looking around, "I see no signs of poverty."

"Yes, I receive a purse regularly from the Bishop of Ely; he is Richard's chancellor in England. It is more than enough to cover all our expenses, and I have even put some aside."

"Well, that is something at least. Nothing speaks so plainly as money, and this allowance clearly says that you are officially England's queen. Now: have you ever actually confronted Eleanor and demanded the recognition that is due you?" He was warming to his role as inquisitor.

"One does not 'demand' anything from Eleanor," Berengaria said bitterly.

"But what harm would be done by trying? She could hardly banish you from her court, if you came to her and said you were going to stay in Poitiers — which is, after all, in Anjou, and as Richard's wife you are Countess of Anjou. It might not be altogether pleasant, and you might not want to stay long; but you would at least have the satisfaction of knowing you had laid a claim to your rights."

She thought with distaste of an encounter with her mother-in-law. She was so convinced that Eleanor disdained her that she could not imagine any good coming of a confrontation.

Sancho went on. "Or, of course, you could go to Richard and simply announce to him that, as his queen, you believe you should be by his side. You were with him on crusade; how much more logical that you join him in his own patrimony? You are also Duchess of Normandy, if I am not mistaken."

Berengaria exploded. "No, no! I could not possibly do that. Sanchito, how can you suggest that I go begging to the man who has treated me so basely? I still have my pride!" She jumped from her chair and paced up and down, glaring at him.

"So I see! And if you would accost Richard with as much spirit as you show now, he might change his mind about you. Now calm down and listen to me. You must not go on sitting quietly here in your comfortable little corner, hoping for the best and feeling sorry for yourself. You must do something!" Sancho pounded his knee and looked almost fiercely at her. She sat down and tried to compose herself. Sancho went on, more reasonably. "If you went to Richard, your purpose would be to claim your rightful place at his side, and to be with him when he travels next to England so your subjects there may come to know you. After all, you need not demand that he take you back into his bed."

Berengaria felt her face burn but she kept her eyes fixed on him.

"There is plenty of precedent for such a royal marriage. Look at Eleanor and Henry, Richard's parents. They ceased to be bedfellows years before Henry's death, yet everyone saw her as a sovereign, even all those years while he kept her in prison."

He rose and stretched. His arms almost reached the ceiling. He folded them and stood looking down at her while she sat deep in thought. Then she looked up and spoke. He had expected something like "But I am not Eleanor!" but to his surprise she was no longer on the defensive.

"Sancho, I will have to admit that you are making me see things differently. I am not sure I am ready to go beard the Lionheart in his castle, even though I agree it is good advice. But I will really think about what you say, and start trying to strengthen my backbone."

"You can do it, Berenguelita, you know you have always had plenty of determination once you made up your mind to something. Remember the way you wore our father down until he let you go to the monastery?"

"Yes, I was insufferably stubborn then. But I think these last few years have destroyed most of my self-confidence."

He sat down again and pulled on his boots. They sat quietly for a minute, both considering. He spoke first.

"You know, there is something you could do while you are strengthening your backbone that would not involve a confrontation. Ask the Pope to use his influence with Queen Eleanor and with Richard. That might soften them up before you approached one or both of them."

Berengaria looked doubtful.

"I know Pope Celestine is a good man, and he was certainly kind and solicitous when we stayed at his palace in Rome. But that was five years ago. He must be ninety by now — he has probably forgotten all about me."

"Well, a few months ago he acted with the firmness of a Pope in his prime, when I asked his help in making the truce with Castile and Aragon."

"Of course he is interested in keeping the peace when kingdoms war with each other. But why should he do anything for me? I am not at war with anyone."

"Berenguelita, I must be blunt. It would not surprise me if Richard tried to divorce you, on some grounds or other — perhaps even consanguinity; there were some common ancestors long ago, I believe. The Church abhors divorce; but Richard and Eleanor could be persuasive enough, if you kept silent and the Papacy had not heard your side."

"Divorce," she said, barely audibly. "Yes, I have been afraid of that. I do not think I could stand the humiliation."

"Well then, you should take the initiative, and go on the attack so it will not happen. That's what we soldiers do when we see danger ahead."

She laughed weakly. "Oh Sanchito, you are the warrior in the family, for sure! I have never thought of myself as a fighter. But maybe I can learn, if you help me. You have given me a lot to think about."

He drained his goblet, stood and took her hands to help her from her chair. He looked down at her slight figure, and her face raised to his in hope and friendship instead of the anger and distress of a few minutes ago. They both smiled.

"Well, sister, I have spoken to you like a cross old brother, but somebody had to. And we can talk more calmly at dinner — I am sure you plan to offer me dinner? And a bed for the night? And I will do my best to teach you how to be a fighter."

By the time Sancho left the next day, Berengaria had agreed to what she saw as the least difficult of all her hard choices. She would tell her story to the Pope.

s good as her word, after Sancho left Berengaria wrote to Pope Celestine. She approached the task with all the care that she gave to her work as a scribe. First she got out one of her largest wax tablets, solidly framed in good Limousin oak. She took up her favorite stylus and worked on her draft. She was not worried about her command of Latin but she rubbed out and rewrote extensively, trying to strike the right tone — self-confident but not proud, pleading but not begging.

When she was satisfied, she set out her finest sheet of parchment and her pens and ink. Before she began to copy, she studied the tablet again. Was it well phrased? She had misgivings. But who could reassure her? Héloise?

She had still not opened her heart to her lady in waiting about Richard, but by now Héloise must have a good grasp of the situation. If she did not, the letter would speak for itself.

After breakfast the next morning, she asked Héloise to come up to her chamber and led her to the work table where the tablet was propped.

"Now, my friend," said Berengaria, "I need your help. I have written a letter to the Pope, and I would like your opinion. Is it properly respectful? Is it too subservient? Is it too long or too short? Please say what you think."

"Good heavens!" said Héloise, astonished and then amused. "I have never written to a Pope, how can I know what to say?" But she sat down at once and looked over the letter.

After the usual salutations, it ran:

Your Holiness,
I remember with great gratitude your kindness to us when Queen Joanna of Sicily and I were overtaken by

winter in Rome, and you gave us shelter. I hope that you
also remember that occasion, and if so you will recall that
while we were there we learned that my husband, King
Richard, was being held prisoner in Germany.

He was freed but he has come to see me only once in the
past six years. He spent Christmas of 1196 with me at my
castle in Beaufort-en-Vallée. After that he left here for
Normandy. I am ignored by him and by his mother, Queen
Eleanor. I am denied my place at Richard's side as Queen
of England.

I believe Richard's wilful desertion of his wife is, if not
a sin, at least to be condemned by the Church, as a violation
of the wedding vows. I have borne it until now in silence,
but I can remain silent no longer. I plead with you to
consider my unhappy situation, and to use your influence
with King Richard and Queen Eleanor to bring an end to
this unnatural state of affairs.

I will count on your wisdom and compassion.
Your obedient daughter in Christ...

Héloise read slowly — her knowledge of Latin was not equal to Berengaria's. Then she looked up. Berengaria, standing by the table, nervously brushed a stray lock off her forehead, and waited to hear her response.

"It is an excellent letter — not too long, but saying all that needs to be said." She hesitated. "Or nearly all. You did not mention the need for an heir to the English throne, and the Papacy always likes to see peaceful successions in royal houses. Did you mean to leave it out? I know it would be painful to write about."

"I know, I know. I should have said something, but you are right, it would have been so hard! Still, you have hit on the one thing I was most worried about omitting. I will try to add a sentence or so. Thank you, my dear friend. And to force me to act quickly, will you send for a messenger to come early this afternoon?"

Alone again, she sat down and after some thought, added this at the end of her second paragraph:

"If their disdain of me is due to Richard's and my failure to have a child, I would point out that if Richard had spent more time with me, this might have been remedied."

She paused momentarily, then forced herself to add:

And it still may not be too late.

Then, without letting herself think further, she made her fair copy, rolled the parchment up and impressed her seal: "Berengaria, Queen of England."

After the messenger bore it off on its month-long journey to Rome, she tried to put the whole sorry affair out of her mind for the time being.

When the reply finally came, it was not much more than a formal acknowledgement.

We thank you... we have the greatest sympathy... we will keep a prayerful watch on your situation... we beg you to write again if at any time... believe in the mercy of an all-seeing God..." etc., etc.

Berengaria was sure that some papal secretary had written it, not the aged Pope. It certainly did not require an answer. She had followed Sancho's advice, and stated her case to the Papacy. Now what?

Later that same fall came a brief, cryptic letter from Joanna, the first word since their reunion in Poitiers.

My dear friend:
Now I have been the Countess of Toulouse for nearly a year. Raymond and I were married in the Basilica of Saint-Sernin. It was a rather subdued wedding. My mother sent word from Fontevrault that she did not feel well enough for the journey, but she sent me a beautiful jeweled girdle. As for Richard, I have heard nothing though I wrote to him last summer about my marriage. I think perhaps he does not approve. Have you seen him, has he come back to you as

*they say the hermit bade him? Please write to me! I am very
lonesome.*

Hardly a word about Raymond, the man she had married because
she counted on him to take care of her.

Berengaria sat down at once and tried to write a cheerful
letter. She related briefly and without recrimination or self-pity the
story of Richard's "repentance" and speedy departure.

She managed to make her life at Beaufort sound busy, calm
and contented — as indeed it mostly was. She concluded:

*If you ever need or wish a change, and would care to
visit a friend who longs to see you, remember that here at
my little castle a chamber is always ready for you.*

There. Did that sound too much as though she sensed Joanna
might like to escape from Raymond? She hoped not; but it was
most important to let her know that she had a place of refuge.

But Joanna did not write again.

The months, each just a little less dreary than the one before,
passed inexorably. The pile of manuscripts on her table ebbed and
flowed, as she found time to make her meticulous copies and send
them back to Leyre. She liked the translating from the Arabic best
— the beauty of the characters never failed to fascinate her, and the
subject matter tended to be much more interesting than the Latin
treatises and homilies. She liked the Muslims' long lyrical poems,
and their fantastic tales of travels to faraway places she had hardly
heard of.

Except for what Héloise learned when she went to Saumur to
see her new grandchild, or to Poitiers when bidden by Eleanor, all
the news they had of the outside world came from wayfarers
passing through the village. In late 1198, one such traveler told the
innkeeper, who told Carlos, who told Berengaria, that Richard had
at last finished his Saucy Castle and was using it as his headquarters for sallies in Normandy against his enemy King Philip
Augustus.

"Thank you, Carlos," his mistress said calmly. Then, with
hardly a pause, "And did you remember to ask the weaver if he has

finished the length of wool that I ordered?" Upon which Carlos rightly concluded, and later told Cristina, that their lady appeared to be well over her sad time, and that Richard's name no longer could hurt her.

However, beneath her stoic demeanor she was not content. She was tiring of this life without a future. She had not forgotten Sancho's stern advice to take matters into her own hands. She had made that one attempt to enlist Papal help, with no luck. She still could not bear the thought of chasing after Richard. But perhaps she could stand up to Eleanor? She was working herself up to a decision to go to Poitiers, or Fontevrault, or wherever the Queen was at the moment, and announce that she intended to stay for a time. Then Héloise unwittingly brought matters to a head.

It was a bleak day in early spring of 1199. Gusts of wind swept around the castle, whistling through the bare-branched trees and creating little whirlwinds of dust in the recently plowed garden. Berengaria and Héloise sat with their embroidery, glad to be inside and warm, though sometimes the wind swooped down the chimney and threatened to put out the fire on the hearth.

A messenger for Héloise was announced and she went down to the reception hall. When she came back, she said, "My lady, I may have to leave you for a time. The word from my son and daughter-in-law in Saumur is that they are planning the christening of my grandson. When the child was born, Queen Eleanor promised me that she would stand as godmother when the time came. So with your permission, I will go to Poitiers and ask the queen when we may have the ceremony."

The answer was quick — as though the words had formed long ago, and were waiting for just this chance to be spoken.

"Of course you must go. And when do you think of leaving for Poitiers? I will go with you. There are some matters I too wish to take up with Queen Eleanor."

22

ust as they were ready to leave for Poitiers, a
messenger brought word that Hugh, Bishop of
Lincoln, was coming. Berengaria wondered why and
in spite of the honor, she was a little annoyed. They
would have to postpone the trip. She hoped her newly
strengthened backbone would not weaken with the delay.

The message simply said that Hugh was on his way from
Angers to Fontevrault, but was making a side trip to Beaufort
because he had urgent news, and would appreciate an interview.

"Why would he come to see me?" Berengaria asked Héloise.
"He was in Cyprus when I was married, but I hardly had a chance
to get to know him, there were so many people and everything was
so confused."

"We will soon know; the messenger said the bishop was very
near to Beaufort."

Berengaria received him in her hall. She had put on her crown
and a fine brocaded robe, as was only right when one received a
prince of the Church. Ever since deciding to stand up to Eleanor,
she found a regal bearing came more easily. (I wish Sancho could
see me now! she said to herself.) She asked Héloise and Carlos to
stay with her, the closest she could come to a proper court.

When Hugh entered, she could hardly believe this was the
august Bishop of Lincoln. She remembered him as one of the three
sobersided, scarlet-clad, intimidating dignitaries who had assisted
Bishop John at her wedding ceremony. Now she saw an unassuming man in a serviceable brown wool habit and cape who
looked more like a country priest than a high prelate. With a warm
smile, he held out his hand and greeted her like an old friend.

"How good to see you again, Queen Berengaria," he said as
he bowed to kiss her hand, and she felt he meant it. "I have always
regretted that on the occasion of your marriage to my king, we had

no time to converse and become acquainted. But I am pleased to see you in good health and, if I may say so, even more beautiful."

"Thank you, my Lord Bishop, and welcome to Beaufort." She was polite, but apprehensive about his "urgent news." He looked very grave. "Now, what brings you to this out-of-the-way spot?"

"I will come to the point at once. And there is no way to soften the blow. Your husband and my liege lord, Richard, was grievously wounded while besieging a castle at Chalus near Limoges, and died as a result of his wound three days ago. I am on my way now to Fontevrault, where he is to be interred. I have heard the account from those who were with him, and if you wish I will tell you more."

She stared at him for half a minute in silence, in shock. The words had not yet sunk in. She needed time. If he kept talking, perhaps she could come to believe that what he said was true.

"Please do tell me more."

She listened dry-eyed, as he told of the king's death.

"According to what some have told me," Hugh said, "Richard heard that his vassal Aimart had discovered a trove of golden coins buried on his lands and claimed it as his own. But Richard maintained his superior claim and tried to take the treasure by force, and it was during his siege of Aimart's castle that he received his fatal wound."

"It does not sound like Richard to take such desperate measures for such a meager prize," said Berengaria. "He had his faults, but he was never greedy." She was still stunned, and hardly knew what she was saying.

Hugh said gently, "I agree. But I have heard from others a different explanation of why he attacked Aimart, and it seems more logical."

Apparently, as Hugh related, Aimart had recently paid homage to King Philip instead of to his rightful lord, Richard. Furthermore, Aimart's half-brother Ademar was still playing the rebel to the south, in Aquitaine. Berengaria remembered vaguely that her brother Sancho had spoken of this Ademar's disloyalty and said he would warn Richard.

So Richard (Hugh went on), wishing to put down all these insurrections, left Normandy in March to confront and subdue Aimart. Then he planned to go on to take care of Ademar.

"And madame," said Hugh, "we all know that our late king, your husband, was wont to act swiftly when angered and to strike like a lion. Which is what he did to his rebellious vassal Aimart, whatever the reason. While he was besieging the castle a bolt launched by a crossbowman on the ramparts found its way past his shield and into his shoulder. The arrow broke as they tried to pull it out. The wound festered, and in a few short days he was dead."

Now Berengaria turned quite pale and her eyes were bright with tears. But she still sat straight in her chair and looked directly at Hugh.

"And did he die there at Chalus?"

"No, Queen Eleanor had him brought to Fontevrault. She was with him at the end, and so was his brother John."

"Fontevrault. So near. Only a day's journey from here," she murmured, and now there was a quaver in her voice and he could see that she clenched her hands to keep them from trembling. "I could have been there, if Queen Eleanor had troubled herself to send me word."

The bishop said nothing. There was no way he could condone Eleanor's lack of consideration, nor did he wish to. His heart went out to the brave woman, struggling to keep her composure.

"And you, my lord bishop. I think you said you are now going to the funeral?"

"I am, madame; and I would be honored if you cared to accompany me. Will you come?"

Berengaria sat perfectly still, looking down at her hands. The silence went on for such a long time that Hugh was about to repeat the question. But she raised her eyes and replied, in an expressionless voice, "No. I thank you, but no. If Queen Eleanor has not seen fit to bid me come, I will not go. I can mourn Richard here as well as anywhere."

She rose, still amazingly calm. "Will you give me your blessing before you leave?"

She knelt before him and he placed his hand on her head and spoke such words of comfort as he could command and bade her continue to trust in God's goodness to the bereft.

After he rode away, she called Cristina and they went to her clothing chest. It was the custom for widows to wear white, and she looked for the snowiest garments she could find, to wear in mourning for the husband she had loved but who had never loved her.

er mourning was strangely detached. She thought sadly of a life so filled with achievement, and promising even more, now so suddenly snuffed out. She grieved, but her sorrow was dull, not the piercing agony she had felt when Richard had left her and set out for Normandy, two years before.

A few days after Hugh's visit she sat in her chamber, taking stock of her situation. The uncertainty and anguish were past history. To her guilty surprise, she felt liberated. Now she could be her own person. Her mind was a jumble of conjectures.

"I will never reign as Queen of England now," she said to herself. "But perhaps the new king will be kinder to his sister-in-law than he is said to be to others. He might even invite me to England and the people will see the queen that Richard never showed them. How I would love to see England! Maybe Blanche could go with me. I will not go if Eleanor is there. But in time Eleanor must die, though I must not wish it. And with the Queen Dowager gone, everything should be easier for me."

She sighed, then scolded herself for daydreaming. She rose impatiently and began pacing up and down.

Héloise came in and Berengaria suddenly stopped. The full skirts of her white gown swirled and settled softly like a cloud. "Héloise, how old is your lady, Queen Eleanor?"

Héloise looked surprised. She had, in fact, been surprised much of the time lately. Berengaria had taken the terrible news so calmly, it seemed; no tears, no retiring to grieve. On the whole, Héloise approved; it was the kind of control she admired.

"I have almost lost count," she said. "Let me see; she must be seventy-five at least. Why do you ask?"

"I was just wondering," said Berengaria. "She has outlived all but one of her sons; do you think she will outlive me too?"

Héloise pursed her lips and drew her brows together, considering. "Only time will tell. When Queen Eleanor has accomplished all the tasks she has set for herself in this life, doubtless she will decide to leave us."

Eleanor, meantime, was busy with one of her more ambitious tasks. She was planning a magnificent memorial at Fontevrault Abbey in Richard's honor. She sent a curt message to summon her daughter-in-law to be present.

"Now that is strange, after the way she slighted me at Richard's death," said Berengaria.

She and Héloise were taking their afternoon constitutional around the garden, assessing the new spring growth of the fruit trees and looking for early blossoms. The clouds were playing a game of chase with the sun, so sometimes they walked beneath grayness and gloom, then suddenly were bathed in brightness and warmth.

"No, it is quite in character," said Héloise. "Say what you will, Eleanor was devoted to Richard and as you know only too well, no friend to you. Your presence at the funeral would have been a bitter reminder of Richard's failure to have a son. Ignoring you was heartless, but it was pure Eleanor. But now, you must be at the memorial, for what would the world think if Richard's widow were not there? Eleanor cares greatly what the world thinks."

"You know your queen very well. And really, I am glad I was asked. It was never my fault that we did not become friends. Now I may be able to start out on a new footing with her. You will come with me, of course, won't you?"

"I will be happy to, because this means I will not need to go to Poitiers to see Eleanor. I much prefer Fontevrault, where there's no formal court and one is left more to oneself."

"I have always wanted to see Fontevrault; you must show me around. I have heard about it from you and Joanna too, but all I really know is that it is a very large abbey, and that Henry and Eleanor have made many gifts, and Joanna was happy there as a child, and the Queen spends much of her time there."

"Well, it is certainly large, and very busy. There are convents for both nuns and monks; and a shelter for lepers, that King Henry founded; and another for fallen women, established by Eleanor and where women are not admitted unless they are repentant. There is a school. Several buildings are lodgings for ladies who wish to retire from the world. And of course, there is the great abbey church."

"It sounds like a little kingdom. Does Eleanor reign?"

"Not visibly. The abbess is supreme, and she is responsible only to the Pope. But of course Eleanor is her real superior. Abbess Mathilde is the aunt of the late King Henry, and has always been absolutely devoted to the Plantagenet family, and especially to Eleanor. I will tell you no more about her — she must be seen to be believed."

Now the clouds claimed the victory and raindrops began to fall. Pulling their hoods over their heads, they ran in to their dinner.

On April 20, 1199, Berengaria arrived at Fontevrault. She was accompanied by Héloise, Cristina, Carlos and the man-at-arms Eleanor had sent. After emerging from a long walled lane that led from the main road they came upon what looked like a veritable city. It was dominated by an enormous church. Tall arched windows pierced its dun-colored walls, and it was crowned with a massive square tower. A half-dozen other buildings stood stolidly around the church, as though rooted in the stone paving; and still more could be seen farther off, along the lanes and paths that radiated from the church courtyard. Encircling the whole, hardly visible beyond trees and buildings, was a high solid wall.

Architecturally, Berengaria thought it even more dour than some of the monasteries in her native Navarre. But at least some of the inhabitants of this austere community had a taste for beauty. A carefully tended garden flanked one side of the church. A few pale lilies had already ventured to show themselves to the tentative April sun, and tulips proudly flaunted their chalices of ruby and purple. A sister walked along the rows, examining the rosebushes. Probably looking for blight, thought Berengaria, who had a little rose garden of her own at Beaufort.

The party dismounted and an imposing figure approached from a long narrow building near the church. She moved deliberately and as she drew near, Berengaria saw that she was very old; her face was a network of wrinkles. She was quite short, but made up for that with a towering white headdress. She wore a loose gray gown and a long black cloak, but they hardly concealed the amplitude of her figure.

"Welcome to Fontevrault, my lady," the woman said. "I am the Abbess Mathilde."

So this was the autocrat of Fontevrault.

"Queen Eleanor bade me greet you and show you to your lodgings. She is resting in her own chambers in La Madeleine" — she gestured to the most distant dormitory — "and asked me to tell you that the memorial ceremony will be at high noon tomorrow, in the church." Berengaria thanked her courteously, but she felt the familiar resentment. "If Eleanor is so indifferent to my presence that she cannot bother to greet me, why am I here?" she thought.

They walked along a poplar-bordered path toward her assigned quarters, Berengaria slowing her pace to accommodate Abbess Mathilde's creeping progress. Behind them, Lady Héloïse, Cristina and the man carrying their bags had to do the same.

As they walked, the abbess made conversation — or rather delivered a monologue. Her voice quavered and Berengaria had to bend her head to hear.

"The king's brother John has just arrived," she said. "But I suppose now we must call him King John. Oh dear, I never thought I would see the day when that one would be king, instead of our glorious Richard. God preserve us." Her voice became even fainter as she brooded on this melancholy situation. Then she became more cheerful. "But we are honored that the Pope has sent his special envoy for the ceremony. He is the Cardinal Pierre de Capoue. The Pope is Queen Eleanor's special friend, and she is very pleased that he has sent this cardinal — a prelate of the very highest rank."

The abbess continued her slow advance as she talked, taking tiny steps, nodding her head repeatedly and making little clucking sounds of approval of the Pope's generous gesture. Berengaria was suddenly struck with her resemblance to a hen crossing a barnyard, and barely suppressed a giggle. She heard Héloïse and Cristina tittering behind her. She turned and glared at them, but her mouth was twitching in amusement.

After what seemed an endless trek along the path, the abbess stopped before an undistinguished one-story building, made somewhat less stark by the clumps of low-growing pines that had sprung up around it. She tapped on the door with her stick and it was opened at once by a gray-clad veiled sister.

"These are your lodgings," Mathilde said, peering up at Berengaria to make sure she was listening. "Sister Genevieve will show you to your rooms, and see to your evening meal." She turned around carefully and began her slow return.

Berengaria did not mind the smallness and plainness of her little room; it reminded her of her quarters at the monastery of Leyre, even to the narrow bed and the south-facing window, with a table under it. But instead of books and writing materials, the table bore only a pitcher and ewer.

Héloïse came in with her, looked around and sniffed in disapproval. "They have taken no pains to put you up in a suitable chamber, have they? I think you must come with me to La Madeleine, where I always lodge. I will find you a room there."

"Never mind," said Berengaria. "This will do very well for the time being. And Cristina will be nearby."

The next day she rose early and took great pains with her attire. This would be her first chance to see and be seen by a whole array of important people, from the new King of England and the papal representative on down. But most of all she wanted to appear at her best in the eyes of Eleanor, who had never seen her in any but plain traveling clothes. She had Cristina brush her hair and pin it into a loose knot at the back of her neck. She was still all in white, even to her head covering — a diaphanous silk veil, not quite hiding her hair and held in place with a delicate silver coronet studded with pearls. It had been her mother's, and was sent by her father when Cristina and Carlos came to her at Beaufort. She had seldom had occasion to wear it.

She had only the small glass she had brought with her and could not get the whole effect. "How do I look, Cristina?" she asked.

"Like the most beauteous widow in Christendom," Cristina answered sincerely.

The abbess sent a lay sister to conduct her to the abbey church, well before the ceremony was to begin. She was dismayed to see that all her pains were nearly for naught. Her assigned place was in an unlighted private little chapel to one side. She would be almost invisible. "So much for pride," she said to herself wryly. "I hope it does not precede a fall."

Still, she had a fine view of the proceedings. Some hundred guests filed into the church and took their places in the vast nave, where clustered columns rose to lofty domes like a forest of marble tree trunks supporting the heavens. Sunlight fell through the high windows but brought no warmth. Tall candles glowed in the corners, and the guests wore bright scarlets and rich furs. Nevertheless, the ambience was gloomy; and the service was cold too.

Berengaria watched as prelates and lords came forward to pay formal, stilted tribute to the fallen king. Each first bowed toward the Queen Dowager Eleanor, who was enthroned just below the altar. She too was in mourning white, but over her gown she wore a robe of gold and crimson, the Plantagenet colors. She acknowledged each speaker with a thin smile and a hand slightly raised from where it rested on the arm of her chair.

This was the first time Berengaria had seen her since their parting in Sicily, eight years ago. Even from her distance she could see some changes. More lines in the imperious face, a slight sagging under the eyes — but the tilt of the chin was as proud as ever and the classic, sharply etched profile was not blurred. No matter what one's opinion of Eleanor as a human being, one had to admire her durability.

The new king, John, seated at her side, was another matter. Berengaria could not see him clearly because he was in the deep shadow of a column. He was dressed all in black. Glitteringly visible, however, were the heavy gold chains around his neck. His head turned often as his eyes darted from face to face. Leaning a little forward, he rested a hand on each knee and his fingers kept up a steady drumming. Once his head turned toward where she sat in her alcove, but there was no sign that he knew who she was.

None of the speakers paid any attention to her except Hugh of Lincoln. Though now wearing the scarlet cassock and white stole of a bishop, he was still the unassuming, sympathetic man who had come to her in Beaufort. Before he spoke he inclined his head toward her and smiled, causing others to crane their necks to see whom he was saluting. I do have one friend here, she thought.

His tribute was short and ended with an assurance of Richard's state of grace at the end of his life. "I pray you to hear his last words," said Hugh, and repeated what Richard had said to his men, while lying wounded at Chalus.

"I know that when the time comes for me to expiate my sins, I shall be hard put to it to escape the pains of hell, be it not for the mercy of God and the prayers of the handmaids of Christ at Fontevrault. Now in my dying hour I commend myself to them. I therefore give you order to bear my body thither and, all unworthy that I am, there to lay it at the feet of my father."

The last to speak was the cardinal from Rome, a small man almost hidden within the stiff, gold- and silver-encrusted robes of a high prince of the church. But his rich baritone voice made up for his slight stature, and rang out and echoed from the stone walls like a message from on high.

"My gracious Queen, King John, my lords and ladies. We are gathered here to pay tribute to your departed king, Richard. You have heard from those who stood here before me of his noble deeds, his fearlessness in battle, his generosity, his devotion to the Church, his brave leadership of the holy Crusade.

"It only remains for me to assure you that Richard, having done penance for his sins in the eyes of God and having received holy absolution before his death, is at peace with his Savior. His earthly remains are interred here at Fontevrault, next to his revered father, Henry Plantagenet. But his heart" — he picked up a small casket from the table at his side and held it aloft — "his heart will go to the cathedral of Rouen to rest there for veneration by the faithful forever. For Richard was duke of Normandy and loved and served that land well. May his soul find eternal peace. And now, go you all with God's blessing." He made the sign of the cross, and the crowd filed soberly out of the church.

Berengaria was transfixed by the brightly polished metal casket, still resting on its table. Now for the first time the reality of Richard's death came home to her. His heart was in that casket: his heart, which she had felt beat in his chest when he held her close to him. In spite of everything, she had loved him dearly — and for a little while, in his own way, surely he had loved her. Tears stung her eyes, and she buried her face in her hands, remembering.

fter a while she raised her head and dried her tears. The church was empty. She went out, hoping to find Eleanor, or perhaps John — it was time she made herself known to him. Neither was to be seen.

The rest of the company stood about in little groups, talking. Wondering what to do and where to go, she caught sight of Bishop Hugh, who was preparing to mount his horse. When he saw her he hurried toward her, smiling and extending his hand.

"I thought you had quite disappeared. I wanted to greet you and tell you how glad I am to see you here. Though it cannot have been easy for you." He saw the signs of recent tears. "You are a good, brave woman. I shall pray that life treats you more kindly from now on."

"Thank you, thank you," she said, touched by his kindness in this strange place where nobody else seemed to care whether she came or went.

"I shall pray for the same thing — and who knows, Bishop Hugh, perhaps I shall call on you in Lincoln one of these days!"

"So you think of coming to England?"

"I would like to very much. I hope to talk to Queen Eleanor and King John about it."

"Perhaps you will then. Send me word from time to time how you are faring."

She watched him ride away, then looked around, again in vain, for Eleanor. Then she caught sight of Cardinal Pierre de Capoue, starting along the road leading to La Madeleine, Eleanor's lodging.

Now, thought Berengaria, now is my chance. I must not let Eleanor and those who toady to her ignore me. I will start with this cardinal.

She caught up with him, fell into step beside him, and spoke. "My Lord Cardinal, permit me to introduce myself. I am Berengaria, widow of King Richard."

He stopped and looked in astonishment at this slender, exquisitely dressed lady. "You are Queen Berengaria?" he asked. "I thought Richard's queen had gone back to her home in Navarre, or was living in retirement in Anjou. Why did no one tell me you were here?" His manner, though brusque, was not unkind. His voice, now that he did not have to make the whole church hear, was more modulated, but still almost musical.

Something about him made her feel she could answer honestly. "Probably because Queen Eleanor is pretending that I am not here," she told him. "Apparently her sense of duty overcame her and she asked me to come for the ceremony — but she has not seen fit to welcome me." The sun was behind the cardinal and his face was shaded by his tall twin-peaked miter, but she could see his black eyes peering from the shadows like shiny ebony buttons.

"And you have something you wish to say to me in private? Let us go back to the cloister and you shall speak freely. Pope Innocent would wish me to bring back a complete report on all that I can learn here."

Pope Innocent! So, she thought, old Pope Celestine has gone to his heavenly rest, and has been succeeded by this new Pope, of whom she knew nothing except that he was Queen Eleanor's good friend, according to the abbess.

They turned and he led her into the small cloister next to the convent of St. Lazarus, an unfrequented haven of peace and quiet. They sat on a stone bench, looking through the carved arches toward the square of green in the center of the cloister. The westering afternoon sun shed a golden sheen on the grass.

"Now, my daughter," said the cardinal, "please tell me about yourself. I do not know much about your situation, except that you were with Richard in the Holy Land and that it did not please God to bless your union with issue. But I have also heard, perhaps not reliably, that your husband seems to have avoided you since he was recrowned in Winchester. What more can you tell me?"

She realized that he must have heard about, perhaps read, her brief correspondence with Pope Celestine. At first she felt diffident about revealing details of her private life, but this was her chance to tell her story to someone who might help her; he was high in the papal hierarchy, and she sensed that he was sympathetic. He did not seem beholden to Eleanor as she had suspected. His beady black eyes were fixed on her, and his face was cocked, awaiting her reply.

She found herself relating, calmly and almost as though speaking of someone else, how she had spent the years since returning from Palestine; how Richard had repudiated her; and how Eleanor had spurned her when she saw that there was to be no heir.

"I have learned to live with all that," she told him. "But now that Richard is gone, I must be realistic and take whatever steps I can to assure my future. I owe it not only to myself, but also to the memory of my father, who put his faith in the honor of the Angevin kings when he agreed to my marriage to Richard."

"And you feel they are not acting honorably?"

"They are not. Eleanor continues to exclude me from the royal family. Thanks to her, I was not with Richard to be crowned at Winchester. Thanks to her, I am tucked away out of sight at a remote castle. I am entirely dependent on my allowance from the English exchequer. Who knows what advice she is giving her son John? In a way, those two hold my future in their hands. I do not despair, I trust in God to watch over me. But I believe I owe it to my faith in God's justice and mercy to do what I can to defend my rights and my honor."

After a moment, she went on. "When my sister-in-law Joanna and I were on our way back from the Holy Land to Poitiers, we spent some time under the protection of Pope Celestine. He was concerned about our welfare, and I felt then that I had a friend in Rome. I would like to think I may still feel that assurance, now that Innocent is on the throne."

The cardinal had come to a decision and spoke briskly. "I can see it has not been easy for you to talk of these matters. But I can also see that you are strong, and so is your faith. You may be sure nothing you have said will be repeated, except in my report to the Pope. He asked me particularly to inquire into the details of the succession to the throne of England, and the welfare of the widow of the late king certainly falls within that body of information. As for whether you have a friend in Rome, be assured that you have at least two — not only will His Holiness take a keen interest in your welfare, but so will I."

The audience was over. They rose. Shadows had fallen on the cloister, and she felt the chill; she had no cloak.

"I thank you from the bottom of my heart, Lord Cardinal. You have been kind to listen to me and to give me comfort. Now I must go back to my lodgings — the evening grows cool."

"But will you not be joining us at dinner?" he asked. "I hear that the Abbess Mathilde has ordered a remarkable meal, to take our minds off our grieving." He looked at her quizzically, and she recognized a churchman's joke. The mood at the service had hardly been one of grieving, rather one of patient forbearance if not boredom, while a necessary ceremony ran its course.

"I think not," she replied. "Queen Eleanor has not bidden me to be present. I will dine in my chamber."

"You need not wait for an invitation from the queen, you know," he said. "In the eyes of God I believe I outrank her, and I hereby invite you to join me at dinner. I would be honored."

She liked this man — his forthrightness, his humor. But she suddenly felt almost weak with fatigue. "Forgive me, but it has been a long hard day, following on the hasty journey from Beaufort. I want only to go back to my room and rest. But I feel we will meet again."

So they said their farewells, and the white-clad widow, feeling far less desolate than when she left the church, set off along the path to her lodgings. Cristina, who had been standing by and waiting for her to finish her talk with the cardinal, met her with a cloak. Back in their chambers, the maid helped the weary queen to take off her formal clothing and brought her a warm wool robe.

Genevieve served her a simple meal, without a word; the nuns were sworn to silence. Berengaria did not mind. She had much to think about. When she had eaten, she leaned back in her chair and closed her eyes, reliving the ceremony in the church. She wondered if the casket with Richard's heart were already on its way to Rouen. She went over her talk with the cardinal and his words of encouragement. She practiced the speech she would deliver to Eleanor the next day.

Emotionally exhausted, she went to bed. But before she slept she prayed God to help her remember Richard the generous king and noble warrior who had been memorialized this day, rather than Richard the faithless husband; and she thanked Him for bringing Cardinal Pierre de Capoue to Fontevrault.

erengaria was awakened the following morning by the raucous crowing of a rooster. For a minute she thought she was back in Beaufort. Then when she opened her eyes and looked around the bare little room, she wished she were. It seemed far less welcoming than the day before when she was so worn out. Could she really be feeling homesick? She curled up under her warm coverlet and counted the places she had lived: Estella, Pamplona, Tudela — all those cities in Navarre where King Sancho had taken his family as he progressed around his kingdom. Then the monastery at Leyre, where she had been so content to study and learn the art of the scribe. Then St. Jean-d'Acre in Palestine — better left unremembered. Finally, the modest castle at Beaufort-en-Vallée.

Of them all, Beaufort seemed most like home. It was there that she had come to terms with the strange turns her life had taken, and had found a measure of peace. Now, it was to Beaufort that she wished to return.

Musing on the changes time can bring, she jumped out of bed and put on a robe. "If Beaufort is where I want to be," she said to herself, "then we might as well leave today, as soon as I have seen Eleanor."

She did not look forward to that meeting, but she had promised herself she would go through with it.

At a tap on the door she called, "Come in."

It was Cristina, surprised to see her up. "It is still so early, madame — have you had a bad night?"

"No, I slept very well, thank you, Cristina. But a lusty, loud-mouthed rooster woke me and I thought I might as well get up."

"I heard the cocks crowing too, while I was bringing your breakfast back from the kitchen," Cristina said. Her serious, respectful face broke into a grin. "And I wondered if they were calling to the abbess!" She giggled and Berengaria joined her at the memory of Mathilde's resemblance to a fussy hen.

Cristina ran out to come back with a tray bearing bread, honey, a bowl of steaming oat porridge and a jug of milk. She set it on the table by the window and Berengaria sat down to eat while Cristina tidied the room. Looking out, Berengaria could see the fields beyond the walls, where a brown-robed monk, his cowl pulled up to keep his head warm, guided a horse-drawn plow over the dark loamy ground. She supposed the grain for the excellent bread she was eating came from those fields.

"Fontevrault is wonderfully self-sufficient, I think," she said to Cristina. "They must grow everything they need, right here."

Cristina seemed in a mood to chatter. "And cook it too, madame. You must visit the kitchen! I've never seen anything like it. It's a big round building, just on the other side of the abbey church — and to my way of thinking, it's far handsomer than the church. Carlos thinks so too."

"The cook must be very busy, providing for the dozens of nuns and monks and clergy," said Berengaria. "To say nothing of all the guests."

"Oh, there are many cooks," Cristina said. "One for each dormitory and convent, and each cook has her own hearth with its own chimney, and they keep running back and forth and calling out to each other. It's nothing like our little cubbyhole of a room at home, where the cook keeps falling over the water barrel. And it's all full of wonderful smells of roasting meat and bread a-baking."

"And a good bit of smoke too, I dare say, what with all those cooking fires," said Berengaria. Cristina's enthusiasm made her curious. "Well, after breakfast I will go see this wonder for myself; then I think we will get ready to go home. I hope to be through with my business with Eleanor by this afternoon."

When she had finished her meal and Cristina had helped her dress — again in the white gown but without the crown — they walked to the much-admired kitchen. She found she was right about the smoke, in spite of all the chimneys that poked their heads through the peaked slate roof like miniature towers of a fortress. Still, it was a cheerful place, partly because — unlike the rest of the abbey where the rule of silence was observed — here the nuns were permitted to speak. A wise exception, Berengaria thought. How could one prepare a decent meal if one could not say, "Oh, Sister Anne, I have no more onions. Could you let me borrow three?" Or "Who will taste my beef and barley soup and tell me if it needs more pepper?" All this and more Berengaria heard during her quarter-hour there, admiring the cooks' skill. At first they were surprised at a visit by such a fine lady but soon they were chatting with her companionably, pleased at her interest.

She had just finished tasting Sister Antoinette's soup and pronouncing it exactly right when the abbess entered. Silence fell like a shroud and there was suddenly a great stirring of pots and stoking of fires and peering into ovens.

"Ah, there you are, madame," Mathilde said. Today she was less like a nervous fowl and more like a querulous, disapproving schoolmistress. "I would never have thought to find you here. But we looked in your room, and the church, and the refectory, all in vain." Every line of her aged face quivered in reproach. Perhaps she had learned this expression from her royal patroness. On her plump face it became a caricature of a childish pout.

"The Queen wishes to see you. If you have finished your business in the kitchen" (her eye dwelt on the ladle still in Berengaria's hand), "I will conduct you to her. We would not wish to keep her waiting longer, would we?"

"I will see you back in our lodgings, Cristina," Berengaria said. Outwardly meek but inwardly amused by Mathilde's self-importance, she followed the abbess to La Madeleine, where they went up to Eleanor's quarters on the second floor.

After the austerity of the rest of the abbey the lavish elegance of Eleanor's rooms was almost shocking. It was said she had given her most precious belongings to the trove collected for Richard's ransom, to show the English that she too could make sacrifices; but clearly she had clung to a few treasures. Berengaria's eyes were drawn at once to the headboard of the high canopied bed, and to the chest at its foot. Every inch of the polished dark oak was carved with likenesses of flowers, vines and mythic beasts. The petals of the flowers were mother-of-pearl and the eyes of the beasts gleamed with gold. It was fully as ornate as anything she had seen in the papal palace in Rome. Still more gold, and silver too, glittered here and there: from the enormous candlesticks placed in each corner and the goblet and ewer on the table to the great gilded and jeweled Bible on its ornate stand.

Berengaria could not take all this in at once and in any event was too polite to stare. Yet by the end of her thirty-minute audience she had memorized every detail. She owed Cristina a description, after the maid's insistence that she see the wonderful kitchen.

Eleanor was as resplendent as her surroundings, in a robe of wine-colored velvet with a high ermine collar. Berengaria had observed that as beautiful women aged their garments and adornments grew more dazzling. And, seen at closer range than yesterday in the church, Eleanor had indeed aged. Her skin was like crumpled parchment. She moved with more deliberation.

The abbess had left after ushering Berengaria into the room. Eleanor raised her head and surveyed her, from her seat near the window. She beckoned Berengaria to approach and to seat herself in the window embrasure.

She was as abrupt as ever. No welcome, no pleasantries.

"Good morning, Berengaria." Her voice had lost none of its resonance. (At least she doesn't call me "my girl" any more, Berengaria thought.) "I had thought to see you at the banquet last night." It sounded like an accusation.

"I would have been glad to come, if you had bade me be there," Berengaria answered with spirit.

Eleanor darted a sharp look at her, then went on.

"Well, now that you are here at Fontevrault, you may stay if you like. You could make yourself useful by helping in the school. I understand you are skilled in Latin. And Joanna would be glad to have you."

"Joanna? Is Joanna here then?"

"No, of course not. Do you not think she would have been with us in the church yesterday if she had already arrived? No, she will not be here for another week." As always, Eleanor did not waste time or energy in explanation.

"Will Raymond be with her?"

"That villain!" said Eleanor bitterly. "He has cast my daughter out, though she is bearing his child." Her anger overcame her reticence. "He accused Joanna of treason and she had to flee for her life." She told the whole sorry tale, her voice dripping with the contempt she had been bottling up.

It seemed that earlier in the spring while Raymond was far away from Toulouse on some business or other, a group of disgruntled nobles had risen up against his rule. Joanna, like the good Plantagenet and true helpmeet to her husband that she was, had gone out with loyal troops to try to put down the revolt.

"Oh, poor Joanna!" Berengaria cried. "What a hard thing to have to do!"

"Save your pity, the story gets even worse," Eleanor said. "Her husband's own knights betrayed her and joined the enemy. She barely escaped an ambush and somehow got back to Toulouse. Raymond returned but refused to see her and accused her of stirring up the revolt. He is a true son of his deceitful father."

Then, the queen continued, though exhausted and ill, Joanna had fled from her unhappy adopted land to seek help from Richard, but when she reached Niort, some hundred miles to the south of Fontevrault, she learned of her brother's death. She almost collapsed, but managed to send a desperate message to her mother. Eleanor had sent people to bring her to the haven of the abbey as soon as she was well enough to travel.

"So you see, she will need care and attention when she is here. I must be away from Fontevrault for a time. But I know that you have been a good friend to my unfortunate daughter. I will give you that, though in other respects you have not brought me the satisfactions I hoped for when you married Richard."

Berengaria fought the impulse to make an angry reply.

Eleanor, perhaps brooding about what might have been, seemed lost in thought. Then she looked directly at her daughter-in-law. Her voice was no longer frosty, and her next words were almost an entreaty.

"But that is all past now. Will you stay, for Joanna's sake if not for mine?"

"Of course I will. Joanna is as dear to me as my own sister, and if I can give her any comfort I will do so."

"I know that she thinks of you as a sister, too. I thank you." For the first time, Berengaria thought she saw a glimmer of human feeling in those cold blue eyes.

She is really grateful, Berengaria thought; after all, she loves her daughter and I believe she means those thanks. Perhaps this would be a good time to say what I came here to say.

She spoke quickly before she could think better of it. "And I thank you also, for giving me this chance to become part of your family. It will be the first time since I married Richard that I have been offered such a role. I hope it means that from now on I will be treated less like a poor relation to be hidden away in a corner, and more like the acknowledged widow of your son, the king of England." She looked unflinchingly at the Queen.

Eleanor's eyes flickered with surprise and she pressed her lips together and narrowed her eyes. Then the corners of her lips rose slightly. It might have been a smile.

"So. You have decided it is time to assert yourself. I wondered when you would. Well, we will talk more about this later. While you are at Fontevrault, you will be lodged here in La Madeleine. I have asked Abbess Mathilde to prepare suitable rooms for you and your people."

She rose. Berengaria went back to her room, to tell Cristina and Carlos that they would be staying in Fontevrault for a while. She did not know whether to be encouraged or not, and began planning what she would say the next time she saw Eleanor.

She did not have a chance for another talk. The very next day, to the amazement of even those who knew her well, the indefatigable queen set off on a military campaign. Berengaria, from her comfortable new apartments in La Madeleine, heard the hubbub of jangling harness and stomping hooves. She hurried down the stairs and found Héloise also going out to the courtyard. They were just in time to see Eleanor, in the midst of a party of mounted knights, disappear down the lane. The small crowd that had assembled to watch the departure was dispersing. A sudden quiet fell over the courtyard as the noise of the troops receded.

"She is going to war!" Héloise exclaimed. "Will that woman never admit her age?" Her words were overheard by the abbess, standing nearby and leaning on her stick. She looked reprovingly at Héloise.

"Age has nothing to do with it, Lady Héloise. Thank heaven, Queen Eleanor still has her health and knows her duty.

And if she does not act, and quickly, who will? Not King John, you may be sure."

"But where is she going, who is the enemy?" Berengaria asked.

The abbess, proud of her position as confidante of the queen, did not mind sharing her inside information with these ignorant women. Her voice became less tremulous and her little eyes, almost buried in her fleshy face, snapped. One could see, now, traces of her Plantagenet heritage.

"The same enemy as always — Philip of France. That miscreant wasted no time after Richard died, and took possession of Angers. If he's left there without a fight, he'll go on to seize even more of the Angevin Empire. So the queen has assembled a hundred of Richard's fighting men, and is off to take the city back."

And so she did. Word soon reached the abbey that her forces had achieved a swift victory. Then, to remind her subjects who their sovereign was, she began a royal tour through Poitou and Aquitaine, stopping at all the important towns to greet her vassals and hear their grievances.

She was still away when Joanna arrived. When the two old friends met they held each other close before speaking.

"Five years, Joanna — that's how long it's been since we were together, in Poitiers. Oh, I am so glad to see you! Come, let us go out to some quiet spot to talk. I have become quite fond of the little cloister of St. Lazarus. Come, and we will tell each other everything." She tried to keep talking so Joanna would not notice her pity and dismay at her altered friend. The merry face was merry no longer, but drawn and lined with care. The slight body seemed too weak and frail to bear the weight of the unborn child.

They sat in the cloister, talking quietly. Joanna filled Berengaria in on the details of the story that Eleanor had told in stark outline. She did not complain or bemoan her fate, simply stated the facts of her efforts to help her husband, and his unwarranted rejection of her.

When she had told it all, she sighed deeply. "Of course you were right about Raymond. I had built up a picture of him that proved completely unrealistic. But I thank you for not saying 'I told you so,' because you did try to warn me. But as usual, I was too stubborn and did not want to listen." Then she brightened a little, and her sideways glance at Berengaria and her half-smile recalled for a moment the old Joanna who could make fun of herself.

"Ah well," said Berengaria, clasping Joanna's hand and trying to think of words of comfort, "at least it is all over now, and surely you will be able to love your little one, no matter if his father is such a renegade. What will you do, Joanna, stay here until your time comes? It cannot be long now."

Joanna sighed again. "Yes, I will stay here — where else could I go? But as for loving my child, I do not know if I can but I will surely try, for God tells us to love one another." Berengaria was about to reply, but Joanna went on. "There is something else I must tell you, sister. I have decided to take the veil of the Cistercian Order and to enter their house here as soon as I can, even before the babe is born; and yield the child to others for upbringing. I see no future for me in the world and I long for a life of service and silence."

Berengaria was incredulous. She could think of a dozen reasons why Joanna should not take such a drastic step and began to remonstrate.

"The Cistercians will never, never permit that, Joanna, not now, when you are about to give birth. And your mother would be horrified."

But Joanna began to sob and Berengaria could not go on. She put her arm around her friend's thin shoulders and soon Joanna was able to speak. "I have thought and thought, Berengaria. I am sorry to leave my mother, though she will certainly find strength to withstand the loss. I am even more sorry to leave you, for our friendship has been one of the most joyful things in my life. But I am determined. If they say no, I will just keep after them until they are worn down and tired of saying no." She had never seemed so adamant about anything.

Keep after them she did and wear them down she did. Presently Joanna said her last farewell to Berengaria, donned her gray gown and her veil and disappeared into the house of the novices of the Cistercian Order. There was nothing Berengaria could do.

Saddened, disheartened at this severing of the last real tie she had with the Plantagenets, she sensed it was time to go. There was no way of knowing when Eleanor would reappear, and the next confrontation would have to wait. She returned to Beaufort to try to pick up the strands of her own life. A few weeks later she heard the tragic postscript. Joanna had given birth to a son. The mother died the next day; the child survived only two days more.

ife in Beaufort took an unpleasant turn in the early summer of 1199.

Berengaria was working in the newly restored room she had taken to calling her scriptorium. Héloise was in Saumur, and Carlos was in charge of the household funds. He came in with the account books in hand. He habitually wore a serious expression, but now he was unusually grave as he held out the books.

"My lady, I dislike worrying you, but I feel you should be told how we stand. Your allowance from the English Exchequer is two months past due, and if it does not arrive soon we will not be able to pay the butcher or anyone else."

Berengaria held out her hand for the books, and was shocked at what she saw. She had come to depend on the allowance without giving it much thought. Had Eleanor, or John, instructed the Bishop of Ely to stop it? If so, what now? She had no one to advise her.

The answer, of course, was to go to see Eleanor. "Thank you, Carlos," she said, as sober as he. "You were right to tell me this. Will you please prepare to go with me to Poitiers tomorrow? I will find out what can be done."

She was quite sure that as Richard's widow she was entitled to his possessions in Gascony. Up to now she had not thought much about them — she had not needed to. She was uncertain about what they amounted to or how to obtain their revenues. Nobody had ever given her a copy of her marriage contract, though she supposed her father, as well as Richard, had had one. Women of her status were ordinarily spared the burden of learning about their financial affairs. But Eleanor, no ordinary woman, would certainly know all about the provisions.

And so they hurried to Poitiers.

The Queen Dowager received her in her ornate Great Hall. She was no help at all. Any possibility of the rapprochement that Berengaria had hoped for, during their last meeting at Fontevrault, had vanished. Eleanor sat on her resplendent throne, almost lost among the cushions and robes. Her elbow rested on the arm of the chair and she propped her head up with her hand. Her shoulders were bowed. Beneath her half-closed eyelids her blue eyes glittered with all the penetration of the hooded eyes of a hawk. She heard the story; then she answered briefly, in such a tired voice that Berengaria sensed that this indestructible woman might at last be feeling her years.

"I know nothing of all this. John is now king of England. He deals with all claims against the crown's treasury. Go see John. He is at Chinon. I cannot help you. I am sorry."

She did not sound sorry. Berengaria had meant to mention Joanna's death and extend her sympathy, but she had no chance. Eleanor waved her out of the hall. That was that.

Now her only hope was John. Back in Beaufort, she composed as polite a letter as she could, saying she was sorry she had not had an opportunity to talk with him at Fontevrault and asking for an interview in order to discuss her position as Richard's widow.

Hardly had the messenger left than another rode into the courtyard, with a joyful message from Blanche. She was now securely affianced to Thibaut of Champagne, and was to be wed at Chartres in a few weeks' time. She implored Berengaria to come, to take part in the ceremonies, and to wish her joy. And could Berengaria, afterwards, accompany her sister and her new husband to their home in Troyes in Champagne, and stay for a time?

She sent a reply at once, saying that she would with the greatest pleasure come to the wedding, and go on to Troyes. If necessary, she said to herself, I will sell some of my jewels to keep us solvent. Then she called for Carlos and Cristina to tell them to prepare for the journey. She sent word to Héloise, who was in Saumur, asking her to join her in Troyes if she could.

The journey went quickly. She forgot her money problems and her quarrels with her in-laws, in the anticipation of seeing her sister. Within a week they were almost in view of Chartres, only a few days' journey to the northeast from Beaufort but a world away from her customary life.

On the last day the way led through a beech wood where branches met high overhead. When Berengaria looked up, she saw no sky, but a green vault. Her horse, a well-behaved gray called Grimaldo the Seventh (she always chose a gray, and named him Grimaldo after her favorite steed years ago in Estella) clip-clopped sedately along the narrow road, its surface pounded hard by many hooves. When they came out in the open, she caught her breath at the sight before her. Looming hazily in the distance, an enormous tower floated above the tawny fields of ripening grain. Nothing she had heard or imagined had prepared her for this first view of Chartres Cathedral. The closer they came the more awesome the prospect. For a long time, only the tower, growing steadily larger, and the fields from which it seemed to spring could be seen. Then they could see the tops of the taller buildings of the town, some of them two or three stories high. As they drew nearer, the town hid the tower from view.

Not only was this unexpected vision hard to comprehend; so was the new turn her life had taken, so quickly. Here she was, riding into a city she had heard of all her life but never dreamed she would be able to visit.

The entrance hall of the chateau of the Count of Blois in Chartres was like a beehive as preparations for the next day's wedding intensified. Servants scurried toward the kitchen, bearing casks of wine and plucked geese. Purposeful clerks, laden with parchments and stacks of wax tablets, went to and fro. Early-arriving wedding guests wandered about, hoping to glimpse the bride and groom. Some of them cast curious glances at two women in lively conversation near the door. One was fair and rosy-cheeked, in a sky-blue gown and flowing white cloak. Tendrils of golden hair escaped from her hood. The other had just entered. She was older and darker-haired, but there was a resemblance. Both women were laughing, their words tumbling out.

"How stylish you look, Berenguelita!"

"Yes, I do, don't I?" She pirouetted in her narrow-skirted white gown with its cape of dove gray that reached just below her waist. "I thought since I was coming to the wedding of a princess to a count I should dress to suit. Tomorrow you will really become Countess Blanche of Champagne! I never doubted it for a moment."

"It might never have happened, if the good Countess had not died last year. Finally Thibaut could speak for himself, and so he did."

"But why is your wedding here in Chartres, Blanche? Why not in Troyes, which is Thibaut's home as Count of Champagne?"

Blanche explained that the Countess of Blois, Thibaut's aunt, had volunteered to act as official hostess for the wedding. The Countess had decided on Chartres because neither Troyes nor Blois held a cathedral so famous and splendid as that of Chartres.

"And besides, she and her husband, the Count, maintain a chateau here as well as in Blois, and she thought this one would be more suitable for the festivities. She is the most kind-hearted woman you can imagine, but she does love splendor and show and the good opinion of the world."

Chatter and footsteps and the clatter of crockery resounded off the stone walls of the cavernous hall. Blanche took Berengaria's arm. "Come, sister, let's go out where we can hear each other talk and not be stared at so. I have nothing to keep me here this afternoon. Thibaut has gone off on some business or other, and Aunt Thérèse is so busy getting ready for tonight's festivities that I won't be missed. We'll go without a servingman, just the two of us — though if Thibaut knew he would scold me."

Feeling a little daring, they walked out into the town. The narrow streets were crowded, for Chartres attracted visitors the year around who came to see its audacious cathedral, still incomplete, and its precious relic, the veil of the Blessed Virgin. The sisters went unnoticed as they made their way with the throngs toward the cathedral. Berengaria teased her sister.

"And did he praise your flaxen hair and your blue eyes? And fall on his knees and declare his love?" Blanche blushed and turned her head aside, and Berengaria laughed.

"Do you know, at your age I had already been married three years? And I know everybody said then that considering my advanced age of twenty-nine, it was a mercy anyone would have me? Indeed, it is high time you were wed! Tell me, how many suitors did you have to keep at arm's length while you waited for your Thibaut to claim you?"

Before Blanche could answer a closed litter displaying the insignia of the king of France approached, borne by four smartly stepping footmen and preceded and followed by liveried horsemen. The pounding of hooves and cries of "Make way there!" made conversation impossible. Like everybody else crowded back against the walls, they looked at it in curiosity, but the royal person inside remained hidden.

When she could be heard Berengaria said, "Do you think that could possibly be King Philip?" She wondered what it would be like to see him again — would he be as ostentatiously courteous as he had been in St. Jean-d'Acre?

"He has of course been bidden, but I have no idea if he will come. But as for suitors, there were only two or three, and none of such high birth or so handsome as Thibaut. I think Sancho would have liked to affiance me to one of his companions in arms, but he never got around to it. He has been away so much lately — have you heard the latest about our brother? I think he can sniff out a good war from hundreds of miles away, and off he goes!"

She told Berengaria how Sancho had recently journeyed to the land that the Muslims held in the south of the Iberian Peninsula. In spite of the fact that the Christian kings of the north were offi-cially at war with the unbelievers, rumor had it that Sancho was fighting alongside the Muslim caliph in putting down a rebellion by some of his tribesmen.

"They even say," reported Blanche, "that the caliph's beautiful daughter fell madly in love with Sancho; and that he agreed to help her father in his battles, in exchange for her hand in marriage."

"Now that is a fantastic tale indeed! I am not sure I would want an unbeliever, no matter how beautiful, for a sister-in-law."

"Nor I. But we will have to wait until he comes back to learn the truth of it all. I sent him word about my marriage and asked for his blessing, and in his message of reply he said he heartily approved. He had met Thibaut at some tournament and admired his horsemanship."

"Perhaps he was glad for other reasons too. Because now Count Thibaut can relieve King Sancho of the burden of keeping you in silks and laces."

They had come to the square in front of the cathedral and there was so much to distract them that they had to leave off their banter.

"I heard there had been a terrible fire here," said Berengaria, "but I did not know they would have to rebuild so much." An enormous pile of stones and charred timbers lay on the ground off to their left. Stonemasons were noisily plying hammers and chisels on massive chunks of limestone in front of a truncated tower. Workmen perched at the top of the scaffolding that surrounded it, hoisting timbers and fitting them together. A companion tower still stood, sturdy and immense: the one she had seen as she approached Chartres.

"And what a blessing that this whole side was unharmed. Just think, Berengaria, tomorrow our wedding party will pass under that magnificent arch in the center, and won't we be grand?" They stood before the soaring façade, its three arches crowded with carved figures both Biblical and fanciful, and a few that Berengaria did not recognize as either. She was puzzled by a remarkably lifelike stone figure on the south arch, a man with a wise face, a high forehead and a book in his lap. It was like no one in the Bible she could think of.

She was about to ask Blanche if she knew who it might be, when they were distracted by a growing hullabaloo behind them. Following the sounds, they came onto a square where merchants were setting up their stalls. It was market day. Farmers, weavers, potters and tinkers were vociferously crying their wares, in competition with the quacks and squawks of caged poultry. The sisters wandered through the maze, inspecting and exclaiming and holding up their skirts to keep them out of the dust and mud. Berengaria stopped to admire an artistic display of red apples and white turnips, arranged in a checkerboard pattern, when Blanche, who had gone on ahead, came back and plucked her sleeve.

"Come see, sister! I have found such beautiful flowers. I must have them for my bridal bouquet." She led Berengaria to the flower stall with its fragrant, single-petaled roses, glowing calendulas, snowy lilies, royal purple and parchment-white fleur-de-lys, and more. "Shall I have lilies, or a mixed bouquet? My gown is rose-colored satin. What do you think?"

They settled on a center of lilies, surrounded by pale-pink roses and white marguerites. When it came time to pay, Blanche discovered she had brought no money. Berengaria saved the day. Inside the back cover of her beloved psalter, which she always carried with her, she had long ago fastened a small purse in which she kept a few coins for just such an emergency. She held out the little trove in her hand and asked the flower merchant, who had been pretending not to listen, if it would suffice.

"Not quite, my lady," he said soberly. "You lack three sous." But before they could turn to leave, disappointed, he added with a grin spreading over his broad peasant's face, "But for two such pretty ladies, one of whom is to be married tomorrow, I will gladly forgive the rest of the price. What is more, I will throw in this spray of lilac to add fragrance to the bridal chamber." He bowed gallantly to Blanche, wrapped the flowers in straw matting and beamed as they thanked him and left.

"A very good omen," Berengaria said. They hurried back to put the flowers in water.

Since, in all the flurry at the chateau, nobody had seen them go or noticed their return, there was no occasion for a scolding.

he splendor and show that the Countess of Blois so admired ruled that evening's celebrations in the chateau's Great Hall. Berengaria, used to quiet and solitude, was at first unnerved by the throngs of gorgeously clad guests. (Parading up and down like a flock of peacocks, she said to herself.) It seemed that everybody knew everybody else and had greetings and gossip to share, at top voice. Blanche introduced her to the countess, then the latter carried Blanche away to present her to her fine friends. Berengaria stood for a while taking in the noisy, brilliant spectacle.

She was not alone for long. Thibaut, seeing her standing by herself, left his aunt's group and came to greet her. He was a well-built, mannerly young man, as blond and blue-eyed as Blanche. A jaunty feathered hat rested on his mop of curly hair, and his luxuriant golden mustaches reached toward his ears like a pair of wings, ready to bear him aloft. He bowed and introduced himself.

Berengaria appraised him. Almost too pretty, she thought; but then he disarmed her, for few women mind compliments. Thibaut took her hand and said as though he truly meant it, "I am so glad to meet you at last! Blanche has told me so much about you, and now I see that she is not the only beauty in the family. May I call you sister?"

As they stood talking he was attentive, but often his eyes strayed to Blanche, across the room. He was clearly devoted to her, as well he should be. Berengaria decided she was going to like this brother-in-law.

"You are an object of curiosity, you know," he told her. "People are wondering who this lovely stranger is. And when they find out that you are the widow of King Richard, they will flock around you like bees to honey." Sure enough, guests began coming up to Thibaut, asking for an introduction.

- 173 -

She was presented to Reynaud, Bishop of Chartres, who was to preside at tomorrow's wedding; and to Garnier de Trainel, Bishop of Troyes, who had come to assist in the ceremony. Both offered condolences on her loss of Richard, which Berengaria politely acknowledged.

After Bishop Reynaud took his leave, Bishop Garnier, a short, very worried-looking man, remained, apparently wishing a private word. If so, he had trouble getting it out. He looked at her with such a pained expression that Berengaria was afraid something was terribly amiss; was her tiara slipping off, was there a smudge on the end of her nose? Before long, though, she decided this was his habitual expression.

Finally he spoke, first in short bursts, then pouring out the words. She realized that he had a tendency to stammer and once he got his start, had to keep going at top speed.

"I am glad to make your acquaintance, Queen Berengaria. There is something I wish to take up with you. But first, what do you think of this fine city? Have you had a chance to see the cathedral? What a terrible tragedy the fire was! It will be years before they can finish the restoration, but on the other hand, it is a heaven-sent opportunity to make it even more glorious than the old one." He paused, out of breath and words.

"Yes, my sister and I were there this afternoon. Actually, you are just the one to settle something for me. Of all the wonderfully carved figures on the façade, there was one that puzzled me, in a niche on the south arch. He looks like a scholar, his hair rather hangs down over his forehead, and he holds a book. Who can it be?"

"I think you must be describing the likeness of Aristotle; I deplore it, deplore it. What can they have been thinking of, to place a secular, non-Christian man in the company of the saints and prophets?" He looked more pained than ever, and Berengaria (who privately thought it quite an honor for the saints to have such erudite company) felt it wise to change the subject.

"But my Lord Bishop, you said you had something to ask me, and I have strayed from the subject. Forgive me."

The bishop's face cleared somewhat, and he spoke again, now with less speed and more in command of himself. "Yes. I have heard from my friend in Rome, the Cardinal Pierre de Capoue, that he made your acquaintance at the services for King Richard. He told me of your precarious situation. He especially asked me if I ever met you to inquire about your present welfare. Have you been in touch with King John or King Philip?"

Berengaria was gratified that the cardinal still took an interest. "I have been to see Queen Eleanor, but she had nothing to suggest except to write to King John," she said. "And I did so, but I left Beaufort before receiving an answer. For the time being, there is not so much urgency, because I will be staying for a time with my sister and the count in Troyes."

"Very good, very good! So I shall undoubtedly see you there, and I shall look forward to it." He took his leave, his brow again deeply furrowed with worriment.

Thibaut at once stepped up and presented a group of lords and ladies who had been waiting to meet her. Berengaria was bemused at finding herself almost a celebrity. The new acquaintances would say a few words, then make their escape in order to boast to their friends that they had met the widow of Richard the Lionheart. She actually overheard one lady who had spent two minutes with her exclaiming to another, "And such a charming person! As you see, very plainly dressed, but they say she has not yet come into her inheritance. Oh yes, we became quite good friends."

Presently the group around her melted away except for one couple who had been standing quietly to the side. She had noticed them because they were so unlike the others in dress and manner. They reminded her of the unassuming men and women who used to frequent her parents' court.

The man stepped up and said, "I had hoped to ask the young count, with whom I am acquainted, to introduce us; but he has escaped me, so I shall have to do it myself."

He was sturdy and not much taller than Berengaria. His brown hair was close-trimmed. His eyes were brown as hazelnuts, and he had a bristly square mustache. He wore the look of a man who more often than not finds life amusing.

"Queen Berengaria, I am Pierre Savary de Colombiers, and this lady is my wife, Solange. We are from the Touraine."

He bowed slightly and his wife inclined her head. Berengaria looked up at this striking, ash-blonde lady. Solange was not only somewhat taller than her husband; she also seemed a few years older. She was very thin, almost frail. Her pale hair was brushed back smoothly from her high forehead, to disappear under a blue velvet cap. Berengaria thought she looked a little like one of the long-bodied angels carved on the cathedral portal: but there was more humanity than saintly remoteness in her expression.

"You are a long way from home," Berengaria observed.

"We are, and no doubt you wonder how we came to be here," said Pierre. " As I said, I am acquainted with Count Thibaut. I have vineyards and other properties in Champagne near his domains and my affairs often take me there. He very kindly invited us to be present at the nuptials."

His wife added in her soft voice, "And I am glad he did! We have no such elegant parties in Colombiers, and it is wonderful to see how other folks live."

"I can say the same," said Berengaria. "I am far more accustomed to the tranquility of my little castle in Beaufort-en-Vallée and I find all this high society a bit daunting."

Solange lowered her voice. "So do I! Tell me, did you ever see so many peacocks indoors before?" Berengaria laughed and admitted that she too had thought of this comparison when she first entered the room.

"And with voices to match," added Pierre. Indeed, some of the conversation and laughter sounded like the raucous squawks of those gorgeous but prideful and unmelodious birds.

She would have liked to talk to them longer but Thibaut came to whisper that another guest had asked to meet her and should not be gainsaid. He presented her to Louis, heir to the throne of France, who was representing his father, King Philip Augustus. She realized it had been his litter she and Blanche had seen in the town. He proved to be a pallid, foppish youth, encased in blue satin, who lost interest in her when she did not fawn on him in the manner to which he was doubtless accustomed. After two or three sentences and without a word of farewell he left her and went across the room to an elderly lady leaning on a cane, who was peering at the company with nearsighted eyes. Berengaria could see them whispering and looking at her.

"That is his grandmother, Adèle of Champagne," Thibaut told her. "She is also my aunt, but not one of my favorites. She is a great matchmaker, and had a royal bride all picked out for me and has not forgiven me for making my own choice. I imagine she is assessing you as material for her marriage mill."

Berengaria felt she was learning more than she wanted to about these people, and was glad when the Countess of Blois left, Blanche still at her side and Thibaut on her other arm. That meant the rest of them could retire too. Her feet were beginning to ache with so much standing, and she felt her face was frozen in a permanent smile.

Blanche paused to press Berengaria's hand as she passed her and murmured, "Wasn't this a wonderful evening? I am so glad you are here. Until tomorrow and my wedding day, sister. Rest well!" Despite the long, tiring day, she was still fresh-faced and vivacious. Berengaria on the other hand felt decidedly old and wondered if she were suited for this strenuous life at court.

Once in her room, she went straight to the glass on the wall to see if she looked haggard. To her relief, the face that stared back at her, though not that of a young girl, still showed no lines of aging or exhaustion.

"Maybe I am good for a few years yet," she said to herself. And her spirits rose at the prospect of the coming journey to Champagne, another new land to explore. She thought of the handful of people she had met tonight who seemed genuine and without guile: Thibaut, Pierre Savary and his wife, and the Bishop of Troyes, among others. Perhaps she could find some true friends in this unfamiliar world that she seemed on the verge of entering.

erengaria propped her elbows on the stone wall above the canal and supported her chin with her clasped hands. She looked toward the city of Troyes which spread out to the south on the other side of the canal.

Above the red-tiled and brown-thatched roofs jutted the bulk of the Church of Ste. Madeleine. She stared fixedly at the scene, trying to realize that this would be her home for a while instead of the familiar, circumscribed world of her castle at Beaufort. She turned to survey the tall residence behind her, and its massive door that bore the coat-of-arms of the Counts of Champagne: the house of Thibaut, her new brother-in-law. She was waiting for Thibaut and Blanche to come out and join her.

She herself had come out through that door half an hour ago, leaving Blanche and Thibaut still at table, plucking grapes from a silver dish and popping them into each other's mouth. Thibaut sometimes pretended to nibble Blanche's fingers, and she giggled. Watching them, Berengaria had felt a spasm of envy. "Will I never have this sweet companionship with a husband?" she cried to herself, and jumped to her feet before they could see her distress.

"I will just go out and get a breath of air," she said.

"Do, sister, and we will join you in a few minutes." Blanche spoke without looking up.

Calmer now, Berengaria mused on the events of the last few days.

First, the wedding — and what a wedding! The bride was a vision in rose and white as she walked demurely toward the altar in the vast nave. Her left hand rested lightly on the arm of the portly and solemn Count of Blois. Her gown was edged with pearls and her long golden tresses were capped with a pearl circlet. Around her neck was the silver crucifix that had belonged to her mother and that Berengaria had loaned her. In her right hand she held her bouquet of pink-and-white blossoms.

Behind these two marched the Countess of Blois, beaming with goodwill. Berengaria smiled at the memory of how the countess, giving up any pretense of imperturbability, looked right and left to see how her guests were receiving the spectacle. After her paced Thibaut with Berengaria on his arm. For this happy occasion she had decided to vary her usual costume. Over her customary widow's white was a long plum-colored coat with a regal train. She wore the crown that had been placed on her head at her own wedding in Cyprus.

Afterwards the bishop asked her to sign the official registry as witness to the wedding. "Berengaria Regina, daughter of Sancho, King of Navarre, and Queen of the late King Richard of England," she had written in a bold hand.

Then the journey from Chartres to Troyes had not been unpleasant, thanks to Thibaut's thoughtfulness for everybody's comfort, and the fine homes of his friends where they stopped along the way.

She was aroused from her reverie by her sister's voice, as she and Thibaut approached along the quai.

"I have never been a countess," Blanche was saying. "Thibaut, will you school me?" She was only half joking, for she took her new responsibilities seriously.

"But, Blanche, you have been a princess — isn't that sufficient schooling?"

"Oh, it is not the same thing at all." By now they were standing beside Berengaria and Blanche appealed to her sister, "Being a princess in Navarre is nothing like being a countess in Champagne, is it, Berenguelita? Our life there was so much more subdued, and our parents had no taste for feasting and parties every night. But sometimes I wished they had!"

"She is right, brother," said Berengaria. In the short time she had known him, she had come to think of Thibaut as her brother just as much as Sancho was, and felt perfectly comfortable accepting his hospitality here in Troyes. "She is quite right. If you had ever been south of the Pyrenees and seen our Basque Country you would understand. Our folk are not given to show or ostentation; and our father's court was" — she searched for a word — "it was serious."

Blanche nodded, and added, "But we did have good times. There were tournaments in Pamplona, and the pilgrims who came to stay with us on their way to or from Compostela — they always had tales to tell. So did the troubadours. And sometimes we would all go with my father when he traveled around the kingdom to hold court in Tudela, or Pamplona, or some other city."

"And often — remember Blanche? — jugglers and comedians would come to entertain us, and earn their night's bed and board. We loved to watch them. And you and Sanchito and I would go out the next day and try to jump about like the acrobats, but we only fell down and got black and blue."

Blanche added, "Or we would toss balls in the air like the jugglers, but even Sanchito could never manage more than two at a time." Both women were laughing like little girls, almost convulsed with their memories.

Thibaut put his arm around his bride and she turned her pretty face up to his. "I see," he said. "Your pleasures were indeed simpler than ours, and I wish I could have known you when you were a little lass trying to juggle."

Then he became the serious young count. "But this is what I was about to say. Here we are here in Champagne, almost next door to Philip Augustus and his elegant court in Paris, and we must do our best to be the kind of count and countess our people expect."

"What do they expect?" asked Berengaria.

"They hope to see us put on a brave show, at least as brave as Philip's court. People are fickle, and if we don't pay enough attention to our vassals they might weaken in their loyalty and flock to Paris, and Champagne could be swallowed up by France. My mother was known all over Champagne for her elegant dinners and receptions, so we must live up to her example." He pulled on his mustache as he pondered, then addressed Berengaria.

"Will you stay on a while and help us, sister? Can you shed a little of your Basque sobriety and adorn our court for a few months?"

It seemed a frivolous prospect. Berengaria remembered what she had read about how the Roman emperors kept the populace content with bread and circuses. But she could see why it was important to Thibaut that his subjects should remain happy and amused and proud to be part of his court. She was intrigued. "Surely I have earned the right to enjoy myself for a while," she thought. "And there is certainly nothing to take me back to Beaufort."

"If both of you think I could be of use, of course I will stay. But how could I help?"

The three of them, standing there by the canal, put their heads together to plan a brilliant fall season at court. "First we must have a state dinner," said Blanche, "though I haven't the faintest idea how to start or whom to invite."

"Don't worry," said Thibaut. "My mother's ladies-in-waiting have stayed at court ever since she died. I think they are wondering what to do and hoping we won't send them packing back to the country. They know all about these things."

So they did, and were only too glad to instruct their new countess in the fine points of entertaining.

"Now we will see some life again," said Lady Aline to Lady Charlotte. "Just like it was when our dear old Countess, may she rest in peace, was young and first married the Count."

Charlotte de Vendeuvre was to attend Berengaria until Héloise arrived. Charlotte's husband Hugh had a fine chateau on the River Barse, a day's journey to the east, and was content to stay there, but Charlotte preferred to spend her time in Troyes. Berengaria thought her superficial at first.

As for Charlotte, she was impressed enough by the fact that she was serving a queen, but she clearly doubted if this woman from some probably barbarous kingdom at the other end of the world would prove sufficiently cultured and sophisticated for the high life at court.

"She seems pleasant," said Charlotte to Aline, "but perhaps too modest and retiring."

"We will take her in hand," said Aline to Charlotte.

The first task was to assess Berengaria's wardrobe. Charlotte was soon won over when Berengaria asked her advice. After two hours of inspecting gowns and cloaks and jewels, and making lists of the necessary additions, they developed a respectful if tentative mutual regard.

Héloise arrived, glad to rejoin her friend and full of gossip about Eleanor's health (not good) and her grandchild in Saumur (thriving, already talking at ten months). "Now," thought Berengaria, "perhaps I could send Cristina and Carlos back to Navarre for a time. They feel out of place here; and there are plenty of others to take over their few tasks."

True friends rather than merely servants by now, they thanked her sincerely, for they had indeed been very homesick in Troyes. Cristina embraced her mistress, while a rare smile spread across her husband's face.

"We will come back the minute you ask, madame," Cristina said. "And you must let us know how you are getting on, and say if we can send you anything from home. Perhaps some salt cod, or some good Pyrenees cheese with a proper heft and bite to it?" Cristina had never taken to the soft life or the soft cheeses of the French, which she considered effete.

"Of course I will write and you may be sure that when I am ready to go back to Beaufort, I will need you. But that may not be for some time."

How long, she wondered? Was she taking the path of least resistance, staying on here in Troyes? No, she decided. She was seizing a chance to turn her life in a new direction and to be of service to her sister by learning the ways of the courtly world.

And maybe — the thought was well buried, but it was there — she might, in this new world, meet someone who would look at her as Thibaut looked at Blanche.

he day after Cristina and Carlos left, in a flurry of tearful goodbyes from Cristina and impatient reining in of his horse by Carlos, Berengaria received a message from Bishop Garnier. She had almost forgotten about him but now he reminded her that he had promised to be in touch when she arrived in Troyes. He asked if she would care to call soon, perhaps that very afternoon? Of course she would.

One of Thibaut's footmen accompanied her on the short walk to the bishop's house. He had moved from the episcopal palace into an ancient, narrow dwelling, in order to be near the site where the new Cathedral of Saint Pierre-et-Saint-Paul would rise. This new cathedral had been the bishop's main concern for five years and it seemed likely to continue to be so for the rest of his life.

He received her in his study, where plans for the cathedral covered almost every surface. Apologizing for the disorder, he seated her in a highbacked chair facing his cluttered table, then apologized again for not getting in touch with her sooner. He was as nervous as he had been when she met him at Chartres. He kept picking up papers and tablets and looking at them, with the same worried expression she had seen then. She wondered why, with so much on his mind, he bothered with her affairs.

Soon, though, he found what he was looking for. He placed a few sheets of parchment in front of him and folded his hands on them, then gave her his full attention. As before, he showed more self-possession as soon as he got to the meat of the matter. He leaned forward and glanced down occasionally at the papers.

"As I told you in Chartres, the Papal office takes an interest in your welfare, so I am speaking for the Pope as well as for myself. He has sent me instructions to assure you that the Church will

- 183 -

support your claims to your rightful share of Richard's estate. Furthermore, he told me to help you make a formal claim if you have not already done so."

He sat back to await her reply.

"I have not made a formal claim. I have been trusting to the honor of Eleanor and John, who are surely aware of my rights. I believe that, according to my marriage contract, all of Richard's possessions in Gascony were to come to me after his death, but Eleanor continues to hold them."

The bishop seemed ill at ease. He cleared his throat. "Hm. Yes. Eleanor. Ah. Speaking frankly, Eleanor of Aquitaine is a law unto herself and there is little we could do, or would venture to try, to budge her. In most respects she is an exemplary daughter of the church — generous and zealous. If she sees fit to claim these lands in the south — which, after all, were hers long before they were Richard's — the church has little recourse but to look the other way. And remember, she is seventy-seven; she cannot be with us much longer."

That is what they have been saying since she was sixty-five, thought Berengaria darkly. But she said only, "Very well. Let us forget Eleanor, and Gascony. Does not Richard's brother and heir, King John, have some duty to me?"

"He does indeed," said Garnier eagerly, glad to leave the subject of Eleanor. He shuffled through his little stack of parchments and picked one up. "He does; under English law you are entitled to one-third of Richard's personal estate. Unfortunately, John's first act after his accession was to seize everything in Richard's treasury. So far he has not seen fit to yield any of it to any of the rightful claimants — of whom there are many, but your claim is the largest."

"Of course!" Berengaria was stung to sarcasm. "Why should he give anything up? After all, he is the king. Who is to say him nay?"

"Do not underestimate the power of God's vicar on earth," said the bishop, fixing her with a fierce eye as though she, not John, were the transgressor. "The Pope's holy duty is to protect the helpless and innocent against the predations of the powerful who dare to break God's law."

"And especially," she said with a knowing glance, "if the helpless and innocent happen to be highborn and devout, and if those powerful ones who take advantage of them threaten to dispute the Papacy's supreme authority?"

The bishop looked at her appreciatively and told her that she had grasped the situation. "I will speak frankly. The church will champion you not only for the merit of your case, but also because John has already shown signs of rebellion against the Pope's authority. Success for us in this matter will strengthen the Papacy's position of sovereignty over secular rulers in regard to their Christian conduct."

The words were pompous, but Berengaria understood perfectly. "Thank you, my Lord Bishop," she said as she rose to go. "You have encouraged and heartened me."

"You are a sensible and an intelligent woman, my daughter," he replied. "We will send a message to King John at once, telling him you are here in Troyes and affirming your claim. We will let you know if any answer comes. You will be with your sister for a time yet?"

Berengaria assured him that she would, and hurried back to ask Blanche to be sure to invite the bishop to the dinner they were planning. And while they were at it, why not invite that nice Pierre Savary and his wife, if they were in Troyes? Not all the guests need be of the upper nobility; and did she not have some say in the matter, if she was to sit at the high table?

The first grand party went very well. A dozen dignitaries, including the bishop, were in attendance, as were all the "peacocks," as Berengaria still privately called them. She was disappointed when Pierre Savary sent his regrets because of the illness of his wife. Still, the banquet was a great success, and so were the second and the third. The beautiful sisters from Navarre were the talk of the city and the fame of the brilliant court in Troyes spread as far as Paris.

The weeks grew into months and winter was almost upon them. Berengaria found she was not in the least bored with her new life. Blanche had generously provided funds for a new wardrobe.

After consulting with Charlotte about gowns and jewels, Berengaria would go down to the Great Hall to stand with Blanche and Thibaut to greet their guests. She worked at associating names and faces; she perfected the art of polite, meaningless banter; and she accepted compliments gracefully.

Sometimes she felt a qualm and wondered if she too were turning into a peacock. "But this cannot last long," she would assure herself. "In time all the curiosity about Richard's widow will evaporate; and meantime, why not enjoy myself? What harm does it do that I am admired? And one of these days I will write to Brother Anselmo and ask him to send me manuscripts to translate again." But she kept putting that letter off.

Certainly, she was admired; in fact she was acquiring suitors. Several of the neighboring nobility began dropping in with the pretext of taking up some matter with Thibaut, then sought out his sister-in-law.

"At my age, Blanche, really! What can they see in me?" she demanded of her sister. "I shall not take them seriously."

"Nobody is asking you to take them seriously," said Blanche. "Just enjoy the attention. You have always belittled yourself, Berenguelita. Why not admit that you are attractive? You are, you know. Even at 'your age.' Isn't she, Thibaut?"

Her husband had just entered the Little Hall where the sisters sat; the room was easier to heat than the formal Great Hall. They were keeping warm by the fire on the hearth, each hemming an end of a soft blanket that lay on the floor between them. Blanche had recently discovered she was to be a mother, and everybody was happily preparing for the great event.

"Of course," Thibaut replied, caressing his wife's cheek and letting his hand fall on her shoulder. "It runs in the family. And the little one who will be warmed by that coverlet will be the handsomest of all!"

Blanche reached up to squeeze his hand, but her mind was still on Berengaria's suitors. "And another thing, sister. It's just possible, you know, that your admirers really do enjoy your company. You have the good grace to let a man do the talking and you don't parade your learning and opinions or boast about being the widow of a famous king. You let them feel important."

"While all the time, if I'm not mistaken," put in Thibaut, "you are busy sizing them up and maybe laughing at them, behind that pretty face."

"Oh no!" protested Berengaria. "I am the most charitable and tolerant person in the world. I do like them, most of them — well maybe not that Jean de Brienne, who is so remarkably boastful. Do you know, the other day he told me that he and the king of France are almost like brothers — that Philip hardly makes a move without asking his advice? A likely story! But by and large, they are pleasant and gentlemanly."

There was a pause, and she felt bound to add, "But I would not want to spend more than half an hour with any of them."

The other two laughed.

"Still," said Thibaut, "though my sister-in-law is the second most beautiful woman in France, we should not forget that she is a queen, widow of a rich and powerful king. For all these gentlemen know, you may be drawing a royal pension. That same Jean de Brienne, for example, is about as poor as a lord can be, and may well have his eye on what he sees as an income for life. So may some of the others. Be careful, Berengaria."

"Maybe," she said, "we should simply make a public announcement that Queen Berengaria is destitute, living on the charity of her brother-in-law, and no suitors need apply."

She meant it as a pleasantry, but there was a hint of bitterness beneath her light tone. Nobody said anything for a minute.

Thibaut, not quite changing the subject, asked, "Has the bishop received a reply to his message to King John?"

"None," she replied. "So let us forget my problems for now, and see what plans Blanche is brewing for our amusement."

As it turned out, Blanche did have a plan: that they should take a little holiday from the court and ride down to Isle-Aumont to spend a few days in the old chateau. "You must see it, Berengaria. Thibaut's mother took me there while I was visiting last year. It's a grand old chateau, and it's been in Thibaut's family ever since the first counts of Champagne, hasn't it Thibaut? And just next to it is a beautiful church, and the monastery, and there's a lovely green meadow running all the way to the river."

Thibaut said the trip would suit him very well because he was eager to see how the workmen were coming on repairing the moat. So it was decided that in a few days they would set out for a week in the country.

However, the next day a royal messenger arrived to announce that King Philip planned to honor the count of Champagne with a visit.

"We will not change our plans," said Thibaut. "We will simply invite the king to Isle-Aumont instead of to Troyes. It will be salutory for him to see that we have such a well- fortified castle, so near to Troyes."

Berengaria was curious. "Does it bother you, Thibaut, that you must pay homage to King Philip? After all, your lands, with Blois and Tours as well as Champagne, are twice the size of his."

Thibaut looked at her gravely, pulling on his mustaches while he considered. "No, I do not mind. He is my lord, I am his vassal. As long as he treats me fairly, as he has always done, I willingly acknowledge his supremacy. But who knows, in this imperfect world, when I might have just cause to rise up against my king? Such things happen. And it is well for him to see how prepared I am to defend myself."

"God have mercy on us!" exclaimed Blanche. "How serious we are becoming! Come, Berengaria, let us go tell our ladies to begin the packing."

Berengaria hardly had time to familiarize herself with the chateau at Isle-Aumont before the flurry of preparing for the king's arrival claimed everybody's attention. The banquet was the first concern. Though it was known that the king ate sparingly, his entourage would not hold back. The cook sent men to scour the countryside for sides of beef, haunches of pork, and all the pheasant and quail they could find. The baker fell to preparing pigeon pies and dozens of loaves for the oven. A small army of recruits from the village swept and scrubbed the hall, then laid sweet-smelling fresh rushes to soften the stony floor. Thibaut, with his seneschal in Isle-Aumont, Guillerme Lavalier, inspected every inch of the walls and the fortified gatehouse, lest the king's sharp eye detect a chink in his defenses.

The chateau had not seen such activity since the days when the first count built it a hundred years before.

The royal visit was brief. Philip arrived just after noon, and Thibaut took him on a tour. Then came the dinner and with it some polite conversation. After one last goblet of wine, Philip assembled his retainers and was off. He was on his way to Orléans, where the Duke had been showing signs of restiveness.

"I think he was impressed, though he certainly didn't show it," said Blanche the next morning. "But he did tell me that the fig pudding was excellent. I must tell the cook; that will set him up for life."

Blanche was taking advantage of her condition and sat with her feet on a stool and a shawl over her legs. Thibaut was at her side, and Berengaria opposite. Lady Charlotte and Lady Aline were nearby, stitching little gowns for the future count or countess. Guillerme Lavalier was half in, half out of the group as he supervised the servants who were clearing off the high table and bringing the room to rights. He was a tall, beak-nosed, balding man, very devout, not much of a talker but a sharp listener, and devoted to the count.

"I hardly spoke to him," said Berengaria. "When he first came and we greeted each other, I had hoped to remind him of our days in Saint Jean-d'Acre, and thank him again for his kindness to Joanna and me, when he arranged for us to be lodged so comfortably. But he changed the subject before I could get started, and told me he was pleased to see me looking so well in view of my recent loss, and said he remembered what a valiant warrior Richard had been, both as companion in arms and later as worthy adversary. I suppose that was by way of making sure I knew he resented Richard's conquests in Normandy, after he came back from the Crusade. Then he turned away without waiting for a reply."

"Such a strange man," Blanche said. "You never quite know what he's thinking. And all the time, he keeps looking around as though some enemy might be lurking behind his back."

"Well," said Thibaut, "I had more conversation with him than either of you, while we were touring the fortifications. After he made sure I was still loyal and content, he began talking about you, Berengaria."

"About me! Whatever for?"

"I'm not sure, but I have an idea. He was full of questions, asked me how old you were, how long you would be in Champagne, even if I knew if you had ever been with child and miscarried."

Berengaria listened in amazement. The ladies-in-waiting were all ears.

"He did say that he found you much handsomer and more assured than the insecure young bride who came with Richard to the Holy Land nine years ago. Then he asked me what your prospects were, meaning, I suppose, had you received any pension as Richard's widow. I told him as little as I could of that; not his business, I say."

"What a meddler!" said Blanche. "None of it was his business. What can he be thinking of?"

"Here's my guess. His last questions put me on what may be the right track. He asked if any of the nobles around here had been paying court to Berengaria. I said she was much admired by many men, but by none, to my knowledge, more than by any others. Then he asked if Jean de Brienne was often at our court. I said he was indeed. And the king said, 'He is one of our most loyal vassals.'"

Guillerme Lavalier groaned eloquently. Lady Charlotte could not contain herself. "He is scheming to marry our queen off to someone of his own choosing! How monstrous, if it's to be that odious Sir Jean!"

Berengaria was quite pale. "Can Philip actually order me to marry anybody he likes, against my will?"

"Of course he can't," said Thibaut. "You are not his vassal. But he can connive, oh how he can connive. And my guess is that he sees you as a person of consequence whom he might manipulate somehow to serve his own devious ends."

All six were silent, thinking their own thoughts. Then Lady Aline spoke up. "He asked me before dinner why my husband was not here. I told him I had been a widow for two years. He asked me if I had inherited my husband's properties in Vendeuvre. When I said yes, he looked me up and down and left me. At the time I thought him merely rude and inquisitive, but now I suppose he might try some day to marry me off to one of his retainers, just to keep our lands under his thumb."

"He reminds me of a spider," said Blanche. "Spinning webs, waiting to see who gets trapped, then deciding how to dispose of them."

"Come now," said Berengaria. "I have more cause than anyone to be alarmed, but I intend to think well of King Philip until I have reason not to. Let us not borrow trouble. And if it comes to a showdown, I will certainly have the Bishop on my side as well as all of you, and, I trust, the good Lord above."

"Amen," said Guillerme Lavalier.

lanche's child was born in May of 1200. Mother and father were enchanted with their tiny daughter, from the fuzz of blond hair on her round little head to the ten perfect miniature toenails on her plump pink feet. They named her Bérengère.

Life at court became calmer, with less entertaining. Thibaut began to think that with such a competent wife to serve as his surrogate, it might be possible to fulfill the vow he had made long ago, and go on crusade to the Holy Land; especially if Berengaria would stay on in Troyes. There was nothing calling her elsewhere, so she agreed. Thibaut began rounding up his men and laying in supplies.

Nothing more was heard from King Philip. Jean de Brienne, though frequently at court, seemed no more and no less persistent in his pursuit of Berengaria, if that was what it was. She found him less and less prepossessing, with his close-cropped head of black hair like a furry egg, and his wild black eyebrows and square, bristly face — he always looked as though in need of the services of his barber.

As for King John, the bishop had heard nothing since forwarding her claim, though John's Chancellor of the Exchequer had sent word that the matter was being looked into. Then after months of silence, a message arrived: an invitation from John to come to England to talk about the settlement he proposed to make. He addressed her as "Dear Sister" and offered apologies for the delay in his reply to Bishop Garnier's letter, blaming it on the pressures of war and government.

"But now that our affairs are running more smoothly," he wrote, "we intend to give you complete satisfaction." He offered her a safe-conduct, since she would have to travel through some of the lands which he claimed but which Philip was trying to reconquer.

Her first reaction was intense pleasure. At last she could visit the unknown country of which she had been queen — if unacknowledged by nearly everybody. Then she had second thoughts. Could she believe the king of England? She tried to remember everything she had ever heard of John Lackland, as he had been called before he fell heir to England and the Angevin Empire. "I must talk this over with Thibaut and Blanche," she decided. "And Bishop Garnier too." She hurried off to find Blanche, and to ask Charlotte to see that a message went to the bishop.

Two hours later, the little council met in Thibaut's chamber with its tall windows looking out to the fields and forests north of the city. But their thoughts were not of the peaceable view but of the militant king of the land across the channel.

"At first I thought of course I should accept his invitation," said Berengaria, "because I want so very much to go to England, and to see my affairs settled. But what do you think, my friends? Can I take John at his word?"

Thibaut was for caution. "Remember, Berengaria, King Henry imprisoned his wife Eleanor for fifteen years, to keep her from meddling in his affairs. What would stop John from the same rough tactics, once you're in England and far from any protectors?"

Berengaria in her first enthusiasm had not thought of that. Then she remembered, and told them, what Richard had once said about his younger brother: "He's as slippery as an eel and as mean as a ferret." And she told them it was really because of John that Richard had agreed to the truce and cut short his Crusade — because he knew John and Philip were conniving to seize his lands.

Bishop Garnier added, "And I have heard that Richard distrusted John so much that for a time he considered making his young nephew Arthur his heir rather than have his kingdom fall into the careless hands of John. In the end he changed his mind, knowing that the result would only be a bitter war."

The consensus was that Berengaria should not go to England. But how to refuse, without closing the door to further parleys?

Blanche thought she should sit tight and wait for John to make another move.

"But why should he?" asked Thibaut. "He has everything to gain by letting the matter drop. What if you asked him to come here instead? That would show him that you consider yourself his equal and you intend to set your own terms."

The bishop was more practical. "John has more sense than to come to Champagne, where the count is a dutiful vassal of John's deadliest enemy, the king of France. No — suggest a meeting in Chinon. The castle there is the historic seat of the Plantagenets. It is still in John's hands and at least now, Philip is not threatening it. If you wish I will help you frame a reply."

Among them they composed a firm but diplomatic message, thanking John for his promise to make the settlement, declining with no explanation the invitation to England, and restating Berengaria's position. Then she proposed the meeting in Chinon — which she explained she had heard so much about from Joanna and had always wanted to see. "And I am sure that you, brother, would be the guide who could show it to me the best."

The letter sent, there was nothing to do but sit and wait. With fewer social duties and more leisure, she had no excuse to put off resuming her life as a scribe. She wrote to Brother Anselmo, and he immediately sent her a book of homilies to copy. She set up a work table in the Little Hall, complete with inkstand, piles of parchment, quill pens and a small pearl-handled knife to sharpen the quills. She slipped comfortably back into the familiar routine.

Blanche was amused. "I would have thought that by now you would have gotten tired of all that drudgery, Berenguelita. But here you go again, staining your fingers black and bending your back over the books like a ploughman over the plow."

"It is not drudgery to me, Blanche. I know you can't see it, but this is really how I love to spend my time. It takes me back to those days with the monks at Leyre, when I had so much to learn and Brother Anselmo taught me so patiently." It was, she reflected, actually the only thread that had run through her life from those days as a girl at the monastery, until now when she was approaching middle age.

Still, she was always glad to stop work and tend to little Bérengère, now nearly a year old. The child was everybody's darling. The ladies-in-waiting vied for the privilege of dressing her, brushing her baby curls and singing to her when she cried. But Berengaria had first claim after Blanche, and loved to serve as baby-tender whenever Blanche had to accompany Thibaut on some state business.

Once she had harbored a hope that some day she might be a mother. Now that hope was all but dead. So it was a deep joy when this little niece came into her life. With every month that passed she took more delight in watching as she grew. When the child put her little hand trustingly in Berengaria's and took her first toddling steps, or nestled in her lap, gazing solemnly up into her aunt's face with eyes as blue as cornflowers, Berengaria felt an outpouring of love like nothing she had ever known.

Late one afternoon she was busy with pen and parchment, taking advantage of the last light that slanted in through the window and fell on her table. She wore a loose robe of forest green — she had given up her widow's white except for public occasions — and, as usual when at home in the palace, let her hair fall unconfined without any covering. She was comfortable and absorbed, and not too displeased with her efforts; her neat lettering was far more legible than the work she was copying. She sat back, holding up a page and admiring it. A very fair copy indeed!

There was a commotion at the door. She turned to see Jean de Brienne squeezing past Lady Charlotte, who had been trying to get in to announce him before he pushed her aside.

"Ho, the queen and I are old friends by now, Lady Charlotte. No need to be formal when I come calling." He strode in and sat down with a thump in a chair near the work table. Charlotte stood by the door with her mouth open in bewilderment. Sir Jean appeared to be inebriated.

Berengaria spoke as calmly as she could. "Lady Charlotte, will you be so good as to tell the Count that Jean de Brienne wishes to see him in the Little Hall?" Charlotte gathered up her skirts and ran to fetch Thibaut.

"We don't need Count Thibaut," growled Sir Jean. "It's you I've come to see, my pretty one." He tried to smile, but it was more like a leer. Berengaria thought he looked rather like a black pig.

He sat staring at her, the unpleasant grin frozen on his stubbled face. He seemed to have forgotten what he meant to say next.

"Perhaps you should come back another day when you are feeling better, Sir Jean."

"Nonsense, I feel perfectly well." He rose unsteadily to his feet. "Come, let's settle this right now. You must know, don't pretend you don't, that we are meant to be man and wife."

He stumped around the table. To her astonishment he seized her hands and pulled her to her feet, then roughly put his arms around her and tried to kiss her. She jerked her head aside so his mouth landed closer to her ear than her lips. He reeked of wine. She screamed, and struggled out of his arms. With all her force, she slapped his face. He staggered against the table, knocking over her ink bottle and in horror, she saw the dark stain spreading over the page she had just finished. She looked at him in rage.

He glared back at her with his little pig eyes. "So that's the way it is, my high and mighty queen. We'll see if you don't sing a different tune one of these days. I have friends in high places, you know."

At that moment Thibaut ran in with two burly knights and took in the situation at a glance. The knights escorted Sir Jean unceremoniously from the room, each holding an elbow and pulling him along, while he protested loudly. The last thing Berengaria heard as he disappeared was a muffled roar, "King Philip will hear of this!"

"Are you all right?" Thibaut asked anxiously. "He has not harmed you?"

Berengaria, still in a daze, shook her head.

"Then I must go see that he leaves and understands that he is no longer welcome at our court. Here is Lady Charlotte, and I'll send Blanche to you."

She looked around her. It had all happened so fast. She felt shamed, defiled by his touch. Then her eyes fell on her table and the page she had worked on all day, blackened and illegible, lying in a pool of ink.

That was almost more devastating than Jean's beastly behavior. She sank into her chair, buried her face in her hands and wept.

It took her days to recover her equanimity. She could not forget the horror of that brutish embrace.

"I think you need distraction, sister," said Blanche, "and you shall have some. Bishop Garnier sent word that he would call this morning. Maybe he will have some news."

The bishop had no news of King John, but he did bring a welcome suggestion. "I know that you are interested in Arabic manuscripts. Would you like to visit the Rachi Synagogue School?" he asked her without preamble and with hardly a stutter, as soon as he was in the hall. It seemed that as he got to know one better, speech came more easily; but he still spoke in paragraphs.

"It was founded a hundred and thirty years ago by Rachi, Rabbi of Troyes. He was a learned commentator of the Bible and the Talmud, and he made the school famous. Its library has hundreds of rare manuscripts in Latin, Arabic and Hebrew. I would be glad to take you there and introduce you."

Berengaria was too polite to tell him that of course she had heard of the school, and had been wishing ever since coming to Troyes that she might have entrée to it. "I would dearly love to go, Bishop."

In two days' time the bishop kept his word, escorted her to a marble-pillared building in the center of the city, took her in to introduce her to Rabbi Josef, who would be her guide, then left. The rabbi was a deliberate man with a white beard that almost reached his waist: the very picture of an Old Testament prophet, Berengaria thought. He greeted her civilly and, almost on tiptoe, led her into a spacious, silent chamber where a dozen serious men sat at tables, scrutinizing important-looking bound volumes and rolls of parchment. With great ceremony the rabbi unlocked a drawer to show her some of the treasured documents, and permitted her to sit down at a table to examine them, while the chief librarian looked suspiciously on.

Presently it became clear to that scholar and the others in the library that this well-born woman with the unusual interest in their precious books was unlikely to mark them or tear out pages to secrete on her person. From then on she was welcome to visit and join the studious group.

She looked forward to these sessions, to the chance to lose herself in reading. One day she came on a compendium of medical treatises that looked familiar. She recognized the translator's initials: one of her fellow scribes at Leyre. She remembered how excited Brother Anselmo had been when the tenth-century Arabic manuscript arrived, on loan from the copyists' school in Toledo. He had put his most skilled scribe to translating it into Latin. Now that translation had found its way here and would be translated into Hebrew. She sat staring at it, entranced. What a small world is this world of learning, she thought — then corrected herself: what an immense world. This manuscript's story spanned three centuries of history and thousands of miles of geography. She felt blessed to be a witness to its travels.

How foolish she was to be distressed by one loathsome little creature like Jean de Brienne, in comparison with so many lives devoted to passing on precious knowledge from generation to generation.

Nevertheless, she still felt a shiver whenever she remembered his words, "We are meant to be man and wife... King Philip will hear of this!"

oward the end of May in 1201, Blanche, Berengaria and the baby Bérengère went down to Isle-Aumont again. Thibaut said he would join them in a day or two, after meeting with the nobles who were to go with him on his crusade. He planned to leave for the Holy Land soon, but not before the birth of his second child, which was imminent. Everybody hoped for a boy. Even little Bérengère, now a precocious one-year-old, had learned to say *"petit frére"* — baby brother.

At the chateau they set up a couch for Blanche in a shady spot under the beech trees. To one side, the tall stone building gave shelter from any errant breeze. To the other, a sweep of grass descended to the old monastery and the church. Lying there, Blanche could hear the soothing murmur of the river.

But she was not soothed; the weather was warm, the air close and sticky. She missed Thibaut and she was uncomfortable. By the third day she was untypically fretful.

"I am so glad you are here, sister," she said to Berengaria, who sat near her, working at her embroidery. "What has happened to my temper? Even the baby annoys me when she tries to climb up and get my attention, but the poor child means no harm. Thank you for taking on so much of her care."

"You know I'm always glad to. And of course you are short-tempered, after all these months of waiting and with your time so near. Now Charlotte and I will take the little lass to see the birds flying in and out of the dovecote. Just close your eyes and think peaceful thoughts."

Blanche smiled wanly and tried to obey, but no sooner had she closed her eyes than a soldier came galloping through the gate and toward where she was resting. He reined in his horse barely two feet from her couch.

Startled, she raised her head. Even before dismounting he shouted, his voice cracking with anguish at his terrible message.

"Oh Madame, I bring sorrowful news. There has been a dreadful accident. Your husband the count was thrown from his horse as he was leaving the city. He struck his head against a stone balustrade and before we could reach him he died."

Blanche turned white and fell back in a faint. The flustered man looked wildly about. Berengaria, Héloise and Charlotte had come running when they heard the clatter of hooves. The baby girl toiled behind them as fast her short little legs would allow. Berengaria reached her sister in time to hear the man's words, and glared at him for the brutal way he had delivered this awful news. She supported Blanche's head with one arm, while trying to quiet Bérengère, who had begun to wail at the sight of her stricken mother.

Charlotte ran to the well and brought a pail of cool water. She dipped her kerchief in it and laid it on Blanche's brow. When the countess came to her senses, she was pale as death and clung to Berengaria, moaning and sobbing. Then she cried out and doubled up with a sudden pain. The others looked at each other. "Yes, I think it has begun," said Charlotte quietly.

There could be no thought of getting her back to Troyes. That evening after a long and difficult labor she gave birth to a son. Charlotte and Héloise were invaluable. Charlotte found a midwife in the village. (Berengaria was ashamed to remember she had once thought her empty-headed and frivolous.) Héloise, the experienced grandmother, knew how to help the midwife and tend to the infant.

Ten days later, back in the palace in Troyes, Berengaria and the ladies watched while Blanche nursed the tiny child and smiled into his intent, pursed-up little face.

"I was afraid that she might resent him, somehow blaming him for his father's death," said Aline. "You know how we women get these silly notions, and no help for it. But the Blessed Virgin be thanked, Countess Blanche is as loving a mother as our little Thibaut could wish for."

The child had, of course, been named for his father — and his grandfather and his great-grandfather. He had been christened Thibaut IV, Count of Champagne, as soon as they returned.

His father was buried in the crypt of the Church of St. Etienne. Blanche had these words engraved on her husband's tomb:

"Par ce tombeau dont elle voile le comte, Blanche, fille des rois de Navarre, devoile tout l'amour dont elle brûle pour lui."

(With this sepulchre where she buries the count, Blanche, daughter of the kings of Navarre, bears testament to her overpowering love for him.)

Then, to everybody's surprise, she put grief behind her. Like the true Basque princess that she was, she did not let private sorrows interfere with her duties as a ruler. She threw herself into her new calling: to pick up the reins of government and carry on, almost as though Thibaut were advising her from beyond the grave. She was firm, just and tireless.

After a month of official mourning, visitors were again welcomed to the court, and the countess and the queen received them in the Little Hall. To everybody's relief, Jean de Brienne was not among those who came to offer condolences.

Then came a disturbing message from King Philip.

To our good vassal Blanche, Countess of Champagne and widow of our loyal Count Thibaut III, whom we sincerely mourn:

We have heard with sorrow that Sir Jean de Brienne fears he may have offended Queen Berengaria with his over-effusive suit. He has assured us that he regrets this unfortunate incident, and that his conduct will be exemplary if he is permitted to pay his respects to you and your sister again. It is our wish, therefore, that Sir Jean be again welcome at the palace of the counts of Champagne."

Blanche showed it to Berengaria. "What do you think?"

"Well! Apparently he does have 'friends in high places.' I wonder why King Philip is so solicitous of a man like that? Still, I suppose you will have to let him in if he comes; this is really an order, not a request."

"I suppose I will. But I shall make sure that several stout men are in the same room with him."

So black-bearded, porcine Sir Jean — half laughingstock, half threat — presently came to call, when the hall was filled with people and his presence was not conspicuous. He avoided Berengaria, for which she was grateful. "Perhaps he is no more than an ill-mannered buffoon who misbehaved under the influence of drink," she told herself.

However, as the hall emptied with the approach of the dinner hour, and only a few people lingered, he came over to speak to her, bold and brusque as ever. "Have you heard anything from King John lately?" he blurted.

A rather strange way to open a conversation, she thought. But she recognized it as a ploy to learn her prospects of receiving her inheritance. She answered politely, concealing her amusement at his transparency. "No, not for many months, Sir Jean. Why do you ask?"

He seemed not to hear her, stroked his bushy beard, said "Harrumph," and walked across the the room to where Lady Charlotte and Lady Aline sat, each with a child on her lap. Berengaria could not quite hear the ensuing conversation, but she saw with surprise how Sir Jean turned away and stomped out of the room. When he was gone, she asked the ladies what had happened.

Lady Aline giggled. "He came up to us without so much as a greeting, and barked that he had come to pay his respects to Blanche and asked when we expected her to join the company. He was quite put out when I explained that she would not be back from Epernay until tomorrow, and he attacked that poor beard and pulled on it as though he meant to tear it off his chin. He glared at me so accusingly that I almost felt responsible for his disappointment. He said, 'Be so good as to tell her I was here,' and off he went."

"Be prepared, Blanche," Berengaria told her sister the next day. "It's your turn to receive the attentions of our ambitious friend. He's obviously decided that a widowed and well-endowed countess in the hand is preferable to a penniless queen in the bush."

Penniless, or almost, she certainly was. Thibaut had tactfully provided her with a small regular pension so she could keep herself with some independence, and Blanche continued the practice. But it pained her to be so beholden. Bishop Garnier seemed to have run out of ideas. With the business of the new cathedral almost entirely on his shoulders, he had much on his mind besides her welfare. It was hard not to give in to discouragement. She thought wistfully of her native land.

"Maybe when Richard died I should have gone back to Navarre," she said to Blanche. "It would have been so easy to forget all about my rights as widow of England's king. I could have married some little lord or other and settled down in his valley domain. Then today I might be rocking the cradle, helping my husband worry about whether the rain would hold off until the laborers got the hay raked and what price wool would fetch in the fall."

Blanche looked skeptical. "What a lot of nonsense, sister. You could not possibly have been happy, buried away so far from the world."

"True. For better or worse, I've become accustomed to this life and I really like it. But I shall never, never give up my fight to get my inheritance so I need not depend on your generosity for the rest of my days."

"Now that's nonsense too. You know how happy I am to have you with me, and the children are so fond of you. Don't even think about any other home."

The fit of despondency passed. "God must have had some purpose when He created me the daughter of one king and wife of another — though He failed to provide me with a kingdom," she mused to herself that evening while preparing for bed. "Perhaps He is not revealing His purpose because it is my turn now to do something. Very well, I will send again to King John and tell him I am coming to Chinon, with or without an invitation."

he did send the message.

In midsummer John replied that he had received her letter and would be pleased if she could come to Chinon, where he planned to spend some time early in August with his young bride, Isabelle of Angoulême.

Berengaria accepted with gratitude, expressing her pleasure at the prospect of meeting him and his queen. She asked Hugh de Vendeuvre, Charlotte's husband, to accompany her. A stodgy but astute man, he usually preferred his country estate to the pomp of the court in Troyes. But after Thibaut's death he had loyally offered his services to the widow and moved to the palace. This pleased his wife as well as Blanche, who found Hugh a sturdy, sensible advisor.

On a hot August day Berengaria, Hugh, Charlotte and their attendants rode up the rough stony road to the castle at Chinon. As their steeds plodded along, Berengaria looked around her at the poor hovels clustered on the hillside that rose from the River Vienne, as close as they could get to the protection of the castle that loomed above. The massive fortress was strung along the cliff, hugging the edge as though to claim this rocky precipice as part of itself. She felt a chill, despite the warmth of the day, and her thoughts returned, as they had done ever since this journey had begun, to the king she was about to meet.

Charlotte, who rode beside her, said, "I wonder what our reception will be like. I only hope that there will be a breeze and that the king will offer us some cool beverage when we arrive — this heat is hard to bear. What do you think, Berengaria? Will your brother-in-law be more gracious as a host than he has been as a correspondent?"

"I can hardly say, Charlotte. I know him only by reputation, and I have seen him only once and then from a distance, where he sat beside Eleanor in the Fontevrault church at Richard's memorial. He did not look particularly gracious then."

She remembered the occasion vividly. John had been seated far from her but as she observed him she formed a picture of him in her mind: as a less attractive version of Richard — perhaps not quite so tall and robust, and darker and smoothshaven. But uneasy — she remembered how he had kept turning his head to eye the guests in the church as though looking for an enemy. She expected to find that he had all the assurance and arrogance of the Plantagenets. Would she be able to stand up to him, if he proved as cold as Eleanor?

Then she had a sudden thought: Eleanor had resented her because she did not give Richard an heir. But if she had produced a son, John would not be king of England today. He should be grateful to her! She smiled at the irony of the situation; and as they entered the formidable gates of the fortress, she thought she could meet John without trepidation.

The vast oval expanse of the castle grounds within the protective walls lay baking in the sun, grass brown and gardens wilting, with no life visible except for some listless workers bearing buckets of water to the parched rows of cabbages. A pair of black-robed clerics disappeared into the chapel. A servingman, peering out from a doorway in the nearest building, bobbed his head and ran into what must be the royal lodgings, in a tall circular tower.

As Berengaria's party waited for what would happen next, the tower door opened and there emerged a short, stout man, red-haired and perspiring. In spite of the heat he wore a heavy crimson cloak over his doublet and leggings. He was loaded with so many golden chains and jeweled rings that he jangled. He gestured sharply to the man to help the ladies down from their horses.

"Greetings, sister, and welcome to Chinon. The heat is unbearable but there is nothing I can do about it. You may find it more comfortable in your chamber. We will meet at dinner." He ordered the servingman to conduct the party to their quarters and went back inside before they could even respond.

Berengaria, Charlotte and Hugh looked at each other in bewilderment. Then Charlotte laughed. "So much for our gracious reception!" They followed their guide through a narrow arched door to their austere lodgings. Berengaria thought her dark chamber, cramped and with no softening tapestries on its gray walls, seemed more suitable for a prison than for a royal guest.

Later they were summoned to the small, airless royal dining room. John had changed into a costume of princely black, which set off his golden embellishments even better. For this journey Berengaria had resumed her snowy widow's garb, determined to dress the part of the deserving queen, loyal to her husband's memory.

Queen Isabelle sat on John's right. Berengaria and Charlotte had thoroughly discussed the young queen on their journey, comparing notes on the gossip they had heard.

"She had been promised to Hugh of Lusignan, they say, when John caught sight of her," Charlotte remembered.

"And didn't John snatch her away almost on the eve of her wedding? I wonder what she thought of that! Maybe she was flattered to catch the eye of a king."

Here at the king's table, Isabelle looked hardly more than a child. She was modest and retiring but very pretty. She said "I am delighted to meet you," to Berengaria, Charlotte and Hugh, like a girl who has been told to mind her manners in company, then spoke no more. Every so often, John would look at her and his face became that of a lad in love; he often caressed her smooth blond hair, or placed a choice morsel on her plate. It gave this sour king a whole new dimension.

"Why, I believe he is positively besotted with her!" thought Berengaria. She caught Charlotte's eye; Charlotte winked.

The only other member of the party was Philip, Bishop of Durham, a stocky smooth-faced man with pale blue eyes that missed nothing but gave no hint of his reactions. He wore ecclesiastical finery to rival the royal garb of his king. He sat beside Berengaria and greeted her with a reminder: "I was present at your wedding to King Richard in Cyprus, but I did not have the pleasure of conversing with you. But I remember how lovely Richard's queen looked on that occasion, and I am pleased to see you looking so well today, in spite of the sorrow of losing your royal consort."

"Thank you, my Lord Bishop," she replied. "But what brings you to Chinon, so far from your English bishopric?"

"King John asked me to be here because I was a witness to your marriage settlement, and I am familiar with the terms, which will probably be discussed during your stay here."

John, at the head of the table, was listening glumly to this exchange. He gestured to the steward for more wine. Raising his goblet he said, in his high rasping voice, "To your health, sister. We are pleased to welcome you to Chinon, and we are only sorry you felt unable to visit our court in England. If you had come, we could have taken care of these trifling matters sooner."

"Thank you, brother." She took a sip of wine to acknowledge the toast. "I am sorry too that circumstances kept me from traveling to England. As England's queen all these years, I have always wished to visit the land of my husband's birth."

"Perhaps your circumstances will soon change for the better and you will be able to travel more widely. I am sure that improved prospects would please your friend Bishop Garnier of Troyes. He has made himself a confounded nuisance, always writing to me. And so has his Pope." His voice had become a whine.

"But the Bishop was only acting with my consent. If he has been a nuisance, it was on my behalf and I am the one to blame."

"Never mind, never mind." John banged down his goblet. "Tomorrow we will meet with Bishop John and with my chancellor and they will explain the settlement we propose to make. I think that you will be completely satisfied."

And that was as far as they got that evening. John had drunk more wine than he should have and, a little tipsy, took his wife's hand and retired.

Next morning he was all business when they assembled in his audience hall. Like all the rooms in this dour castle, it was cramped and unwelcoming. The round oaken table nearly filled the room. Hugh de Vendeuvre sat at Berengaria's side while Bishop Philip read in a droning monotone the pertinent terms of the marriage settlement. Though they were vague ("If Richard should predecease his queen, his heir is to make adequate provision for her and her issue,") they seemed incontrovertible.

John listened, expressionless, while the chancellor got down to details. He told Berengaria that John would grant her 1,000 livres a year from his English treasury and, in France, the city of Bayeux, the castle of Segre, the town of Montbazon and the formal right to Beaufort. She was surprised to learn that the little castle she had lived in so long had been legally hers, granted to her under the marriage settlement. All that time she had thought she was living under Eleanor's sufferance in Eleanor's castle.

When the chancellor had finished, John folded his arms and watched while Berengaria and Hugh conferred privately and briefly. Then she looked at the King and chose her words carefully.

"This seems more than adequate. I am grateful that at last I will receive what has been due me ever since Richard's death."

John flashed a mean look at her, recognizing the veiled accusation; but he only said, "Good. We thought you would agree. The settlement is generous, but of course no more than what is due you. My chancellor will draw up the formal transfers at once, and he will send you the first payment on our return to England."

He got up to leave but turned back and said gruffly, as though remembering his manners, "You are welcome to stay as long as you like. Unfortunately, we must leave today for Normandy, but our people here will make you comfortable."

When the others had left Berengaria and Hugh looked at each other, amazed at such a swift resolution to what they had expected to be a lengthy wrangle. Berengaria was relieved — and puzzled. What kind of a monarch was this? John was like a caricature of a Plantagenet king. He knew he should be firm, but he did not know how to combine majesty with diplomacy.

They left the cool but dank and oppressive castle hall to find Charlotte, seated on a bench in the garden, fanning herself languidly and surprised to see them so soon. When they told her the outcome and that John had more or less invited them to stay at Chinon, it took no more than a minute to agree on a speedy departure. They had achieved what they had come for; why stay?

"Still," said Hugh as they rode down the cobbled road they had ascended only the day before, "it did seem remarkably easy. I am not too sure if that King John means everything he says."

heerfulness was in short supply at the palace in Troyes, the following summer. There had not been a word from John, much less any thousand marks a month, since the visit to Chinon some eight months ago, when Hugh had gloomily predicted that promises would not be kept. Moreover, the weather was horrid. Mid-June might as well have been March.

For weeks rain had wrapped the city in swirling curtains of damp gray. Cold winds whipped through the leaves of the poplars along the canal. Sensible people stayed indoors, fortifying themselves with mulled ale and complaining about the unseasonal weather.

A little after noon on such a day, a horseman, his hooded cloak wet through, rode across the bridge and along the quai, looking for the house that bore the insignia of the counts of Champagne. When he found it he dismounted and handed the reins to a groom who had come running from the stables. Before the visitor had time to lift the massive brass knocker the door opened.

"You must be Pierre Savary de Colombiers," said the serv-ingman.

"I am," said Pierre. "Who else but a country bumpkin from the Touraine would be so foolish as to come calling on a day like this?"

The man, not accustomed to raillery from his mistress's guests, did not smile. "You are expected. The ladies are in the small reception room." He gingerly took Pierre's dripping cloak and his soaked leather gloves.

Pierre smoothed back his unruly brown hair and entered the room where Blanche, Berengaria and several of their ladies sat sewing and gossiping. A candelabra had been placed by the blazing hearth and draperies hung over the windows to hide the dismal rain. The room was bright and cheery. Pierre blinked a little in the light and warmth, and his spontaneous smile embraced the whole company. Blanche put down her needlework and rose, hands outstretched. Her graceful stance was somewhat marred by an unnaturally large billow in her voluminous skirts, where her little daughter had hidden herself. Pierre took her hand and she cried, "Why, you're all icicles! Come here by the fire and dry yourself, Sieur Pierre. We received your message yesterday, and we are pleased that you are able to take time to visit us while you are in Troyes."

"Thank you, Countess. You are good to take in a man you doubtless hardly remember, and one so wet and bedraggled!"

"But I remember you well, and so does my sister." Berengaria, whose white headdress had fallen loosely about her shoulders, quickly pulled it up over her hair and fastened it, then smiled up at him in agreement. Blanche went on, "We often think back to that happy evening in Chartres, and in fact Berengaria has more than once told me we should invite you and your lady to visit us. We were sorry her illness prevented it last year."

"Your wife is not with you, Sieur Pierre?" asked Berengaria. "I remember how much I enjoyed our conversation in that crowd of wedding guests where I hardly knew a soul. I hope sometime soon you will bring her, so we may renew our acquaintance."

Pierre told them, matter-of-factly, that his wife had died a year ago. "She had been unwell for some time, and it was God's mercy that her suffering could end."

He plainly was not asking for sympathy, and Berengaria sensed that it would have been painful for him to speak further of his loss. So she only said, "Oh, I am so sorry!" and Pierre went quickly on.

"I know you too have had a loss, Countess; your husband was a good man. Champagne has been deprived of a noble ruler, and I have lost a worthy friend."

Bérengère had crept out from her mother's skirts to get a look at this large stranger her elders seemed so glad to see. She stared up at him, solemn and round-eyed. Blanche, proud mother, introduced her and Pierre bent to bow gravely over the hand of the shy little girl.

"What a pretty gown you are wearing, Bérengère; it is just the right blue to set off your golden curls. I can see that you are going to grow up to be as beautiful as your mother and your aunt."

She gave him a dimpled smile, and was about to hide again but Blanche led her away to turn her over to her nurse.

Settling into the chair beside Berengaria, Pierre stretched out his long legs toward the hearth and sighed with pleasure. Steam rose from his rainsoaked boots and leggings.

"It is good to be here and not pounding along on that rough-gaited horse of mine," he said. "Let me advise you, Queen Berengaria, never to venture to ride from Sens to Troyes in one day, in the rain."

"I doubt if I am likely to try it, especially since I cannot imagine any reason to be in Sens in the first place. May I ask what brings you so far from your home in the Touraine?"

"My business is not very exciting. I have a small property near Sens and my overseer sent word that the vines were withering for no apparent reason, in spite of all the rain this spring. So I thought I had better have a look. Else we may have none of our fine wine to bring to the fair next year, and that would be a disappointment to the good people of Champagne." His broad face, more that of a countryman than of a courtier, broke into an infectious grin.

"And what did you discover about the mysterious ailment of your vines?" asked Berengaria. She did not know much about vineyards and was curious.

"Well, I found them with hardly any new growth and disgracefully shriveled. I told them to mend their ways, or I would tear them up by the roots, which I suspect we will have to do unless my man can come up with some miraculous remedy. But enough about me and my silly vines. We surely have more important matters to talk about." He fidgeted and recrossed his legs.

"Tell me how you are. You are looking very well, I must say. So is your sister. How do you occupy yourself? Do you go out in the city very much? Troyes is a fine town, and I expect you feel quite at home here now. Has King Philip come to visit since Thibaut died? Or perhaps you have been to Paris?"

"Wait, wait!" Berengaria laughed. "So many questions! How can I answer them all? I would never have thought you such an inquisitor!"

"I beg your pardon. It is just that you — you and your sister, that is — have made me feel so welcome, and I am genuinely concerned about you both, especially since the count is no longer here. I will now be more circumspect." He stroked his brown mustache, pursed his mouth and frowned as though considering weighty matters, and cleared his throat with a preparatory "Ahem." When their glances met, she saw the twinkle in his eye.

"First, we shall take up matters of state, namely King Philip. Champagne is certainly crucial to his peace, and I should think he would have come to see how his vassal's widow was getting on."

"We have not heard from him for some time. He came only once, soon after our arrival in Troyes, on a formal visit to Thibaut, but it was very brief. He did, however, send a proper message of condolence when Thibaut died, and also his congratulations when little Thibaut was born."

"And well he should. The infant will be Count of Champagne some day. Philip would do well not to ignore this land just because it is now ruled by a woman; he may not realize what a very capable woman she is." He turned to Blanche, who had just seated herself on his other side. "Every one I talk to seems full of compliments for your energy and ability, Countess."

"Why, thank you, Sieur Pierre. I am lucky to have good advisors — and a most supportive sister." She looked across him at Berengaria, and he saw the affection in both faces.

"Well, I must say you have both been most supportive of this poor wayfarer, and I thank you for taking me in out of the rain. Now do tell me, Queen Berengaria, how you are enjoying your stay in Troyes. Do you follow the progress of the new cathedral, and take note whenever it rises by an inch? And have you been to visit the famous Rachi Synagogue School?"

"Yes, on both counts. Bishop Garnier keeps me thoroughly up to date on his cathedral, in fact I am almost overloaded with information. And he was good enough to introduce me to Rabbi Josef. I was quite flattered when the very proper rabbi and all those serious men with their long beards decided it was safe to let me poke about in their library."

He chuckled. "I am sure they were not hard to persuade. They must have been delighted to have such a comely visitor, and a scholar to boot."

"Now where have you heard that? It's true I have done some copying and translating, but you could hardly call me a scholar."

"Well, we will argue about that another day. Now, Countess," rising and turning to Blanche, "I do not wish to outstay my welcome, and they will be expecting me at the inn. May I come back in a few days' time, before I leave for Colombiers?"

After he had left, Blanche and Berengaria looked at each other in wonderment. Then Blanche erupted in helpless laughter. Her pink cheeks became even more pink, and she raised her blue eyes to heaven. "Oh sister! We seem to be blessed with another suitor, and will you have him, or shall I?"

Berengaria considered. "I think I shall claim him," she said. "After all, he sat beside me all that time, waiting for his boots to dry; though once or twice he did try to bring you into the conversation."

"Still," said Blanche, "I am his hostess. And I was the one he asked for permission to return, and very properly too. I think he must be mine."

"We are being most uncharitable," said Berengaria. "He is probably a very good man. Just because he doesn't dress like a fop or chatter like a magpie, like so many of the men who come to your court, we need not laugh at him."

"Perhaps not. I suppose he is just lonely, he misses his wife, and he has simply come to call on two old friends — if that; two acquaintances, whom he knew in happier times."

"Anyway, I am glad he is coming back. Maybe he will have better news about his vines."

erhaps because she felt guilty for laughing about him with Blanche, Berengaria dressed with care and greeted Pierre with particular cordiality when he called again. Blanche had gone out with the children, for the weather had briefly cleared and she said she might not have another chance to show them what the sun looked like for the rest of the summer. So Berengaria and Pierre were alone in the hall except for two ladies who were preoccupied with their work at a loom at the far end. The welcome sun, so long absent, streamed in the windows, which had been opened to air out the hall. Outside, the fresh-washed leaves of the poplars and planes that stood in a row along the canal danced and glimmered like flocks of green butterflies. Berengaria's highwaisted gown, almost the same color, clung to her breasts and fell straight to her feet in loose folds; her headdress and the scarf loosely knotted about her neck were of shimmering yellow silk.

Pierre's immediate thought was that she looked like the first daffodil of spring, and he impulsively told her so, then wondered if he had been too bold. She did not even blush; she was used to compliments by now. She led him to the two chairs drawn up before the hearth where a modest fire burned. "We hardly need the fire, but Blanche insisted on having it lit; it is still not full summer. And she said to tell you she was sorry not to be here to greet you."

This was not quite true. Blanche had actually said she supposed they would have to light the fire, because undoubtedly Pierre would have been out in the rain and gotten his boots wet again. She added that she was sorry not to be there to get more clues as to which sister he was pursuing.

When they were seated he was all seriousness. "Now to continue with my inquisition. How are you really getting on? How do things stand with King John?"

She looked at him in surprise, then annoyance. "So, have you heard rumors of my difficult situation?" Her voice became icy. "Is all the world talking about how Queen Berengaria is living off charity?"

"No, no, all I know is what Thibaut told me, of how John kept putting you off and that his unkindness made you unhappy. Believe me, I am only thinking of your peace of mind. Forgive me if I was too abrupt."

She was mollified and before she knew it, she found herself recounting her interview with John, and the broken promises.

"Is anybody helping or advising you?"

She told him how Bishop Garnier had at first done all he could, but seemed to have run out of enthusiasm.

"So just a few weeks ago I decided to take matters into my own hands. I remembered how my brother Sancho once lectured me severely, when I was in despair about another difficult time in my life — far more painful than this." She looked off toward the window, her thoughts far away — remembering those anguished days when she had to accept Richard's desertion. Then she looked back at him, managed a smile and spoke again quickly, as though afraid to stop and consider her words.

"What Sancho told me then was, in brief, that it was up to me to take charge of my affairs. So I did, and I have remembered his advice to this day. Three weeks ago I wrote directly to the Pope, and reminded him that it is three years since Richard died, and not a penny of his estate has come to me. I am sure that the good Bishop in his letters probably did little more than set forth the facts, expecting them to speak for themselves. But I was quite shameless, and presented my case as that of a helpless woman, throwing herself on the mercy of the Church."

She was surprised at how much she had confided. But she felt that he would understand. At the end of her recital, he rose and took a step toward her.

"Well done, Queen Berengaria!" he said heartily, and seemed about to clap her on the back but caught himself and sat down again. "Now do not let grass grow under your feet. Keep after Pope Innocent. If there is anything I have learned in my life as a countryman, it is the value of persistence. You must not give in to discouragement, whether it is a hay crop ruined by rain, or a vineyard that stops producing. 'If you fall on your face while chasing a hen, pick yourself up and go at it again,' as the farm folk say in the Touraine."

Realizing that this was not entirely appropriate and that he had strayed somewhat from the subject, he hurried on, "What I mean is, if the Pope ignores you, you must simply pick yourself up and try again. In fact, it would do no harm to write again at once, just to keep him fully aware that you are not going to give up. Remind him that you are royal by birth and by marriage, and that John, by his perfidy, is in effect displaying his scorn for every royal personage in Christendom!"

"You are very eloquent, and your maxims ring true. I seem to have found another brother, as wise as my Sancho."

"I will be pleased to try to fill his shoes, but it may be difficult because I am well past youth and unlikely to grow any more. And I have heard that your brother is very large and very tall. I expect both my feet would fit in one of his boots!"

Berengaria laughed, then asked, "Would you like to help me compose my next letter? You seem so sure of what is my proper course."

"I would not," he said. "That would be presumptuous, and I have already presumed on your kindness by inquiring so closely about your affairs, and speaking my mind so freely. Besides, I see already, though our acquaintance is short, that you are a woman of extraordinary competence — which is only exceeded by your beauty." Again discomfited by his impulsiveness, he rose quickly, saying brusquely, "Now I must go."

She rose too and they looked at each other for a moment. Berengaria thought to herself, "What a kind man! I am so lucky to have his friendship."

She put her hand on his arm and asked, "Will you come back soon, and perhaps I shall have some progress to report?"

"I must leave tomorrow, but even if you have no progress to report, I shall hope to hear from you. Please thank your sister again for her hospitality." He seemed about to say more, but then with a quick pressure of her hand, and an abashed smile, he bowed and left.

Berengaria told Blanche the whole conversation that evening.

"Aha," said Blanche, sniffing. "Now I am not so sure about this Pierre. He must be after your money, sister; why else would he urge you so strongly to keep asking for your inheritance? It is none of his business, after all. He is not a rich man, and he is looking for a fortune. Be careful, Berengaria."

Berengaria looked at Blanche in surprise. "I am sure you are wrong. He is simply trying to help me. I can tell."

"Maybe. But Berengaria, you are a very trusting person. Remember that you have been hurt before by a man whom you believed in. I am merely suggesting that you go slow in thinking of Pierre Savary as a disinterested friend."

Berengaria had thought the pain of Richard's repudiation was long behind her, but now it came back like a knife in her breast, all the worse for the fear that again she had laid herself open to disillusion.

Without replying, she left the room and very slowly climbed the stairs. Could Blanche be right? Was Pierre not the sincere man she had thought but a conniver, using her to pull himself up in the world — as Richard had used her to try to father an heir to his throne? Was he merely a fortune hunter like that base Jean de Brienne?

She felt a sudden desolation. She had been so glad to think that she had found a new friend. But yes, Blanche could be right. Pierre's eagerness to help could indeed be due only to his own hopes of material gain.

Slowly she undressed and put on her nightdress. She climbed up on the high bed and pulled the covers up to her chin. Staring into the darkness, she thought over her conversation with Pierre and what Blanche had said. She was still unwilling to believe he was as grasping as Blanche thought. Yet, there was that clumsy compliment about her beauty. She had thought little of it at the time, but it was untypical of him. Was it his inept attempt to play the courtier?

Her head had begun to ache. She turned on her side and curled up, hoping for sleep. Just before she drifted off it came to her that there was nothing wrong with Pierre's advice, no matter what his motive. She decided that she would compose another letter to Rome, the very next day; and that she would follow his suggestion and exploit the fact that she was a proud queen, albeit a poor widow, who was being victimized by a king who had made promises he had failed to keep.

"There," she said, as she affixed her seal to the rolled-up parchment. The seal bore the letters "B.R." — Berengaria Regina — in brilliant red wax. "As Pierre might say, 'Nothing ventured, nothing gained.' No matter what he's up to, that maxim is as true for me as for him."

he news of the death of Eleanor of Aquitaine reached Troyes by a slow, roundabout route. When she died at Fontevrault Abbey in March 1204, by all accounts quietly and without suffering, Abbess Mathilde was with her queen until the end. She sent word to King John of England and to Queen Eleanor of Castile, the only two surviving children of Henry and Eleanor. Presently the news reached Paris and quickly circulated through King Philip's court, where Adele, the old queen dowager and Philip's mother, heard it. At sixty-six she tended to be forgetful. So it was some time before she mentioned the matter to her crony Jean de Brienne, who was in Paris to ask her help to get an audience with Philip Augustus.

Jean hurried back to Troyes and went straight to the palace. He strode into Blanche's reception room, hardly waiting to be announced, at the hour when he knew it would be most crowded.

He stood in the doorway, arms akimbo, feet apart, his black-capped head swiveling from side to side. "Well, my friends. Have you heard the news?" He paused for effect. "Queen Eleanor is dead."

The announcement did not arouse the attention and questions he had hoped for. Everybody had been expecting this for so long — after all the queen was eighty-two — that it was an anticlimax. Still, there were murmurs and conjectures. More than one of those present looked at Berengaria, wondering if this might mean an improvement in her prospects.

The question was on Jean de Brienne's mind too. He hurried across the room to where she was conversing in low tones with Blanche and Hugh and Charlotte de Vendeuvre. "I agree," he heard her say. "I shall go at once."

"If I were you, madame," Jean interrupted, "I would go nowhere except to Paris. King Philip will be seizing all of Eleanor's possessions he can get his hands on, before John does. If you are to come out with any of the spoils you had better get access to his ear as soon as possible. If you like I will put in a word for you."

"Thank you, Sir Jean," she said with some coolness. "Your advice is excellent. In fact we had just come to the same conclusion. And thank you for your offer of help, but I believe I will be able to arrange an audience with King Philip without assistance."

She set off for Paris the very next day, accompanied by Hugh and Charlotte, after sending a swift messenger ahead to let King Philip know they were coming. Charlotte had never been to Paris and was beside herself with joy at this chance to visit such a famous and fashionable city. Even Berengaria was caught up in the excitement, in spite of her resolve to be calm. She took great pains with her preparations. She wanted to strike just the right note with Philip; she did not want to appear as a drably dressed supplicant in widow's weeds. With the help of Héloise and Charlotte, she selected her most becoming gowns and a few of her most precious jewels. But not too rich, or too many jewels — she must not look overly prosperous.

When Hugh saw the dozens of saddlebags that the two women proposed to take, he grumbled. "Are we going to Rome then, and for a year, instead of simply to Paris for a week?" He went off to command three more mules.

All during the two-day journey Berengaria thought of what she would say and do when she met with Philip, and went over it with Hugh.

First, she would kneel. This was correct, since she was the widow and heir of Richard, who had owed Philip fealty for his possessions in Normandy.

Then he would probably ask her what she wished of him, though he would doubtless already have a good idea. She must have her reply firmly in mind: a sober, respectful request that he recognize her rights to those of Eleanor's possessions that were part of Richard's dowry to his queen. Then, she hoped, he would assent. But would he? She had learned from her few encounters with him that Philip did not always behave as one expected.

Paris was as splendid as Charlotte had hoped. They rode along streets lined with haughty palaces and crowded with citizens dressed is such finery that Charlotte thought it must be a holiday.

Berengaria said she believed this was the usual thing in Paris. Hugh muttered, "Show-offs!"

At last they crossed a graceful bridge that led to the Isle of Lutèce in the Seine, site of the ancient Capetian palace. They were expected. A pair of gorgeously costumed footmen ushered them to a magnificent throne room. It rivaled the Pope's palace in Rome, but Berengaria thought it was in better taste. Philip seemed to prefer unostentatious elegance to gaudy display. The tapestries glowed with color, the satiny wood of chairs and tables was decorated with delicate silver filigrees and the golden candelabra were as graceful as the tendrils of a vine. She looked down at the soft royal-blue Turkish rug on which she stood, with its subtle patterns of rose and turquoise. She suspected that despite his hasty departure from the Holy Land, Philip had found time to acquire treasures to take back to France.

As they entered the room, Philip stepped down from the high throne at the other end and advanced to greet them with the utmost courtesy. Unlike John, he was restrained in both dress and speech. Where John stuttered and bumbled, Philip spoke suavely and confidently. Where John blurted his words curtly and without a trace of tact, Philip was circuitous, walking around a point before pouncing on it. And unlike John, he listened.

The interview did not go exactly as she had envisioned. There seemed no point in kneeling, when Philip stood before her and engaged her in conversation at once.

"We welcome you to our court, Queen Berengaria, and you also, Sir Hugh and your lady," he said smoothly. "We remember with pleasure our visit to the home of the late Count. I hope the Countess is well; I am sorry she could not accompany you but I know how demanding her duties must be."

"My sister was sorry too, and asked me to convey her respectful greetings."

"Of course. Now, we trust you will be comfortable in your lodgings in our palace. Are you finding Paris agreeable?"

Berengaria assured him that from the little she had seen of it so far, Paris was quite agreeable — in fact, wonderful.

"It is not like any other city I have ever seen," said Charlotte.

"I should hope not," said Philip, the semblance of a smile raising the corners of his lips. "We like to think that here in Paris we set the standards of culture and civility for the rest of the world. But come, we must not keep you standing. Let us seat ourselves." He led the way and ascended his throne.

Berengaria was invited to a velvet-cushioned chair facing the king, with Hugh and Charlotte seated on either side. Several of Philip's courtiers flanked him, standing silently during the interview.

Philip resumed, "Now tell me, how may we serve you?" His sallow, sharp-featured face showed no expression beyond a polite curiosity.

"You may affirm to me, my lord king, that certain lands of my late mother-in-law, Queen Eleanor, will be duly recognized as mine. According to my marriage contract they were to come to me and my heirs at her death, if Richard predeceased me."

"To what lands do you refer?" Philip asked. ("As though he did not know!" she thought.)

"To these only," she said, referring to a small parchment that Hugh handed her. "The provostships of Falaise and Domfort, and the viscounty of Bonneville-sur-Touque. These demesnes, all in Normandy, should now rightfully be, I believe, in my dowry." She looked at him with composure but her mind was racing ahead to plan what she would say if he raised an objection. She hardly expected he would agree outright.

He did not. Neither did he object. Instead, he changed the subject.

"Tell me, cousin. Are you in touch with your brother-in-law, King John?"

Why did he address her as "cousin?" She was wary. "Not often. Why do you ask?"

"Because I understand that the Pope has ordered him to make restitution to you for what is due you from Richard's estate. Has he done so? And if he has, why are you so in need that you must hasten to my court to beg, when your mother-in-law is hardly cold in her grave?"

She was shocked. He must have spies everywhere! How did he know that she had indeed heard — finally — from Pope Innocent, telling her that he had ordered John, under pain of punishment by the Church, to keep his promises? And if he knew that much, he also knew that John had not complied. He was playing with her — but how did he dare to insult her by telling her she was "begging?" Yet it would not do to antagonize him. Not now.

With a great effort to appear as controlled as he, she replied, "In answer to your first question, John has not sent me a word or a farthing. As for my appearing here to beg, I assure you that I came only in order to present my legitimate claim to what is lawfully mine. I believe it is a claim which the king to whom I owe allegiance is bound to honor."

Philip simply looked at her, but she thought she detected a touch of admiration in his fixed regard. Into her mind's eye flashed the picture of Pierre de Savary as he congratulated her with a "Well done, Queen Berengaria!" She felt a surge of confidence. The discussion was off to a good start.

Philip, however, seemed to have tired of the game. "Very well," he said, rising. "We will talk about this again in a little while. It is still only midafternoon, and I recommend to you a stroll along the river; the views are very fine. Meantime, I will summon my secretary. You have, after all, given me very little notice so it will take some time to assemble the necessary documents."

The resplendent footmen ushered them from the room.

When they met two hours later Philip was less the remote, unapproachable sovereign and more the efficient man of business. When Berengaria and Hugh entered the audience chamber (Charlotte had elected to go out into the city), they found the monarch seated at a long table. Several scrolls and what looked like charters with impressive seals were arranged neatly on the polished surface. Philip's only attendant was a man who kept picking up the documents and peering at them shortsightedly — undoubtedly the secretary.

"Again, welcome, cousin, and Sir Hugh," Philip said as soon as they were seated opposite him.

Once more he called her cousin. She and Hugh and Charlotte had wondered at this. Berengaria supposed it referred to the fact that Richard's mother Eleanor had been the first wife of Philip's father Louis. This hardly made them cousins, but she took encouragement from it; maybe he would consider her case favorably due to kinship, far-fetched as it was.

He got to the point at once.

"Unfortunately I cannot grant you the three cities you claim in Normandy. I have already taken possession of them and I intend to keep them."

He paused and looked directly at her, as though awaiting some reaction. Something about his tone made her believe this was not the end of the matter. She did not reply. He gave his characteristic slight smile — which she had learned did not necessarily indicate amusement.

"You may wonder why I refuse, since it is true that you have a legal right to them. I will show you.

He placed a map on the table between them. "Here is Domfort, here is Falaise and here is Bonneville. As you must know, John and I are disputing all this part of Normandy. I have full confidence in my ultimate victory. In fact, I have already taken a key stronghold, Chateau Gaillard on the Seine."

She started.

"Yes, it fell to our forces last month."

Mention of Chateau Gaillard brought back the memory of how Richard had loved his "Saucy Castle" more than he loved her. But the bitter recollection was overborne by gratitude that Richard had not lived to see his beloved fortress fall.

Philip went on. "It was — it is — a formidable castle and was bravely defended for seven months. It cost us many men. Your husband was a master at designing fortresses. But not even he could have foreseen the way we finally breached its defenses."

"And how was that?" asked Hugh. "I have seen that castle, and I thought it was impregnable."

"Why, one of our clever fellows found a drainpipe that led from the cliff where we were encamped up to the castle privy. It was big enough to crawl through, and so he did. Once he was inside the walls, he opened a gate for the rest of the soldiers, and then it was just a matter of time; the garrison was weakened by the siege and we soon overpowered them."

Hugh chuckled in appreciation, but Berengaria did not — this seemed an undignified way for such a mighty fortress to fall.

"Still," Philip went on, "if Richard had been the general in charge of defending Chateau Gaillard instead of his feckless little brother, he might have pushed that soldier back down the drain and our French troops might still be there besieging it." All three were silent for a moment, imagining what might have been.

Philip went on, "But the past is past. I have a word or two on the future that I think will interest you."

Hugh, who had been waiting patiently for some concrete offer, straightened up and listened attentively.

"You will understand that I cannot, in the interests of France, release these strategically located cities in Normandy to you. But I uphold the French law, which requires that the lord who denies a vassal's legitimate claim to a property, for whatever reason, must provide a substitute of comparable value." He paused and looked at Hugh, then Berengaria, as though to increase the suspense. "So I offer you, madame, instead of the Normandy demesnes, the city of Le Mans and its revenues, for your lifetime."

"Well!" said Berengaria, nonplussed and with a gleam of hope.

"Well…" said Hugh, nonplussed and puzzled. He looked at her warningly, and her first enthusiasm gave way to suspicion. Why should Philip make such a favorable settlement? She knew Le Mans was the fairest city in Maine, renowned as birthplace of the counts of Maine and Anjou from whom Richard was descended.

The King had been watching them. "I can see that you wonder why I make this offer. There is no reason not to tell you frankly. If you hold Le Mans, your brother-in-law would hardly dare to try to take it from you by force — that would bring down on him the full wrath of the Church, far more than he has already received and ignored. And if John attacked, it might even persuade your brother Sancho to intervene with an army. To say nothing of my own resistance on behalf of my vassal. So with you securely in charge there, I can turn my attention elsewhere. Do you see?" Hugh was looking less resistant. Berengaria thought what Philip said made a great deal of sense.

"And there is more. Since the city is yours only for your lifetime, it reverts to the crown of France on your death, which we trust will be far, far in the future." He bowed to her slightly. "Thus it is certainly in my interest to secure such an important possession, by such peaceful means. Now, perhaps you would like a few minutes to discuss this."

He tactfully removed himself while they talked the proposal over. Cautious Hugh reminded her that Henry, Richard and now John had all fought Philip for Le Mans; in fact only the year before Philip had regained the city from John and his allies among the barons of Maine. Why should Philip give up this hard-won prize?

"He may prove to be another John, making promises he does not intend to keep."

"I think he means what he says, and his reasons ring true." She convinced Hugh that they should accept, but he insisted that they ask Philip for more details before a final agreement.

Berengaria walked to where Philip stood at a window looking north to the cathedral of Notre Dame, its square twin towers and arrow-like spire silhouetted in black against the crimson sunset sky.

"My father began building that cathedral forty years ago," Philip said. "It goes so slowly — yet I hope to see it completed in my lifetime. Already — do you not agree? — it makes a magnificent crown to our city."

"It does," said Berengaria. "When we walked along the Seine, it quite astonished us with its size and grace. It reminded me of Chartres Cathedral." She added diplomatically, "I expect when it is finished it will be even more beautiful."

They walked back to the conference table, and after all were seated, Berengaria said formally, "We appreciate your generous offer, Philip. We are inclined to accept, but could you spell out the terms for us?"

The secretary took over. In return for the possession of the city and the right to collect revenues therein, Berengaria would do homage to Philip as his vassal, and he as her lord would defend her rights against all. The bishopric of Le Mans would retain the right to collect its own revenues, as would those barons who were still vassals of Philip. Everything else was Berengaria's.

The residence of the Counts of Maine would be made ready for her whenever she wished.

"This was the home of your husband's forebears," Philip said. "There is also an old royal castle in the city, but John almost destroyed it in 1199, and anyway it was quite drafty and cold; you will find the Counts' palace much more comfortable."

"My lord king, or may I say cousin?" He shot her an appreciative glance. "I have no objections to these terms, and I am as grateful for your generosity as I am admiring of your skills as a ruler. Perhaps I can learn something from you!"

"So shall we sign the documents?"

Berengaria was now Dame of Le Mans. Such an immense change in her circumstances — it would take some getting used to.

36

"Why are you crying, Aunt?" asked three-year-old Thibaut. The family were gathered in Blanche's bedchamber to hear the news Berengaria had brought from Paris. Thibaut stood with his sturdy little legs apart and looked up at Berengaria in puzzlement. "You said you were happy."

She wiped her eyes, then knelt down and hugged him. "Yes, I am happy, Thibaut, because I am going to have my own home at last. But I am sad too." She looked up at Blanche and tears filled her eyes again. "I will be leaving your mother, and you and Bérengère, and I shall miss you all very much!" She kissed him and stood up, half laughing through her tears. Bérengère climbed down from her mother's lap and clutched her aunt's skirt, whimpering in sympathy.

"Here, here!" said Blanche briskly. "No more crying. Your aunt is moving to her new home, children, but we will certainly go to see her, and she will come back to visit us, too. Now we must all help her get ready."

Wrenching herself from this comfortable haven would be hard. Before she did anything else, Berengaria had one small task, which she had decided on during the trip back from Paris. She sent a brief message to Pierre Savary, to tell him of her new circumstances.

"I owe him that much," she told Blanche. "I did promise to keep him informed."

Blanche was still suspicious. "Mark my words, when he hears that you're Dame of Le Mans, he'll come running to ingratiate himself with you."

"I'll deal with that when the time comes." She quickly changed the subject; she herself was not sure how much she should trust Pierre Savary. "Now I must really start sorting through my belongings. Blanche, how could I have accumulated so much? But dear me, it has been five years, hasn't it? Remember when I first came, and we thought it would be a visit of just a few months?"

Héloise helped her pack and so did Charlotte, as well she should; thanks to her encouragement, Berengaria had practically doubled the size of her wardrobe. But she had nobody to blame but herself for the quantities of books and manuscripts, enough to fill a whole chest. Some, she realized guiltily, should be returned to the library of the monastery at Leyre. She wondered if Brother Anselmo were still alive. She had had no word for a year. She would have to write when she reached Le Mans.

And should she not go collect the belongings she had left at Beaufort? She dreaded the thought of returning to the place where she had been so happy and later so miserable. Then she brightened, remembering Cristina and Carlos, who had served her faithfully there. She could ask them to join her again, and fetch her things on their way.

She wrote them at once, and in a few weeks received an answer in Carlos' painstaking hand — he had learned to write, after a fashion, at the cathedral school in Pamplona.

> *Esteemed lady:*
>
> *I would be honored to enter your service again. Cristina and I will go to Beaufort, which we remember very well, and carry out your instructions. I should tell you that my wife and I now have two sons. Will there be room for us in your new house? They are quite small and very well behaved.*

She smiled, picturing two diminutive dark-haired Basque boys, creeping about the halls of the palace in Le Mans, trying not to be noticed.

Carlos's letter concluded:

> *Cristina asks me to tell you that we have often spoken of you and wondered how you were. She says she has never forgotten her long journey to the Holy Land with you, and that life here in Navarre is not nearly so exciting. We will arrive in Le Mans by Michaelmas, God willing.*

God was willing and they duly arrived, two days before Berengaria herself, and were standing on the palace porch with their little sons behind them when she saw her new home for the first time. It was impressive, this residence of the Counts of Maine and Anjou, and far more like a palace than that of the Counts of Champagne. It was taller, more massive, with two towers and a ten-foot-high wood door set in its pale-gray stone facade. Above the door was the coat-of-arms of the Counts of Maine and Anjou, freshly painted and gilded.

Carlos and Cristina ran from the porch to help her down from her horse. Both were a little shy, but Berengaria pressed Carlos' hand and embraced Cristina warmly, deeply touched.

"And you are now a mother, Cristina, with these two little ones. Yet you do not look a day older!" Berengaria marveled, looking affectionately at the bright-eyed face and the cloud of curly brown hair.

Cristina could not say the same. This dear mistress, whom she had always thought of as forever young, now looked her years. She was as slender and shapely as ever and her dark chestnut hair was as lustrous and carefully arranged, the gaze of her green eyes as direct and kind. Her olive complexion, tinged with rose, was as smooth and blemish-free as that of a girl. But the cheekbones stood out a little more, there were dark shadows under the eyes, and two lines were etched on her brow (as though she had been thinking too much, Cristina suspected).

"You need not say the same to me," Berengaria said quickly, reading Cristina's expression. "I am nearing forty, and I look it, I know. But with you two here I already feel younger. Now you must help me to get properly settled."

Within a fortnight she became fairly well acquainted with her new home and her new city. The former was wonderfully spacious. It had a hall of noble proportions for state events and council meetings, with a tall, broad arched window that gave on a small town square, which was lined with other stately houses but none so grand as hers. There was a whole suite of rooms on the first floor for the administration of the city and county. Her apartments on the floor above were commodious. Next to the bedchamber was a large room with three tall windows, looking over the ramparts toward the south where the city was spreading beyond its walls onto the plain. She decided this would be her private audience chamber, and a study where she would resume her book work, when she got around to it.

As for the town, confined within its thousand-year-old Roman bulwarks, she first thought it a hopeless muddle of dwellings and shops, some centuries old and some new and pretentious, jammed together along narrow streets that twisted about as though they had once been cowpaths, as perhaps they had. She was pleased to find the private chapel of the counts in a corner of the square. Exploring the city, she oriented herself by the two tallest structures — her own palace, and the Cathedral of Saint-Julien.

On her first visit to Saint-Julien she was struck by the resemblance of the carvings on the main portal to those at Chartres. It was almost as though they had been carved by the same hand. Inside she met an aged, stooped sacristan, who was shuffling about in the gloom replacing candles. He looked up at her with a crooked smile when she asked him about the portal.

"You have a good eye, my lady. It's true, the carvers from Chartres came here to study our cathedral, before they did their own." He stopped for a coughing spell, then went on. "You know our Saint-Julien is much older than Notre-Dame de Chartres, and we make it more beautiful all the time. Soon we will finish our magnificent new choir, twice as large as what you see." He gestured toward the far end of the vast space where the high altar stood, gleaming with gold.

She thanked him for his time and pressed a coin into his hand, then walked slowly along the broad nave. Worshippers and pilgrims were quietly praying or simply standing, taking in the majesty and peace. She felt a gentle tug on her sleeve. It was the little sacristan, with a final word.

"I see by your dress, my lady, that you are in mourning, perhaps for your husband? If you say a prayer to Saint Julien for the soul of the one who has died, he will listen most attentively; this is St. Julien's Day." She thanked him again and gave him another coin, for the candle she would light. Then she went to kneel before the altar.

Although she daily said a perfunctory prayer for Richard's soul, this day seemed different — the beginning of a new life, when she could cast off the bitterness and anger that so often assailed her when she thought of him. She bowed her head and let peace and forgiveness flow through her. Unwittingly, he had proved her benefactor, for it was because she was Richard's widow that she found herself now so miraculously rescued from penury.

"Blessed Saint Julien," she prayed, "intercede with our Lord for the heavenly rest of Richard; and know that his widow will from now on try to remember only his bravery, his generosity and his fierce championship of Christianity. May he abide forever in the Grace of God."

She lit her candle, then knelt again to give thanks to God and to pray for guidance. She was not above reminding Him of what He owed her. "Since You have given me new duties and unfamiliar responsibilities, dear Lord, You must also give me increased wisdom and strength. I have never been the ruler of a city. Watch over me and guide me to be just and to do Thy will."

She soon found she would need all the wisdom and strength she could muster.

She wrote to Blanche, a few months after her arrival:

> *Some days I might have given up and come back to Troyes to knock on your door. But somehow I have endured until now and I am determined to go on. Let me tell you as quickly as I can what has happened. The seneschal who was here when I arrived, one Guillaume des Roches, whose duty it is to collect the revenues and hand them over to me, proved to be keeping a good half of the money for himself. Then I learned that King Philip had confiscated the city of Chateau-du-Loir. It was in my dowry but somehow we did not discuss it in Paris. He had given it to the wicked seneschal Guillaume. I was angry, but what could I do? Well, Blanche, you may be proud of me yet. I thought of you, ruling so well in Champagne; and I thought of our father, the wise King of Navarre (I wish I had paid more attention to how he dealt with his problems); and I prayed.*
>
> *Then it came to me: suggest a compromise before Guillaume becomes an enemy. So I told him I would give up all my claims to Chateau-du-Loir if he would leave his post*

as seneschal here. He agreed, maybe a trifle too easily. I do have misgivings. But now I have appointed my own seneschal, Herbert de Tucé, from one of the old noble families, and I have great confidence in him. What do you think, have I begun well as Dame of Le Mans? When can you come to see me? I miss you all very much.

She was fortunate in Herbert de Tucé. With his encouragement, most of the lords of Maine pledged their allegiance, and brought their ladies to call. All were curious about this woman with the fascinating past. They knew her story in broad outline. She was the daughter of Sancho the Wise, late king of the Basques. Married to Richard the Lion Hearted, whom she accompanied on the Crusade. Sister of Blanche, Countess of Champagne, and of King Sancho the Strong of Navarre. Tragically widowed, unfortunately childless. And apparently a favorite of King Philip Augustus since he had given her Le Mans to hold as her fief entire. And still so handsome, despite her age.

Many came forward to offer their services: "Only say the word, and I will do your bidding, whatever it is." Empty words, she thought. Among them, though, she found one man whom she was inclined to trust. This was Paulin Boutier, who came one day and asked for an audience. She received him in the council chamber.

At first she thought him undistinguished and dull. He was middle-aged and middle-sized, with medium-brown hair and an unassertive presence. He had a wispy mustache, a tendency to squint and a sharp nose, and she tried to repress the thought that he looked like an inquisitive mouse.

He bowed, and she asked him, "How may I serve you, Sieur Paulin?"

"By permitting me to serve you, my lady. You are new here, unacquainted with your people, whereas I have lived here all my life and know the city and its ways very well. I would like to put my knowledge and counsel at your disposal." He was more self-possessed than she had expected.

"And why should you do this? I have no great wealth, and could not recompense you as you doubtless deserve. I appreciate your offer, but you must tell me more about your reasons."

"I have no need of wealth. I have extensive lands outside the city, and I live as well as I care to. As for why I wish to serve you, the story goes back a long way." He paused. She saw that he was a methodical man, who took thought before he spoke.

"My father served with your father-in-law, King Henry, a score of years ago. Besides being King of England, Henry was also Count of Anjou and he rightly claimed Maine and Le Mans but was disputed by King Philip. My father fought at Henry's side in many battles against the French king and was true to him until the end. I grew up with my family's loyalty to the counts of Anjou as my example. I was glad to serve Henry's son, your husband Richard, if briefly, before his death. Now I would like to put my humble abilities at the disposal of Richard's queen."

She looked at him, considering; she liked what she saw and what she had heard. His words had the ring of honesty. He reminded her a little of Blanche's counselor in Troyes, Hugh de Vendeuvre — steady, almost stolid, but sensible and trustworthy.

She rose from her chair and reached out her hand. "Sieur Paulin, I accept your offer, and I am grateful. You shall be the first man of my council, and I will be glad of your advice in finding others to serve me." He bowed, and their long association was launched. Over time she found him totally dependable and a fund of down-to-earth advice and guidance.

Paulin had two other assets: his sisters. Both were widowed and childless, with little to occupy them. They were eager to serve as ladies-in-waiting to this interesting queen. They were as different as sisters could be. Marie-Louise Vaudun was little, dark and quick, garrulous as a magpie. The older sister, Henriette de Coulaines, was a plump fading blonde and more like her brother in personality — undemonstrative, a good listener, ready to offer an opinion but only if asked. Neither could replace her old friend Héloise (who had elected to go back to Saumur) or the good Charlotte, whom Berengaria missed greatly, but she was glad to have found these new friends.

These three, with Herbert de Tucé, formed a nucleus around which she acquired a court. Her first request of them was for advice about her shaky finances. The palace expenses were heavy and her revenues, because of Guillaume's depredations, did not yet meet them. For the first time in her life, she desperately needed money and had no one to turn to. If her own personal survival had been the only thing affected, she would not have been so worried. But now she was responsible for a court, a palace, a city. She told them how King John refused to yield her the third of Richard's estate that was due her.

"That wicked man pays no attention to the Pope?" Marie-Louise asked, indignant.

"None," said Berengaria. "The last word I had was that he had turned the matter over to the bishops of Ely and Worcester, but they have been silent."

"I expect King John is too worried about the way he is losing his lands to Philip to give much thought to your affairs," said Herbert de Tucé. "I hear that Normandy is going to Philip, town by town."

"We would do well to send him another request, so he will not think we have given up," said Paulin.

They did so and finally in 1206 a messenger came from John:

> *The king addresses you as his dear sister, and assures you that he has received your messages, and has heard them with affectionate interest. He urges you again to come to see him in England so the two of you can talk of these matters and agree on a settlement. He will gladly grant you a safe-conduct, and he will receive you with brotherly friendship, as he has so often assured you before.*

She did not think she should go, but she asked her council.

"Certainly not," said Paulin Boutier, his lips pinched in disapproval. "Everybody knows that John's safe conducts are not worth the parchment they're written on."

"And he makes no mention of providing the wherewithal for you to make the journey," said Herbert de Tucé. "Your treasury could not bear the expense of a trip like this, with all the attendants who would have to go with you."

She knew they were right; but none of them had an idea about how to deal with this slippery king. She dismissed them and sat for some time in the darkening council chamber, eyes cast down, hands folded in her lap and shoulders bowed. She was almost lost in the big chair that had been designed for the burly counts of Maine. She found herself thinking wistfully of Pierre Savary. If he was the disinterested friend he seemed to be, why had she not heard from him since coming to Le Mans? Had he some inkling of Blanche's distrust, and was he silent because he did not wish to be seen as a fortune hunter? If so, she thought the better of him for it. But now she longed to pour out her troubles to some one. Maybe she would send a message to this "other brother" and tell him he would be welcome at Le Mans.

Or maybe not. She sat up straight, and placed her hands on the carved arms of her chair, as though about to rise, but remained motionless for a few minutes, remembering who and where she was. She felt herself absorbing the strength of those who had sat here before her — and almost literally sensed that her backbone was stiffening. Who was Pierre Savary, that she should think of him as her only savior? He had ignored her for half a year; very well, she was not going to make overtures to him. She would think of some way out of her dilemma on her own.

A servant who had come in to light the candles started when she rose from the chair, like a white-clad wraith in the gloom.

"Your pardon, Joseph. I was just sitting here thinking."

She had indeed, of a sudden, thought of her next move. She would write a conciliatory letter to John, thanking him for his invitation and accepting it — provisionally. She would ask him to send an installment on his debt to her first; it could be small, but would serve as a token of his good faith, and would help defray the expense of her journey. She would tell him that when she received it, she would gladly begin planning the trip. If by some miracle he agreed, she could decide then what to do next. She could dissemble as well as John!

The Dame of Le Mans did not need advice from Pierre Savary, or anyone else.

he Dame of Le Mans read the message, cried "Oh joy!", jumped up from her chair and did a little dance step, almost tripping over her gown. Cristina entered the room just in time to view this caper and her mouth dropped open. She almost forgot what she had come for — to see if there were any reply for the messenger.

"Cristina!" Berengaria waved the scrap of parchment, laughing at the maid's amazement. "I have good news, and I am rejoicing."

Cristina did not remember ever seeing her mistress rejoice quite like this. Though she was older and presumably wiser, it seemed to Cristina that after six years in Le Mans, she was far less concerned with what others thought of her than when she was the self-conscious young queen.

"What is the good news, madame?" she asked politely.

"We are to have visitors. My sister Blanche and her two children will be coming from Champagne to spend Christmas with us, and Blanche sends word in advance so we may be prepared."

"How wonderful for you, madame! I haven't seen your sister since she came through Beaufort all those years ago. And now she has two little ones, just imagine!"

"Not so little by now, Cristina. Why, when I was in Troyes two years ago, I could hardly believe how they had grown. And now — bless me, Bérengère must be ten and little Count Thibaut at least eight. It will be so good to see them again, and dear Blanche."

Cristina decided the hop and the skip were entirely appropriate. Her mistress needed cheering up, considering how many cares seemed to weigh on her thin shoulders here in Le Mans.

"Now we must get ready for them," the maid said practically. "I will go tell Carlos the good news. Shall I ask your ladies to come up?"

First they had to settle who would be lodged where. Then they began to think of entertainments. "We must show Blanche that we are not dull here in our out-of-the-way city," said Berengaria to Marie-Louise and Henriette. "We must have a grand banquet. Maybe even the Bishop will come!"

She was not really optimistic about that. She never knew from one day to the next how the Bishop regarded her; their relations had been far from cordial, ever since her arrival. It all had to do with disputes over taxes. For years, with no Counts of Maine in residence or paying attention, the bishops had gradually added citizens' names to their lists, at the expense of the secular government. Herbert de Tucé had labored mightily to bring the old tax rolls up to date, but every time he removed a name from the cathedral's register and added it to Berengaria's there was a squabble.

However, she would not let that upset her now. With or without the Bishop, Berengaria intended to celebrate Christmas in style.

"What about those mummers from Tours, do you think they could come to our holiday banquet?" Henriette said she would find out.

"And we must have the musicians who were here in September," rhapsodized Marie-Louise, rolling her eyes. "They played so beautifully, I am dying to hear them again!"

And the Christmas feast had to be planned, and provisions laid in, and a guest list made out. Even the two small sons of Cristina and Carlos, Cristiano and Carlito, were pressed into service. Now eight and nine, curly-haired and with melting brown eyes, they looked like a pair of mischievous cherubs. They were instructed that they were to amuse and assist the little count and countess.

Blanche and her entourage arrived two days before Christmas, in a snowstorm. All were wet and tired and some were out of sorts. Charlotte and Hugh de Vendeuvre were in the party and Charlotte was disappointed that they had not come through Paris, but had instead taken the faster southern route by way of Orléans. Thibaut was cross because he had not been permitted to bring his new puppy.

After drying out and warming themselves by the fires, however, they all revived. The children ran off to explore this big new house with Carlito and Cristiano. The elders were taken on a tour by Berengaria.

"It is far grander than we are in Troyes," Charlotte said afterwards to Hugh, with just a touch of jealousy.

"Yes, it is," Hugh replied. "And I cannot think of anyone who deserves a fine home like this more than Queen Berengaria."

The Christmas banquet was blazingly successful, from the warmth and crackle of fires in almost every room, to the brilliance of the musicians and jugglers. Besides the palace contingent, Berengaria had invited a half-dozen of the local nobility and their ladies, who turned out in their finest. The Bishop had declined, pleading a previous engagement in Tours, but perhaps the gathering was the merrier for his absence. Festoons of pine branches hung on the walls of the dining hall, and the seldom-used candelabra had been fitted with new candles. The holiday table groaned under roast fowl, giant barons of beef, steaming pitchers of mulled wine and raisin-studded suet puddings. There was even a suckling pig roasting on the hearth, filling the hall with its rich aroma. The children giggled at the piglet and the rosy apple in its mouth. Their elders were unanimous in saying they had never had a jollier Christmas.

"You will have to live on bread and water for months to pay for all this," warned Herbert de Tucé.

"Gladly," said Berengaria. "My sister has been so generous to me in the past that I can never, never repay her. This little extravagance is the least I can do to show her my love and gratitude."

Every penny seemed well spent when Blanche, on New Year's Day, told her, "I can hardly believe this is my reserved Berenguelita! You are quite transformed, here in Le Mans."

They were walking by the river. The weather had finally cleared on this almost mild day, and a sizeable party had wrapped up well, then gone out to take the air. It was Berengaria's first chance to show her sister the city. Also in the group were Hugh and Charlotte, Marie-Louise and Henriette, as well as a few others from the court, and the children's nurses. The four little ones scampered about, running circles around their more sedate elders like frolicsome puppies. The party straggled through the town, inspected the cathedral and the old Roman gate, and went down a long flight of stone steps to walk along the River Sarthe. Blanche and Berengaria, arm-in-arm, had fallen behind the others.

"How am I transformed, Blanche?" Berengaria asked. "Not into an old shrew, I hope. Sometimes I feel like one, when I have to quarrel with the Bishop and the canons of the cathedral."

"Not at all," Blanche replied. "In fact, I wish I carried my years as well as you — see how plump I am getting, and it seems there's a new wrinkle in my neck almost every day. Yet you have only one or two gray hairs, and your figure is as delicious as ever. But what I particularly admire is how self-confident you have become; you seem to be enjoying your position as dame of the city. Look at the way you have taken over the whole palace and found good people to serve you."

"One does what one can, Blanche. You have certainly proved that. Life has not been easy for either of us, but sometimes I think it has been harder for you because for so long you had Thibaut at your side, and then had to adjust so quickly to his loss and learn to make your way without him. I may be alone, but at least it has been that way from the day I arrived here. No ambitious Prince Charming has come along to offer to share my life. Which reminds me — are you still plagued by that unspeakable Jean de Brienne?"

Blanche laughed. "No, thank the good Lord. He soon saw that I was no more likely to accept his suit than you were, and has fled the fields of Champagne for the bright lights of Paris. Charlotte heard somewhere that he is thicker than ever with old Queen Adele, and we have all decided that it was she who asked King Philip to order us to receive Jean again. But never mind all that. What of you — has your country squire from Colombiers been to call?"

"You mean Pierre Savary? Not a word from him, these two years and more. Before that, there was one short, polite letter, congratulating me on my gift of this city from King Philip." She did not tell Blanche that she had answered that letter, thanking him and asking him to come see her if he found himself nearby. She had been piqued when her invitation drew no response, and embarrassed at being so forward.

"So you have not seen him? That is a surprise. I thought surely he would come buzzing about like a bee after honey, when you became Dame of Le Mans. I wonder why not."

"Perhaps because he is a good and honest man," Berengaria answered drily. "I believe there are a few such left in the world. I would like to think he sees how unworthy such a transparent suit would be." But she halfway wished she could say that yes, he had come to call, and let Blanche make the most of it. She began walking faster. "Come, let us catch up with the others. What can all that shouting be about?"

"I hear Thibaut whooping loudest of all. I hope he has not found another stray puppy."

It was not a puppy, it was a kitten — lost and bedraggled and mewing in a tiny piteous voice, with no sign of a mother. The ladies in the party were unanimous: it must be taken back to the palace and dried and fed. Bérengère and Thibaut alternated in carrying it, squabbling about whose turn it was; Blanche had to remind them that they must behave like little ladies and gentlemen.

In mid-January Blanche and her party left. The kitten, now christened Petite-Grise, was lodged in a strong basket and entrusted to Hugh de Vendeuvre, as the most responsible rider.

Berengaria kissed the children goodbye. "I will try to come see you before that little ball of fluff becomes a cat," she promised them.

"Bring Carlito and Cristiano when you come," called Thibaut as his pony bore him around the corner and out of the square.

With the Christmas holidays now really over, it was time to come back to hard realities. The day of reckoning Herbert de Tucé had gloomily warned her of was upon them, and the whole palace went on an austerity regime. Wood for the fires was doled out carefully, the soups became thinner, and wine flowed less freely. Herbert impressed on the tax collectors the need to be diligent and firm.

By March, all this effort began to pay off. Berengaria was heartened when she won an argument with the fractious cathedral chapter about taxes. A few days later she, Herbert and Paulin settled down to go over the accounts. A late snow had fallen overnight and covered the turreted roofs and the bare-branched trees; the winter's accumulation of filth and rubbish in the streets was hidden by a blanket of pristine white. The city looked like a fairyland, but the cold was penetrating.

"Brrr!" growled Herbert, pulling his woollen cloak tighter about him.

"At least we will not be likely to doze off," said Berengaria, trying to make the best of it.

Just then a servant came in and announced, "A messenger from King John of England is here and inquires if you can see him."

The three of them exchanged puzzled looks.

"Send him up at once," she said, and to her companions, "I have not heard from John for months and months, not since I told him I would come to England if he would send me an advance on what he owes me; surely he has not agreed at this late date? Maybe he is finally beginning to fear for his eternal soul."

"As well he should," said Paulin, "seeing that the Pope excommunicated him last year."

The messenger came in, stamping his feet and slapping himself to restore his circulation, and handed her a rolled-up parchment. She read it carefully, then passed it to Paulin and Herbert.

"Another maneuver that will come to no good end," said Paulin when he had finished. "But we must pursue it and send representatives to Winchester, as he asks. You have too much at stake, and you have invested too much of your energy and time in this business to give up now."

"I agree," she responded, "though like you, I have not much hope. Still, if his representative is the Bishop of Winchester that is a good sign. I believe he is as righteous as any in that land."

"John says here that the Bishop will have full authority to negotiate," said Herbert. "I suppose we have little to lose, and it would be a fine thing if our men came back with something in their pockets."

"Whom do you think we should send?" she asked.

Paulin suggested Guillaume de la Trappe and Garsie Leclerc, both canons of her private chapel, Saint-Pierre-la-Cour.

"We can be sure of their loyalty even if they may not be as crafty and shrewd as the canons of the cathedral."

The next day the sun came out, the snow melted, and spirits rose. Optimism was in the air. But Paulin was stern and his pointed nose twitched menacingly as he instructed the two canons before they left for England.

"The Bishop of Winchester will try to get around you, so be careful. Make sure you forget none of the Queen's claims, see that they are all set down in the agreement and that the bishop signs."

They promised to be watchful.

"And remind the Bishop that the Queen requests as a sign of John's good faith that you come back with at least a token payment of what he owes her."

They said they would so inform the Bishop.

"And beware if anybody offers you that wretched English wine. Take my advice, drink nothing but ale."

They nodded, and off they went.

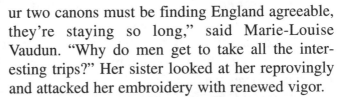

"ur two canons must be finding England agreeable, they're staying so long," said Marie-Louise Vaudun. "Why do men get to take all the interesting trips?" Her sister looked at her reprovingly and attacked her embroidery with renewed vigor.

They were in the large pleasant room Berengaria had taken to calling her library, next to her bedchamber. While Marie-Louise and Henriette sat on a bench by the window, plying their needles, Berengaria stood before a cabinet where she had stowed her books and manuscripts. She was dressed for comfort in a simple knitted gown, dark brown, straight and unadorned, with a cowl neck. She had brushed back her hair and pinned it up in a knot. From the back she has a very monkish look, Henriette thought, looking up from her work.

Berengaria had hardly touched her books since coming to Le Mans. Now that there was little to do but wait for word from England, she had decided to find a book of psalms she wanted to copy, and see if her hand had lost its skill.

Something about Marie-Louise's words had a familiar ring to her. Then she saw herself thirty years ago, standing at the palace door in Estella with her mother. Young Sancho was riding off with their father on a journey over the mountains to France. "Why do the women and children always have to stay at home?" she had complained to her mother. Queen Sancha had said, "That is just the way it is, little one. And besides, you would not like it at all, up there in the cold windy mountain passes." She had not answered, but silently vowed to herself that some day she too would set out on adventures.

She stood there, musing and remembering. Since that long-ago day she had been on many a journey and suffered many a hardship, but with more damage to her young and susceptible heart than to her resilient body. She told herself she was very lucky to be so comfortably settled here in Le Mans, secure and well beyond the days when love had consumed her.

As she became more involved with governance of the city and as Herbert de Tucé's tax collectors grew more adroit, even the long, dreary battle with King John and the English exchequer was losing its urgency. Now it was more a matter of principle than survival. Still, she wished they could know what was going on across the channel. Only one brief message had come from Guillaume and Garsie in three months. They said they had met with their English counterparts, and their discussions had been productive.

She had a notion and turned around. "Why don't we take a little walk to Saint-Pierre-la-Cour? Maybe they have heard something from the two canons." She was always glad of an excuse to visit her private place of worship, modest and familiar, a far cry from the overweening cathedral.

The ladies seized on the suggestion and they all quickly put on their cloaks and set out. The air was bracing and they told each other that the little walk was going to do them good. Just as they emerged from the palace door, a tall, handsome roan horse clattered into the square. The rider's blue velvet cloak flowed almost to the ground, and on his head he wore a dashing hat with a long blue plume that curved down over his shoulder.

"Now who can that popinjay be?" asked Berengaria, turning back. The rider pulled up his horse and dismounted, waiting to greet her. There was something familiar about the solid figure and, as she came nearer, the square-jawed face with the broad smile under the neatly clipped brown mustache. To her astonishment she saw that this vision was none other than Pierre Savary.

"Sieur Pierre! This is a surprise. Welcome to Le Mans. What brings you here?"

Along with his new finery, he seemed to have acquired fashionable manners, quite unlike the modest man she remembered. He took off his hat with a flourish, made an exaggerated bow, took her hand, raised it to his lips and kissed it, looking soulfully at her. But the smirk on his lips told her he was playing a part. She entered into the game and simpered as fetchingly as she could, spread the skirts of her cloak and made a deep curtsey. They both burst into laughter.

Pierre looked with unfeigned admiration at her face. The fresh air had brought a pretty rosiness to her cheeks, and her eyes sparkled with fun.

Watching from a respectful distance, Henriette and Marie-Louise thought she suddenly looked ten years younger. They noted the way this mysterious stranger held her hand so long, and looked at each other in surmise.

"I know it is most uncivil of me to burst in on you like this, but I had several pieces of news for you and since Le Mans was only a little out of my way as I came back from Paris, I thought I would chance your forgiveness for an unannounced visit. And" (he smiled broadly) "I also thought I would chance your welcome to a country squire who tries to look like a king's courtier. Believe me, the real Pierre is still here, beneath it all. I can explain everything."

"Then come in, and begin explaining. You have been such a stranger — I am delighted you came this way, and I'm eager to know what all this news can be."

She asked Marie-Louise and Henriette to come and be introduced. All four entered the palace, where a servant took their cloaks. When Berengaria invited Pierre to come up to her private apartments, her two ladies were left with much to discuss.

Berengaria preceded him up the steps. "The last time we met, we sat in the hall at Troyes, and you gave me wise advice, which I followed," she said over her shoulder. "I have often wondered why I did not hear from you after I wrote you that you would be welcome in Le Mans." Pierre did not answer. She suddenly felt self-conscious, aware that her thin gown might be too revealing. She hurried ahead to open the door.

"This is my library," she told him. "One of these days, I will find time to get serious again about my work. But meantime, it does very well as a place where I can relax and receive old friends." She sat in a chair in front of her copying table, and he took the chair on the other side.

"I am indeed honored that you consider me an old friend, in view of my deplorable silence, ever since you wrote me so kindly. But you have no idea how often I have thought of you." Then he looked down, unable to meet her eyes.

"Do you have bad news, Pierre? You seem worried."

"Not bad news for you, I hope. And my only worry is how you will take it; but let us get it over with."

She waited during a half-minute of silence.

"Yes, I am honored that you think of me as an old friend," he repeated. "We have not seen each other since those days in Troyes, but remembering them always gives me pleasure. Lately, though, you may have assumed I had forgotten you. But after I left Troyes in 1204, my affairs took a turn for the worse. My wretched vines in Champagne never recovered and I had to replant the whole vineyard. Then I had several crop failures at Colombiers. I could not afford to pay my laborers, so I had to do much of the work myself. I do not mind hard work, but farming does not give me much time for socializing."

She smiled sympathetically. She still had no idea where this was leading. "And then?"

"Then not long ago King Philip asked me to come to Paris. He had heard of my troubles and he knew I had always been a loyal vassal. I proved it when I joined in his battle against John in 1203. He was worried because some of the other landowners in Poitou and Touraine were not so loyal, and he knew John was promising them castles and lands if they would come in on his side. So Philip gave me two properties. Of course what it amounted to was a bribe to make sure he could still count on my loyalty. But I was only too glad to accept."

"Of course you were."

"And to make doubly sure, he has just ennobled me and made me a Chevalier Banneret. That was why I was in Paris — for the investiture. And that is why you see me dressed in this ridiculous way. It seems the costume makes the man, when one becomes a Chevalier."

He paused and looked directly at her. She felt she should say something. "This is good news indeed. I hope it has meant better fortune for you."

"From a material point of view, yes. But for my conscience, no. When Philip made his gift, I did not realize to whom Montbazon really belonged."

"Montbazon!" she exclaimed. "So Philip gave you Montbazon?" She remembered this as one of the castles in her dowry that John had promised her at their meeting in Chinon. At the time, she did not even know where it was, and since he had not kept any of his promises it had been easy to forget about it. Now Philip had seized it and given it to someone else!

"He did. He gave me what was not his to give, but that should not surprise us. How often does Philip act in a straightforward manner? Later I found out that it was in your dowry. I have come to give you what is rightfully yours."

At last he had told her, and he drew a deep breath. She could hardly comprehend what he was saying. "You mean that, in spite of Philip's act, you will give up this Montbazon, and its revenues, to me?"

"Exactly. It is now yours, with no conditions or caveats. I placed the documents transferring the rights to collect its revenues in the record office while I was in Paris."

"I do not know what to say, except thank you from the bottom of my heart. This will mean so much to me."

Without taking thought she reached across the table and took his hand. His discomfiture had disappeared, and she could read in his face his relief that she had accepted so gracefully. She felt an unaccountable pleasure at his warm, firm clasp, and did not take her hand away until he released it.

"But why were you worried about telling me? Surely this generous act reflects very well on you; how could I take it but the way it was meant?"

"I was afraid you would think I was like Philip. He as much as bought my loyalty. You might think I was trying to buy your goodwill. Or your regard. You must be aware that you would be a highly desirable match for some swain hoping to better himself."

She blushed, and seeing her discomposure, he went on quickly, "You need not worry, I am not that swain. And I am only glad Montbazon will help you. I take it that being Dame of Le Mans does not automatically bring riches? How about bad King John — has he made restitution at all?"

She told him about John's latest ploy: the meeting of her representatives with his, in England.

"But I have very little hope anything will come of it. And with what you have done for me today, it will not matter so much."

"I am glad to hear it. I know what a worry that wicked man has been to you."

He rose and walked over to the cabinet across the room and stood surveying the contents, hands clasped behind his back. "Now tell me, what do you plan to do with all these formidable tomes? Do you intend to read them all? Or perhaps you have already done so?"

"Oh no," she laughed, coming to stand beside him. "But I do plan to copy several for my own library, before I send them back to where they belong, the monastery at Leyre in my native Navarre. I lived and studied there for five years, and the monks have been generous ever since with the contents of their library."

He looked startled. "You lived in a monastery — whatever for? Were you fleeing from the world to live in silence? I had heard you were a scholar — was that when it began? I find I know very little about you, and you keep surprising me."

She assured him that far from fleeing the world, she had gone to Leyre to find out more about it, through books. "I learned so much, and I had a wonderful teacher. Leyre was always like home to me, and I loved it because it was founded by one of my ancestors, four hundred years ago. I even began to dream I myself might found a monastery some day."

"I think perhaps you regret leaving."

"No, not at all; but I still, sometimes, long to go back to those days with Brother Anselmo, when life was simpler and my goals were more clear." She had returned to her chair. "I will tell you all about it some day, perhaps. But enough about me. You said you had several pieces of news. You're a Chevalier and a knight of the realm; you have made Montbazon over to me; is there more?"

His cheerful mood vanished and he gave her such a look — was it part despair, part something else?

"I told you I would not be your suitor, because I would not wish you to think I was so mercenary as that would appear. But there is another, more serious reason. I do not know how to lead up to this, so I shall simply say: I have remarried."

This was the last thing she had expected. It came as an unpleasant shock. All of Blanche's chiding that this man was an undeclared suitor had colored her idea of him, much as she laughed at the notion. Now he had chosen another.

"I wanted to tell you at once, before you learned of it from someone else. Please hear me out." He walked to the window, turned his back and looked out toward the ramparts. "My wife is Femo, daughter of Gautier, the Count of Montsoreau. I have nothing but respect for her. But the marriage was arranged, in fact ordered, by King Philip. Montsoreau is just on the border of Poitou and Touraine, where he fears an uprising."

He turned quickly to glance at her. She was listening intently. He turned back. "You have probably passed through Montsoreau on your way to Fontevrault, so you can understand that the location is a perfect one for Philip to have a friend. It could be disastrous for him if it were occupied by an enemy. Philip has doubted Gautier's loyalty, and hit on this uniting of our two houses as a way to ensure it. He knows well enough he can count on me. And now that I have my title, this marriage to the daughter of a count is quite appropriate."

He paused. She wondered if he were through and if so, what she could possibly say. Congratulations on your marriage? Please bring your wife to call?

He turned toward her again and she saw with a shock the misery in his face. "This is what I beg you to believe, Berengaria. It is a political marriage. I had never even met Femo until we went to the church two months ago. She maintains her residence in Montsoreau, and I still have mine in Colombiers. She is a good and worthy woman, and I suppose we will have to live together eventually, but I do not love her."

She could hardly hear his next words, spoken as though wrung out of him. "I do not love her as I love you."

She stood up, confused, wondering how to bring the interview to a close. Pierre was silent, but his eyes searched her face. She brushed a wisp of hair from her forehead and the next thing she knew, he had swiftly crossed to her and placed his hands on her shoulders. She was transfixed, unable to think of anything except the dear face so close to hers. He kissed her lightly, briefly, like the brush of a butterfly's wing. Her arms involuntarily went around him and his around her. Her head found his shoulder and rested there for what seemed an age, while he held her. It was an avowal of love and a renunciation of love, both at once.

Then she came to herself and withdrew. With a groan he let her go. They looked at each other dumbly, trying to deal with what had just happened. Pierre spoke first.

"Berengaria, I think I have loved you ever since that day in Troyes when I came in like a drowning rat and we sat by the fire together. You were so lovely, and you were so kind to me. But I did not dare to hope that you felt the same."

"I do. I did not know it until now, but I cannot hide it. But all this comes too late. Now you belong to Femo."

"Yes. And what I have just done was very wrong. I cannot ask for your forgiveness. But I can tell you that I love only you, and that will never change. Now I had better go."

"Yes, I think you must." Her voice was very small.

"But my dearest, surely this need not be goodbye. We are grown people, not lovesick youngsters. May we not still be friends? May I write to you?"

"Yes — no — I don't know! Just go!" She turned away, afraid he would see the tears in her eyes. Quietly, he let himself out.

39

month had passed since Pierre had come and gone so quickly, leaving a tempest in Berengaria's heart. She could not still it, no matter how sternly she chastised herself. She felt like two people, engaged in a perpetual argument.

"He is nothing but an unprincipled scoundrel, to make advances to you when he has just told you he is a married man!" This was her head.

"But it was hardly an advance. And he was as appalled at his behavior as I was. And if he loves me as much as he says, he truly could not help himself," said her heart.

"You should have repulsed him at once."

"I know, I know — but his embrace was so sweet! I can still feel the touch of his lips on mine. I could not help myself any more than he could."

"You should be ashamed of yourself, a forty-five-year-old woman imagining that she is in love."

"What has age got to do with it? I have been waiting all my life for a man like this."

"But he is married. Have you not always believed in the sanctity of the marriage contract? Have you forgotten the example of your mother and father, true to each other for thirty years? So what are you going to do?"

"I don't know. What can I do? Try to forget him."

"See that you do."

She tried. She labored at the copying of her book of psalms. She took renewed interest in her finances. When she discovered that the Bishop's men had been collecting customs duties from merchants who came into the city, she ordered Herbert de Tucé to tell the bishop to cease and desist and impress on him that these levies were due to the Dame of Le Mans. She pestered her long-suffering seneschal so much that before long he wished she would confine her interests to copying and embroidery. She took long walks through the city, with Carlos to attend her, and spoke to her people.

She visited the chapel almost daily but it did not seem that God heard her. In the midst of a prayer she would suddenly see Pierre's weather-tanned face, his eyes crinkled in a smile, those brown and searching eyes, and she would long to feel herself held in his arms again.

One night she awoke suddenly from a vivid dream. Quickly, before the cloudy memories should fade and disappear, she tried to reconstruct them. First she was in her library with Pierre. He took her in his arms, but in her dream it was not a sorrowful renunciation; rather a hopeful, glad embrace. He put his arm around her protectively and led her to her bedchamber. He lifted her effortlessly and laid her on the bed, and she reached up her arms to welcome him.

Then the scene changed and she was in Richard's arms at Beaufort, still trembling with the ecstasy of their lovemaking. Blessedly, in her dream she was spared the awful memory of his rude departure that used to torment her, waking and sleeping. She awoke feeling deeply contented and dearly beloved. But in an instant, she was overcome by desolation because it had been only a dream.

She stretched and half sat up, leaning back on her pillows with her hands clasped behind her head. Dawn's light was just beginning to chase away the shadows. She pondered.

She could understand the Pierre part; that was the way she would have wished their encounter to be. But why should the other memory intrude, of that brief time so long ago, when she was convinced of Richard's love? She had thought it thoroughly buried. Could it be that in spite of her newly acknowledged love for Pierre, she missed the helpless passion that had kept her heart enslaved by Richard all those years? Or did she wish that Richard had been as devoted and faithful as Pierre? Or was this a sign that some day, somehow, she and Pierre would be able to love each other without restraint?

She could not sort it all out. Still, the strange dream seemed to have exorcised whatever demon had been destroying her peace of mind. She rose and dressed, feeling a faint hope that she was getting some balance back.

It was the middle of April now, and the sun was shining bravely every day and had dried up all the puddles. Green blades of grass were poking up between the cobblestones in the square, and in the tiny garden at Saint-Pierre-La-Cour, the daffodil buds were almost ready to burst into bloom. Townsfolk walked about with fewer layers of wool between them and the weather. Warmth, brightness, greenery — spring had come at last.

The ladies of the court decided they would like an outing, and Henriette and Marie-Louise tried to persuade Berengaria to join them. They had talked endlessly about how to bring their lady out of her doldrums. "I wish that Pierre Savary had never come!" said Henriette. "He must have behaved quite wickedly."

"You have been looking far too morose, my lady," said Marie-Louise. Her plump face shone with sympathy. "What you need is a change of scene. Do come with us for a day in the country."

Berengaria could hardly think of a plausible reason to refuse, and had to admit that perhaps she did need a diversion. So the cooks were instructed to prepare hampers of cold beef, bread, cheese and wine. With Cristina and Carlos to take charge of transport of the provisions (somewhat assisted by Carlito and Cristiano), off they went. Some of the gentlemen of the court thought it would be nice to come along, but Marie-Louise said no, this was a ladies' party.

But as they were preparing to ride out, Carlos came to Berengaria with a slender, somewhat travel-stained rolled-up parchment, just delivered by a messenger. Without breaking the seal, she was sure it had to be from Pierre. He had asked if he could write her; she had not exactly said he must not; and she had been trying to suppress the hope that he would.

She wanted desperately to stay behind and read it, but she was unwilling to hold up the party, and to appear so eager. Remember, you are trying to forget him, she told herself. "Use some self-control." So she put the letter in her bag and joined the others.

They rode out of the city by the Paris road, and then for half an hour followed an obscure track across the fields and through the trees to the little River Huisne, a tributary of the Sarthe. Berengaria knew the Sarthe well, the sizeable river that flowed along under the city wall of Le Mans. But she had never been to this spot, and she was enchanted. They went down a gentle incline, and a secret green hideaway opened before them. They came out of the forest of elms and oaks to find a flower-sprinkled meadow sloping down to the banks of the placid stream, where the willows leaned to meet their reflections in the unruffled water.

The ladies exclaimed with delight as they dismounted and looked around.

"Is it not charming!"

"Look at all the daisies and buttercups! I will pick us each a nosegay."

"And there is a fine level spot just by the river, where we can spread our picnic."

On the other side of the river they could see an old stone mill that looked abandoned. "How picturesque!" cried Marie-Louise. "I wonder if anyone lives there — perhaps some hermit who has said goodbye to the world."

"If so, he would do well to stir himself and get the millwheel turning again," said Henriette. "Our bakers in the city could use the flour."

Berengaria smiled at this typical interchange between the sisters. It reminded her a little of herself and Blanche when they were girls: the one sensible and sober, the other seeing romance at every turn.

Cristina set out platters and jugs, knives and napkins, and the party seated themselves on thick woolen rugs spread on the grass, though even so some complained that it was a little damp and cold.

Berengaria said she was not yet very hungry, and went apart from the others to read her letter. She sat on a fallen log and with eager hands broke the seal and unrolled the parchment.

It was not from Pierre. It was from Father Eximino, abbot of the monastery of San Salvador de Leyre, hundreds of miles away in her native Basque country. The cramped, precise writing recalled the man himself — severe and withdrawn, with a towering self-importance. They had never become real friends, but by the time she left the monastery, they had come to share a mutual respect.

She read:

*To Queen Berengaria, Dame of Le Mans, our Daughter in
Christ:*

*The message this letter brings is a sad one for us all.
Our Brother Anselmo has died, after three-score years of
faithful service to God. You will remember his achievements
as a scholar, which brought renown to our monastery and
from which you yourself, as his pupil, benefited.*

*It was his wish to be buried at the Benedictine Abbey at
Cluny, where he spent his early years before he came to us.
The service will be at Pentecost. I shall attend, as will
several others from here whom you may remember. I tell you
this so you may have time to arrange to make the journey
yourself, if you wish.*

May God continue to bless you.

Pentecost was only two weeks away. This message must have made
a very slow journey from Navarre to Le Mans; no wonder it looked
so bedraggled. She sat staring at Father Eximino's words, remembering. How skeptical Brother Anselmo had been when she said she
wanted to learn to be a scribe and to master Arabic! Yet she had
managed to convince him that she was serious, and he had taught
her gladly. Few people had had such an influence on her life.
Somehow, she had always hoped she might go back and see him
again. Now it was too late. He was gone.

She sat perfectly still, her skirt falling like marble-white
drapery to her feet, her head bowed in thought, hardly hearing the
chatter of the ladies; it was like the twittering of birds in the trees.
She felt ashamed of her foolish obsession with Pierre, while this
dear friend was dying. Still, how could she have known? But now
she did know. She raised her head. I must go to Cluny, of course,
she said to herself.

Cristina, ever vigilant, saw how her mistress sat alone, in
evident distress, and came hurrying over to ask, "Madame, is
anything wrong? Will you not come and take something to eat?
Have you had bad news?"

"Yes, I have, Cristina; a dear friend has died. But I will join
you now. Have you left me any food?" She managed a smile, and
walked over to the gathering. The ladies, sitting on the grass with

their skirts spread out around them, could have been a flower garden — roses, buttercups, marguerites. They rose to welcome her and made a place for her. She felt a lump in her throat as she sat down among them.

How fortunate I am to have these good friends, she thought. And I have a loving sister and my dear niece and nephew. And brother Sancho, wherever he may be. I have made a good life as Dame of Le Mans. And I was blessed to have Brother Anselmo for my friend. So why do I waste time pining for that inconsiderate Pierre, who has trifled with my heart and who has not even seen fit to send me a single word?

All the way back to the city, she rode in silence, planning. Cluny was in Burgundy, a good ten days' journey. She would have to leave at once if she were to arrive in time.

As for Chevalier Pierre Savary de Colombiers, if he wrote to her while she was away and she could not answer, serve him right.

t's good to be home."

Berengaria settled into the high-backed chair at the head of the long table in her library, on her first day back from Cluny. At her left sat Paulin Boutier, fidgeting a little, ready to fill her in on what had happened during her month's absence. At her right Herbert de Tucé was still busy going over his figures so he could bring her up to date on her finances.

It was indeed good to be home, here where she was surrounded by familiar furnishings. Some, like her mother's embroidered wall hangings, had been brought from Beaufort Castle years ago. Some, like the chair she sat in, had been made especially for her here in Le Mans. It was smaller than the huge ornate chairs on which the counts of Maine, her predecessors in this palace, had been enthroned. The seat and arms were cushioned with soft woven wool instead of cold leather. Across the room she could see through three tall windows the top of the old Roman walls and a tower that marked one of the city gates. It was a view she had come to cherish. Without turning around, she sensed the presence of the cabinets with her parchments, vellums, tablets, pens, inks and precious books. Along the far wall were the capacious chests containing the sorry records of her dealings with John, and the city tax rolls and accounts. Here, only Herbert dared to delve.

She sighed with contentment. "The older I get, my friends, the more I appreciate my own bed and my own rooms. After two nights in a monk's cell, I could hardly wait to leave."

Herbert looked up at her words. "I hope you did not find your trip a waste of time. It would be too bad to spend so many weeks and so much energy without some gratification." (To say nothing of the expense, he privately thought.)

"Not at all. I was glad to be able to pay my last respects to Brother Anselmo, and to see the Cluny Abbey. It's even larger than Fontevrault, imagine! And there were old friends to greet. One of the brothers who worked in the scriptorium while I was at Leyre had come, and we had such a time, reminiscing. We both had stories to tell about Brother Anselmo, and how much we had learned from him."

She fell silent. Paulin looked at the pensive unguarded face, the clear green eyes fixed not on anything present but on a picture called up by memory. He thought he saw a glimmer of what this woman must have looked like when young and untried by life's vicissitudes.

He cleared his throat. She came to herself.

"I beg your pardon, my friends. We are not here to brood on the past, but to deal with the present, yes? So tell me, what news?" She looked curiously at the document that Paulin was unrolling. It bristled with official-looking seals.

"There is some news, madame. Our two emissaries returned from England, their purses as empty as when they left. But they had a very impressive treaty — the most impressive yet, promising you the moon, as usual. The Bishop of Winchester signed it and John signed it; now you are to sign it and have it witnessed, and off it will go to His Holiness in Rome."

"I might as well do it at once; the sooner it is on its way the better." She read it carefully. It held no surprises, only John's worn-out promises to meet his obligations to her.

"You will note, my lady, that it still has that clause that you especially wanted: the one reserving to you the right to reclaim any lands on the continent that belong in your dowry, no matter who holds them. You were wise to insist on that. You may be glad if John ever gets back any of the lands he's lost to Philip, and some that should be yours are among them."

"Yes, I am learning a great deal about devious diplomacy, am I not? With two such examples as John and Philip, I should." She grimaced, dipped her pen in the horn inkwell and signed her name. She handed the document back to Paulin. "You had better ask Herbert de la Marche and Gervais de Pringé to witness it, along with yourself and our good seneschal here. Then the Pope will see how serious we are about all this. I fear, though, it is just another useless move in the silly game we play with John."

She saw that Paulin had another parchment, of which the seal had been broken. It could not be a letter from Pierre; they would not have opened that.

"Then just three days ago," Paulin went on, "a message came from John himself. We took the liberty of reading it; you had instructed us to do so, if any word came from him while you were gone."

"Quite right, Paulin. Will you just tell me what he says? The same old meaningless compliments and plausible excuses, I suppose."

Paulin unrolled the parchment. "He begins with the usual greeting: 'The King to his beloved sister Berengaria, once Queen of England, greetings and the sympathy of sincere love.'

"Then he goes on to tell you that Philip's son Louis has brought an army to England. He complains that this is a sore trial not only to his military forces but also to the royal exchequer. He says he cannot now pay the installment he promised in the treaty that has gone to Rome. He begs you to bear with him 'until the dark cloud is cleared away from us and our kingdom rejoices in full tranquility and we, with the greatest thanks, will make you a full account of the money we owe you.'"

"If Prince Louis is really attacking him in his own land, he has reason to feel under a dark cloud."

"He has more troubles than that, we hear. Guillaume and Garsie, our two canons, told us that some of John's own lords in England are rising against him. And the nobles are insisting in a body that he agree to a solemn charter, guaranteeing their rights. They are calling it their 'Magna Carta.' Apparently they've lost patience with his high-handed ways."

"Dear me. One is almost inclined to say, poor John. But I am afraid he has brought all this on himself. Well, fortunately we are getting on well enough without him, are we not, Herbert?"

The seneschal had finished his summing up. His normally long and worried face was almost cheerful. "We are indeed, madame. Our revenues here in Le Mans are quite satisfactory, much more so than even a year ago. We have seventy-five more names on our tax rolls, and almost all of them are paying up without a quibble — and without any objection from the cathedral chapter. Would you like to see the accounts?"

"No, I do not need to; you are a good man, Sir Herbert. My compliments." She reached over to press his hand, and was about to rise when he went on.

"May I return the compliments? There is more and even better news. Thanks to the revenues coming to you from Montbazon, which you have held now for less than a year, we have been able to put money aside as a reserve." He peered at her quizzically. "I do not know how King Philip came to return that property to you, but it has made a world of difference to your situation."

She turned a little pink. She had not told them how Montbazon had come from Pierre, not Philip, fearing that they might misconstrue it; might assume she had given Pierre some favor in return. Well, let them wonder. They would probably not believe her if she said that Pierre had returned her property because he believed in justice.

So she simply smiled, and thanked them both for their time. They gathered their documents and left.

Now what? She sat on, wondering why she felt so discontented. The affairs of the city were in good shape. She had a loyal, efficient, even zealous council. Relations with the Bishop and chapter of the cathedral were quiescent. In short, nothing required her attention. She did not even have to decide what to do about Pierre; painful as the realization was, he had settled that question with his silence. The friendship, love affair that might have been, whatever — it was over.

She stood, and idly she let her eyes wander around the room. They lingered on the cabinet with her manuscripts.

"Dear God," she said aloud, "What am I thinking of?" There was her answer. For years, she had told herself that she longed for the day when she would have time to devote herself to her copying, seriously and without interruption. Many a time she had made a start, with high hopes of sticking to it, but something always intervened. Now the day had come. She surveyed the contents of the shelves. There were the two beautiful books of Islamic poetry that, years ago, she had begged from Brother Anselmo so she could make copies for her own collection. He had never written to ask when they would be returned, but he must have wondered. She owed it to his memory to get at them at once.

Then there was the book of psalms that she had begun to work on in her despair after Pierre had left her. She had not looked at it for months.

"Dear God," she said again and folded her hands. "I thank You for bringing me to my senses. There is plenty to do here to occupy me until I join You in Heaven."

She fetched her inkpots, her pens, the few pages she had already completed, and the psalmbook. She sat down at the table, found her place and dipped her pen in the inkwell. Something seemed wrong.

With pen in air, she looked around and knew at once what was missing. If she were to be as serious about her work as she had been in Leyre, she needed the proper scribe's equipment: the tall desk with the slanting top, and the stool. She knew just the man to make them: the fine woodworker who had crafted her comfortable chair. Carlos would know how to reach him.

She jumped to her feet, picked up her skirts and ran down-stairs like a girl, looking for Carlos. He was at the outer door, super-vising the entry of four stout men, each bearing on his shoulder a heavy oaken cask. He was directing them toward the kitchens, and impressing on them the need to walk carefully and avoid stumbling and spilling the casks' contents. At the door to the kitchens stood her chief cook, giving them the same advice.

"Whatever is all this, Carlos?" she asked in bewilderment. "Are these wine casks? Why do we need so much all at once? Who ordered them?"

"I do not know who ordered them, madame. But I know who sent them: these fellows say they come from Sieur Pierre Savary."

"Right you are, master," spoke up one of the burly delivery men. "His instructions to us were to take four casks of the finest wine from the 1212 vintage in Sens to Queen Berengaria in Le Mans." He grinned happily at her and bobbed his head, while balancing his heavy burden precariously.

Carlos suspected the man had been sampling his wares along the way and hurried him on to the kitchens. Berengaria stood stock-still. Pierre was sending her a message with this unexpected gift, she was sure of it. He was recalling their conversation about his vines in Champagne, all those years ago in Troyes; the time when, as he had told her later, he first began to care for her.

It would not do! She had just taught her heart to forget him. Furious, she turned and went back up to her library. She realized belatedly that she had not told the men to thank their master; that would have been only common courtesy. She stood in indecision; what message should she send? As she considered, her lips twitched, and she found herself smiling. How like Pierre, who seldom did the expected, to come up with such an unorthodox means of communication! Her anger faded and she told herself she could certainly accept his gift as a thoughtful sign of his regard.

She went down again and asked the men to tell their master that Queen Berengaria thanked him for his generous gift, and that she would have a cask opened at once so she could drink his health that very evening.

That was not the end of it. For the next year, a cask of wine arrived every two months, as regularly as sunrise. Each time the bearer — the same jolly man who had delivered the first message — recited his master's words as accurately as he could.

"Pierre Savary will drink the queen's health with this same vintage, and trusts this will meet with her approval."

Or "Pierre Savary respectfully sends this latest from his vineyards and informs the queen that his wines grow ever more worthy of respect and admiration, like her gracious self." If the message was sometimes garbled by the bibulous fellow, Berengaria always understood perfectly the intent of the sender, and sent her thanks.

s she entered her fiftieth year, Berengaria often felt grateful that she was a daughter of the Basques and had inherited her ancestors' tenacity. Her campaign to get justice from her English connections was going nowhere. A new bishop at the cathedral was disputing her authority and relations with the chapter were beginning to sour again, after years of relative calm.

The sporadic interchanges with Pierre were almost the only relief and she found herself looking forward to each arrival of wine. She imagined him thinking up a cryptic message, looking pleased with himself when he had it right, then making the messenger repeat it until he was satisfied.

She also imagined a shadowy wife in the background. Though she knew nothing whatsoever of Femo, she pictured her as a jealous older woman who kept an eagle eye on her husband — hence no letters could safely be sent. That made the clandestine "correspondence" all the more titillating.

Then came the death of John, in the autumn of 1216.

A most unexpected messenger brought the news. Berengaria and Marie-Louise were on their way home from the cathedral, where they had gone to inspect the work on the new choir. They walked down the narrow, steep street that led to the Palace Square, to come out into a noisy sea of activity.

Here was the lively center of the whole city. It seemed even busier than usual, perhaps because winter was just around the corner and everybody wanted to make the most of this fine, sunny day. Throngs of townspeople were crisscrossing the square, chatting, shouting over the heads of their fellows to greet each other, buying a rabbit or a length of linsey-woolsey from the stands set up here and there. Some hungry citizens had brought their loaves of bread, claspknives and jugs for an impromptu meal, seated on the cobblestones that held the warmth of the autumnal sun.

Berengaria loved these chances to mingle with her people. As the two women made their way carefully through the crowd, those they passed bobbed their heads and murmured a greeting to their "Reine Blanche." She smiled in return and often addressed them by name, for by now she was acquainted with many of the towns-people, grand and lowly. They had almost reached the palace when she saw, coming directly toward them, a man from the past: Jean de Brienne. Catching sight of her at the same moment, he removed his hat and bowed. Her first quick look showed her that his black hair had turned iron-gray and he wore it longer; his face was more composed and not so openly pugnacious as she remembered.

"Queen Berengaria! What luck to find you here. I was just on my way from the palace; they said you had gone out. If you are on your way back, I hope you will permit me to come in and pay my respects." Even his voice was more mannerly. She remembered that Blanche had told her Jean had left Troyes for Paris. Apparently his years at King Philip's court had moderated his truculence.

Since he was being so civil, she would have to reciprocate. "Certainly. Do come back with us, and tell us what brings you so far from Paris. This is my friend Lady Marie-Louise Vaudun. Marie-Louise, this is Sieur Jean de Brienne; I was acquainted with him in Troyes."

Marie-Louise smiled thinly. She remembered Chevalier Pierre Savary, that other former friend who had come to see her queen and who had left her so distressed. She hoped this was not to be repeated.

Half an hour later Berengaria received Jean formally in the state reception rooms. She had needed the time to change her clothes; she did not want Jean going back to tell Philip that the Dame of Le Mans looked shabby. She had capped her white coif with her gold and pearl circlet and put on a blue velvet cloak over her white gown. When Jean came in she was seated in a chair similar to the one she had ordered for her own private rooms, but this was more like a throne, with a higher back and cushioned in red velvet. She had asked Paulin to join her and he stood at her side.

Looking at the outwardly transformed man before her she tried not to think of the hideous occasion when he had tried to force himself on her; she was willing to give him the benefit of the doubt and believe his character might have improved. She was fairly sure that he would hardly remember the event; he had been so deplorably drunk. Today he appeared perfectly sober, and the soul of politeness.

She nodded to him, indicating that he should seat himself in the chair drawn up before her. "Very well, Sir Jean. Pray tell us your business with us."

"First let me say how happy it makes me to see you looking so well and even more beautiful. I will gladly report to King Philip that your years as Dame of Le Mans have obviously agreed with you."

She nodded again in acknowledgement of the stilted compliments. She knew they were meaningless, but she did not mind hearing them.

"Of course you wonder why I have come to your city," Jean continued. "There are several reasons. King Philip sent me, first of all, to make sure you had heard the latest news from England."

"I have not had a word from King John for a year. In fact, I have quite given up any hope that he will ever live up to his obligations."

"Then you do not know that two weeks ago he died, and he has been succeeded by his son Henry. I regret to be the first to bring you this sorry news; after all he was your late husband's brother."

She looked up at Paulin, wide-eyed; both could hardly believe what they heard. Somehow she had thought she would be burdened forever with her recalcitrant brother-in-law. She had expected him to linger on as long as his mother had, making mischief to the end.

"This is a surprise, Sir Jean. Tell us, was it a death in battle? We have heard of his troubles at home, and that his barons had rebelled and joined forces with the invading army of Prince Louis, your king's son."

"Nothing so noble. The doctors say John ate too many fresh peaches and drank too much new cider, causing a torment in his stomach that brought on his death."

While they thought this over, he went on. "But there are others who surmise that a merciful God finally decided that he had done enough deviltry on earth, and took pity on those he had misgoverned for seventeen years."

Berengaria smiled slightly, partly with appreciation of this judgment, partly with bitterness.

"This must be welcome news to your king," said Paulin. "Unless John's successor is as determined as he was to fight Philip for the few lands the English still hold in France."

"That's hardly likely," said Jean, with a sneer — the elevated upper lip and bared teeth made him look more like the pig-faced rascal Berengaria remembered. "Henry is only nine. His mother and his elders hold the reins, and they are far too busy fending off the army of Prince Louis to think of anything beyond the Channel."

"You are very thoughtful to bring us these tidings. I hope you will tell Philip that we appreciate his efforts to keep us informed. You may also tell him that I trust that he will not think of reclaiming Le Mans, because of this new development. When he gave the city to me, it was with the understanding that I would be diligent in keeping the County of Maine loyal to him, even if John should attack and try to regain it. I have kept my part of the bargain, and I am sure he will keep his, even though the Plantagenet threat may be less."

Paulin looked at her in admiration. "She knows when to speak out boldly," he thought.

"On the contrary," said Jean. "He asked me particularly to tell you, after you have had time to accustom yourself to this grievous loss, that more than ever he counts on your loyalty as his vassal here in Maine. In fact, he hopes you will continue to be content with your present holdings, and will cease to try to reclaim your so-called dowry lands from others of his loyal vassals."

He squinted at her with his little black eyes, expecting her to react angrily to his accusation.

She did not. She looked straight at him, motionless and wordless. She waited for him to elaborate.

Disappointed at her silence, he continued.

"You may well ask why I make such a charge. It has come to our attention that Chevalier Pierre Savary de Colombiers has turned over to you his demesne of Montbazon. This was King Philip's gift to Sieur Pierre as a reward for his years of loyal service. King Philip is displeased.

"We do not know how you persuaded Sieur Pierre to make the gift to you. But we can guess. It is well known that he has no particular love for his wife and that he visited you after his marriage. Perhaps you would care to explain what happened then." His manner had lost its polish. Again the sneer. This was the Jean she remembered.

Paulin, normally as imperturbable as a saint, could not contain himself. Berengaria had not told him much about her acquisition of Montbazon, but he knew her too well to suspect her of any wrongdoing. He took a step forward and glared at Jean.

"Enough! Sir Jean, I cannot believe that you speak for King Philip when you insult Queen Berengaria like this. On your honor as a knight, can you tell us that your king instructed you to come before her with such rude insinuations?"

Jean snapped, "Who are you to disbelieve me?" Then he winked cunningly. "But I could go back and assure him that his suspicions are unfounded, in exchange for certain considerations."

Berengaria cut him short. She was as outraged as Paulin, and her voice dripped with scorn. "If you were truly in your king's confidence, you would know that he has been well aware for two years of the transfer of this property to me; perhaps he was not pleased but he has made no objection, then or since. It is my opinion, Sir Jean de Brienne, that you are a paltry self-serving spy who pretends to be on his king's business but is actually nothing but a common blackmailer. You may leave us now."

She rose and stood beside Paulin until Jean de Brienne, affecting a swagger and sending a black look at them from the door, left the room.

Paulin and Berengaria looked at each other, dazed at the way the interview had gone. Berengaria spoke first.

"Paulin, you are a wise and true friend. I am sorry I never confided in you about Pierre Savary's gift of Montbazon. When he found it was actually part of my dowry, he honorably gave it to me. You rose magnificently to my defense, even without knowing all that. Thank you."

"He is a scoundrel, that Jean de Brienne, but you were more than a match for him. May I say, I have never seen you more queenly."

"I was quite surprised at myself — but something about the man brings out my rage. Some day I'll tell you what he was like at my sister's court. But now, Paulin, we must talk of this news of King John."

They sat down to confer. Berengaria took off her crown and pressed her hand against her forehead.

"It makes my head ache just to think of starting over again with this new English king. Maybe I should forget all about my claims." Her shoulders drooped.

"Certainly not! Think of your honor." Steadfast, upright Paulin looked at her in disapproval. "We must write quickly to Pope Innocent and ask him to remind the young king and his council of the agreement that all of us, including the Pope and John, signed. He must impress on them that they are honor-bound to abide by it."

Events overtook them. Innocent, that doughty warrior of the Lord, died before their message arrived in Rome. Berengaria had never met him, but she felt she had lost a strong ally. Who would support her as he had done, so unflaggingly, so determined to see that God's justice would protect her?

Fortunately his successor, Honorius III, proved an equally patient and protective champion. When he fully understood the matter, he wrote to Henry, to Henry's mother, to the bishops and to the papal legate in England, urging a settlement. They did not say yes, they did not say no: another impasse.

There was one tragi-comic note. Paulin, who had his own ways of learning what went on, heard that Jean de Brienne had, while the worse for wine, fallen into the Seine and drowned. When he told Berengaria, she said, "I know I should pray for his soul, but I cannot bring myself to." Then she wrote Blanche to tell her they would not need to be concerned with this onetime suitor any more.

Inexplicably, about this time the deliveries from Pierre stopped. Berengaria was puzzled, then resigned and saddened. If it had not been for the progress she was making in her scriptorium — as she had taken to calling the working end of the library — she might have spent even more time in wondering why. But as the sheets of parchment, covered with admirably straight and legible lines of Latin, piled up, she felt smugly pleased. She was well into the books of Arabic poetry by now, and had sent for François Lemonds, a gifted artist from the Illuminators' Guild in Tours, to come help her with the ornamentation.

"I am no artist," she told him. "I can copy and read and even translate, but I have tried my hand at illustration, and I cannot produce the pictures I see so clearly in my mind. Between us, we will create something beautiful!"

They were hard at work on their collaboration one afternoon in May of 1217, when a servant knocked, then entered at her bidding to tell her that a man had come from Pierre Savary, and had asked if he could come up to deliver his message.

This was unusual — ordinarily she went down to talk to the man. Perhaps he had something to say in private. She was flustered; seeing this, François tactfully said he had an errand in the town, and would go out for a bit, with her leave.

A moment after he had gone the door opened, and there stood Pierre.

"Pierre Savary sends himself to Queen Berengaria, and though he brings no wine, he trusts that she will be pleased." He mimicked the singsong speech of a messenger delivering his memorized words.

He came in, closed the door and stood quietly, giving her a moment to get over her surprise.

For months she had asked herself what she would say if she met him again. She would thank him for the wine. She would inquire about his wife. She would tell him that the revenues from Montbazon were arriving regularly, and express her gratitude.

All her well-rehearsed speeches flew away and she only stared at him dumbly. Somewhere on the borders of her consciousness was an inward smile at his unorthodox greeting. How like Pierre to lighten the solemnity of this meeting!

She saw that he was dressed more soberly than the last time she had seen him, when the splendor of his attire contrasted with the sorrow of their parting. She saw that the solid figure had thickened a little, but the bronzed, square-chinned open face, the neatly trimmed mustache, the rather bushy head of brown hair, the steady gaze of the hazel-brown eyes, were just the same.

Even from across the room, she could sense his tension, like an arrow fitted to the bow and waiting to be released.

Then he walked quickly over to stand across the table from her. Now he was very serious.

"Before you say a word, please let me explain why I am here."

She sat up straight, her hands pressed flat on the table, as though she were ready to rise and escape. Her face was pale, but there were spots of red on her cheeks.

"My wife Femo has died, Berengaria. It was five months ago. There was never any love between us, but I tried to respect her. As time went on it got harder. She was not easy to live with. She was ten years older than I was, and she must have sensed that I had an attachment to someone else. But now she is gone, God rest her soul. Now at last, my dear, I am a free man. Free to tell you I love you."

He moved around the table, took her hands and raised her gently from her chair.

She found herself staring at his lips, and the memory of that bittersweet, fleeting kiss when they last met blotted out everything else. She wanted nothing except to taste those lips again. Her eyes flew up to meet his and he read their message. There was no need for words. Gently, then with passion, his strong arms came around her and pressed her to him. She gave herself to his embrace, like a wild creature that has been lost and is now home again. He placed his hand under her chin and tipped up her head. Their lips met — softly, like a prelude. He released her and with his arm around her, led her into her bedchamber. He lifted her effortlessly and laid her on the bed, and she reached up her arms to welcome him.

42

erengaria could not remember when she had felt such happiness. With Pierre at her side, sure of his love, she bloomed. Everyone at her court noticed it. She did not try to hide the liaison with Pierre, but nobody questioned it. It was not at all unusual for a royal person to take a lover, and those close to her were happy for her.

"She looks years younger!" marveled Marie-Louise. "Have you noticed how her face is not so drawn, and she smiles so often?"

"When I think how that Pierre left her so miserable, when he came to see her two years ago, I think it's simple justice that he should be the one to set things to rights," said Henriette.

"Our queen continues to arouse my admiration," said Paulin Boutier to Herbert de Tucé. "She has so much more assurance — not that she lacked it before."

"I can see even more reason to be glad she has this new friend," said Herbert. "From all I have heard, Pierre Savary has a good reputation as a sound and sensible man, and frankly, I hope that before long our lady may find him as valuable at the council table as she does in her private rooms."

Only Cristina, who clung to her Basque probity, had reservations. She too was glad for her mistress, but she would have preferred to see her properly married.

"But she was married once," pointed out Carlos. "And look how it turned out for her. I can't think God will grudge her this good fortune, even if it bends His rules a little."

As for the two lovers, they soon settled into a comfortable routine. Pierre came whenever he could remove himself from his obligations in his several demesnes. His affairs were prospering and needed frequent attention. He was always admitted without announcement to the queen's private apartment. They usually dined there alone.

The question of marriage came up only briefly. About a month after their reunion they were sitting on a bench before the southwest-facing window, watching the shifting bands of saffron, crimson and gold in the western sky. Pierre's arm was around Berengaria's shoulders, and they leaned comfortably against each other.

"I have never seen such a beautiful sunset, I swear," said Berengaria. "But then, the whole world seems more beautiful now. Who could have guessed that at my age, I would at last find my true love?"

"Your age indeed! How about this grizzled oldster you have taken into your bed? Let's forget about our years and be thankful that we have come together at last."

They looked at each other and laughed for no real reason, just as though they were as young as they felt.

"The sun has nearly retired, don't you think we should follow his example?" He softly traced the oval outline of her face with his fingertips, then cupped her breast in his hand. He leaned to kiss her. But she put her hand over his lips and stopped him.

"My dear Pierre, we must talk about something we have both been avoiding. But we must face it. Should we marry? Let me speak first; I have been thinking about this for some time."

He sighed and sat back. "So have I. But yes, you speak first."

"Well, I believe it would only stir up all kinds of troubles. Those English would probably claim I was no longer entitled to anything from Richard's estate if I remarried. And I do want to keep that suit alive and get the recognition that's due me, no matter how long it takes. With this new king, I think my chances are better — anybody would be better than John."

Pierre agreed, but for different reasons. "Besides that, my dear love, what a comedown for a Queen of England to marry a lowly chevalier of France — it is not such a lofty title, you know. King Philip has been creating chevaliers right and left. What would people say? They would be condemning you from here to Rome."

"I don't care what people say. If I did, do you think you would be here beside me? No matter what we do, we will be gossiped about. I'm sure we are already the talk of Le Mans."

"No doubt; but there's another, even better reason against our marriage. King Philip is a watchful monarch. He has kept very quiet since Femo died, but he might fly into a rage if his loyal vassal married the widow of his worst enemy."

So they agreed to stay with the status quo. "There's no need to light a fire under a sleeping rooster," as Pierre with his store of homely country aphorisms put it.

While Pierre spent about half his time away, Berengaria presided over her city, kept up her sparring with the cathedral chapter and the bishop and continued to create "something beautiful" with her collaborator François. The latter was proving well worth the money she paid him. He had studied at the Basilica of Saint Martin in Tours, then joined the Illuminators' Guild and found plenty of occupation with ecclesiastic and lay commissions. He worked quickly and without fuss, his head of short gray curly hair bent attentively over his page, where the colors of the richly embellished initials blazed like captive rainbows.

Pierre did not pretend to understand what they were doing, but sometimes he looked over their shoulders and uttered appropriate murmurs of admiration.

It became harder and harder for Berengaria to find the time to produce enough pages to keep up with François.

"You are too efficient and I am too slow. I must translate as well as write, and I don't want to hurry for fear of making mistakes. What do you think, should we find another copyist to come in and help? Do you have any friend to suggest? He would have to read Arabic, you know."

Yes, François did; in fact two. "I knew them well when I was at the school at Saint Martin. They are serious and well trained; but you should probably see their work before you decide."

Berengaria thought a little journey to Tours might be just the thing. The Bishop was becoming more demanding and she needed some respite from the niggling negotiations. Pierre said he had to go away too, to see about his affairs in Montsoreau. So with François and the ever-faithful Carlos and Cristina, she set out to seek a scribe. It took ten days; besides interviewing the men and studying their work, she prevailed on François to take her to see the Illuminators' School, and to let her browse in their library. Stepping into the atmosphere of study and quiet application, she felt she was back with Brother Anselmo at Leyre, and said a private prayer for her old friend.

Once her choice was made and the man engaged, she could not wait to get back to Le Mans, where Pierre would undoubtedly have already returned. She insisted on riding far into the evening, so they made the return journey in only two days.

"Sometimes I think she is trying to be another Queen Eleanor," complained Cristina to Carlos.

Not until she entered her palace did Berengaria realize how tired she was. She flung off her cloak, pulled off her coif and ran her fingers through her hair. She sank into the nearest chair and gladly accepted the cool drink of water Marie-Louise brought her.

"Thank you. I was quite parched. How have things gone in my absence? Has Sieur Pierre returned from Montsoreau?"

"He has not returned, madame, because apparently he never went, but we have not seen him." She looked flushed and seemed temporarily at a loss for words.

Henriette took over. "We have heard, madame, that he has bought a house nearby and he is busy moving in."

"He has sent you a message," said Marie-Louise. "He said that whatever day you returned, we were to tell you that he invites you to breakfast with him the next morning, and he will send his man at nine."

Berengaria was confused and a little annoyed. "Will one of you please tell me just what is going on?"

"All I know is what our brother Paulin has told us," said Marie-Louise. "He says that he helped Sieur Pierre find the house two months ago, but Paulin had to promise not to tell anyone until Sieur Pierre said he could."

"And where is this house?"

"It is on the Rue des Chanoines, the third house from the cathedral square," said Henriette. Over the years the sisters had solved the problem of both wanting to talk at once by taking turns.

"You know, the tall narrow one where Sieur Charles Bonnard used to live," her sister added.

"And then Sieur Charles left it to his daughter when he died, but she wanted to stay in Angers and never lived there."

"And now Pierre has bought it and made it quite comfortable, Paulin says."

"And he has two good servingmen, and guess who they are!"

Before Berengaria could guess, Marie-Louise told her. "Why, they are Carlito and Cristiano, the sons of our Carlos and Cristina. And they both say they are blessed to have found such a kind master."

What a lot had happened in the ten days she had been gone! Berengaria was too exhausted to sort it out and went to bed. She could not imagine what had gotten into Pierre to do this without saying anything to her.

When Pierre's man appeared the next day — it was Carlito — she was dressed and ready to be escorted to her breakfast engagement, a five minutes' walk up from the palace square. Pierre met her at his door, without a word and trying to look guileless. He dismissed Carlito and led her from the dark entry up the steep wooden stairs to an airy chamber with windows looking down onto a small courtyard, crowded with trees and bushes that had not seen a gardener's shears for some time. He bowed, and gestured to a chair drawn up to the table laid for breakfast. "Will you do me the honor, my dear, of joining me for our first meal together in my new house?"

"Oh Pierre!" she exclaimed. "It's beautiful! But why didn't you say a word to me about all this?"

"Because I wanted to surprise you, of course. I have decided it was time for me to stop living like a kept man, and to instead give you a chance, now and then, to be a kept woman."

She burst into laughter and hugged him.

"So you don't mind and you will come to see me often?"

"As often as you come to me. I expect we will wear out the cobblestones between the palace and — Pierre, does your house have a name?"

"Nothing more than La Maison de Charles Bonnard. But I had thought of calling it La Maison de Mon Bonheur — the House of my Happiness."

here came a day, four years into the reign of the new English king, when Herbert de Tucé staggered up the stairs to Berengaria's library, straining with the weight of the heavy copper chest he bore in his arms. He had grown more portly over the years, but he would accept no help. He wanted to be the first to tell her the news.

"My lady Queen! The English have sent you 1,000 livres; it is all here in this coffer." He set his burden down with a thud on the table and pulled a cloth from his sleeve to mop his brow. Berengaria looked at him in amazement, then stared at the sturdy chest, well bound with leather straps.

Herbert was still puffing and wheezing but he could not wait to tell her more. "The man who brought it had four armed guards and I couldn't think what could be the reason for so much protection. He gave me the chest and tried to tell me what it was, but I could hardly make sense out of his wretched French. Then he gave me these documents and I saw that this is the first year's installment of what is due you, and that the arrears will be paid off at the rate of five hundred livres a year."

He sank into a chair and looked at her with what could only be described as a foolish grin. "Madame, did you ever think we would see this day?" She had never seen sober Herbert let down his reserve so much, but she knew exactly how he felt and her smile was as broad and bemused as his.

Vindication at last! She told Pierre, who congratulated her. She wrote to Blanche, who had been her confidante and supporter during the whole dreary twenty-year struggle:

Sister dear, glorious news! The King of England is an honorable man. He has agreed to pay me what is owed me

from Richard's estate, and I have actually received the first
payment. I can hardly believe it.

At last, the world will see that a princess of Navarre and
Queen of England has been properly recognized by those
haughty Plantagenets. I hope our father is looking down
from his seat with the angels in heaven, and applauding this
tardy justice to our house.

Now with this money, I may be able to do some of the
things I have been dreaming of — perhaps even build a
monastery, as our mother did.

How are affairs with you? Can you remove yourself
from your duties for a time, and come pay us a visit? You
could help us celebrate.

She had not yet told Blanche about Pierre's place in her life and she
was afraid her sister still clung to her earlier distrust of him. A visit
and a chance to get to know him better would surely put all that
straight.

However, Blanche sent word that her affairs in Champagne
were so topsy-turvy that she would not dare to go away, even
briefly. Several of the high nobility were restless and showing signs
of joining forces to dispute her authority as Countess.

Just because I am a woman, they think they can threaten
me! Even if I have to go into battle against them, I shall
show them they are wrong. King Philip is on my side. But
for now, I must be here. When I can come, I will.

Berengaria's adversaries — the Bishop and the chapter —
were not nearly as bellicose as Blanche's, but they were getting
more and more worrisome. It seemed that no sooner was one cloud
lifted than another hovered.

One day when Pierre had just returned from Colombiers, she
told him there was something she needed to talk to him about and
suggested they go out for a walk beside the River Sarthe, below
the walls. The street down to the river was crowded and many of
those they met smiled and murmured respectful greetings. Most
of them did not know who Pierre was but they were getting used

to seeing him, and thought him a proper solid sort, a fitting escort for their lady.

The riverside path was one of Berengaria's favorite walks: on one side the quietly flowing Sarthe and beyond it, fields and forests. Today they displayed every shade of green and golden-brown. Slender pale-green poplars stood like candles among the still leafless oaks. Farmers' fields were beginning to show faint mists of green over the rich brown earth, where the wheat was just coming up. It was a landscape of renewal and hope on this fresh April day. Turning her eyes upward in the other direction, she saw the thousand-year-old Roman walls that enclosed the old city. How many people, she thought, must have gazed at those towers and that impregnable stonework, and reflected on how fleeting is our time on earth, while the ancient walls look down uncaring, century after century?

She shivered a little, not from cold but from her sudden glimpse of the weight of time and history. She drew her long white cloak about her and pressed closer to Pierre, her friend, her refuge, her heart's companion. She squeezed his arm and looked up at him to see him smiling down on her.

"Well?" said Pierre. "Have you come back from wherever your thoughts were taking you, and are you ready to tell me what we are to discuss?"

She started. "I am sorry. I was just thinking how much it means to have you by my side. I need your advice, Pierre."

"My advice? Not again! I recall that only twelve years ago when you were in a quandary I suggested that you write to the Pope for help in approaching King John. And now once more you need my counsel. Am I to have no peace? What kind of trouble are you in now?"

"Very funny, but I am serious. I truly need to know what you think I should do about that bothersome Bishop."

"Perhaps if you started at the beginning I could dredge up some pearls of wisdom. Why is the Bishop suddenly so bother-some?"

"It's not sudden; he has been a worry ever since he came to Le Mans, two years ago. That was before you came back into my life. I shall never forget my first meeting with him!" She looked grim at the memory. Pierre saw that she was indeed serious and waited for her to go on.

"As you so wisely suggest, I will start at the beginning. I went to pay my respects to Bishop Maurice soon after he arrived. He was not at all what I expected. I have met many churchmen in my life, but none quite like this. He did not even dress the part. He wore doublet and hose like a lay nobleman, and he had thrown a stole carelessly around his shoulders, in token of his churchly office, I suppose. It was too bad of me, but my first thought was that he looked more like a hawk than a holy man. His eyes were yellowish-gray and I never saw him blink. His nose looked like a beak."

"And did he swoop on you like a hawk, and try to carry you away in his talons?"

"On the contrary. He permitted me to kiss his great ruby ring, and said only, 'We thank you for your visit, and we hope you will prove to be the dutiful daughter of Christ that the Dame of Le Mans must be.' I did not think this was the time to complain about the chapter's highhandedness in taxing my people. I simply said I would indeed pray for a dutiful attitude, and left. And those were the last civil words we said to each other."

"And now?" They had turned, and were pacing back toward the steps that would take them up into the city.

"Oh Pierre, I am sorry to keep boring you with all this. But you are the only person I can talk to with complete frankness. My counselors have my interests at heart, goodness knows; but they have lived here all their lives, getting along with the chapter as best they could. They've learned it's easier to compromise than to fight."

"So. You are inclined to fight, and you want me to encourage you. What shall we fight about?"

"It started as such a little matter. It seemed almost silly to make a fuss about it, but sometimes I feel I have to take a stand."

As they walked up the steps, she poured out the story. A certain Julien Laurent, one of her bailiffs, had collected a tax on animals sold in a section of the city which lay between the area governed by the cathedral chapter and that by her administration. It was an area long under dispute. The canons of the chapter demanded that Julien Laurent yield them the money he had collected. He refused.

"They asked me to make him return it, and of course I refused too. Herbert de Tucé says that place is absolutely within my fief. Now they are threatening to place the entire city under interdict, just because I held to my principles and refused to give up a paltry five farthings! Why, it's hardly enough to buy two loaves."

"So what did you do?" Pierre's attitude had changed from indulgent amusement to concern.

When they reached the palace, the footman standing at the entrance quickly opened the heavy door and they walked in, Berengaria still talking distractedly. "I have not done anything yet; I have simply worried. If they carry out their threat, that will mean that none of the churches in the city will be permitted to hold services; not even Saint Pierre-la-Cour. How could I stay here when those dreadful people wouldn't let me attend services in my own chapel? I would have to leave the city."

She sank into a chair, and looked up at him. He saw that she looked tired, drawn. Yet the beauty that came from within, the simple goodness that shone from those clear green eyes, still moved him, just as it had fifteen years ago, when they sat by the fire in Blanche's hall.

"What must I do, Pierre? Paulin says I should pay the money, but send word to Pope Honorius and if he supports me, demand that they acknowledge that they were wrong. Gervais de Pringé is not sure, but thinks I should refuse to pay anything and wait to see if the bishop means what he says. And Herbert says I should give them the bit of money and end the affair, even though I'm in the right."

"No! You are a woman of principle, Berengaria, you always have been, and you must not back down." Pierre had become almost as incensed as she was. He hated to see her so tormented. He was quiet for several minutes, frowning, thinking.

"If I were on your council, I would advise you not to pay them; to leave the city to show your defiance, and at the same time to write to the Pope and ask his help. Do not give in even though the amount of money is so small. That would only encourage them to make more demands. As we say in the Touraine, 'Give a beggar a groat, he'll ask for your coat.'"

Berengaria took the advice. She left to stay with Paulin Boutier's old mother at Saint George-du-Plain, a half-day's ride south of the city. She sent an urgent message to Pope Honorius; then she waited.

The impassse went on for three months. All that time, not a mass was held in all Le Mans; not a marriage was consecrated; not a body was given a Christian burial. At last the Pope appointed Abbot Bernardo of Josaphat as his legate to come and adjudicate the matter. The abbot acted quickly to end the confrontation. He decreed that the interdict should be lifted and that Berengaria should agree to come back to her city. The matter of the five farthings was to be decided later by all parties, when presumably tempers would have cooled.

It was a triumphant return. Canon Guillaume of Saint Pierre-la-Cour escorted her to the city from her exile, with a party that included Herbert de Tucé and the queen's "Grand Ami" — Great Friend, as Pierre was beginning to be known. The whole chapter of Saint Pierre met her with great ceremony, and conducted her to her palace where the papal legate and the two judges, one appointed by the Bishop, one by the judiciary, were waiting.

Berengaria and her counselors held a brief conference before the meeting. They told her what they recommended: return the five farthings, but state publicly that the bailiff had been within his rights in collecting it.

"That will make you look statesmanlike and magnanimous," said Paulin solemnly, placing his forefinger alongside his pointed nose and peering at her, looking quite statesmanlike if not magnanimous.

The meeting with the dignitaries in the palace's state chamber began civilly. Abbot Bernardo presided, with the two judges at his side. Berengaria and six of her counselors sat on one side of the room; the Bishop with members of the cathedral chapter on the other. A small crowd of leading citizens and churchmen stood at the back of the hall, near the door.

Abbot Bernardo raised his hand for silence, and the murmuring stopped. After expressing gratitude to all present for laying aside their differences and agreeing to his terms, he nodded to Berengaria, who rose to speak. All eyes were on this slim, white-clad woman standing as straight as a birch sapling.

"My Lord Abbot, my Lord Bishop, and all those present, welcome to our palace. I am well pleased to be back in my home, and I am gratified that the city no longer lies under an interdict. I am sure we can quickly resolve any few differences that remain."

She signaled to Herbert de Tucé, who formally handed a leather purse containing five farthings to the Bishop's representative. Bishop Maurice fixed his yellow eyes on her and his thin lips stretched in a malicious smile. So! She had decided to give in after all and return the money.

Berengaria was still facing the Abbot, and Paulin indicated to her with a nod of his head toward the spectators that she should turn so they could hear her clearly. She did so, and went on with her remarks, speaking now more loudly so all could hear.

"So we thank God that the churches of Le Mans are again open to the citizens, and that the differences between the Dame of Le Mans and the chapter of the cathedral have been amicably resolved. In order to come to this peaceable conclusion, we have gladly presented to the chapter the money in question, which was collected by our bailiff from a merchant in the Rue du Pilier Rouge. But we do not admit that the tax was wrongfully collected, and we are confident that from now on, it will be acknowledged by all that the Rue du Pilier Rouge is rightfully within the domain of the city of Le Mans and not the chapter of the Cathedral of Saint Julien."

Bishop Maurice's face became suffused with an angry flush, and he was on the verge of making a heated retort. The Abbot was quicker, and began speaking while still rising from his chair. He was not going to permit this whole dispute to erupt again.

"Thank you, Queen Berengaria, and thanks to you, Bishop Maurice, and to all those who have come here this day. We will return to Rome to report to our Holy Father that God's benevolent mercy falls again on the people of Le Mans. Now go you all in peace." He made the sign of the cross, and there was nothing to do but disperse.

This whole affair had two results. For one thing, the long enmity between city and cathedral sputtered to a close. Both sides were exhausted after years of controversy, and tacitly agreed to put it all behind them.

Secondly, from then on, Pierre Savary was a regular member of the queen's council. It seemed only right, after the part he had played in rescuing her from her dilemma. Pierre was pleased; he had rather enjoyed his fling at diplomacy, and this honor legitimized his position as an advisor to the Queen.

Herbert de Tucé, who had early on predicted that this might happen, solemnly congratulated Pierre when he formally joined the others for the first time. Herbert de la Marche and Gervais de Pringé, by now regular members of the council, nodded agreement. Paulin Boutier added, "We will all benefit from your presence. Anyone the queen trusts as she does you, and anyone who has served her so well, is sure to prove a wise counselor." There were no hidden barbs in the words, or subtle references to Pierre's status as the Queen's Grand Ami. Paulin was too honest and fair for that. He beamed with genuine pleasure.

Pierre was almost at a loss for words. But his years in the countryside came to his rescue again.

"Gentlemen, I thank you all. As for wisdom, I promise to listen more than to talk. After all, even a donkey can look wise, so long as he refrains from braying."

t was some time before the city settled down after the lifting of the interdiction. Some of the citizens had been grumbling, blaming their Dame for the disgraceful closure of the churches all those months.

But when those who had been present at the hearing before the papal legate told what they had seen, and word got around of how their lady had stood up to the Bishop and adroitly outmaneuvered him about the taxes, their affection and respect returned.

Only one thing was lacking for Berengaria's peace of mind: a rapprochement between Blanche and Pierre. In 1223 she again wrote to Blanche, asking her to come for a visit.

Blanche replied quickly. Yes, her affairs had taken a turn for the better. Thibaut was now twenty-one and officially Count of Champagne. So Blanche's years as regent were ending. It was a good time to go traveling. She was on her way and would arrive in ten days.

When they met, the sisters assured each other that they had not changed a bit, then laughed at themselves. "Of course we are older, and we show it," said Berengaria as she led Blanche up to her chamber. "I have wrinkles in my brow, and my hair is going gray. And you, sister, aren't the slender lass you used to be — but you still have that peaches-and-cream complexion. How I envy you!"

"And I envy you your slim figure. Really, though, I don't mind saying I think we are both remarkably well preserved, considering our age and what we've been through. Remember what our mother used to say? That once she reaches her prime, a Basque woman does not change much? I think she was right."

"So do I — about that, and so many other things. Now here is your room, Blanche, and I hope you will be comfortable. When you are settled, come into the library and we will have a good talk before Pierre comes to supper." The mention of Pierre's name hung in the air, but neither pursued the reference for the moment.

When Blanche entered the library she saw that it was almost filled with three scribes' tables and stools, book chests and the big rectangular oak table. "What have you done to this beautiful room, Berengaria? I would have thought the Dame of Le Mans had no time for all this bookish folderol."

"Quite right, I don't have time. So I have engaged a copyist and an illuminator. In fact there is François, hard at his labors." She gestured toward the man, absorbed in his work at the far table. He looked up abstractedly, brush raised from his paintpot, nodded and again bent his head over his work. Even from where she stood Blanche could make out a thick-shafted, ornamented red-and-gold letter "A" on the page before him.

"I know you have never understood why I go on with this 'bookish folderol,' Blanche."

"When you insisted on going to the monastery and becoming a scribe, I thought it was just some youthful phase and you would grow out of it. Yet here you are, worse than ever. What on earth do you see in it, sister?"

"I will try to explain. When I make a fair copy of a book of the Scriptures or the writings of the fathers of the Church, I am creating something beautiful and useful that will give pleasure and comfort to others for years to come — long after I am gone. When I translate from the Arabic to Latin, I am doing something truly original, that no one has ever done before. I can bring the songs, the learned treatises, the histories of that culture alive for all of us here in the West. Don't you see, Blanche? This work gives me a sense that I am doing what God gave me the ability to do, and it becomes my reason for being." She stopped, embarrassed at having become so carried away.

François had put down his brushes to listen. He rose and approached the women. "She is quite right, Countess. It is God's work that we do here, and we are creating a priceless legacy to leave to future generations. But what Queen Berengaria does not tell you is that she herself is recognized as one of the best Arabic translators in France. You should be very proud of your sister."

Blanche was surprised. Her sister, a noted person of learning? Berengaria blushed. "Thank you, François, that is gratifying to hear whether it is true or not. Now we will leave you in peace." They passed on to the bedchamber.

As her library had become a crowded scriptorium, Berengaria had made her own chamber more of a sitting room. Her bed, off to the far side, was draped with dark blue curtains. Two well cushioned chairs were placed by the fireplace, with a small table between them. She had hung one of her mother's weavings on the wall; it was bordered in gray, with a center of twining rosevines, their pink blossoms peeping out from the green leaves. Blanche exclaimed when she saw it.

"That was in the room you and I shared when we were little girls in Estella, wasn't it? I remember counting the rose blossoms, and I never got the same answer twice. What a pretty little nest you've made yourself. I would spend all my time here, if this were my room. And I suppose this is where you and Pierre have your meals," pointing matter-of factly to the table by the fireside.

They seated themselves. "It is," said Berengaria, a little flustered. "That is, when we are not down in the hall with guests. So, Blanche, you have heard about Pierre and me, but how?"

"My dear sister, you are a personage of some prominence, and you cannot expect to keep such an affair to yourself. It is discussed in Paris, as I found out during my last visit, just before King Philip died. Everybody was well aware of it and couldn't wait to ask me what my sister's 'fiancé' was like. But I doubt if Philip was interested in what you and Pierre were up to. After all, he'd been king for forty years, and he was mostly worried about his failing health and the dubious abilities of his son and heir Prince Louis."

"Well, that is encouraging, I suppose. Pierre and I might have married, Blanche, but we thought Philip would be angry. We couldn't afford to alienate him. Now I wonder. Maybe it would have been all right. Maybe we still should."

"I wouldn't be too sure. Louis is a lot like his father. He's capable of stirring up trouble if he thinks it would serve his purposes. But never mind all that, Berenguelita. The important thing is whether Pierre is the man you deserve. Is he as good and trustworthy as you always maintained, and as I doubted?"

"He is, absolutely. He truly loves me, and I love him."

Blanche rose to embrace her sister. "I am so glad for you. I grieved over your anguish with Richard, and I prayed you might find a man you could love as much as I loved my Thibaut."

Berengaria looked up at her, close to tears — tears of joy that she could share her happiness with her sister. "I never would have thought it possible, but there it is. The last ten years have been the happiest of my life."

Just then the man in question entered, in time to hear her last words. He grasped the situation: the sisters had been exchanging confidences, and he was the subject. The moment promised to be awkward. All three spoke at once.

"Sieur Pierre!" said Blanche.

"I am so pleased to see you, Countess," said Pierre.

"Oh, here you are, Pierre." said Berengaria.

"You are looking very well," said Blanche.

"Welcome to Le Mans," said Pierre.

"We were just talking about you!" said Berengaria.

Then all three laughed.

"Shall we start again?" said Pierre. "Since I am the one who interrupted your tête-à-tête, I shall try to make amends. Countess, you are indeed welcome to Le Mans, but I shall hope to say so with more authority when I receive you in my own home, which I hope will be soon."

"Well said, Sieur Pierre! I had no idea you had your own residence here, and I am very glad to know it. And you are indeed looking well. We have all changed but I think you less than any of us." Appraising him, she thought his bearing was much more polished and self-confident than she remembered. "I am happy that my sister has such a stalwart ally."

Berengaria sighed in relief. Apparently they were all to be friends.

"Shall we call for our supper?" she asked.

Blanche and Berengaria spent all the next day together, catching up. Pierre left them to it. Towards evening they went to vespers at Saint Pierre-la-Cour and walked slowly back through the square, where townsfolk were hurrying home before dark and rooks were settling into the treetops, quarreling loudly over the best spots. On the way, Berengaria had finished telling of her last confrontation with Bishop Maurice.

"Our stories are not so very different, are they?" said Blanche when they were back in the palace and settled in Berengaria's room. "Though my enemies were not the hierarchy of the church, but noblemen who had an inflated idea of their importance. It took them a good ten years to get it into their heads that this was not a weak-willed woman they could push around. They certainly didn't expect me to send armed troops against them!"

"Did you actually go into battle, brandishing a sword?"

"I would have if it had been necessary. But I had help from my good deputy Guillerme de Lavalier and of course from Hugh de Vendeuvre, my right-hand man whom you remember. Guillerme assembled half a hundred knights and several brave captains to lead them. Off they marched in good order and took the rebels by surprise early one morning, before they had staggered out of their tents. They didn't put up much of a fight; my captains thought they were still recovering from too much wine the night before. Now, one by one, they've all come skulking back to pledge their allegiance to me."

Berengaria heard all this with wide-eyed admiration. "My sister the general!" she exclaimed.

Blanche laughed, then rose and walked about the room, looking at her sister's possessions. She caught sight of a little psalter on a table and picked it up.

"Oh Berengaria, you still have this psalter, and how worn it has become! Some of the pages are quite ragged. And look, most of the jewels have fallen off the cover. Surely you could engage someone to make you a new one? You have so many friends in the monasteries."

"But I love my little psalter; it reminds me of dear Brother Anselmo who gave it to me when I left Leyre. I need reminders of my friends and family about. And that reminds me." She took the psalter and opened it to a picture of a very tall knight in armor, brandishing his sword at a small, terrified devil. "This always makes me think of brother Sancho. Have you heard from him lately? I have not, for two years. His last message said he was going to retire to Tudela and try to get over his infirmities. But he did not say what they were."

"No, and I am worried, too. Our nephew Ramiro de Tolosa used to keep me posted while he was a chancellor in Provins. His duties often brought him to Troyes."

"Ramiro!" said Berengaria. "I had quite forgotten that he had a post in Champagne. I wish I knew him. After all, he's our brother's son, even if Sancho never married his mother and we don't even know who she was. Does he look anything like his father?"

"A little, but he is not nearly so tall or broad. His mother must have been a dainty little maid! I became quite fond of him; he is really a good man. He knows he can never succeed as King of Navarre, so he has supported Thibaut's claim. Which looks stronger all the time; I doubt if Sancho will marry and have any legitimate children now. But Ramiro has not been in touch with me since Sancho made him Bishop of Pamplona."

She laid the psalter down. Suddenly Berengaria jumped up.

"Blanquita! We should go see Sancho. Why not? Thibaut can handle affairs in Champagne, and now that things have calmed down here, I could leave my good counselors in charge for a few months. What do you say?"

They talked it over, and agreed now was the time to see their native land one last time — "before we're too old and crippled to climb on a horse!" said Berengaria.

Pierre worried, and said he should go too — but Berengaria told him she could not possibly feel comfortable about leaving unless he were in Le Mans, looking after her interests. So it was agreed: as soon as Blanche could go back to Troyes and arrange matters, she would return and they would set out.

erengaria, Blanche and their retainers, including four men-at-arms and a captain, set out on a bright September day in 1225. Cristina was in the party — Berengaria could not imagine taking such a journey without her faithful maid. So was Cristina's son Cristiano, on leave from his duties with Pierre. He was old enough now to serve as squire to the captain. The dark-haired, taciturn young man looked amazingly like his father Carlos, as Berengaria remembered him when he first joined the household staff in Pamplona. But Cristiano had a little more dash. He puffed out his chest in pride at his new leather jerkin, and firmly clasped the carved hilt of the short sword he wore in his belt.

When Pierre told Berengaria goodbye, he held her close for a minute, then looked at her with his steady brown-eyed gaze, his face as solemn as a bishop's. "There is only one thing I am worried about, my dear love."

"And what is that, are you afraid I will fall off my horse? Remember, I will be riding my sturdy and surefooted Grimaldo the Eighth."

"Nothing so inconsequential. There will be plenty of people to pick you up if you do. No, I am afraid you will be so glad to see your brother and the places where you were so happy as a child, that you will stay in Navarre. And since I could not bear living without you, I would have to come join you, and I really do not want to move to Navarre."

As she set out, Berengaria smiled to herself, remembering Pierre's words, missing him already. The road they followed was at first familiar, leading southeast to Tours, then joining the main route of the pilgrims bound for Saint-Jacques-de-Compostelle, as the French called Santiago de Compostela. The road was narrow, and the party rode in single file. Berengaria was lulled by the peace and warmth as they rode past tawny fields where harvesters were gathering in the oats and barley. The sun shone on autumn-gilded oaks and beeches. Grimaldo paced placidly along, as tranquil as his mistress.

Then the road rose toward the Forest of Bercé and they passed from sunlight into the shadows of giant oaks that dwarfed the little party and filled Berengaria with a sense of her insignificance. Her sleepy calm gave way to questions, conjectures and memories of other journeys. What would it be like, to go back to the land of her youth which she had not seen for so many years? To relive, as she must, the wrenching yet hopeful departure when she left Leyre with Queen Eleanor to travel off to Sicily and Richard? Then there was the journey from the Holy Land back to France, when she still thought she and Richard might find happiness. Who could have guessed that she would still be in France thirty-three years later? That she would never see the country of which she had been crowned Queen? Or that in all this time she would never return to Navarre? Where had all the years gone?

She sighed. A squirrel ran across the road, chattering in excitement. She wondered if he had as many squirrel-sized concerns as she had for a human. "Probably more," she decided. "For him, it's vital to find enough nuts for winter; while I have no worries about starvation."

On the seventh day as they neared Toulouse, she saw the massive octagonal tower of the Cathedral of Saint-Sernin rising ahead of them. She and Blanche were riding side by side.

"I hope we will have no trouble here," Berengaria said.

"Mercy me, why should we? Does the city not accept visitors gladly?"

"It is just that I have never trusted the counts of Toulouse, ever since my poor Joanna was treated so dreadfully by Raymond. I have heard that the new Count Raymond has been warring with King Louis, just as his father did with Louis' father King Philip. This new one is Joanna's son but he hardly knew his mother, so I suppose he takes after his father. He may think we are here to spy for King Louis."

The city looked calm. No arrows were flying over the walls or siege engines poised to launch their projectiles. Berengaria spurred

Grimaldo to a trot and caught up with the captain of the guards to ask his thoughts.

"No need to worry, my lady," he assured her. "I have already received word by the messenger I sent on ahead. The city is quite safe. Count Raymond is away in the south, and his truce with King Louis still holds after two years of peace. Lodgings are waiting for you at a hospice near Saint-Sernin."

Sure enough, they proceeded without incident. As was their custom, they ate a simple meal and retired early. Even when they traveled slowly, they were tired and eager for bed at the end of the day.

The next morning, Berengaria decreed that they would not leave until noon. She wanted to see the famous Basilica, one of the main stops on the road to Compostela.

"Never have I seen such an enormous church!" Blanche marveled as they stepped inside. "Why, it seems twice as large as Chartres, and I thought that was the biggest in the world."

Hundreds of pilgrims were in the church. Some were hearing Mass at the altar, others were wandering around the ambulatory with its five chapels, each dedicated to a different saint. Still others waited in lines to view the holy relics of Saint Jacques or Saint Sernin. Yet the interior was so vast that it seemed almost empty. Berengaria thought of Joanna, walking down that long nave to be married to Raymond and trusting in his love and kindness; how soon she had been disillusioned! She lit a candle and said a prayer for the soul of her long-gone friend.

She would have liked to stay in Toulouse longer, to see the palace of the counts and to walk the streets and think of Joanna; but the road ahead was still long.

From Toulouse they traveled southwesterly until the first jutting peaks of the Pyrenees appeared, the familiar mountains of their youth. Blanche was delighted. "Now that we see our own Pyrenees, the end of the journey can't be too far off; but with all these folk on the road, not to mention cows and sheep, we may not travel very fast."

The way was indeed becoming more and more crowded. Besides bands of pilgrims, there were merchants, jongleurs, mendicant monks and the occasional herdsman, bringing his flock of sheep down from the mountains to grazing lands on the plains. For these, everybody had to stop while the bleating, balky creatures were herded to the side of the road.

Berengaria had seen pilgrim bands many times before, but Blanche kept exclaiming in surprise.

"Listen to them singing as they go! They look so happy. Isn't it wonderful, Berengaria, that so many pious folk are taking this long hard journey, to show their devotion to the saint?" Just then a swaggering, ragged pilgrim, dancing along and nodding his head in time with the song of his fellows, looked up, grinned and shouted something unintelligible at Blanche as she rode past him, and gave her horse a friendly slap on the rump. The horse neighed and reared, and Blanche had to clutch his mane to keep in the saddle.

Gasping, she pulled her cloak closer about her. "What did he say, Berengaria? I did not understand a word. I think it was not civil."

"I don't know either; these people speak in tongues I've never heard. But never mind, sister. I don't think he meant any harm, and we shouldn't begrudge them a little amusement as they go."

"Perhaps they are not all as pious as I thought," said Blanche.

Presently they left the fields and gentle hills of Béarn to find themselves riding up a road that seemed aiming for the sky. They crested the rocky heights by way of the Pass of Somport, and then it was all downhill, following the River Aragon. Now everything they saw took them back to their childhood.

"Remember when we used to come up into these mountains for the dove hunting with father, and how sorry we felt for all the poor birds caught in the nets?" Blanche asked. "I swore I would never eat a dove as long as I lived — oh dear, I did not stick to that very long."

"Yes, and then sometimes we went into the woods to gather chestnuts; we didn't have to feel sorry for them. I remember how good they tasted, roasted over a fire back in the palace. I have never thought the French chestnuts could compare."

The farther they went, the more the memories came back. On the hillsides, they saw where diligent farmers had planted hayfields on slopes so steep they looked impossible to mow, and where they had laboriously cleared pasturages for their hardy cattle and sheep.

"Remember when Sanchito told us that all the cattle up here were born with their legs on one side shorter than the other, so they could stand up on the hills?" laughed Berengaria. "And for years I believed him."

The route went down through tight little valleys. Wherever there was a bit of level land by the river a tiny village of square red-roofed houses huddled. Here and there a larger house, surrounded with outbuildings and gardens, displayed a coat of arms, a sign that this was the home of a lord of the valley.

With everything so poignantly reminding her of her youth, Berengaria felt a sting of doubt. Was she wrong to have deserted her native land? It was a land that demanded much, yet it repaid every ounce of effort, if not with riches, then with a sense of worth, and pride in the homeland. She wondered again, as she had wondered before, if she should have renounced her claims as Richard's heir and come back here to live out her years — perhaps as the lady of some Navarrese noble, or as an impoverished widow, depending on her brother Sancho for support.

No. That would have been cowardly. No matter how hard the struggle had been, she had won in the end, and she felt immensely strengthened by the ordeal.

Besides, she would never have met Pierre! Smiling a little, she said to Blanche, "God moves in mysterious ways."

Blanche too had been musing on "What if?"

"I know exactly what you are thinking, you are wondering what it would have been like to grow up and grow old in our homeland. Yet I know both of us are glad we lived our lives as we did, where we did."

"God save us!" exclaimed Berengaria. "We sound as though we were teetering on the edge of the grave. Let's be grateful for good health, and stop dwelling on the past, and think how wonderful it will be to see dear Sanchito."

"Who may be the one teetering on the edge of the grave. I am so worried about how we will find him."

They had more reason to worry that night when they arrived in Sangüesa, one of the five royal seats of Navarre. This would be their last stop before reaching their destination, Tudela. They went directly to the palace — which was hardly a palace. It was, rather, the most substantial house in the town, therefore the one where the kings of Navarre customarily stayed when they visited Sangüesa. But no such guests had come for years.

The owner of the house was a bent, wrinkled man — once tall, now with a back so bowed he had to peer up to meet Berengaria's eyes. He greeted his guests warmly, not in the quavering voice one might have expected, but in the firm tones of a man accustomed to commanding attention. They realized he was not as frail as he looked.

"Welcome to Sangüesa, Queen Berengaria and Countess Blanche. I am Francisco de la Huerta, and this is my son Jaime. We heard only an hour ago that you were on your way, but we have tried to get ready. I knew your sainted father well and his good Queen Sancha, God rest their souls." Jaime bowed gravely; he was a man of perhaps thirty, with little to say.

"I am sure I often heard my father speak of you," Berengaria replied, though she was not at all sure. "You are most hospitable to take us in, on such short notice."

By now they were in the dining hall, being helped out of their traveling cloaks and invited to sit by the fire. The room was musty, and it was plain that the whole house lacked a woman's touch. Candles were still being lit, and tables and benches dragged out, and through the door to the kitchen the cook and his helpers were seen and heard as they hastily tried to assemble a proper meal for a party of twenty.

It was not too bad a dinner, considering, consisting mainly of an enormous meat stew served in wooden bowls with wooden spoons. ("I do not know what could have happened to our silver spoons," Francisco said plaintively.) Berengaria and Blanche agreed later that the stew undoubtedly consisted of all the leftovers that could be found in the larder; but with plenty of onions, garlic and pepper, and thick chunks of bread to soak up the juices, it served very well.

As they ate, Francisco told them what he could of their brother the king, their first concern.

"I have not seen him for five years, and even then he was not well. He used to be so vigorous, but he seemed to have lost half his strength. Now, they tell me, he has shut himself up in his castle in

Tudela and refuses to budge. He has let it be known that if anybody — prince, bishop, counselor, friend — wishes to see him, they must climb his hill and then climb some more, to the topmost room in the castle."

"Why so high, so hard to reach?" wondered Blanche. "As I remember that castle, there are several comfortable rooms on the first floor."

"I believe it is because he has become suspicious and fearful of traitors. From that tower, he can see every inch of land where friends or enemies could approach the city."

The next day the sisters were climbing Sancho's stairs, and feeling their years.

"Do you remember, Blanche, when we were children and our parents brought us here, how we would run up these steps to see who could reach the top first? Sanchito always won, of course. Now it is all I can do to put one foot in front of the other, much less run."

"What I remember best" (Blanche paused and her plump bosom heaved as she tried to regain her breath) "is counting as I went because it was hard to tell how far we were, since we could see neither top nor bottom as we ran up the tower in circles. There were ninety-five steps."

When they reached the top, gasping, the manservant who had trudged up behind them knocked on a massive door and pushed it open. They saw a lofty chamber, bare except for a chest against one stone wall and a huge bed placed near the tall arched window. From here the bed's occupant could keep one eye on the door and the other on his city at the base of the hill, where the cathedral loomed over the lesser buildings. Just visible off to his right was the bridge he had built across the Ebro River, with its formidable tower at either end.

The great mound in the bed stirred and a big bald head turned toward them. They recognized the piercing brown eyes, the noble nose, the wide and generous mouth. When the fat face was split by a smile like a crescent moon, they knew this was — however changed — their dear brother, and that they were welcome.

"So there you are. What took you so long?" His voice was gruffer than they remembered, but Berengaria thought he was trying not to show sentiment. "I saw you crossing the bridge an hour ago. Well, come over here and let's take a look."

He sat up and pushed pillows behind his back. One sister perched on either side of the bed. He held out a hand to each. All three were overcome and unable to speak for a minute.

"I can't get up to greet you properly because of this cursed leg of mine. Never been the same since I took an arrow in the calf, back when we finished off those heathen Muslims at Las Navas de Tolosa. Now that was a battle, sisters!" His eyes flashed with the zeal of a warrior.

"Yes, and we know that you were the hero of the day and it was a splendid victory for all the Christian kings," Berengaria said. "Oh Sanchito, we have so much catching up to do. You must tell us everything."

"But first," said Blanche, looking at him with a disapproving eye, "when are you going to get up from this ridiculous bed and go out into your kingdom, so your people will know they really have a king? We heard them whispering in the town that they haven't seen you in a year. Do you know that they call you 'El Encerrado' — the Imprisoned One?"

Sancho growled, "Never mind that. Even if my leg were to get well, which the doctors say it won't, I can't get about now because I've grown so monstrous fat, and I'm monstrous fat because I can't get about. And I've lost all my hair — I don't care to be known as 'El Calvo' too — the Bald One. Now let's have no more on that subject and get on to more important things. Have those niggardly English ever done right by you, Berenguelita?"

Then he interrupted himself. "But first you must be made more comfortable. I'm not used to being a host. I'll send for some chairs." He rang a great iron bell that hung from the bedpost and they jumped at the deafening clang. "I don't keep chairs in here because I don't want my counselors to sit easy and stay too long. After they stand here for ten minutes they're glad enough to leave and get on with their work." A servant entered and Sancho asked him to bring two chairs. "And while you're at it, fetch us a fresh loaf and some apples and a flask of my best Rioja wine."

When they were settled, Berengaria could answer his question. "Yes, King Henry is better behaved than his father John, and the English have indeed finally begun to repay what is owed me."

"And what will you do with all your wealth, sister? We could use a little help in finishing our cathedral, you know." Sancho was half joking but she took him seriously.

"Perhaps I could help, Sancho. I remember they were just beginning the sculptures on the portal, the last time I saw it. Have they finished?"

Blanche remembered too. "I always liked the sinners better than the saints. They seemed to be having more fun."

Sancho harrumphed, and said he had to agree, but maybe it was because he was a sinner himself.

Then he wanted to know all about his nephew and niece. What did they look like?

"Well, you would hardly know they had a drop of Basque blood in their veins. Bérengère looks like me, they say, but Thibaut is his father all over again; and turning into quite a famous troubadour, though he can't find much time nowadays to make up his little songs. He's now Count of Champagne, you know."

"I wish he could have come with you," said Sancho, draining his wine and looking meditatively at Blanche. "How do you think he would do as King of Navarre? I won't be around much longer."

Berengaria felt a catch in her throat and Blanche paled but answered quickly — there was no point in denying Sancho's words. "Naturally, I think he would do very well. He is really quite sensible, in spite of his taste for frivolous verse. I am prejudiced, of course. Still, he has shown some signs of being a firm governor and he has my good counselors to help him. I had no qualms at all about leaving him in charge while I came here."

Sancho looked doubtful. "It wouldn't do, you know, for him to hang about up there in Champagne, singing songs, instead of spending time here where the kingdom will need a firm ruler. God knows I haven't been able to do much except rule from the shadows, these past years. And you're right — the people want a king they can see and talk to."

He was silent a minute, frowning. "And there's the matter of whether they can in fact talk to him. Has he any knowledge of our language? It's not so easy to pick up." All three had been talking in Basque, which Berengaria and Blanche found came back to them quickly, in spite of years of speaking French.

"I've tried to teach him some, but I haven't had much success. He says it has no melody to it. But I'll work harder at it when I get back."

"Well, we will see," Sancho finally said.

Then he announced that it was time for his dinner, which he was used to taking alone, but said he had ordered a good meal to be served to them below. They thought he was probably in pain and did not want them to see how he suffered, and took their leave.

"But we will see you tomorrow."

he sisters stayed in Tudela for a fortnight, but they gave up trying to persuade Sancho to leave his bed. He was in great pain much of the time and, though stoical, often had to ask them to leave the tower.

Then they would sometimes walk down the castle hill and wander through the city, surprised at how much it had grown since their girlhood. They went first to the cathedral, heart of the city and gathering place of rich and poor, noble and commoner. They returned several times, for services or simply to admire the majesty and workmanship. The great Portal of Justice was, as they had hoped, completed. On its concentric arches, a hundred stone figures stood out in bold relief. Those on the left looked pious and calm, knowing they were on their way to heaven. The unfortunate reprobates on the right grimaced and wept, anticipating an eternity in the inferno.

"The sinners don't look as jolly as I remembered them," said Blanche.

"No, they don't. But then, the sculptors were just beginning when we were here. Maybe some bishop cautioned them that sinners should show more suffering."

One day they visited the Muslim section of town and found it little changed from their earliest memories. In the Jewish quarter they looked for the humble house of the world traveler Benjamin of Tudela that their father had taken them to see, when they were very young. But although they asked several merchants and passersby, nobody seemed to know anything about Benjamin or his house, and they never found it.

Berengaria remembered that once she had thought she might learn Hebrew so she could read the journal that Benjamin kept during his travels. Yet, even if she had succeeded, she did not know where she might have found a copy. Another regret.

"Remember, Blanche, how our father told us about the strange foreign lands where Benjamin traveled? And how I wondered if I would ever have a chance to see them — or even to leave Navarre?"

"As it turned out, you traveled farther than anyone else in our family — all the way to Sicily and the Holy Land, and almost to Jerusalem."

"But Sancho did cross the sea to Africa," Berengaria reminded her.

"Well, as for me, the only traveling I am concerned with now is getting back up this hill and to the castle. The sun is well into the west. Sancho will be wondering where we are."

Berengaria briskly began the ascent and Blanche, not quite so vigorous despite being the younger, followed. The patient manservant, who had been wondering how long these two elegant ladies would linger in such a lowly quarter of the city, brought up the rear.

By now Sancho had decided they could join him for meals, and when they reached his room at the top of the tower they found a great repast had been spread on the table. Sancho was sitting up in his bed, drumming his fingers on the coverlet.

Berengaria brought him a platter with a brace of stuffed partridges, a mountain of suet pudding and chunks of rock-hard, pungent cheese. She and Blanche drew their chairs up to the table and served themselves more moderately, watching Sancho in awe as he chewed meat off the bones and washed it down with gulps of wine.

Presently, when he had demolished one bird and dropped the greasy bones on his plate, he looked up, sighed in contentment and let out a sonorous belch, with a belated effort to cover his mouth. Blanche looked pained, but Berengaria laughed.

"Sanchito, sometimes you're just like the naughty little boy that our mother tried so hard to teach manners to."

"Well, it's a bit late for me to mend my ways now, isn't it? And that brings me back to how time is passing. Blanche, you might as well tell Thibaut that I would be glad to receive him if he can manage a trip to Tudela. It would be a good idea for him to learn something about this land where his ancestors lived, and meet some of our people. Just in case."

"I will urge him to come as soon as I am home."

Clearly, Sancho was thinking more and more about his death. Berengaria quickly changed the subject.

"Sancho, you have told us practically nothing about your days as a warrior with the Muslims. We've heard that you spent more years with them, as friend or foe, than here at home in Navarre."

"Yes, and now you must at last tell us the true story of the Moroccan princess," Blanche said.

Sancho, between mouthfuls, told the tale with as much relish as he attacked the second partridge.

"Well, as you know, sisters, I went off to Morocco looking for adventure, not long after our father died and I inherited his crown. The sultan asked me to come help him in his battles, and I thought, why not? Those Muslims down there across the sea were not our enemies, like the ones who had held Andalusia for so long; and nobody seemed to be threatening Navarre at the moment. So off I went. The sultan was so good to me, and the fighting went so well, that I just stayed on."

"But what about the Muslim princess?" asked Berengaria. "Did she have nothing to do with your staying so long?"

Sancho grudgingly admitted that there had indeed been a young girl, daughter of the sultan, who thought she had fallen in love with him. "But she was far too young to know what she was talking about; she was only twelve and got carried away by her romantic notions. Of course, sisters, I was not the wreck you see now — that was years ago, after all; more than one lass thought me a fine figure of a man and worth the pursuit."

"So you discouraged the poor little girl, did you?" asked Blanche mischievously. "And what did she think of that — did she die of a broken heart?"

"Hardly." He barked in laughter at the memory. "Within two days, the dark-eyed little minx had decided her heart's desire was one of her father's warriors and by the time I left Morocco, a few weeks later, she had forgotten all about me. It was not so very flattering, to tell you the truth."

"So it isn't true that the sultan offered you half his kingdom if you would marry his daughter?" Blanche asked. "That was what we heard in Troyes."

"Not so," Sancho said, hacking off a slice of pudding with a formidable knife. "In fact, our relations got much cooler after that. I told him I couldn't stay any longer because I had heard that King Alfonso was marching into Álava and it was time I went home to watch over my own kingdom. He didn't take that news very graciously. So I left. But without a word of goodby from the fickle little princess."

They all laughed, but Sancho's merriment turned to a groan from a sudden pain in his ulcerated leg. He rang the bell and the servant came to remove the remains of the meal and to send for the surgeon to come and change his dressings.

Not speaking, the sisters negotiated the ninety-five steps and emerged in the great hall of the palace. "I think it is time for us to go home," said Berengaria. "We cannot do anything for Sancho by staying here — perhaps we are harming him, by interrupting his repose. Only heaven has the power to help him now."

Blanche agreed. "I can't help thinking, though, that if he had not buried himself away and given up his active life, he might not have fallen so ill. Still, there's no point in looking back now."

"Anyway, he has been a good king for a long time, and we know he is beloved, even though they do call him 'El Encerrado.' If Thibaut should indeed inherit this kingdom, he will have some very large shoes to fill."

"In more ways than one! Did you see that coat of mail Sancho used to wear — the one in the palace armory? You could put two Thibauts in it."

They decided they would tell Sancho the next day that they were leaving. Immediately, Berengaria felt a terrible urgency to be off. She wished she could go to bed in Tudela and find herself in Le Mans in the morning. It had been good to come back to the land of her birth, but it was no longer her home. Her home was where the good citizens smiled when they saw her and called her their "Reine Blanche." Where Paulin Boutier and Herbert de la Tucé and the others served her with such loyalty and wisdom. Where she had fought and won so many battles.

And where Pierre was waiting to clasp her in his sheltering arms.

wo weeks later a weary Berengaria walked into her palace after a long day of riding through wind and rain. Marie-Louise Vaudun hurried to greet her, talking at top speed. Her plump face was pink as a berry with the pleasure of seeing her lady again.

"How good to have you back, madame! We have been so lonely without you! Henriette will be here in a moment, she is just sending the man up to light the fire in your chamber. We knew it must be you when we heard all the clatter out on the square. Now let me help you off with that wet cloak, and here's a chair and a stool for your feet. We'll have a warm drink for you in a minute."

As the traveler sank into the chair and looked up at her friend with a strained smile, the babble stopped. Marie-Louise, seeing the pale, almost gaunt face, said in concern, "Oh madame, you really are not well, are you? I will go and see what is keeping that girl with the wine."

Just then Henriette, who had taken the tray from the serving girl, entered the hall. Marie-Louise hurried to her and whispered, "Henriette, our lady doesn't look herself, not at all. Come see what you think."

Henriette thought Berengaria should go up to bed at once and said so. Without reply, Berengaria bent over to inhale the spicy aroma of the wine, then drank it slowly. Some color came back to the wan cheeks. When she spoke her voice was faint and she faltered. "I must have been more tired by this journey than I knew. I suppose I hurried too much. But I was so anxious to get home." She sighed, leaned back in her chair, and closed her eyes. After a minute she forced herself to sit up.

"Forgive me. I am better now. And safely home, praise God. Tomorrow I will go to the chapel and give thanks. But now" — her voice was stronger — "now let us go up and sit by my fire for a bit, and you must tell me all the news. Has anyone sent word to tell Sieur Pierre that I am back?"

She began to rise, but sank back on seeing how the sisters looked at each other in confusion. Marie-Louise, at a nod from Henriette, spoke hesitantly.

"We would have of course, madame, but Sieur Pierre is not here. We have sent for our brother Paulin because he asked us to let him know the moment you arrived, so he could come and explain everything."

"What do you mean? Pierre promised he would be here when I got back. What could possibly have happened to take him away?" She began to think of all kinds of disasters. Was he sick? Had he had a dreadful accident?

By now she had again become quite pale. Marie-Louise tried to get her to take another cup of wine but she shook her head. The sisters looked around distractedly.

"I think I hear Paulin coming now," cried Henriette.

The majordomo hurried in, came straight to Berengaria and with uncharacteristic familiarity, took her hand in both of his.

"Welcome back, my lady. Let me tell you at once about Sieur Pierre. You must not be so distressed. He is not hurt or ill. Five days ago a messenger came from King Louis looking for Sieur Pierre…"

"Very rude he was, too," muttered Marie-Louise. "Came stomping in here in his great boots without so much as a by-your-leave, then when we told him where Sieur Pierre lived, he became quite cross because he had to walk five minutes up the hill."

"…and the messenger told Sieur Pierre," Paulin went on, "that King Louis ordered him to Paris at once. He hardly had time to throw some things in a bag and saddle his horse, much less write you a message. So he asked me to tell you where he had gone…"

"And who knows when we will see him again, poor man, having to go off and fight those wicked heretics?" Marie-Louise interrupted again.

Berengaria's eyes widened in alarm and Paulin's narrowed in annoyance.

"Now, now, Marie-Louise, let me finish. Madame, Sieur Pierre asked me to tell you this: the King is calling on his vassals to come to Paris and join his crusade against the Albigensians down in the south, the folk in Languedoc who are disputing the authority of the true Church. 'I have no choice but to obey my King,' he said. 'But tell her I cannot believe it will be much of a fight, and she is not to worry. I will send a messenger as soon as I can.' And he leaped on his horse and galloped off, but he called back to me, 'And tell the Queen I love her dearly and will count the days until I see her again.'" Paulin looked discomfited at having to repeat this, but he was duty bound to do so. "And that, my dear lady, is all I can tell you."

Berengaria leaned forward, listening intently. It was a relief to hear that Pierre had come to no harm, but she frowned in puzzlement. What was the King up to, that he had to call on a vassal as minor as Pierre to help him?

"I thank you, Paulin. You are a true friend, to repeat so carefully everything he said. Now what do you know of this crusade? I have heard there were heretics in the south, and I know King Louis had sent men against Count Raymond. But when we came through Toulouse there was no talk of any more fighting and they said a truce was still in effect. Why should King Louis begin the whole dispute over again, and call all his men to Paris?"

"I know hardly anything about it. Perhaps this new king is a young hothead trying to live up to his father's reputation as a strong ruler."

"He may be a hothead, but he cannot be very young. I remember seeing him at Blanche's wedding in Chartres in 1199. He seemed about twelve or thirteen then, so he must be at least thirty-eight by now. I remember I didn't like him at all. He was rude and conceited." She could still see the sneer on the foppish youth's face when he broke off their conversation, having decided she was a nobody.

"But what about these Albigensians? People in Toulouse seemed to think they were simply harmless, misguided folk who had strayed from the true path of Christianity, not a band of militants threatening the safety of the King of France."

"From what I have heard, King Louis' real quarrel is with Count Raymond and the counts of Foix and Carcassonne, and he accuses them of supporting the heretics. But we may learn more soon. At your chapel, Saint Pierre, they say that a cousin of our canon Garsie Leclerc is expected daily. He is a monk from Carcassonne. He may be able to tell us what is really going on."

Berengaria gazed at the floor, deep in thought. The others waited, exchanging a few words in low voices. They were used to her silences when she was turning a matter over in her mind. Now she raised her eyes and spoke calmly.

"Well, I will go to the chapel in the morning and see what I can find out. I thank you all for sharing my anxiety, and let us all hope and pray that it is unwarranted. I am sure that our good Pierre will return to us soon, and no harm done." She spoke with more confidence than she felt.

When she woke in the morning Berengaria felt somewhat refreshed after a good night's sleep in her own bed. She was still a little stiff from days in the saddle, but the weakness and faintness of the night before had disappeared. She walked to her window and leaned out to look eastward, where the most glorious sunrise she could remember bathed the sky in rose and orange. Who could be a pessimist on a day like this?

After breakfast she walked over to the chapel and asked about Garsie's cousin Robert Le Clerc, the monk from Carcassonne. He had arrived the night before, they told her, and would be glad to talk to her.

He could not tell her much, as it turned out. He confirmed that Count Raymond was taking the side of the heretics against King Louis and that (people said) the King was enraged at this and had declared war on the Count and his "raggle-taggle band of malcontents." That was why he had called up his vassals to join in his so-called crusade. When Brother Robert had left the south, no army had yet appeared, and though Count Raymond was trying to muster his troops, the Albigensians themselves were doing their best to present a low profile.

"They keep to themselves, and try to live their lives in peace, and I for one do not see why the Pope and all the bishops are so upset about them. They do nobody any harm, though I am sorry for them because it is a sin to stray from the true faith and they will suffer in the afterlife. But let that be on their own heads."

They were sitting on a bench in the chilly foyer of the chapel, and Brother Robert rose and walked up and down. He crossed his arms and tucked his hands into his long loose sleeves. He looked at Berengaria, his thin brown face filled with sorrow at the plight of his countrymen.

"I could be one of them, you know. I was born in Béziers and my own brother and his wife have embraced the heresy. I took one road, they took the other."

"Thank you, Brother Robert. At least I know a little more about this affair, and I am glad to hear that so far there has been no fighting. We will just have to hope a messenger comes soon. Do you think you will get any further word while you are here?"

"Ha!" the monk laughed bitterly. "No, I do not. Because I did not tell anyone where I was going. People were beginning to look at me strangely because of my brother, and I was sure my abbot was about to call me before him for an interrogation. So I left quietly, and thought I would stay here with my cousin for a time."

"I am glad you had this safe place to come to. Let us hope that the whole thing will blow over. And of course you will let me know if you do hear anything."

She walked slowly back to the palace. She felt a little easier in her mind, and tried to assure herself that Pierre had to be all right, or she would have heard something. As he himself might say, "No news is good news."

Meantime governance of her city had to go on. She had asked Paulin to call a meeting of her council at two hours past midday, and now she wished she had set it for tomorrow. Her weariness of the day before had returned. Followed by Cristina, she climbed the stairs and looked longingly at her empty, quiet library where the scribe François had neatly arranged his pens and inks on his table, and where rows of unexamined manuscripts awaited his and her attention.

In her own bedroom she was afraid if she looked at the big canopied bed she would give in and lie down, so she went resolutely to her clothing chest to find something suitable to wear.

As she grew in years and experience, Berengaria attached more importance to her appearance. She believed that by dressing like a queen she helped her counselors to feel that they were participants in matters of great import, and that should make them more judicious in their acts and advice.

So today she wore royal purple. At her throat a white lace fichu was fastened with a gold brooch in the shape of a lion — a reminder to all who saw it that this was the widow of King Richard, whose coat of arms bore three lions sautant. She did not put on a crown — that was for state occasions — but her hair was contained by a white silk wimple. Looking in the mirror, she was not displeased. Like a soft cloud, the wimple framed a face that showed assurance and control. A few wrinkles furrowed her brow but her cheeks were pale and smooth, though there was a slight sagging under the still-starry green eyes. Her lips were set firmly, almost severely, but they were rosy enough. Not too bad for a woman of sixty, she thought and smiled at her reflection, then went down to the meeting.

In the council chamber, she sat at the head of the long table. The half-dozen men who had been waiting then seated themselves. Besides Paulin Boutier and Herbert de Tucé, those present included Herbert de la Marche and Gervais de Pringé, the two barons of Maine who were vassals of Berengaria and who kept residence in the city; Gautier de Perseigne, her chaplain; Garsie Leclerc; and the representative of the cathedral chapter, Arnaud Duverne.

"It is good to be back with you all. It was a great pleasure to arrive home from Navarre and find everything much as I left it. Except, of course, for the departure of Pierre Savary to serve the King. I know you all join me in wishing him a safe return."

There were nods and murmurs of agreement, and Herbert de Tucé said quickly, "We do indeed, madame. I am certain that when it comes down to it, King Louis will not pluck up the courage to take an army down to Languedoc, where he has so many enemies."

"Besides," said Herbert de la Marche, "he would need the approval and blessing of the Pope for such a crusade. And His Holiness would far rather see him go on a crusade to Palestine, where the infidels still hold Jerusalem, than to Languedoc."

He may have meant this as reassurance, but Berengaria shot him a look of alarm. "To Palestine?" She stared at him and clenched her hands tightly together to keep them from trembling. She knew Palestine. She knew its dangers. Her heart constricted with new fears for Pierre's safety.

She must not show weakness. The business of the council had to go on.

"Well, let us get on with our discussions. I have been giving a great deal of thought to the welfare of the cathedral of Saint-Julien. We are pleased that a representative of the cathedral chapter is now a member of our council." She bowed slightly toward Arnaud Duverne. "As token of our desire to live in peace and harmony with those of Saint-Julien, we are proposing to assist them in the construction of the new portions of the cathedral. In particular, we wish to contribute the necessary funds to complete the arc-boutants that will support the walls of the apse."

This statement was met at first with silence. Herbert de Tucé cleared his throat, and Berengaria knew he was about to raise an objection.

"Pardon me, madame, but what is an arc-boutant? And why does the cathedral need them?"

"I am not an expert in these matters, Sieur Herbert, but I have heard that these modern supports for walls are now being used on some cathedrals, to good purpose. Garsie Leclerc has some knowledge of architecture, and perhaps he can enlighten us."

The canon obliged. "The architects tell me that buttresses are quite essential to support the walls, and these new 'flying buttresses' are extraordinary because their design makes it possible to put up walls far taller than heretofore. So we shall have a cathedral that reaches farther toward the heavens than any other."

Berengaria added, "And if we act now, though it will be many years before the task is completed, we may be able to get our cathedral soaring heavenward sooner than that of King Louis in Paris. I know his father Philip Augustus had high hopes of seeing arcs-boutants gracing the cathedral of Notre Dame in his lifetime, but he was disappointed. When he died they were still not finished. Perhaps his son will be equally unfortunate." She calculated — correctly — that this veiled invitation to compete with the King of France would have its effect. Nobody raised any serious objections, though Herbert de Tucé felt it his duty to introduce a prudent word. In his measured monotone, he said, "Madame, this is a noble aim. The magnificent new choir will be even more splendid, with those leaping buttresses adorning its exterior and its high columns inside."

He paused. She knew what was coming. "It will also prove very costly. Can your treasury bear the burden?"

"Sieur Herbert," Berengaria replied, "I am glad you recognize the need for caution before we commit ourselves to such a long and expensive endeavor. But as the man most familiar with our finances, have you not assured me that our revenue from the forests of Maine has been higher than ever this year? And are our tax collectors not bringing in ample funds, more than enough to pay our daily expenses? The English have been conscientious in sending their remittances, which I have always designated not for my own needs but for works that redound to the glory of God. What better use for this gold to than the strengthening and beautification of one of God's temples? All Le Mans will share in the glory."

Herbert was satisfied; he had had his say. Paulin Boutier, who had seemed on the verge of seconding the seneschal's cautious warning, changed his mind.

However, Gautier de Perseigne, the chaplain, did not hesitate to speak. "Such a generous gift is more than a noble gesture. When we are long gone, this magnificent cathedral will demonstrate to all men that here in Le Mans, in the year of our Lord 1226, there were men who had vision and a generous spirit."

Arnaud Duverne nodded emphatically and everybody beamed at this promise that posterity would honor them.

So it was decided, and the eloquent Gautier, with Arnaud Duverne, was delegated to begin discussions with Bishop Maurice, the chapter and the cathedral architects about the project and the costs.

Berengaria retired. Every muscle was crying for rest. She sank gratefully onto her bed. Thinking over the meeting with her council, she decided it had been a good afternoon's work. Then she permitted her thoughts to turn to Pierre — she was sure she would lie awake for hours imagining the perils that might be facing him; but hardly had she envisioned him on his horse riding off to battle than she fell into the sleep of exhaustion.

48

t last, in the middle of March of 1226, Pierre came back to Le Mans. He went straight to the Queen's chamber. He took her in his arms, her head rested on his shoulder; no words were needed. He saw the signs of strain in her face and through her gown, thick wool as it was, he felt how her slender body had become even thinner.

"I can hardly believe it — you are safely here. No matter how firmly I told myself you would come to no harm — I was so terribly worried!" She clasped him tighter, assuring herself that this was her Pierre, come home.

"Of course you worried, my dear one," he said gently. He took her hand and led her to their favorite bench by the wide window, overlooking the city walls. They sat as they had done so often, with his arm around her shoulders. "But I must tell you at once that I am here for only a day."

She stiffened. "Oh no! I thought surely King Louis had given up his foolish crusade and sent everybody home."

"King Louis is a shilly-shallerer, I am afraid. First the army was to march in February, then he kept finding reasons to put it off. But he has ordered all to be ready by the end of the month. I think now he means it."

"But Pierre, you are not a fighting man, not any more. You have done your service for France. Why should you have to go? And after the war in the south, will it be Palestine next? We heard the Pope wants Louis to lead a crusade to take Jerusalem. Is that his plan — to take you away from me for months or years?"

He looked at her quizzically and placed a finger on her lips. She realized that her voice had become almost shrill.

"Oh dear! I sound like a selfish whiny old wife, don't I? I am ashamed. You are the one in danger, not I. Now I will stop complaining and be quiet and you will tell me everything."

"First of all, King Louis is not going to Palestine. He proclaims" — Pierre's voice rose to a resonant high-pitched tenor and he raised a clenched fist — "it is his duty as a Christian monarch to stamp out the evil Albigensian heresy in the south, and in order to do so he must subdue the wicked lords who are championing the heretics." He resumed his normal voice. "At least, that is what the herald shouted out when all the King's men met in the palace in Paris. But those who are close to Louis know that his real quarrel is with Count Raymond of Toulouse and the Count of Foix. The purpose of this whole adventure is to expand the territory of the French crown."

She sniffed. "He is as full of intrigue as his father was. You could never quite believe what Philip said, either."

"I think we must accept that duplicity comes with the crown, if a monarch means to get the best of his enemies. Did you ever know of a king who was completely honest?"

She was quiet a minute, then spoke in such a low voice that he had to bend to hear her. "Yes. King Richard of England." She paused. "At least in his public life, as a king and a leader of an army, he meant what he said, and kept his promises. Even his enemies knew that Richard's word was to be trusted."

Though the light was fading fast, he could see that her face was strained. She looked up at him quickly, then bowed her head. "But in his private life, it was something else again."

During all their years of intimacy she had never brought herself to confide in Pierre about her marriage to Richard. She was never sure why. Was it that she wanted no shadows of the past to intrude on the happiness she had at last found? Or a reluctance to speak ill of a man whom the whole world remembered as heroic? Or shyness about disclosing the private and painful events of her marriage — such as it had been? If she told anything, she would have to tell all. So she had told nothing. Pierre had never pressed her, sensing it was a distressing chapter in her life that she did not wish to reopen.

He tightened his arm around her. "My own love, I know that Richard was not a good husband to you, but that is past, long past, and now you and I have each other. I have always respected you for your loyalty to him in spite of painful memories. Do you wish to talk about it now?"

She hesitated, then turned to him and took both his hands in hers and said earnestly, "Yes, I do want to talk about it. I always wanted you to know my whole story, yet as the years went by it did not seem so important, and the time never seemed right. But I think now I should like to tell you."

There was a knock at the door. It was Cristina. She peered into the shadowy room. "Madame! Here you sit in the dark — why didn't you call for candles, and tinder for the fire? And you must be wanting some supper, both of you." She bobbed her head at Pierre. "We are so pleased to see you back, Sieur Pierre." She called the servant to bring lights, then Berengaria asked her to have their supper brought.

The moment of confidences was postponed until their meal had been served. They sat long at table, while she talked and he listened, breaking in now and then with a question or a word of sympathy, or rising to add fuel to the fire. She began with her earliest memory of Richard, when he came to Pamplona for the tournament and she was so dazzled by him. She told of the trivial matter of the sprig of yellow broom she had given him as his prize, and how he had carelessly lost it. "If only I had realized it then, that was Richard through and through — a charmer who cared nothing for those who cared about him."

Some of the story Pierre knew in outline — how Eleanor had come to remove her from the monastery and take her to be married to the crusading king, and how as his queen she had gone with him to Palestine. But he heard with shock how the drunken Richard had treated her on their wedding night, how he had then avoided her, and his betrayal of her with poor little Maria.

"I wonder what ever happened to her," Berengaria said wistfully. "She was really a dear, and he took advantage of her."

"I do believe I heard something about that Maria," said Pierre, "while I was in Paris. I had no idea she was a player in your history, or I would have paid more attention. But there was some talk of a Flemish adventurer who married a Cypriot princess. His notion was that they could go back to the island and reclaim it, with her as its queen. Nothing came of it of course; the island was firmly held by the Lusignans. It was a curious tale, and I asked what happened next. But nobody knew."

"Poor Maria, she deserved better than that."

"And you deserved better than the life you led with Richard."

They were still seated before the fire, and the hour was late, but Berengaria felt compelled to go on. She told Pierre that while she lived at the castle at Beaufort, she still hoped that Richard would come to take her to live with him as his queen and that she would see England; and then — of his ultimate deception, when he professed to love her, then went off to build his "Saucy Castle." She never saw him again. At that point, she could not hold back the tears. She covered her face with her hands, and her shoulders shook.

"I am not crying for myself, Pierre," she said, looking up and wiping her eyes. "I am crying for the child we should have had, but God decreed otherwise. I have never said this to another soul, but the greatest sorrow of my life has not been Richard's unkindness, but the fact that I was not granted the gift of motherhood."

He rose and stood behind her chair, his hands on her shoulders, trying to find words. "I know. I mean I understand. I have no children either. It is a sorry prospect to know you will leave this world, with no child to mourn you and bear your name and try to finish the tasks you left undone."

She stood and they faced each other. Berengaria felt drained. Her whole body drooped. Even Pierre — strong, sturdy Pierre — looked diminished. He spoke slowly, choosing his words carefully.

"This has been hard for you to share with me. Nor was it easy for me to hear. But I think it only strengthens the bonds that tie us together. Now I know you better and love you even more."

She nodded and they looked at each other, not touching. She could not speak. Along with the pain of recalling the whole sorrowful story, she felt immense relief and gratitude for Pierre's understanding. She sensed that their love had taken on a new dimension — beyond the physical, even beyond their deep friendship. Now she wanted only to rest. It was time for him to go.

"Berengaria my dear, now we must part again for a little while, but I will send word as often as I can. Soon we will be together, for the rest of our lives, God willing." He kissed her gently, briefly, and was gone.

She stood there in the gloom, head bowed. "For the rest of our lives, God willing," she repeated.

49

"S o that is an arc-boutant," said Berengaria to Arnaud Duverne. "Somehow I had expected it to look more like an eagle on the wing, or failing that, perhaps a goose." She had walked up to the cathedral to inspect the first flying buttress to be completed and Arnaud, representing the chapter, was showing her around.

"It may take some imagination, madame," he said, "but if you squint at it, you can imagine a wing, curving from the cathedral wall out to that parapet."

She squinted with as much imagination as she could muster. "Thank you, Arnaud. I think I see what you mean. Now let us go in and take a look at the new choir."

Nothing had been heard from Pierre for weeks, and the visit to the cathedral was one of the many tasks she was setting for herself, to avoid idle moments when worry about him might take over her mind. The palace ran smoothly, thanks to Carlos's attentive and conscientious management. Administration of the city did not take much of her time, what with the amicable relations with the cathedral chapter and the efficiency of her council. So she made herself spend several hours a day in her scriptorium, absorbed in the demanding task of translating lyrical Arabic into sober Latin.

She began to take more interest in the welfare of the city's churches. When Garsie Leclerc pointed out to her how her own chapel was sorely in need of repairs, she persuaded Herbert de Tucé that they could afford to shore up the walls, and perhaps put on a new roof. She helped to establish or renovate several other churches and abbeys, and brought the Jewish schools under the protection of the cathedral chapter. Sometimes she thought wistfully of creating something completely new, something more dramatic than roof repairs or even arcs-boutants. She remembered her half-formed dream of founding an abbey where scholarly pursuits would be fostered. However, she could not contemplate beginning that ambitious project without Pierre's help.

Every time she went to her chapel she thanked God for giving her the opportunity to glorify His temples. Then she would say a special prayer for Pierre. "I must trust that God will keep him safe," she said to herself. "There is not a blessed thing I can do except keep that faith."

"No news about Sieur Pierre?" Cristina asked her one day.

"Not a word, since that message a few weeks ago that told us they were still marching south. But I am sure he will be able to take care of himself. He is a clever man, and he wants to come home in one piece as much as we want him to."

Cristina nodded, thinking her mistress showed a shocking lack of anxiety about her Grand Ami. "I pray for his safe return every day," she said and hobbled out; over the years of faithful service Cristina had acquired aching joints.

She went down to the kitchen to tell Carlos what she thought. The big room was filled with the sounds and smells of the palace business. There was a great to-do of cooking, stirring and chatter around the huge fireplace where bubbling pots hung from hooks. Whenever a lad threw another log on the fire, smoke bellied from the hearth. Gardeners strode in with baskets overflowing with cabbages and turnips. At a long table against one wall, craftsmen were busily sewing at leather garments and women were knitting and mending. Here sat Carlos, now a somewhat stooped fifty-year-old, bent over his work.

"I shall never understand our lady, never," Cristina said to him. "Here she is, calm as an oyster, no idea where her man is or when he'll be back, and all she's thinking about is filling the chinks in the chapel walls."

"Hmm," said Carlos, who was busy mending his boot.

"I can remember when that wicked King Richard left her, she stopped eating and moped around for weeks. Yet now Sieur Pierre — and him worth three of King Richard — is off who knows where, in all kinds of danger, and you'd think he had just gone out to take the air."

"Women!" said Carlos, pounding a nail into his boot's heel. He took the boot off the last and looked at it critically. "What do you think, Cristina? Good as new, no?"

She glared at him, muttered what might be agreement, and went to ask the cook to be sure to put a bowl of his richest broth on her mistress's supper tray. "Sieur Pierre won't thank us if he comes home to find her a bag of bones," she said to him.

Four months after the army's departure, a most unlikely messenger, Count Thibaut of Champagne, brought news. Berengaria had not seen her sister's son for years, but when he was shown into the scriptorium she knew him at once. He looked very like his father, with the same incredibly handsome face and a head of curly golden hair, but where Blanche's husband had sported a flamboyant mustache, her son was clean-shaven.

She rose and stretched out her hand, then impulsively hugged him. He blushed.

"Don't mind me, Thibaut. Certainly an aunt may hug her nephew, especially if she knew him when he was a tiny babe. Now come sit down, and tell me what brings you so far from Champagne. No bad news about my sister, I hope."

"My mother was in good health when I saw her in the spring. She had no idea I would be seeing you, or I'm sure she would have sent a message. But I have just come from Avignon, where I was serving in King Louis' army while he besieged the city. I come to bring you word about Pierre Savary."

Berengaria's heart gave a lurch. All of her boasted equanimity about Pierre's safety was gone like a puff of smoke. If Thibaut was here with a message from Pierre, it could only be bad news.

Thibaut saw her anxiety. "Your Pierre is alive though sorely wounded," he told her.

"Thank God he is alive," she breathed, putting a hand to her heart. "But how badly hurt? Tell me, tell me everything."

He began by explaining that he too had been called by the King to join the crusade but had stayed only two months.

"I will tell you more about that later. When I decided to leave the siege, I sent my chevaliers on ahead to Champagne since they were anxious to get home. I set out alone. On my first night I reached an inn just across the Rhone from Avignon, in Villeneuve."

He described it: hardly more than a humble house on the outskirts of the town, whose owner had a couple of extra rooms for travelers, and was willing to cook for them. At the inn he met another man who had left the siege. He had been wounded — an arrow in his thigh — and had somehow made his way this far, with only his servant to help him; fortunately both their horses had survived the battle. But he was too weak to go farther.

The two had gotten to talking and his new acquaintance asked Thibaut if his travels would take him anywhere near Le Mans, because he wished to send a message to the Dame of the city.

"Why, that is my aunt, Queen Berengaria!" Thibaut had exclaimed. They quickly discovered their connection through the Queen. Pierre remembered that when he visited the Countess's palace in Troyes, Thibaut had been a shy, pretty little boy. Thibaut had only a vague memory of Pierre, but he had heard from his mother that his father had known and liked Pierre, and that now he was his aunt's Grand Ami. He saw at once that it was his duty to help this good man — his uncle, as it were.

He conferred with Cristiano, Pierre's faithful servant and squire. They both felt it would be some time before Pierre would be well enough to travel. He had lost a great deal of blood, Cristiano said, and there was danger that the wound could fester. Though with help he could slowly make his way from his bed to the next room where the innkeeper served meals, he grimaced and sweat beaded his face, the pain was so great. They had been unable to find a surgeon to look at his wound.

"And it was a very deep wound, Aunt; the arrow went almost to the bone and although Cristiano was able to pull it out, the flesh was badly torn."

He was sorry at once that he had been so explicit. Berengaria's eyes were almost wild, and her hands trembled. "And he was there when you left, with no one but Cristiano?"

"No, he was not, thanks to that generous innkeeper. He helped us get Pierre to the Benedictine abbey, just down the road, where the monks have some knowledge of medicine. I left as soon as I saw him safely there, and that was two weeks ago. I promised him I would make a detour through Le Mans to tell you all this."

Berengaria sat a minute or two, breathing deeply. Now that she realized Pierre was not at death's door — dire as the situation was — she could think more clearly about what to do.

"He pressed me to tell you that you are not to worry," Thibaut went on. "I am to tell you that the brothers and Cristiano are taking good care of him, and he expects to feel much stronger, very soon."

Then he began to describe the monastery, thinking she would want reassurance that Pierre was in the best hands; but while he was talking, she was making plans to leave at once to see to Pierre and get him home.

For a day and a half, the palace was a scene of controlled confusion. Cristina, who remembered vividly how Queen Eleanor had ordered and supervised their travels from Navarre to Sicily, was proud to see her mistress display just as much firmness and energy.

When all was ready, the rescue party, led by four men-at-arms and with two others bringing up the rear, set out toward the south. There was no ceremony to the departure, just a crisp "Off we go, then," from Paulin Boutier, who had insisted on taking charge of the logistics of the journey. Cristina and Carlos, and their son Carlito, had also demanded places in the party. Pierre was beloved by many.

Thibaut rode beside Berengaria; he would accompany them as far as Orléans. Now that she had done all she could for the moment, she was full of questions. There was so much she still did not know — of the crusade, Thibaut's part in it, why he had left. Thank God he had — or she would not have had this news of Pierre.

"Let us try to start at the beginning," she said. "Why on earth did you go off to fight the heretics, so far from your own Champagne?"

"At the request of King Louis, of course. He sent word to all his noble subjects who at one time or another had declared fealty to him. The Count of Champagne always does so, though it doesn't amount to much; sometimes we think the King of France should swear allegiance to us! Especially when he manages to lose so many lands to the English that he controls far less of France than we do. However, I thought I should honor this request and my mother agreed — though we have no particular quarrel with the Albigensians, and in fact we have always been friendly with Count Raymond of Toulouse, whom the king hates so. There were other reasons. We thought the crusade would not last long, and my mother suggested that while I was so near, I might go on to Navarre and visit your brother, King Sancho."

"Of course! He would have been so glad to meet you. I am afraid it cannot be long before he dies, and he must make his choice of a successor soon. But you did not go?"

"No, and I was sorry. I have always wanted to see the land of my mother's birth. But what with one thing and another, I decided to leave the crusade."

The account was interrupted because they had come to the Tusson River and though it was not high at midsummer, it was rocky and treacherous. The whole party forded it in single file, giving their horses plenty of time to choose their footing. When Thibaut resumed his place by her side, he was silent and preoccupied. Berengaria thought perhaps she should not pry into his reasons for leaving the crusade, but he suddenly began to pour out a strange tale.

"I think I must tell you the whole story. I have told no one else, and I have been vilified by many. It is hard to keep it all locked up." His somber mood was giving way to anger. She turned to him, all concern and attention. The road was ascending a low hill, and the horses had slowed to a walk.

"For one thing, the quarantaine had long run out — the forty days my men were required to serve. They were anxious to get home to their fields and their families. And the more I thought about it the more I wondered why I was helping King Louis take Avignon, one of Count Raymond's cities. I should be loyal to the King when he is defending himself against invading armies, but why should I take his part when he is attacking my friend and ally — as Raymond is?"

Again he stopped talking. Berengaria began to see that this was a young man of moods, so she kept silent and thought her own thoughts: about Raymond, another Raymond his father, and her dear friend Joanna who had been married to that elder Raymond.

"Thibaut!" she exclaimed. "What a pity you cannot justify your refusal to fight Raymond on the grounds of consanguinity, as so many men and women justify the annulment of their marriages. I have been working it all out. This Raymond, the seventh count of

Toulouse, is your cousin, and who would go to war against his cousin? Listen: He is the son of Raymond the Sixth and Joanna of England. Joanna was the sister of Richard, my late husband. So Raymond the Seventh is nephew to Richard, and by marriage, my nephew too. And since you are my sister's son, are you and Raymond not cousins — of a sort?" She looked at him triumphantly.

Thibaut had trouble following all this, but he laughed. "Well done, Aunt! If King Louis tries to force me back into his army, I will call you to defend me."

Another silence, but a short one this time. The light moment was past. "I know he will not try to make me return, and I might as well out with it. King Louis suspects me of paying suit to his wife. He is glad to be rid of me."

Berengaria had heard that Thibaut was something of a gallant, and had a reputation as a talented troubadour. She also knew that Blanche, Louis' queen, was said to be beautiful and pleasure-loving. She was intrigued, and asked, "So? Is there any truth to his suspicion?"

"Yes and no. I admire her very much, and she has been kind to me whenever I visited the royal court in Paris; but she is kind to any chansonnier who can sing a pretty song. Especially if it is dedicated to her. So when I wrote a song to 'La Dame au Clair Nom,' and sang it one evening, everybody thought it had to be meant for her because a 'Clair Nom' — a bright, white name — might well be 'Blanche.' And perhaps it was — a poet finds his inspiration wherever he can. But I certainly had no intention of seducing the queen of France!"

"How did this dangerous song go, Thibaut? I would like to imagine how Queen Blanche, with the bright name, felt when she heard it."

Like most troubadours, he was happy to perform. His ill temper subsided and he laughed. "It was not much of a song, and I have almost forgotten it. But the last few lines I remember well. I think they were what aroused the king's anger."

He let go of the reins so they lay loosely along his horse's neck. He raised his arms, pretending to be holding a viella in his left hand and to move the bow across the strings with his right. He sang:

My lady fair, I have no words for you
Except my song. If you will sing it too,
How full of joy my future life will be!
Come, dearest one, and sing along with me.

He bowed to Berengaria, and she clapped her hands in delight. "It is a lovely little song, and your voice is just right for such a pretty sentiment. I do not see why King Louis was so upset." Privately, she thought there might be more to the story than Thibaut had confessed. Maybe he was on his way now to Paris, where the queen was alone, awaiting her husband's return from the wars. She wished Henriette and Marie-Louise were here so they could discuss this interesting topic.

But she still had questions, more serious ones. "Now you must tell me just why King Louis feels he must besiege Avignon, if his aim is to stamp out the heresy. Isn't the Albigensians' strength far to the west, in Albi, and Carcassonne, and up in the Pyrenees? A monk from Carcassonne who was in Le Mans told me that King Louis was waging war as much for land as for human souls."

"Your monk had it just right. King Louis is determined to break Raymond's hold on the county of Toulouse. The Pope's call for a crusade was the perfect excuse. But Louis could not dare to attack the city of Toulouse at once; the truce that was declared after Amaury de Montfort failed to take it a few years ago still holds. So Louis decided to go after Raymond's second-most important city, Avignon."

"Will he succeed, do you think?"

"That's hard to say. It's protected by two rings of walls, with immensely tall towers all along. When I left, the defenders were resisting as fiercely as lions — but they are much better marksmen than any beast, as poor Pierre can bear witness. The King's troops are sick and hot and hungry. Raymond destroyed everything he could all around the city."

"Oh dear. Why do men see no other way to settle their quarrels than to kill each other?" Berengaria sighed.

Thibaut looked surprised. "What else could they possibly do? Men have always gone to war with each other, ever since the sons of Adam. If God did not want us to fight each other, surely He would have shown us something else to do."

Oh, but there are other ways, she thought. Our Lord's life was proof of that. But she let the subject drop; they were approaching Orléans, where Thibaut would leave them. Then it could be only ten days before she would reach the end of her journey. And Pierre.

erengaria found Pierre in the cloister of the monastery at Villeneuve. He was sitting on a hard stone bench with his hands clasping the head of a gnarled cane. Though she was only a few feet from him, he was staring out into the garden and did not see her. His shoulders were bowed. The signs of aging, which she had not noticed when she saw him daily, were startling. There was much more gray in his hair, and his mustache, once such a rich brown, was peppered with white. He had lost so much weight that his tunic hung on him loosely. His left leg above the knee was wrapped in a cloth that looked none too clean and his hose were wrinkled and sagging. Poor Pierre, who was always so careful about his grooming! His face looked grim and the brown eyes that used to gleam with good cheer and humor were dull.

"Pierre," she said softly.

He looked up and his face was transformed. He made an involuntary effort to get up, but sank back with a groan. She cried, "Oh, let me help you," but he forced himself to his feet.

"My prayers are answered. You came." Supporting himself unsteadily with his right hand on the cane, he stretched out his left hand toward her. She saw how it trembled.

"And what do you find? A poor husk of a man who can hardly rise from his seat. Oh my love, I am so glad to see you." His voice almost broke.

She hurried to him and they stood looking dazedly at each other, hardly able to believe that they were reunited.

"I came as fast as I could after Thibaut told me what had happened." Her voice, too, was unsteady. "Now let us sit down so we can talk." She hardly knew what she was saying in her relief at finding him relatively intact.

"The brother who let me in said you had been using your poor leg far more than you should."

"I wanted to be ready to ride when you came — that is, if you came. So I have been walking five times around the cloister here every day for a week. Now that you are here, I will double the dose, so we can leave all the sooner. Would you care to take a turn with me now and judge my prowess?" His voice was stronger already. This was the old Pierre, no friend of solemnity.

"I would not, thank you very much. And neither will you, just now. I see it is high time some sensible person took charge of you." She kissed him lightly. "Now I will go in to talk to the brothers to see what they say about how you are getting on. As for you, you are to go in and get some rest."

He bobbed his head and grinned. "Your obedient servant, oh most wise Queen Berengaria." He hobbled inside, where Cristiano was waiting to take his arm.

She found Paulin and Carlos and went to ask the two monks who had been taking care of Pierre when they thought he could stand the journey. They were cautious. "He has been forcing himself to do all that walking, though we told him that was too strenuous a regime," said one. "There is still some danger that the wound will fester, because it is still open."

"He is not well enough to ride yet, but if you could put him on a litter, he might do well enough," said the other. "There's no doubt that the sooner he can get back to a place where he can do nothing but rest, the sooner he will recover."

Carlos went off to see to horses and supplies, and Berengaria and Paulin reported the plan to Pierre.

"If you will behave and stay off your leg, I think we could be ready to leave in a day or two," Berengaria said.

"I will behave," said Pierre.

When they told him about the litter, however, he refused pointblank and insisted he was well enough to mount a horse.

"Perhaps you will get on, sir, but once the horse starts moving, you will wish you were anywhere else," said Paulin. "Brother Jacques says that your wound is still open, and could start bleeding again. It is very deep, and it takes time for the flesh and skin to grow back over it."

So Pierre sighed and grumbled but agreed.

When she went into his room to tell him good night, Berengaria sat on the edge of his bed and took his hand and stroked it gently. "I still find it hard to believe that I have found you, and that before long we will be back home and far away from this terrible war. Was the fighting quite dreadful?"

He was quiet a minute, remembering. "Yes, it was quite dreadful. It was bloody, it was murderous and far too many good men died. It grieves and shames me to know that I left my comrades in the midst of the battle."

"What else could you do? You could not fight any more, wounded as you were."

"But I deserted my king."

"Perhaps your king was forcing you into the wrong kind of battle, not in the service of God but for his own selfish ends. Thibaut thinks so."

He was quiet for so long that she thought he had gone to sleep, and she rose. "You may be right, Berengaria. I simply do not know. Good night, my dear."

The next day the men began assembling enough supplies to see them far up the Rhone and outside of the scorched-earth area around Avignon. The monks were enormously helpful because they always kept their storehouses full, and no king would dare to plunder them. They packed up baskets of bread, pickled beef, wedges of cheese and jugs of wine — for a price, of course; but Paulin had brought a pouch fat with coins.

On the second day they were off. Pierre consented to lie down on the litter, but he felt ashamed to be in such an ignominious position and sulked for an hour or so.

Progress was slow, but by midday they had put Avignon well behind them, and could see the broad Rhone Valley stretching northward into the distance — their route for days to come. When they stopped for the noon meal at an inn, Pierre was allowed to get up and join the others.

"Now tell us, Sieur Pierre," asked Cristina, "how was your morning's journey?"

"I will have to admit," he said grudgingly, "that it is an effortless way to travel. There is some jolting, of course, but there is no pressure at all on my wicked old leg, and I seem to feel it mending."

So they traveled on, but progress was painfully slow, so slow that travelers who passed them on the way could bring them news of the siege of Avignon. First, the word was that the attackers were suffering from heat and hunger while the defenders behind their high walls kept up their deadly barrage of arrows and stones. Many of Louis' troops deserted, their required tour of duty being long past.

Then, as the days passed, they heard that the tide of battle was going the other way. Finally, as the party reached Montelimar, the word was that Avignon might fall soon; the inhabitants were running out of food and growing weaker. The crusaders kept pounding at the walls and were close to making a breach.

By now Avignon and its siege seemed remote to all except perhaps Pierre. Everybody was eager to reach Le Mans before bad weather set in. By the end of September they were two-thirds of the way and Berengaria felt they could stop for two days in the Abbey of Fontgombault on the River Creuse. Though Pierre was getting stronger daily and obediently staying on his litter, she knew a day of rest would be good for him. Also, they needed to replenish their supplies.

The party were taking a late supper in the refectory on their second night at the abbey. The monks had left them at table, because it was time for vespers.

One of the men-at-arms spoke. "Queen Berengaria, we picked up some news today of the battle at Avignon. A peddler who left there two weeks ago said that King Louis has forced his way into the city, and the defenders have given up."

Berengaria, still saddened by the very fact of war, was glad the siege was over.

Pierre's face became grim. "I should have been there. I am glad King Louis was the winner, but I should have been there. I am ashamed."

"Well, King Louis was successful, so you need feel no guilt whatsoever," said Paulin. Paulin's whole life had been spent in Le Mans, and he was a partisan of neither King Louis nor the Albigensians. His loyalties were closer to home.

The man who had talked to the peddler had more. "Apparently, from what the man said, King Louis felt beholden to justify his conquest by searching out the heretics and punishing them. He sent his men all over the city to poke about and interrogate the inhabitants. But he could find only one heretic to burn."

This was food for thought indeed. Why such a mighty and costly effort to send only one unbeliever to hell? They were all too tired to discuss it. The meal was over and they rose to go to their lodgings in the monks' dormitory, up the stairs from the refectory. Only Pierre, Berengaria and Cristina had rooms on the ground floor. Pierre told Berengaria good night and she promised to come look in on him before she went to bed. She sat alone for a while, musing and looking idly about her. The room was not as severe and unadorned as most of the monastery refectories she had seen — and she had seen many. Eight stone pillars throughout the room supported the roof. They were graceful, with spreading bases and capitals, and carved with garlands and flowers, rabbits and lambs and other peaceable creatures.

"If I ever realize my dream, and found an abbey at Le Mans," she said to herself, "I will see that it has a room just like this." But that day seemed long distant. Where could she build it? Not within the walls of her city — every inch was occupied. Could she afford to buy land in the countryside, enough for all the buildings she envisioned? She knew what Herbert de Tucé would say: "No." Perhaps King Louis would help her? He was certainly pious — look how fiercely he had fought for his faith; and to build an abbey was a good Christian cause.

She sighed, then brightened at the thought that no matter what, she would have Pierre's help. She rose and went to tell him goodnight. In the dim light of her candle she could see that he was still awake. She sat on the edge of his bed.

"What are you thinking, my dear?" She stroked his brow.

"I was wondering whether you had forgotten me."

"Now that is not like you, old complainer. I was sitting in the refectory, thinking."

"And what were you thinking? Perhaps about some way to keep this cripple occupied, when we get home? Maybe as a scribe's assistant. I could fill inkwells and sharpen quills, if it did not take too much walking about."

"Oh Pierre, don't be silly. Of course you will be fit as ever, in no time, if you take care of yourself now. But yes, I was thinking of how you could help me when we are back in Le Mans. I am not going to say anything about it now, though. You must just wait until the time comes." She bent and they kissed. "Sleep well, my love."

"Do you sleep well too. And when we are back in Le Mans, and sleeping in the same bed, perhaps you will tell me more about what you were thinking in the refectory."

In just two weeks more, they were home. On the very last day, Cristiano — who rather enjoyed his position as guardian of Pierre's health — solemnly told his master his wound was so much better that he might mount a horse for the entry into the city.

51

"If you will not mind the doctors for your own sake, do it for mine. I do not wish to walk about with a one-legged man."

Pierre had come limping in the palace door, Cristiano at his side, just as Berengaria was on her way to the state chambers for the first council meeting since her return. She was happy to see him, but she was exasperated at the thought that he was taking chances with his recovery.

"The doctors said I could walk down, if I went slowly and used my cane. Even Cristiano agreed."

Berengaria looked at Cristiano suspiciously and the young man nodded solemnly. "That is correct, madame. They said he had been so careful for these two weeks that he could go out."

She sighed. She had walked up to see Pierre every day and it was true that he had become stronger and more like himself. Maybe she worried overmuch. She softened her stern look and smiled. "Very well, since you are here, I know the others will be glad to have you with them again. Everybody has been asking about you."

She preceded him into the state chamber and saw with pleasure that someone, probably Henriette, had brought in armfuls of branches flaunting golden autumn leaves, and put them in big copper pots along the stone walls. What a difference they made — it was like sunshine pouring into the gray room.

The counselors crowded around Pierre, assuring him that he was looking very well and congratulating him on his safe return. He took his customary seat at Berengaria's right. The chair at her left was still empty, awaiting Paulin.

Here came the majordomo, walking quickly into the council chamber. He did not usually walk quickly these days, having put on considerable weight. By his pace, and the set of his chin and flush on his cheeks, they could tell that he brought news.

"I have just heard… King Louis has died." He stopped to catch his breath and after the first gasps of disbelief, they peppered him with questions. When? Where? How?

"He died in Montpensier, ten days ago. He was on his way back to Paris, but he suddenly fell ill and within twelve hours he was dead."

"But of what? Surely he was not wounded in the siege of Avignon?" asked Garsie LeClerc.

"No, at least not according to the peddler who was spreading the news in the square just now. The king was quite well when he left Avignon for Paris. But that is all I know."

He fell into his chair and puffed a bit. "Well, almost all." He looked askance at Berengaria, wondering whether to go on. "The man did say there was a strange tale: that King Louis, out of love for his wife, had not touched a woman since he left on the crusade, and that his abstinence brought on a fever."

"Ha!" snorted Pierre, before he thought. "If that's the way it works, then I should not be sitting here alive today." He stopped and looked guiltily at Berengaria. She caught his eye then looked away, blushing and trying not to smile.

She said quickly, "Of course, I will send my sympathy to the king's mother, Queen Blanche. But shall we begin our deliberations? We have a long list of matters to discuss."

Paulin had briefed her on events during their absence: The merchants had asked their Dame to give them a subsidy because rainstorms had devastated the harvest and the price of wheat and barley had risen immoderately. One of the old Roman towers in the city wall had almost collapsed — they would have to decide if it was a danger to passersby, and if so who would see to the rebuilding. The Bishop had asked the Dame to take care of the reroofing of the Abbey of La Couture, saying it was not his responsibility. And so on.

When they at last came to the end of the list the counselors left. Pierre looked tired and admitted that his leg was paining him. She called for Carlos and Cristiano and with their support he started slowly up the hill.

She asked Paulin to stay. "I will need your help, Paulin, in preparing my letter of condolence to the new King of France. I want to establish a good relationship with him. I never really did with his father."

"He is only a child, I understand. Nine, I believe."

"Yes. So his mother, Queen Blanche, will be regent for sometime. But I may be able to make a little claim on her goodwill; her mother, Eleanor of Castile, was Richard's sister, so I am Blanche's aunt by marriage. I will remind her of this, and perhaps she will prove agreeable to a request I intend to make."

With Paulin's help she framed her letter, addressing it to the widow and the heir. She expressed proper regret for the death of Louis VIII and sincere hopes for the success of the new reign. She reminded Blanche of their connection. She continued thus:

> *When your grief permits you to take up the reins of government, I hope you will bear in mind a request which I sent to the late King, but which must have reached him just before his end, if it reached him at all. I do have every reason to believe he would have granted it. I asked him for the gift of a small plot of royal lands near Le Mans. Here I would like to erect an abbey for the shelter and nurture of worthy men who wish to serve God through scholarship and study, away from the evil distractions of the world.*

When she was satisfied with the letter, she sat back and said, "Now Paulin, you are the only person whom I have told about this plan of mine. I have often spoken of my dream of founding an abbey, but nobody, not even Pierre, knows that I have taken any steps to bring it about. I depend on your discretion and silence, until we know whether there is any real possibility of success. I would not like to have talk all over town about this, when it is only a castle in the air."

"Or should we say, an abbey in the air?"

She laughed. Paulin seldom chanced a pleasantry. Perhaps it was a good omen.

He knew that she was telling him in a roundabout way that above all, he should not mention the matter to his two gossipy sisters. He was not one to babble in any case, but he assured her that his lips would be sealed, and that he appreciated her trust.

"I have heard that the little prince, now King Louis the Ninth, has already shown signs of unusual piety. How wonderful it would be if the Queen Regent decided that granting your request would be a demonstration of his religious zeal."

Berengaria hoped so too. To herself, she wondered if her nephew Thibaut's rumored romance with Queen Blanche might cause the queen to think kindly of her — or not.

Whatever the reason, the little prince's mother, in a surprisingly short time, sent word:

> *King Louis will gladly donate to his very dear aunt, the loyal Queen Berengaria, a portion of the royal lands consisting of forty-six acres of forest, seven acres of fields and two acres of gardens, lying along the River Huisne in the County of Maine. He is happy to hear of her plans for the abbey on these lands, and will expect her to keep him informed of her progress.*
>
> *If Berengaria will come to Paris, or send a representative, we will prepare the documents and conclude the donation.*

Berengaria sent Paulin to Paris. By August of 1228, the land was hers. She could hardly believe it — the dream she had cherished so long was going to come true.

52

"So what is so important that you have summoned me to ride out with you in private to hear about it?" Pierre asked.

He and Berengaria had left the city and were riding south into the countryside. His leg, though quite healed, was still weak from months of inactivity. He favored it when he walked and often needed his cane. On horseback, though, he looked his old hardy self — except for graying hair, deepening furrows in his face, and some thickening about the middle, due to little exercise for so long.

At his question she flashed him a smile. "Patience, dear one! We are almost there." Her pale cheeks were tinged with a rosy flush. She looked as saucy as a girl teasing her swain.

They rode down the lane that led to the River Huisne. Berengaria remembered the first time she had come here, during those painful days when she had realized that she loved Pierre, but long before they had become lovers. She had been moping and her ladies had urged her to join them in an outing. And it was here by the stream that she had read the news of Brother Anselmo's death. So many memories! Today, however, she was not mourning the past; she was looking excitedly to the future.

They reached the same meadow where she and her ladies had spread their picnic. She pulled up her horse.

"Now let us dismount, and we will walk to the edge of the stream." She was still playing games with him. He obeyed, mystified but enjoying the suspense.

They stood by the little river, and all was still except for the gurgling song the stream sang to itself as it flowed beside its willow-clad banks. Sunlight and shadows played on the waters. A thrush suddenly pealed its song of rejoicing — "It's summer, it's summer, it's summer!" Across the way was the same old mill Berengaria remembered, now even more of a ruin.

"Here is a convenient log; let us sit down," she said. "Now I am completely serious, and I will tell you why we are here. Do you remember the first time I told you that I hoped to found an abbey some day, where men of learning could live a good and simple life, pursuing their studies and serving God in peace, with no worries about sustenance or lodging?"

"I do remember. It was in your palace, the day I came to tell you about returning to you your rights to Montbazon. I thought it was a praiseworthy notion and I honored you for it, though at that time I had no idea how serious you were about scholarship and all that. I admit I thought it was only a dream."

"So it was, then. But it was a dream I had cherished ever since I was at the monastery of Leyre, when I came to love the quiet life and the little triumphs. While I was learning my Arabic and getting better at copying, I began to see how important it is to have people with the skills to preserve and pass on all the knowledge we have inherited. Nobody thinks much of those toilers, but they are the real links between our past and our future." She stopped and looked at him almost apologetically, aware that she had been carried away.

"My eloquent friend! I am now quite ashamed of myself for never paying more attention to my studies — or I could have been such a link. How have you put up with this idler all these years?"

"Well Pierre, God does not give all of us the same gifts — think how dull it would be if He did. You have your own special qualities, you know." She took his hand. "Still, I think if I had been born a man, I would be a monk sitting at a stool in some scriptorium even now, happily copying away."

"Though I am sure you would have made a very fine monk, I am glad you were born a woman."

She pressed his hand affectionately and looked up into his face. "So am I." He bent his head and they kissed, then sat leaning together, content with each other and the peaceful prospect before them.

"But go on," he said. "What brings us here? Why all this talk of monasteries and abbeys?"

"Because now I can make my dream come true. I have always instructed Herbert de Tucé to keep the money that comes from England separate from the rest of my revenue; it is mine to spend as I please. All my other receipts go to the costs of running the city and the betterment of the life of my people. I have spent some of my savings on the work at the cathedral and the city's churches, but now I have enough set aside to begin building the abbey." She looked at him, eyes shining, then pointed across the river. "And I plan to build it right there."

"What, do you own that land? I thought it was in the royal domain."

"It was," Berengaria said smugly. "But I asked King Louis, and his mother Queen Blanche, to donate some land for this purpose, and they agreed. I now have a charter for most of what I need."

She held up her hand and counted off on her fingers. "First, forty-eight acres of woodland; second, seven acres of fields, ready to cultivate and sow; and third, two acres of gardens. The gardens are behind the old mill, and probably sadly neglected. I will clear enough of the woods to make a grand space for a fine large abbey. And Pierre, I will need all your help."

"Bravo, Queen Berengaria! How have you done so much, without dropping a hint of what you were up to?" He rose and looked around as though searching for his first task. "Of course I will help. What can I do, where do we begin?"

She laughed up at him. "Oh Pierre, you are quite the man of action again! You're ready to go out in the fields and start gathering stones for the foundation right now, aren't you? But that must wait a bit, until I receive an answer from Cîteaux. I have asked the father abbot of the Cistercians if he would send some of his men here to help us get started."

"Cîteaux seems a long way to go to find help. It's way off there in Burgundy."

"Yes, but the Cistercians know more than anyone else about establishing monasteries; they have built so many. They can help us plant our farmlands too; they always cultivate the soil as well as cultivating their souls. I want my abbey to be completely self-sufficient. I can see it now, surrounded with wheatfields and gardens and vineyards." She flung out her arm to encompass all the wild land across the river, in her mind's eye transformed into a fruitful spread of fields and vines.

"Well! Now there is something I know something about, or I used to when I lived and farmed at Colombiers, and when I had those vineyards near Troyes, remember, dear heart? Let me work at figuring how much land we will need for your various agricultural enterprises. And I can find good young vines to bring in."

"Yes, Pierre, do! And start looking for the very best stonemasons, and ask Garsie LeClerc who were those carpenters he had working on the chapel." She was carried away with her enthusiasm. Then a shadow came over her face.

"Oh Pierre, there is so much to do and time is so short!"

"Why do you say time is short?"

"Well my friend, at our age, we never know when God will call us to Him, do we? So we should act with dispatch, to finish our work on earth while we can." It was an evasive answer. She too rose and, avoiding his eyes, began walking back to where the horses were tethered.

A seed of alarm had been planted. He saw that she walked slowly, choosing her steps carefully as though she were afraid of stumbling and falling. He realized that he had begun to notice that when she did not know she was being observed her face looked strained. She saw his eyes on her and the dawning of an anguished doubt.

"Now Pierre, you are not to look like that. I cannot conceal from you that I am not as well as I would like. But do not feel sorry for me, do not look like a mourner already! God will give me strength to finish this good work. And you will give me your support too. More than ever, I need you, Pierre." There was a little catch in her voice and she looked down; to her dismay she was blinded by tears.

He took her in his arms, gently, like a father with a suffering child. He stroked her hair. "Of course you will have my support, dear one. We will go on together."

he new abbey became the talk of the town. When Berengaria went out walking, city folk smiled when they saw their "Reine Blanche." Some came to thank her, and told her they had already been impressed with the magnificent additions she was making to the cathedral. And now this: a grand abbey! It was sure to add lustre to Le Mans. Why, people would be comparing it with Fontevrault.

Her whole council, with Pierre as her chief lieutenant, became engaged in drawing up the master plan.

In response to her request, Robert Abbeville, abbot at Cîteaux, sent an emissary, Brother Jerome. She first met him on an October morning in 1228 when he was admitted to the scriptorium where she and Paulin were conferring.

Brother Jerome was tall and smooth-faced, suave, prolix and assured. "Good morning, Queen Berengaria. Greetings from our revered Father Robert. He begs to express to you his joy at your plan to build an abbey here at Le Mans, and he assures you that he will do everything in his power to assist you. He will gladly send monks to assist in the building, and to stay as the founding members of the abbey. It is all too seldom, I fear, that secular lords seize the opportunity to put their wealth to such a noble purpose…" and on he went.

She assessed him while she waited for him to run down. He was hardly one of the austere, plainly clad monks like her friends at Leyre, though they too were of the Cistercian order. An ostentations silver cross glittered from a silver chain about his neck. His robe was not roughspun wool but of smoothest, whitest linen. Well! she thought. No matter how worldly the rest of the Cistercians have become, at my abbey they will follow the rules of austerity that were set out by St. Bernard, a century ago. They will wear the plain, natural wool robes that he favored.

She realized that Brother Jerome had asked her a question. Something about a name. What would the abbey be called?

"I think we have settled on the 'Abbaye de Piété-Dieu.'" She glanced at Paulin, who nodded. "We plan to make it a center of learning in the service of God."

"Very good. I will so inform Father Robert. Now as to your requests. You have asked for the first contingent to come as soon as possible, to help in the construction. You have also asked that the monks we send from our other abbeys to populate yours may include some skilled in copying and illumination. We will do our best. The only other matter of import is the naming of your abbot. You will be glad to hear that Father Robert has selected Brother Sigismund from Fontenay for the post. He has studied in Paris, and in fact taught at the university there, before joining us."

Her surprised cry almost jolted him out of his self-assurance. "Sigismund! Surely not the Sigismund who wrote that commentary on Peter Abelard's 'Ethica'? He is one of the finest scholars of the age. I had no idea he had joined the Cistercian Order."

"He did indeed, some six years ago. I believe I am betraying no confidence when I tell you that when Father Robert told us he was looking for just the right man to send here, Brother Sigismund asked most fervently to be considered. You too have a reputation as a champion of learning, madame."

"I am afraid I have not done all I could. But we will soon change that, with Brother Sigismund to encourage us. I must remember to call him Father Sigismund, mustn't I?"

Paulin saw that she had tired, and rose to indicate that it was time for Brother Jerome to go. "Please tell Father Robert that we are greatly pleased with his messages, and we look forward to welcoming the brothers and our abbot."

When Sigismund himself shortly arrived, she could hardly believe this was the famous scholar, he was such a comical figure. He was very thin, enveloped in a voluminous robe (undyed homespun, she was glad to note). His round head was bald except for a gray fringe that encircled it, echoed by a sparse beard that tried to conceal a rather insignificant chin. His nose was remarkably large — not pointed but like a little apple in the middle of his face. It was quite red. (She wondered: too much dissipation during his student days in Paris, before he joined the order?) His bright brown eyes darted about constantly, as though trying to take in everything at once.

No sooner had two polite sentences been exchanged than he jumped up to examine the manuscripts on her work table and on the shelves.

"What a fidgety man!" she thought. "Will he ever be able to concentrate on our work?"

However, she found his mind as agile as his body. She asked Pierre and Paulin to join them, and they went over the plans together. Sigismund grasped the overall scope and the smallest details with amazing speed.

"First the wall," he said. "Then the chapter house, next the monks' dortoir — their dormitory. Or perhaps both at once. The church can come later." His finger pounced on the space reserved for the scriptorium. "This is not big enough. If we are to make our abbey the center of learning we all envision, we must have at least six workplaces. We will need a warming room next door, because of course the scriptorium will not be heated. St. Bernard adjured us to labor for the Lord without thought of our own comfort."

"That seems rather harsh," said Pierre.

"Yes, I think we could relax that rule, at least in winter," said Berengaria.

"Not while I am abbot," Sigismund said, his eyes snapping and his nose growing even redder. "There is enough laxity already in our order. What was good enough for the monks a hundred years ago is good enough for us."

Berengaria, who had thought she too favored austerity, but was willing to temper it, was abashed. "Very well. I suppose if there is a warming room nearby, they can go in there from time to time."

"Certainly not! The warming room is for the lay brothers who have not taken the vow; but we will need a little window just here, open to both rooms, so the scribes can pass their inkpots through when the ink freezes, to have them thawed over the brazier."

What a stickler for the rules he was! She did not think God would mind if His servants toiled with warm fingers. Still, she did not argue; there would be time enough to deal with little differences like this later.

But would there be time? She had no doubt now that she was seriously ill. She was not in pain, but she was always tired and fretted when she could not be as active as she wished. Her doctors told her to rest, and suggested one remedy after another: a diet without meat, a daily dose of an infusion of fennel, fasting, poultices of nettles on the brow. Nothing helped.

She was relieved when Pierre and Sigismund proved not only compatible but good working partners. Pierre listened respectfully to Sigismund's views of what a proper abbey should offer, and the latter yielded to Pierre's practical knowledge of what was possible and how to achieve it. Both were bound by their regard and concern for their lady.

"She is an extraordinary woman," Sigismund said one chill winter day as they stood by the river, looking over the ground to select a suitable place to put temporary huts for the workers. The mill had been restored to working order and its wheel turned steadily, creaking and squeaking. Behind them the masons were working on the wall that would surround the abbey. Nearby, a line of monks was passing buckets of water drawn from the river to where the masons were mixing their mortar. There was as yet no well, so the river water was essential.

"Imagine her conceiving the notion of building an abbey here in this desert," Sigismund went on, "and having the foresight to locate it by a river."

"I have known her for twenty-five years," said Pierre. "I am still amazed at her tenacity. Once she decides to do something, she finds a way, and nothing stops her."

Sigismund noticed the carpenter who was bringing planks for the huts, and beckoned him over. All three were soon deep in a discussion of placement and size. Sigismund thought no floors would be needed — perhaps a little straw could be strewn on the ground — but Pierre insisted on wooden floors.

The abbey wall was finished by the fall of 1229 and all the ground within was cleared and smoothed. Structures had begun to arise. Some dozen monks labored there for the glory of God, along with a number of workers and artisans from Le Mans who labored for the glory of their city — and the good wages that Queen Berengaria paid.

As the weeks and months passed, the council met regularly, and Berengaria insisted on being present, though everybody could see that she was not up to it.

Cristina would beg her to stay in bed. "Madame, why not let Pierre and Paulin speak for you, and come report to you afterwards?" Cristina herself was feeling her years, and often wished that someone would urge her to stay in bed. From the time the fire was kindled on the hearth before dawn until the last candle was extinguished at night, she was on the go.

"No, Cristina," Berengaria would say. "I must be there, and know how the work is going. They might lag if I did not. I must keep my counselors' spirits up. To say nothing of my own."

On a bright October day in 1230, the sixty-fifth year of her life, she walked slowly down the stairs, Cristina at her side, to the council chamber. Her friends rose as she entered. She looked almost ghostly, with pale face and white gown, relieved only by the glint of the golden lion brooch at her throat. She sat down, holding herself perfectly erect, and listened as Herbert de Tucé made his usual cautious report on her finances. Never mind how much revenue was coming in today, he chronically expected disaster to strike tomorrow. Then Gautier de Perseigne, the chaplain, said the work on the cathedral buttresses was going as well as could be expected. He confessed that he could see little change from one week to the next, but cutting and carving and hoisting great pieces of stone was a slow and difficult process.

Finally Berengaria turned to the abbot, who for ten minutes had been jumping about in his seat.

He launched into a rapid-fire recital: two groups, one building the chapter house, the other the dortoir, were racing to see who would finish first, and he expected both to do so by Christmas. Soon they could set a date for the dedication. The columns in the chapter house were all in place, just like the ones Berengaria had admired at the Abbey of Fontgombeau. A skilled carver was embellishing the capitals. "But as you all know, the Cistercian Order discourages over-decoration," said

Sigismund. "So we shall not dazzle the Christian world with our carvings."

Berengaria was tempted to speak up on behalf of dazzlement, but held her tongue.

"We do have one little problem, and I would welcome your advice. We try to be good neighbors. But that mill! It is so noisy, twenty-four hours a day. It is so close to our huts that it's impossible to get a night's sleep. I have appealed to Alphonse Buiton, the miller, to give us at least a few hours of quiet every night, between compline and prime, but he says he cannot shut down the wheel without interrupting his production of flour. And the bakers of Le Mans must have deliveries daily. My men are complaining, and flagging in their work. Even I, the calmest and most imperturbable of men, am at my wit's end, for lack of sleep." He threw up his hands and rolled his eyes, looking anything but imperturbable, and produced a gaping yawn to make his point.

They all said they would try to think of something.

Later, Berengaria and Pierre met in her chamber and sat by the fire. She held out her hands, always so cold these days, and rubbed them in the warmth of the flames.

"Poor Father Sigismund! What can we do about his quarrel with the miller?"

"I know Alphonse Buiton," said Pierre, "and he is not unreasonable. He only wants to make a living. If we could find some way to recompense him for shutting down the mill periodically, I am sure he would listen."

"But what about the flour for the bakers of Le Mans? Some morning we might not find their fresh loaves at our breakfast!"

It was a doleful prospect.

Then — "I know!" she exclaimed. "Pierre, our treasury for the abbey is healthy. Why not purchase the mill from Monsieur Buiton for a good price so he may go buy or build himself another, far away from our monks' sensitive ears?"

"Then what would we do about the mill? Let it languish, and go without our bread?"

She looked at him with a glimmer of her old mischief. "Why no. We will give it to the abbey. When the monks hear the millwheel creaking away, they will hear the coins falling into their coffers. And they will sleep soundly."

They both laughed, pleased with this neat solution. But suddenly she gasped and pressed a hand against her breast. She looked at him wide-eyed, terrified. He had never seen her so defenseless.

"Oh Pierre, it hurts, it hurts!"

He called Cristina. Henriette and Marie-Louise came running too. Among them they helped the stricken woman to her bed.

She lay there for three weeks, listless, without appetite, wasting away day by day. The pain was with her always. She would see no one but Cristina, not even Pierre. She asked Cristina to bring her little psalter, and her only diversion was leafing through its pages, studying the pictures (their brilliant colors now faded), rereading the Psalms that she knew by heart, remembering.

54

ierre sent a messenger to Blanche, and she came as quickly as she could. She went straight into her sister's room and stood by her bed. Heavy drapes covered the windows and the only light was from a solitary candle by the bedside and from the fire that flickered on the hearth. Berengaria looked up with the ghost of a smile and stretched up her thin arms to embrace her sister.

"Oh Blanche — did Pierre send for you? Bless him! I was hoping you would come. But Blanche, I am so ashamed to be seen like this." Her voice was so faint that Blanche had to bend over to hear her. "I am worse than poor old Sanchito. At least he ate like a man who meant to stay alive."

"So you should follow his example, because he is indeed still alive, even though he's bedridden. And at least he did not lie in a room as black as the tomb. I can hardly see you! Let us get some light and air in here!"

She went to pull aside the drapes and came back to pick up the tray on the table. "Now look at this good pudding they've brought you, and you haven't touched it." She raised a spoonful and Berengaria obediently opened her mouth and swallowed it.

"But I still think Sancho could have gotten up if he had just set his mind to it." Blanche chattered on, to hide her devastation at the change in her sister. She talked of her journey, of Thibaut and Bérengère, of how glad she was to be in Le Mans again. All this in the cheerful, half-scolding tone she had so often used with her older sister.

"They tell me you don't even ask any questions about the work at the abbey. Don't you want to know how it's going? Pierre says there is great news and he has been coming every day to see if you will hear it. He and Abbot Sigismund are outside now — shan't I ask them in?"

Berengaria passed a hand over her brow, brushing aside a few wisps of straggling hair. "Oh dear, I suppose so. But I hate to have them see me looking like this. I have discovered, at this late date, that I am afflicted with the sin of vanity!" Her weak laugh brought on a fit of coughing. Blanche, alarmed, brought water and when the coughing had subsided, briskly began to make her sister more presentable. She called for Cristina, and they helped her sit up in bed, supported by a mountain of pillows.

Blanche brushed her hair. "Still as brown as ever, with just these few streaks of gray!" Blanche marveled. "And here am I looking like a dandelion gone to seed."

Cristina brought a white lace kerchief for her mistress's head and a soft wool shawl to put around her shoulders. Then the two men were admitted.

Pierre was shocked at the change in the last few weeks. Her skin seemed stretched tautly over her bones. There was something ethereal about the ash-pale face, lit only by her eyes, greener than ever and glowing as though from some inner fire.

Then when she smiled and held out her hand, he knew she was still his Berengaria. He came to her bedside and pressed her cold hand so warmly that she winced. He looked into her eyes, but he could not speak. Sigismund stood at the foot of the bed, immobile for once, his face full of compassion.

It was up to Berengaria to fill the silence. "How good of you both to come! Blanche persuaded me that I was well enough to receive visitors, and perhaps I am. And she tells me that I am going to get better if I will just eat my puddings, so I shall try to think so too."

"Everybody is praying for you, madame," said Sigismund. "At the abbey, at Saint-Julien, at your own chapel and at every church in the city. You are in everyone's thoughts."

"Thank you for telling me. I miss getting out and seeing my people. I shall beseech God to bless them for their caring." She had to stop to catch her breath.

"But you must tell me, what is this great news? Blanche says that you have great news." She looked from one to the other, and Pierre signaled to the abbot.

Sigismund erupted. "Great news indeed! Father Robert is coming from Cîteaux for the dedication of the abbey, and King

Louis will either come or send a representative, and twenty more monks are due any moment now. We are working night and day to get finished in time. The chapter house is beautiful and only lacks glazing in two of the windows, then it will be complete." He beamed and waited for her reaction.

Pierre was heartsick to see how she strove to rise to enthusiasm. "You see, you have gotten along very well without me, and I am proud of you all." She fell back against her pillows and closed her eyes, then with an effort raised her head. "But I must see these marvels. When is the dedication to be?"

Pierre said gently, "I am afraid it is very soon — the day after tomorrow, December 24. And we cannot put it off, because of all the dignitaries who are already on the road. My dear, I am not sure you should exert yourself to come."

"Nonsense!" she said, forcing strength into her voice. "Of course I shall come."

Blanche suggested that a litter was the answer; it was only an hour's journey, and they would get the softest-walking horses in the city, and go very slowly.

"And I will supervise the whole thing," said Pierre. "After all, I have a great deal of experience with litters."

So it was decided. Sigismund rose to go and Blanche accompanied him.

Pierre stayed and sat by her bed, holding both her hands in his, and they looked dumbly into each other's eyes. It was impossible now for either of them to maintain the pretense that she would regain her health.

"My dear, my only love," he said in a voice husky with his pain, "please, do not leave me!"

She raised a thin hand to gently smooth his cheek and trace the outline of his lips with her fingers. "Don't grieve, Pierre. Think of all our years together, the best years of my life." He leaned down to place his cheek against hers so she could not see his tears. "You have given me so much happiness," she whispered, still clinging to his hand. Her eyes closed.

After a long look he kissed her softly, released her hands and left the room, now darkening with the shades of evening.

Sigismund was waiting outside.

"I am glad she will be there for the dedication," he said. "It will mean a great deal to all those who have worked so hard if their patroness is present." Pierre said nothing.

After they were gone, Blanche came in to find Berengaria fallen back on her pillows, apparently asleep. She smoothed her sister's brow and fought back her tears.

Berengaria opened her eyes and looked up. "Don't cry, Blanche. God would not let me come this close to seeing my dream come true without letting me be there for the fulfillment."

The next day she was weaker. Blanche did everything she could think of to help her, from poultices to prayer. She encouraged her to get up and take a few steps, but Berengaria could not manage even with Blanche bearing her weight, and had to return to her bed. Still she insisted she would manage to get to the dedication on the morrow.

That night she drank her broth and managed to swallow a little bread, then fell asleep at once with no turning or tossing or coughing. Blanche began to think she might indeed be able to attend the dedication. She sank onto her cot near the door and into the slumber of the exhausted.

erengaria woke suddenly to find herself floating in the air above the palace, but it did not seem odd. She could see through the roof. There was a motionless figure lying in her bed. "That must be me, but how can I be in two places at once?" she wondered. As she watched, the figure jumped out of bed, quickly got dressed and ran down the stairs to where Pierre was waiting to help her onto her horse — it was dear old gray Grimaldo the First, who had been her mount when she was a child.

As she hovered she saw Grimaldo take his place at the head of a long procession and step smartly along. That other Berengaria sat straight and proud in her saddle, and her flowing white cloak fell in graceful folds almost to the ground. The procession moved down from the city toward the new abbey. She realized they were all going to the dedication, and she was filled with joy. The day had come at last!

And what a lovely day — though she knew it was December, she felt the warm rays of the sun on her back. She could clearly see everybody in the procession. How splendid they all looked! That first one must be the Bishop of Paris, come to represent King Louis. He was tall and portly, as bishoplike as a man can be, robed in scarlet with his mitre gleaming white. After him came Bishop Maurice of Le Mans, and she felt a touch of civic pride to see that he was almost as grand as the Parisian.

Next came Father Robert Abbeville of Cîteaux and dear Abbot Sigismund. In contrast to their lordly superiors, both were in the unremarkable colorless homespun of the Cistercian order. She smiled to see how proud and happy Sigismund looked. His round red nose looked as though it had been polished for the occasion.

Now who were these monks, solemnly marching two by two? Their hoods covered their heads and their robes swung as they walked, all in step, with almost military precision. She remembered that Sigismund had told her the twenty scholars who would man the scriptorium would arrive in time for the dedication. She thought she would glide down to examine them more closely, to see if they looked properly earnest and studious. As she descended, marveling at how easy it was, the whole scene dissolved and she found that she had become one with the Berengaria who was riding Grimaldo.

She turned in her saddle to see who was behind her. There was Pierre, striding along in as forthright a fashion as he could, considering his limp and his cane. His face was closed, stony. Why didn't he look more happy on this joyful day? She tried to call out to him to rejoice, but he did not hear. There was Blanche clinging to his arm, weeping openly. Why were the countryfolk lined up along the road looking so sad?

She thought she would just go back up into the air and survey the rest of the procession. She patted Grimaldo on the neck. "Keep trotting along, old friend. I will be right back." With a gentle push of her feet on the stirrups, she rose and turned to see her council marching solemnly along behind Pierre and Blanche.

They were led by Paulin Boutier and Herbert de Tucé, sober-faced, dignified as ever. Then members of her household: Marie-Louise and Henriette walked unsteadily while tears streamed down their faces. Carlos seemed stoical but Cristina could not contain her sobs. She was supported by Carlito on one side, Cristiano on the other.

"Please don't cry so, Cristina!" she called out. But Cristina did not hear.

A crowd of dignitaries, including most of the city's nobility, followed. Some were in colorful costumes suitable for a festive celebration, which she was glad to see. Others seemed to have hastily thrown on any old black or somber cloak. The procession looked like a dreary winter-blackened field where a few brave poppies and buttercups were raising their heads.

A disorganized clump of citizens fell in behind the official procession. She could hear no chatter, no talk at all; the scene was eerily silent, except for the sound of marching or shuffling feet.

She swam back through the unresisting air to the head of the column. Now Grimaldo was pulling a cart with a long black box on it, draped with a red-and-gilt cloth on which she could make out the three lions of the Plantagenet coat of arms. It looked like a casket.

Before she could wonder whose, she saw that Abbot Sigismund had turned and signaled the marching monks. They stepped onto the new stone bridge across the River Huisne which had been built since her last visit to the abbey. She hovered over it, examining with pleasure the graceful arched supports.

The monks began a dirge-like chant, marching in time to the music until they were just inside the chapter house. Four of them carried the casket to a dais near the windows on the far side. Berengaria floated down and slipped in the door. So this was the chapter house she had begun planning so long ago. It was just as she had envisioned it. The honey-colored stone of the walls, not yet darkened by the years, created an illusion of brightness and warmth. Tall arched windows let in pale shafts of light. She looked around for Sigismund so she could compliment him. There he was, beside that mysterious casket; the Bishop of Paris stood at the head and the Bishop of Le Mans at the foot.

She made her way through the crowd, but strangely nobody seemed to see her. She passed Pierre, and his face was so sorrowful that she stopped to tell him to cheer up because this was a day of celebration. But she was jostled by the crowd and the next thing she knew, she was lying in the dark confines of the casket. She did not know why. But it was warm and comfortable. The cover was open, and she looked up contentedly to where the tops of the supporting columns curved elegantly to the stone ceiling. "We did plan well," she thought. "Pierre and Sigismund and I have created something truly beautiful."

She could dimly hear the Bishop of Paris, saying something about "the wise and benevolent Dame of Le Mans."

Next Abbot Sigismund spoke, more slowly and solemnly than she had ever heard him. She could not see him but she caught every word. "This abbey, which Queen Berengaria planned for so many years as a gift to her people, will stand here long after we are gone. The scholars she has drawn to this place will continue to work, knowing that she would wish it, and so will the generations of monks who come after them. As abbot, I will always keep her wishes in mind. Berengaria has gone to her rest, but what she has begun here will live on."

Quite true, she thought. The abbey is indeed my gift to my good people and those who come after them. But what does he mean, I have gone to my rest?

Now there was the face of the Bishop of Paris above her. He was making the sign of the cross. "Let the casket be closed," he said. The lid descended, but instead of darkness, she was bathed in warmth and light.

On her cot in the Queen's bedroom, Blanche woke groggily, to hear her sister murmuring in her sleep and breathing with difficulty. Then she heard, not loud but perfectly clear, "Yes, my Lord. Now I understand." Blanche lit a candle and hurried to the bed.

In the flickering light she saw Berengaria's face smooth, all tenseness gone. Her eyes were open and her lips were curved in a smile — the hesitant smile of a girl who has had wonderful news but hardly dares believe it.

Epilogue

Sancho VII died in 1234, his ailments having finally conquered his strong constitution.

Blanche lived long enough to see the crowning of her son Thibaut as Sancho's successor, King Thibaut I of Navarre.

Pierre found solace for his bereavement in carrying out Berengaria's wishes for the completion of the Abbey of Epau. He was present at the dedication of the abbey church, which took its place with the chapter house, the dortoir, the scriptorium and the dining hall.

Geoffrey, the new bishop of Le Mans, presided over the dedication and the unveiling of the Queen's tomb by the altar.

Many years later her tomb was moved to the cathedral of Saint-Julien in the city. It bears a recumbent effigy of Berengaria. The face is that of a beautiful, composed young woman. Her hair is loose, partly covered by a veil. She wears the crown of the Queen of England. In her hands is a book, showing her portrait flanked by two torches as though on a bier. At her feet is a lion like the one on Richard's tomb at Fontevrault. The epitaph reads:

"Homage to Berengaria of Navarre, Queen of England and of Cyprus, our good Lady of Le Mans... To the sovereign majesty, beauty and goodness and the virtues of her youth, were added her greatness in adversity and her resignation in sacrifice. Queen, in this sanctified place, may your venerated remains rest in perpetual tranquility."

The Abbey of Epau still stands today, and has been cherished by the people of Le Mans for seven centuries and more as the legacy of their "Reine Blanche." It looks just as Berengaria planned it, and though monks no longer live there and scribes do not toil in the scriptorium, it is a famous center of scholarly and cultural pursuits, a monument to her vision.

A Selected Bibliography

Bridge, Antony, *Richard the Lionheart.* M. Evans, New York, 1989

Chardon, Henri, "Histoire de la Reine Bérengère," in *Bulletin de la Société Agricole de la Sarthe,* Vol.X. Le Mans, 1866

Gillingham, John, *Richard the Lionheart.* Times Books, New York, 1978

Hallam, Elizabeth, ed., *The Plantagenet Chronicles.* Weidenfeld and Nicolson, New York, 1986

Hallam, Elizabeth, ed., *The Plantagenet Encyclopedia.* Viking, Penguin Books, London, 1990

Kelly, Amy, *Eleanor of Aquitaine and the Four Kings.* Harvard University Press, Cambridge, Mass., 1950

Norgate, Kate, *Richard the Lion Heart.* Macmillan, London, 1924

Pernoud, R., *Eleanor of Aquitaine.* Coward-McCann, New York, 1965

Piolin, Dom Paul, "Bérengère, Reine d'Angleterre, Dame du Mans," in *Révue des Questions Historiques,* Vol. IV. Paris, 1890

Richard of Devizes, *The Chronicle of the Time of King Richard the First.* Ed. and trans. by J. Appleby, Nelson's Medieval Texts, London, 1963

Sismondi, J.C.L., *History of the Crusades against the Albigensians in the Thirteenth Century.* 1830

Strickland, Agnes, *Lives of the Queens of England,* Vol. I. London, 1857